TRIPLE PLAY

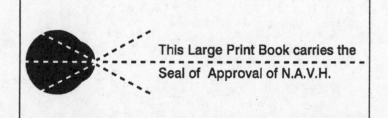

This Large Print Book carries the
Seal of Approval of N.A.V.H.

TRIPLE PLAY

JAMES D. CROWNOVER

WHEELER PUBLISHING
A part of Gale, Cengage Learning

GALE
CENGAGE Learning·

Farmington Hills, Mich • San Francisco • New York • Waterville, Maine
Meriden, Conn • Mason, Ohio • Chicago

GALE
CENGAGE Learning®

Wheeler Publishing Large Print Western.
The text of this Large Print edition is unabridged.
Other aspects of the book may vary from the original edition.
Set in 16 pt. Plantin.

LIBRARY OF CONGRESS CATALOGING-IN-PUBLICATION DATA

Names: Crownover, James D., author.
Title: Triple play / by James D. Crownover.
Description: Large print edition. | Waterville, Maine, Wheeler Publishing, a part of Gale, Cengage Learning, 2017. | Series: Wheeler Publishing large print western
Identifiers: LCCN 2017003549| ISBN 9781432838393 (softcover) | ISBN 1432838393 (softcover)
Subjects: LCSH: Ranchers—Fiction. | Frontier and pioneer life—Fiction. | Large type books. | BISAC: FICTION / Historical. | FICTION / Action & Adventure. | GSAFD: Western stories. | Adventure fiction.
Classification: LCC PS3603.R765 T75 2016b | DDC 813/.6—dc23
LC record available at https://lccn.loc.gov/2017003549

Published in 2017 by arrangement with James D. Crownover

Printed in Mexico
1 2 3 4 5 6 7 21 20 19 18 17

To My Beloved Wife,
Carol

FAMILIES OF *TRIPLE PLAY*

BEAVERS
Tucker Sr., father, born 1833.
Mary, wife, born 1845.
Tucker Jr., born 1865.
Eda B., born 1867, married Joe Meeker.
Zenas Meeker, born 1886, named after his grandfather.
Sue Ellen, born 1869, married Bud Stone.
Nathan, born 1877.

NEALY
Robert, husband.
Presilla, wife.
Lucinda, born 1868.
Green, born 1878.
Joshua, born 1882.

BROWN
James R., husband.
Sue, wife.
Parmelia, born 1862.

7

Rance, born 1865.
Polly Ann, born 1875.

FOREWORD

Tucker Beavers is going to tell you a story, part of which most of you have heard before in a different form. This is the mother of that other story, that is, one portion of this story is what the other story is about. Tucker is going to tell the whole story about his life in and around the Tularosa Basin in south-central New Mexico Territory in the late 1800s. He and his family ran a cattle ranch in the valleys of the Sacramento Mountains near the town of Pinetop. Part of his activities take place in Old Mexico where he spent two years of his life seeking stolen cattle and the killers who took them.

We tend to think that cowboys didn't do anything but herd cows on horseback, eat bear sign, shoot up towns and saloons and chase Indians and bandits. In truth, they loved baseball and every town — and a lot of ranches — had teams. Competition was stiff and those who didn't play watched with keen interest. Baseball plays a part in this story, maybe not as much as do Indians, outlaws, cattle drives and cattle stealing.

Tucker and his family associate with such western characters as Oliver Lee, Eugene Manlove Rhodes, Doctor George Goodfellow, Pat Garrett, Zenas Leonard Meeker and Heiskell and Ma'am Jones.

While in Mexico, he battles the thieves who have his cattle and experiences the great earthquake of May 3, 1887, and its aftermath. The earthquake has a very large part in the outcome of his visit there. Returning home, he is accused of murder and goes through a trial that has a surprising conclusion.

I hope you enjoy his story as much as I have, so with that, I invite you to sit back and enter his nineteenth-century world. While you read, try to recall the other place you have heard the essence of a portion of Tuck's experiences.

For everything there is a season,
And a time for every matter
under heaven.
            The Preacher, Ecc. 3:1

CHAPTER 1
THE GAME

1880

Here he comes, just like I knew he would. Sure as she comes to me in the night, Rance'll be here the next morning. Look at him stopping at the gate to see who has left their tracks. It's always the same way, over and over, first he'll say . . . "Howdy, Tuck, I see she's been here agin. Hope you had a good visit. Don't know why, but she always visits you when her cycle comes around. Hurts so much she can't sleep. Gets up and walks th' floor or sits and rocks there in th' dark. I always know when she leaves, that rocker stops creakin'. Funny how a sound *stopping* wakes you up just as easy as *making* a sound does. Don't know what you-all talk about so much. I sneaked up here once an' listened. Couldn't hear a word.

"Now don't be mad, I don't care if she comes t' see you. Nobody sees, nobody knows but me and even if folks was to find

13

out, I wouldn't care. I know you're just friends — now — and no harm is done." He chuckles.

"Did you hear about our game last Sunday? We beat 'em good. Would have had a triple play if our center fielder had thrown th' ball in quick enough.

"I've got a new goal; gonna figure out how t' get an unassisted triple play for each position on th' field. It's easy enough for second base and short, maybe even third, but things get a little complicated for catcher, pitcher and first base. Seems like they're gonna have t' roam away from their positions some to get that job done. Hadn't thought about outfielders yet.

"Still remember that triple play I had back — when was it — near ten years ago! Haven't had one since you stopped playin'.

"Well, got t' get goin' I'll open th' store a few minutes late this mornin'. Won't hurt nothin' I guess."

And off he goes, never caring *I* might have something t' say to *him*. Seems like "Green Grow the Lilacs" is the only song he ever sings.

I guess you being new around here don't know about that triple play. It was just over ten years ago when it happened, but I should start tellin' you some time before it

14

happened so's you'll get th' whole picture . . . we got plenty o' time.

There were men on first and second when Gene Rhodes hit a line drive straight to me at second. Man, did it sting! I dropped it, but recovered in time to flip it to Rance covering second and force the runner.

"Whasa matter, Tuck, too hot for you?" Gene called from first.

"Try catchin' with this rag an' you'll know!" I replied.

"Dang, Tuck, you catch that clean and we'd a' had a triple play!"

Rance was always figurin' ways t' get a triple play. He'd sit and think up all different ways it could be done. Truth was, we'd be doin' good to get a single out, th' way we played.

"We already had one out, Rance, an' yuh can't carry over any fourth out to th' next innin'," I replied.

"Still woulda been fun."

"Two away!" Sol McGlathery called from behind the plate.

We knew Gene would try to steal on the first pitch so Sol always called for a pitchout. It was so habitual that Bransford just stood in the box and leaned on his bat grinning. Riley Giddens took his stretch and Gene

15

took his lead. Rance and I leaned forward on our toes, ready to cover and backup. Throw to first, Gene gets back. Riley stretches, Gene leads and Riley fakes a throw. Another stretch, long look, pitch, Gene takes off and I cover second. Sol's throw is right on time, but off to the right. By th' time I tag, Gene has both feet on the bag grinnin' at me.

"Yer safe! Strike one!" Ump calls from behind home plate. Buck Jones was umpire. That's all he did because of his age, but he really did know the game. No one who knew him ever argued with his calls, especially when he came out of the box with a bat in his hand. We never called him anything but Ump.

"Strike?" Bransford yells, "I wasn't even ready!"

"You were in th' box an' he throwed a strike."

"You throw a strike, Rile?" Bransford was halfway to the mound.

"Fooled ya, didn't I? Maybe next time you'll put that bat on yore shoulder and pertend yo're gonna hit!"

"That wus s'posed t' be a pitchout!"

"T'aint always th' case enny more, feller." Riley grinned.

"Batter up!" Ump called. "It's gittin' late

an' I got t' milk yet."

Ump points at th' pitcher, Sol gets set. Bransford saunters back toward the box. Just as he taps th' plate and sets his feet, th' ball whizzes by. "Strike two!"

"I wasn't ready!" Bransford yells.

"Rest of us were an' you were in th' box," Ump replies. "Batter up!"

Now Bransford's jaw is set and he's in the box ready an' Riley hasn't even got th' ball yet. It's two to one, last of th' ninth. One more strike an' we win. Riley paces around th' mound, hitches up his britches, grabs a handful of dirt and rubs his hands. Slowly, he approaches the mound, all the while, our batter is like a statue, not moving a hair. I don't believe he has even blinked. He's got t' be tensed up, it's been so long.

"Ball one!" Ump calls.

"I ain't even throwed," Riley yells.

Bransford grins and swings his bat.

"Ye took too much time!" Ump yells back. *"Now play ball!"*

Bransford's ready, Riley doesn't even wait for a signal, just winds and throws. C-r-rack! Bransford hits a fastball high in the zone and it sails out over center. We didn't have any fences, but that one is hit so hard and far, no one is gonna catch it. Home run, game over, we lose three to two.

"I hope your cows go dry!" Rance yells at the umpire who's hotfootin' it for home.

Will Stone comes trottin' in from center field.

"Where's my ball, Will?" Riley asks.

"Where it landed, Riley, it hit a big fresh cow pile an' didn't even bounce. Looked like a big green explosion. Don't think you're gonna want it 'fore a couple o' days o' sunshine."

"Prob'ly flat as mush after those guys got hold of it," I said.

"It's our only ball 'til someone goes to El Paso with some jingle an' buys another one," Riley said, as he trudged out to retrieve the ball. He kicked it out of the crater it made and was last seen kicking it toward the acequia.

"Hope no one needs t' fill their water bucket tonight." Sol grinned.

"It'll just add a little flavor t' th' water," I said. "B'sides, don't they say if water runs over three rocks an' a goose pile, it's clean?"

"That's what they *say*, but I just as soon it skipped the goose pile," Rance said.

"Aw, you know you drank worser," L. O. Vineyard said. "I *seen* you drink out of a cow track."

"I done it through a silk scarf an' you

know that strains out bugs *and* dirt," Rance replied.

"Here comes Cindy with our mounts, Rance, we better get goin', it'll be dark afore we get home, now," I said. I hurried out to hold the horses.

I was named after my pa, Tucker Beavers. They called him Mr. Beavers and I'm just called Tuck.

Cindy's whole name was Lucinda Nealy. Her pa, Robert Nealy, was foreman for our ranch, the Mountain Beaver. I was three years old when she was born at the ranch. About all I remember about that was how little an' red an' ugly she was an' how loud she could squall when she was hungry. Things was different after that. It wasn't long afore she was walkin' an' I was given the job of taking care of her. That's how we grew up, me watchin' her an' her sayin' she could do anything I could.

When the Browns bought Rimfire Ranch, we had a new playmate in Rance Brown. We spent many a day playin' up an' down Shady Creek or chasin' calves if no one was lookin'. Cindy was always with us, or lookin' for us when we ran away from her. She usually found us too.

By th' time we were ten or eleven years

19

old, playin' all day was over for me an' Rance. We were expected t' work, an' work we did. Cindy had less time t' pester us, too, bein' she was expected t' take care of other little ones that come along after us. Still there was time for play but as we grew older that playtime got less and less. About the only time to ourselves was Saturday afternoons or Sunday afternoons after church when we played ball. Mostly it was baseball, but in th' fall we played some football. Cindy would stay in town visitin' her friends then ride home with us after the games.

All three of us had our favorite ponies and we did a lot of ridin'. One of the things that marked change in our lives was when Cindy started ridin' sidesaddle. Rance and I were puzzled by it an' Cindy just told us to shut up and ride. She took a few spills but it wasn't long until she could ride that way almost as good as astraddle. Ma said it was ok for kids to ride astraddle, but young ladies were expected to ride sidesaddle. We didn't think of Cindy as a young lady, but we figgered she was just practicin' up to be one.

When the snow wasn't too deep we would ride into town to school, but most of th' time we couldn't go and Ma would teach us. It was good enough an education and I enjoyed th' diversion from everyday chores.

Pa made a brand for our Mountain Beaver Ranch no one could fiddle with. It was an outline of a beaver sittin' up on his big tail. It took him a long time to make one just like he wanted and when he registered it the registrar said it was the most unusual brand they had ever seen. We never found any of our brands altered, but that didn't keep cattle thieves away. They would just take a few head and hightail it plum out of th' country. Some feller down in Mexico built quite a herd stealin' our cows over time. Didn't even bother to change the brand, just took it for his own an' no one said a thing. Course, no Mexican would say anything, there was so much cow stealin' back and forth across that border, they thought it threw some back in their favor.

One cowboy I knew made a livin' out of stealin' horses. He'd steal some in the US an' run them to Mexico and sell them. When he had used up all his money — usually in a day or two — he'd steal a bunch of Mexican horses and light out for th' border. He told me he once stole the same horses twice, but would never do that again as he had t' find another market in both countries.

When we were fifteen, Rance's dad sold

their ranch and in th' deal, they got one of the two merchantile stores in town. They moved to town and a new owner took over their ranch. I was a full-time vaquero, able to carry my weight an' more. One day Pa an' I rode over t' Far Pasture looking over our range an' cattle there. They were sure a wild bunch, not being used t' seein' riders and every time we made ourselves visible, they would hightail it out of sight.

"Those are th' wildest cows on th' ranch," Pa said. "I'll bet we didn't get half th' steers last spring."

"I saw a lot of mossyhorns last time I was up here," I said. "Probably two out o'ten were over two years old."

"And wild as rabbits." Pa lit his pipe and took a few puffs. "Trouble is that this pasture is pretty isolated from th' rest of our range an' these cows don't mix with tamer cattle an' they *shore* don't see riders much." Pa took a few more puffs. "It's for sure they need more attention." He looked at that meadow and then directly at me. "You're getting' up t' where you need a little more responsibility an' you need t' start thinkin' about what you're gonna be doin' for a livin'. I tell you what, I'm gonna give you th' cows in this pasture. You can graze 'em in this pasture an' on my range for one fourth of th' increase. By th' time you get this herd in shape, you'll know if you want t' make ranchin' your occupation or not. If you do it right, you will at least have a start at whatever you want t' do."

Well, that just about took my breath comin' outa the blue like that. I didn't know what t' say for a minute or two. Pa sat there puffin' his pipe an' waitin' for me to say somethin'.

"There must be near two hundred head in here, Pa, that's a lot t' give away."

"Ain't givin' 'em away, I'm givin' you a boost up toward bein' a man able t' take care of yourself independent of your folks. It's no more than a man should do for his son if he's able an' it's a chance for you t' learn a lot of things about cows and ranchin' — and yourself."

There wasn't any question in my mind that I wasn't gonna take Pa up on his proposition, but it sure did give me pause about what I was getting into. This was goin' t' change a lot of things, some of those things I didn't think I was ready to change. I guess if I had thought about it any longer, I would have talked myself out of the idea, but I didn't.

"Thank you, Pa, that's awful generous an' I'm willin' t' try if you will promise me

23

you'll step in if you see I'm goin' wrong."

Pa held out his hand and said, "That's a deal, son."

We shook and the deal was sealed. Now I had to make plans about what to do with my new responsibility. We rode around talkin' about what needed t' be done to get things straightened out. That pasture only had about three thousand unfenced acres in it. Bein' remote like it was, we depended on natural barriers like woods on two sides and bluffs on the north and east sides to keep the cattle. It worked very well because there wasn't any graze in the woods for miles and cattle had to keep comin' back to graze in the meadows. The east bluff was too steep and rocky to climb and that north cliff was a hundred and fifty feet of solid rock straight up. We called it Mossy Bluff. Top of the cliff sorta marked an end of useful land except for a thin strip of timber between there and timberline.

Rock Spring at the bottom of th' bluff drained into Shady Creek that ran through the pasture. In spring and early summer snowmelt fed the creek and it poured over the rim of the cliff into a pool beside the spring. It was always cool and green around the bluff and there was an old line shack just out of the edge of the woods west of the stream. It was an ideal place for a cabin, cool in summer and warm under a winter sun bouncing off that bluff. We used it at roundup an' sometimes kept a hand up there through th' summer when cow stealin' was in season. That roof didn't shed much water and we slept outside most of the time.

"I suspect first thing I oughta do is fix up that cabin, looks like I'll need t' be stayin' up here some," I said. Turned out I stayed up there a lot — more than I really had to.

"The corral an' small pasture fences need some work." Pa pointed with th' stem of his pipe.

"I'm gonna have t' brand these cows, so I could build a small pen against th' pasture fence an' put a brandin' chute between 'em."

Pa nodded. "Good idea, keeps your hired hands to a minimum. You cut an' set fenceposts an' I'll provide wire, since I'm landlord."

We rode all over that pasture talking about things that needed to be done an' scarin' up cows an' steers like they was deer. The more I saw of them, th' more I wondered what I was gettin' into. They sure were wild.

Goin' back home, Pa said, "You work out th' rest of this week with me an' you can begin on your work Monday mornin'. That will give me time to get wire here for you and be a good time to start since Sunday's th' first of the month."

"Ok, Pa," I said, but it was hard waiting. Pa worked us hard and it made the time go a little faster. By Saturday night, I was about done in and so was Pa.

I found time during the week to work on my brand. Pa agreed t' let me brand the number 2 in th' tail of his beaver brand. I tried it out on a branded board and it looked best when it looked like it was lyin' on the tail. I planned to call it the Mountain Beaver 2, but it got named the Lazy 2 Beaver by other cowhands because that 2 was layin' down.

Sunday morning the family rode to church in our buggy while little Nate an' I drove the wagon to pick up that load of wire at Brown's. Rance helped me load after church an' I told him about the deal with Far Pasture. To my surprise, Pa had ordered enough tin roofin' for the cabin.

"Wow, Tuck, that sounds like fun!" Rance said.

"Looks more like work t' me," I said. "If I need a hand for a day or two, would you help out?"

"You betcha I will — if Dad will let me

26

off from th' store."

"I'm cash poor . . ."

"Don't worry about that," he said, "just gittin' away from here an' ridin' an' feed is all I ask."

The ball field was too wet t' play so I was lucky an' didn't miss a game when I headed back up the mountain to home. At dinner I tried my best to hide my impatience to get it over with so's I could get on, but Mom could tell.

"I made you up a pack of grub to keep you for a week," she said, "you be sure to get back down here Saturday night if not before."

"Yes, ma'am."

"And another thing, I put extra clothes on top. You change clothes a time or two. If you want to, you can bring the dirties back or you could wash them yourself in the creek."

Pa gave me the look that meant *do it yourself,* and I said, "Yes, ma'am."

Me an' Pa walked out to th' wagon and looked over the load. "Pick out a couple more horses t' go with yours an' keep them all in your little pasture. If they run free, they're liable t' head home an' you would be afoot."

"Wouldn't do to be afoot among those

cows," I said.

"Just be sure to keep your horse close at hand when you put your feet on th' ground an' you should be OK. Keep that wagon with you. If anything comes up here, we have that Studebaker to use. Are you sure you have all th' tools you need?"

"I'm pretty sure, but even if I don't, I have plenty t' do without them."

Pa grinned. "You sure do, boy. Be careful. I'll try to check in on you middle of th' week."

We hitched up horses and tied three more to the tailgate and I climbed up on the seat and clucked to the team. Mom and the kids were standin' on the porch when I passed by. Nate was yellin' to go with me an' if he hadn't been seven years old, I would have taken him. He would have jumped off th' porch if Ma hadn't grabbed his galluses. As it was, his feet swung free and he nearly pulled Ma off with him.

Cindy ran out when I passed their house. "Daddy says you have your own ranch, Tucker, is that so?"

"Not really," I said with a grin. "Pa rented Far Pasture t' me an' gave me those wild cows that are in it."

"Do you need any help herdin' — I can help you!" She jumped up on the wheel an'

28

spoke low.

"Somethin' tells me you wouldn't be much use sidesaddle," I teased.

"I can ride as good as you can!" she hissed between her teeth. Then she slugged me on my shoulder — hard.

"Now don't go gittin' mad . . ."

"You ain't seen nothin' yet, Tucker Beavers," she yelled jumping down an' giving th' nigh horse a slap on his rump. "Now get goin' afore I pick up some rocks and send you off good!"

She followed us around the corner of the house and ran ahead into the tack room. Almost as soon as she went in, she was out again with a heavy tow sack. Runnin' up beside the wagon, she threw it on top. I stopped for fear of running over her and she said, "You could have stopped sooner!"

"What is that?"

"You just mind your knittin' an' *git goin'*," she said, and ran back to the house. I clucked to the team and we headed up the mountain.

I was surprised the trip took so long, but I hadn't driven a loaded wagon to the cabin before and it was mostly uphill. Just before we dropped off to the pasture, I stopped the wagon to let my horses get a blow and look the place over. A lot of cattle had been grazing in the open but now every head was turned toward us and they had frozen in place.

"Bet they run when we move," I said to the horses. The only answer I got was a snort. Sure enough, when I slapped reins on their backs and started to move, every cow headed for the brush. It didn't take thirty seconds for that whole pasture to empty and there was nothin' but a little dust hangin in the air t' show that anything had been there.

"Now, that's sure a bad omen, boys. You better get rested up and eat your oats if we're gonna tame those mavericks." The funny thing is that I think they understood what was going on. Cow horses love their job on the whole an' they get excited just like we do when they see cattle work to come. Cowboys ain't th' only ones that love a good dustup.

CHAPTER 2
PECOS PETE

I spent a couple of weeks repairin' the pasture holding pen and buildin' long wings on to it. When it was ready, Pa helped me gather up what stock we could find and drive them in. When th' gate swung shut, we had about a hundred head. Less than twenty head were steers.

"I expect that's about half of your stock in th' pasture," Pa said.

"I was hopin' we had caught most o' those mossyhorns, but I know better," I said.

"That's for sure, an' I bet they's a half dozen o' them peekin' out of th' brush an' laughin' at us right now."

"They'll be laughin' out t'other side o' their mouths when I git them in an' branded!"

"Well, son, it'll take a lot more time catchin' 'em than brand-in' 'em if you're just gonna put that lazy 2 on their second tail. Don't forget t' put another notch in

31

their ear while you got 'em down."

"Some o' those bulls are gonna git worked on th' other end too," I said.

"If they're over three years old or so, cuttin' would go hard on 'em. You're better off sellin' ones you want t' cull. It would give you some cash t' work with an' rid yourself of poor stock an' headaches." Pa lit his pipe an' hunkered down in th' shade agin th' wing wall.

I hunkered down aside him. "Pa, d'yuh think I could sell enough o' them t' buy me a good Durham bull?"

He puffed on that a moment and said, "Possibly, though those Durhams sure come at a premium. You prob'ly need at least two bulls for every hundred head of cows, so I would pick out th' best of what you got an' only buy one Durham for now."

I nodded an' we sat there lookin' at the herd we had caught. There were several older she-cows, some steers an' some bulls. I knew I would cull most of those bulls an' there were several old cows that looked like they needed culling too.

Pa must have been readin' my mind, for he said, "You might wait 'til next spring t' cull out cows. Keep those with calves an' sell those that don't bear. I'll help you pick out some that bear an' aren't good stock."

"OK, Pa."

We sat there a while 'til Pa knocked out his pipe on his boot heel an' stood up. "If I leave now, I'll get in just b'fore dark." He tightened his cinch and mounted up. "Be careful an' I'll see you at th' house Saturday afternoon."

"OK, Pa. I guess I'll look that brush over down th' creek an' see if I can scare out a few more head afore dark."

Pa laughed. "I'll bet b'fore you're done, you'll be doin' some night ridin' t' catch 'em all."

I've heard men talk about the brush country of south Texas but I'm here t' tell you that they don't have any monopoly on brush. Stretches of that creek bottom are just as brushy. The only thing Texas brush country has on our brush is quantity. Riding along th' edge of those bushes, I could hear cattle every hundred feet or so, but I didn't see hair or horn. About the only way I could see t' roust those cows out was to light a fire somewhere downwind. We got t' callin' that area th' Nueces Strip an' everyone knew where we meant.

The sun set on me before I knew it and we had t' hurry t' get back before dark. I didn't think anything about it when I smelled smoke as I neared my cabin. I unsaddled and tried to rub Socks down, but he was too eager to get a drink and roll t' stand around long. I picked up my saddle and headed for the cabin but the sight of a light brought me up short. Someone was in there!

Quiet as possible, I laid my saddle down and drew my rifle from the boot. The door was open a crack and I sneaked up and peeked in. All I could see was the bunks but I could hear someone movin' around at the other end of the room by the fireplace. Slowly I pushed the door open. A man was kneeling on the hearth with his back to me stirrin' somethin'. Without even looking, he said, "Come on in an' shut that door. That air comin' in is causin' such a draft it'll burn th' biscuits."

I took note that he wasn't carryin' a gun and after looking around behind me I shut the door and let th' latch fall. If there were more people around, I wanted to be sure t' take 'em on one at a time. I swear I could hear that man's bones creakin' as he stood up and unbent.

He turned around and said, "Howdy, air *you* th' owner of this fine castle?"

"I'm th' renter, more or less," I replied.

"Some people call me Pete and some call

34

me Pecos. I answer to both." He held out a hand that was hard as horn and had the little finger missing back to the second knuckle. Even so, his three-fingered grip was as firm as any. "Lost it to a rattlesnake when I was only twict yore age," he said as if I had asked him a question. "Bit me when I was gatherin' wood for th' cookie. When I yelled and shook him off in th' fire, Cookie was there with his cleaver an' lay my hand on a log. Whacked off th' finger at th' knuckle clean as a whistle. Don't know how he missed th' others." He chuckled then turned back to his fire.

I stood there like a dolt an' watched him cookin'. I knew about th' hospitality customs of th' range but this was my first time to experience it by myself and I was downright uncomfortable.

My guest must have sensed it, for he said, "Nothin' t' worry 'bout, boy, I'm just an old cowhand lookin' for a dry place t' lay up fer th' night. This place come along at just th' right time. Biscuits an' beans'll be ready by th' time you're washed up."

That invitation was plumb irresistible to a youngster who hadn't had anything but a little jerky since a before-daylight breakfast and I was back in no time, dryin' my hands on my pants legs. Coffee was scaldin' as

35

usual, biscuits done to a turn an' those beans had chunks of beef in them. We ate in silence an' when I finished my second plate, I said, "That sure was good, mister, hope I wasn't eatin' my own beef."

He chuckled. "Not less'n yore brand's th' Rockin' M. Grab that biscuit an' put some of this lick on it for sweets."

While I sopped up molasses with that biscuit, he made t' gather up th' dishes.

"I'll wash 'em up," I said. "You did th' cookin'."

"Good enough," he said, and began spreadin' his bedroll on the dirt floor by th' fire.

"Help yourself to one of those bunks," I said. "My bedroll is out under th' trees an' I'll be sleepin' there."

"Like sleepin' outdoors, do you?"

"It gets stuffy in here with that door closed an' I don't want critters wanderin' in on me in th' night." I didn't mention the pack rats that ran around all night makin' little noises an' stealin' my socks.

He threw another stick of wood on th' fire and said, "I saw those cows in th' holdin' pen — acted mighty skittish."

"They are pretty wild," I said. "Pa give me all th' ones in this pasture just t' get shut of 'em. I guess we got up about half of the lot."

"Sure are a lot o' mossyhorns."

"There's just as many or more hidin' in th' brush out there. I don't know how I'm gonna roust 'em out without settin' a fire."

He chuckled. "That'd be easiest, I reckon, if you didn't burn off th' whole mountain. Looks t' me like you're gonna be doin' a lot of brush poppin'."

"Pa thinks I'll be doin' some night ridin' t' get 'em all."

"He's probably right, how many hands you got t' help?"

"Just me right now," I said.

"Ain't enough."

"I got a buddy said he would come up an' help."

"Two would do a little bit o' good, but you would need four or five t' clean up."

I explained to him the deal I had made with Pa an' he sat thinking about it a minute or two. "Tell you what," he said. "I'll help you out a few days just for bed an' found. It would give my hosses time t' rest up a bit."

"You might be sorry after you look over that brush along th' creek."

"I done right smart o' brush poppin' down south Texas, guess I could git th' hang of it agin."

I didn't mention how much brush poppin' I had done which was zero up to that time.

"You're welcome t' stay. I could use help an' maybe you could see easier ways o' doin' things."

"Don't know's I know that much over hard work an' grit." He grinned.

The fire had died down and I banked it up an' said my good nights.

"I'll try out one o' yore bunks," Pete said. "Bein's I'm a light sleeper, I'll jist leave th' door open for air."

With that, I slipped out to my bedroll and turned in, but I kept my rifle under the covers an' my pistol by my head.

I liked t' jumped outta my skin when Pete yelled, "Come an' git it!" I was sittin' straight up when I opened my eyes an' it was dark as pitch. Only thing that told me I wasn't dreamin' was th' silhouette of Pete standin' in the doorway.

"OK!" I yelled and he turned back to the fireplace. Fast as I could, I rolled up my bed and headed for the cabin. Leftover biscuits were hot like they had just come out of an oven and I decided I had t' learn how Pete had done that. Beans, a slab of salt pork and of course coffee filled out the meal. Pete rolled a cigarette while I cleaned up. "Well, boss, what's on yer mind t' do t'day?"

"Not too sure," I said. "We got those cows in th' little pasture t' brand an' cull, or we could make another run at roundin' up some more b'fore we brand."

"Air ye set up t' brand?"

"Mostly, all I got t'do is get my brands an' gather some wood for a fire."

Pete chewed on that for a minute, then said, "Let's look over your layout afore we start anythin'."

We saddled up and rode over to the little pasture. When th' cattle saw us, their first impulse was t' run, but they could only bunch up at the far end of the pasture agin the fence. That fence had them buffaloed. It's for sure it would have gone down if they had hit it, but they weren't sure enough of it t' try. Those rags fluttering on th' top wire every other span kept them wary long enough t' tame them down somewhat so's they didn't have a runaway ever' time they saw a rider. I showed Pete the squeeze-down chute, an' he nodded.

"Wondered how you were 'spectin' to do brandin' by yoreself. Thet's a good idea. Air ye sure that gate will hold 'em when they git t' th' end?"

"Pretty sure."

"Can't be pretty sure, gotta be positive. If one o' those rannies busts down th' gate, that whole herd will be right ahind him an' you'll play hell gittin' 'em through that chute a second time." He looked at the gate, rattled it, and checked my lock bar. "Pretty good, it'll hold if'n yuh don't let one of 'em git a run at it. Tell you what, let's make a second gate just b'hind this one an' we can squeeze two at a time. We should be able t' brand two at a time without reheatin' yore iron an' that'll save time."

We worked hard building another sliding gate behind that first gate an' gatherin' firewood. By mid afternoon our gate was done, firewood arranged for lightin' an' brandin' irons were hung up ready for use.

"Now, if them cows don't come around an' mess up our fixin's, we'll be ready t' start brandin' early in th' mornin'," Pete said.

I looked up at th' sun. "What you say we ride th' pasture an' see if we can roust out a few more head afore sundown?"

"Sounds good t' me, boss," and we headed for our horses. They were still fresh, havin' done nothin' of consequence all day and we rode to th' end of the big pasture. I showed Pete features of the place and when we had surveyed that brush, he said, "Looks jest like th' Nueces Strip, t' me." And that's how it got its name.

By ridin' hard, we gathered up a dozen head of stock in- cludin' one calf Pete roped in th' brush and dragged out, mammy bawlin' right behind. When we had them well within my wing walls, I rode around an' opened th' gate b'fore Pete hazed them in. The sun was already down when we rode to th' cabin. While I got both horses taken care of, steaks were cookin' an' we sat down t' eat. Supper over, we sat outside on a bench propped agin the wall an' watched a pink sky over th' mountain fade to blue then purple black.

Pete took th' stem of his pipe out of his mouth and said, "Tuck, I havta 'pologize for takin' over like I did t'day. This is yore job an' you ought t' be boss.

"One thing a good range boss does is know th' night b'fore what he's gonna do next. He lays things out t' his crew afore they turn in for th' night, listens t' any questions an' suggestions from his men an' by an' by ever'one knows what his job's gonna be soon's he's up next morning. A good crew will be on to their job soon's breakfast is over without havin' t' say any more.

"If men have t' stand around wonderin' what t' do, onlyest thing they're doin' is wastin' daylight. A boss has t' always be

41

thinkin' ahead — knowin' what comes next an' who is gonna be doin' it. Runnin' a ranch ain't no big myst'ry an' a good vaquero knows what comes next. Most o' th' time he's ahead or right along with his boss. Still, it's th' boss's job t' see that instructions are clear an' timely.

"From now on, I'm gonna be yore crew an' you're gonna be boss, though I do reserve th' right t' make suggestions, seein's how I have a mite more experience than you." He chuckled.

All was quiet for a moment save for crickets chirpin' an' a hooty owl down th' valley callin'. "Thanks, Pete, an' I'll try t' be a proper boss. Tomorrow we'll start brandin' an' cuttin'. All th' brandin' involves just addin' a 2 to the beaver brand an' another notch below Pa's notch in th' ear. I want t'cut all th' bulls we can an' I'll depend on you t' tell me when a critter's too old t' cut. We'll brand 'til all are done then we'll let 'em into that big pasture as soon as we can an' tally as we do."

"Thet sounds like good plannin' an' with that I'm gonna turn in." Pete knocked embers out of his pipe and headed for his bunk.

I rolled my bed out under a tree an' don't even remember when I lay down.

42

CHAPTER 3
NEW HANDS

Gonna hafta t' get t' bed earlier, I thought when Pete called breakfast. *Can't have th' help callin' th' boss up like this.* There wasn't much t' say, since we knew what th' day's work was. We saddled up an' I carried a bucket of coals t' start th' fire. When it was goin' good, I laid irons in an' we started brandin'.

It was slow because I had to mount up and haze a couple o' head into the chute, then come back an' help with th' ground-work. When I got there, Pete had branded one cow an' was headin' for number two. I notched an ear, cut an' doctored the former bull then hurried for th' second cow.

We had branded a dozen cows an' I was mounting when Pete said, "Looks like we got company."

There, riding down from the cabin, came Cindy. That burlap sack she had thrown on the wagon held her old saddle and I had hung it up inside. Getting it down an' exchanging it for her sidesaddle must have been a chore for her.

"Mrs. Beavers sent you some more food and I left it at the shack," she said as she rode up. "I came to help."

"Now what in th' world can a sixty-pound girl do at a brand- in'?" I asked.

"I can do anything you . . ."

"The smallest calf in that pen outweighs you by twice," I injected. "Your pa'd kill me if he knowed I let you rastle these critters." Her jaw set an' I could see her temperature climbin'. "But you could ride an' haze cows into th' chute for us," I added quickly. I was relieved t' see she liked that idea.

"Where's yore tally book, Tuck?" Pete gave a little nod.

"And if you could keep tally for us, it would save us a lot of time too," I added. "This is Pecos Pete, he's helpin' out; Pete this is Cindy Nealy."

Pete removed his hat an' nodded. "Pleased t' meet you, ma'am."

That pleased her and I got my tally book out and we rode down to th' holdin' pen t' catch up with cattle already branded. I showed her how I wanted to keep tally an' we rode back to the chutes and went t' work. "Don't let them run in th' chute," I

44

yelled. "They'll run through th' gates."

Cindy kept th' cattle pretty well bunched and pushed two at a time into the chute. It went a lot faster with her helping.

I knew I was gonna get into trouble with her pa when she saw me cuttin' bulls, but I didn't know what else t' do. She turned red and trotted off when she saw what I was doin'. She stayed away when cuttin' started if she could.

At noon, I changed her saddle to Socks and let her horse rest. We worked hard and with Cindy there, we got over half th' bunch branded by late afternoon. Pete an' I made t' quit early enough for her to get home before dark. I rode with her to the corral and switched saddles for her.

"What are you gonna do with *those*?" she whispered, indicating the bucket of fries I had brought to th' cabin.

"Coyote bait." I lied. "Didn't want t' leave them by th' pens."

She wrinkled her nose disgustedly, blushed and turned toward home. "I'll be back tomorrow to help," she called over her shoulder.

I watched her out of sight and went back to the pens. Me an' Pete worked 'til dark, but it was sure a whole lot slower and more work without that girl helping.

45

By the time Pete called breakfast, I had horses caught up and saddled and as soon as breakfast was over we rode to th' pens. The sun was peeking over th' mountains when Cindy rode up sidesaddle. "Where's my saddle?" she demanded.

"Right here, I brought it down so I could change it for you," I replied.

"I can do my own changing, thank you," but she let me do it for her without any more fuss. We worked steady 'til noon and since we would finish up early, took a break at noon. Cindy and I walked down to the creek while Pete dozed in the shade.

"Ma told me what you did with those *fries*, you *coyote*! Yuck!" she said.

"You won't be so critical an' righteous after you've tried them."

"Never, *never*," she said loudly and punched me hard on the shoulder. My face felt hot and hers was red but there was a little smile she tried to hide.

"Was your pa mad?"

"No, we didn't tell him, but I know the difference b'tween steers an' gentlemen cows now."

She laughed a little and I grinned. I have

always felt more at ease around girls raised on a ranch because they know more about animal husbandry and such and don't make so much fuss or act squeamish about those things where a city girl's *sensibilities* would not allow her to know about steers and geldings and you couldn't call a bull a bull in their company.

We were finished, the fire put out and the irons hung up high by mid afternoon. At the shack, I changed out Cindy's saddle and hung it from the rafter while she rolled up her pants legs and pulled her riding skirt over them. When she had arranged her skirts and mounted up, she turned to Pete and said, "Mrs. Beavers said to invite you to dinner Sunday. We are all gonna eat together with th' Browns. We all insist on you to come, there's going to be doughnuts for dessert."

Pete bowed a little and tipped his hat. "Tell Mrs. Beavers I would be pleased to come." No cowboy ever refused bear sign, no matter how shy he was, not that Pete was especially shy.

I rode with Cindy to the ridge, then me and Pete spent rest of the afternoon doin' little chores and fixin' up around the cabin.

All day Wednesday, Thursday and Friday we built another holding pen for our culls. I dug postholes an' Pete snaked posts down an' set them. By Friday evening, wire was stretched and we had cut three gaps, one to the holding pen, one in th' adjacent pasture fence, and one to the range. Now, there were three pens all connected to each other where we could hold and sort cattle easily.

That night as we sat on the bench we discussed the next week's work, for I planned to ride to the ranch next morning. "I've thought an' thought, Pete, an' I don't see any reasonable way two people can clean out th' pasture an' especially that Nueces Strip."

Pete put that in his pipe and smoked it a little. "Shore looks like you're gonna need a couple or three more hands t' help."

"Rance was gonna try t' get off next week an' come up t' help but that's only one more hand. I'm gonna make Cindy stay home even if I have t' get her folks t' help do it."

Pete nodded. "She's a good rider, all right, but this roundup is gonna be too rough for a girl her size t' handle."

"Yuh really think we still need two more hands?"

"Yup, an' I think I know jist whur t' find 'em."

"I'm cash poor, Pete, how'm I gonna pay 'em?"

"I got a feelin' they'll do it for fun an' found," Pete chuckled. "They shore love a dustup an' th' rougher, th' better. Tell ya what, I'll ride out tomorrer and see if they kin come. I'll see you Sunday an' we'll know then if they're gonna be here."

"If they can't make it, maybe Pa can lend us a couple o' hands for a couple o' days."

"Awful busy time o' the year fer that t' happen." Pete tapped out his pipe and cleaned it with his knife.

"Guess we'll just have t' wait 'til Sunday afternoon t' know," I said as I walked off to bed. When I got up Saturday morning, Pete was already gone. I dug out my cleanest dirty clothes, hitched up and headed for home. Ma wouldn't let me in the house smellin' like that, so me an' Nate headed for the creek with clean clothes an' a bar of soap. After lunch, I saddled up and rode into town to see Rance and possibly get up a ball game. I wasn't far out of the yard when Cindy caught up with me. It was that old "I can go anywhere you go" thing again.

The news was good, Rance would be able t' help with our roundup an' Gene Rhodes had his team ready t' beat us agin. And they did.

It was pitch dark when we got to the barn. I made Cindy rub her horse down before

49

she went home. The lights were off in our house and bunkhouse so I climbed up in th' loft and slept on the hay.

It wasn't uncommon for th' Beavers and Nealy families t' eat together, but addition of that Brown tribe was a whole new proposition and we were all pretty busy cookin', cleanin' an' settin' up.

Luckily, we had already penned up our dogs when Pete rode up, for standin' in his lap, forefeet on the pommel looking like a gargoyle on th' bow of a ship was a little black-and-white bulldog, and trottin' beside was a large mixed-breed dog that looked to be mostly bulldog.

"Got our two helpers." He grinned.

"Well, at least I won't have t' provide horses for *one* of 'em," I replied.

"Neither one, this here's Duke, th' Boston Terrier, an' he'll be on th' ground with Pie there who's more bulldog than anythin' else."

"Pie? He's got a funny name!" Nate exclaimed.

"Short for Piasano which is his long name." Pete grinned.

Pie spied the water trough and ambled over for a drink. When Duke saw the big dog's destination, he jumped off an' trotted after him. I say jumped off, but it was more like he ran down Pete's stirrup and hopped off when he was close to th' ground. Pete's horse shied.

"How many times I gotta tell yuh, dog, yuh git off on the *left* side!" Pete called after him. Duke hopped up on the edge of the trough at a corner and balancing there reached down and got a long drink.

"Guess they were thirsty," Pete observed as he stepped down and led the horse to the trough.

Howls from th' corncrib told us that the ranch dogs had discovered these intruders and they were anxious to challenge their right to be on home property.

"How in the world are two dogs gonna take th' place of two men?" Rance asked.

"Best brush poppers ya ever saw. Might be we'll never have t' go after a cow, jist keep 'em rounded up 'til all's cleared."

"That'd be OK with me!" Rance said.

Ain't gittin' soft are you? I asked myself.

Pie walked back to us and dribbled water on Nate's bare foot. "Yuck, dog!" he yelled. Pie wagged his tail and grinned. The terrier was off exploring, ignoring the challenging yowls from the corncrib.

Just then, Cindy walked up with her dad. "Father," she said formally, "this is Mr. Pecos Pete, Mr. Pete, this is my father, Bob Nealy."

The two men shook hands. "Glad you came, Pete, come on over and I'll introduce you to th' boys." Bob's welcome was sincere and I was glad. I wasn't too sure about how that would go, Pete just showin' up like he did, but it seemed t' me that Bob and Pa both knew of Pete from somewhere, probably another ranch in our area. It was reassurin' that they were easy in their minds about him. I put his horse up and we got up a game of Scrub with th' kids.

A TIME TO LAUGH

It was a fun time and we ate and talked and played the afternoon away. Toward evening, the wash pot was moved off its fire place and a good fire lit. The ladies brought out heaping bread bowls of dough and began to cook bear sign. They disappeared as soon as they were sugared or dipped in the sweet sauce and the cookin' and eatin' didn't taper off until those dough bowls were nearly empty. It looked like Nate and little Green Nealy were having a contest t' see who could eat the most.

"How many's that?" Nate asked.

"Six," Green mumbled as he stuffed a last bite into his mouth. "How many you had?"

"Num'er seven." Nate waved a doughnut with one bite out of it.

"Hah, I kotched ya." Green swallowed the last of num'er six and grabbed another.

As if someone had rung a bell, two mothers turned and asked, "What are you two up to?"

"Green Nealy, look at that shirt, when are you going to learn that clothes are not towels to wipe your hands on?" said the appropriate mother. There were two great arcs of sugar, sauce and crumbs down the front of his shirt where he had wiped his hands.

At the same time, mother number two was admonishing Mr. Nate. "How is it possible for you to get sauce from your hair to your chin like that? It's dripping off your chin and down your shirt!" Her vigorous wiping with a towel only served to smear goop all over. Now it was not only from hair to chin, but from ear to ear.

There wasn't a father in sight and the cooks were showing signs of distraction from their primary purpose. We couldn't let them leave the cooking. "We'll clean 'em up, Ma," I quickly said, grabbing up Green an' carrying him away while num'er seven disappeared into his mouth.

Behind me I heard Nate yelp and glancing 'round, I saw Rance had him over his shoulder. It was a good fifty yards to the creek behind the house and halfway there, Nate called out, "Num'er seven's gone."

"Hah . . . finished . . . mine . . . first," Green hollered between bumps.

Rance jogged up beside me as we approached the rock shelf over the creek, boys thinking a race was on and encouraging us. At the last moment, Green realized our intent and with a yell grabbed my collar as I threw him. I teetered on the edge an' was almost recovered when Rance, who had thrown the totally unsuspecting Nate overboard, slapped me on th' back and sent me in face-first.

Th' girls had been searching for four-leafed clovers on th' bank and followed us down to the creek as we came by. Parmelia, Rance's older sister, stifled Rance's laughter by shoving him off the ledge. As he fell, he turned and grabbed her wrist and carried her with him.

Cindy, my sisters, Eda B. and Sue Ellen, and Polly Ann Brown, seeing the fun came skipping down the hill hand in hand and skipped right off the ledge into the creek. Josh Nealy cannonballed the girls as they came up to the surface.

In less than a minute, there were ten fully clothed kids splashing in the water. We were all having fun splashing and yelling until Nate threw up and Green seeing that threw up too. The pool was evacuated in record time. There we stood, dripping, wringing out clothes and dumping out boots.

"I would swear that was more than seven bear sign, Nate," I said.

"Wasn't nuther, I counted 'em," Green grunted.

Those girls began gagging and runnin' up the hill to the back porch. As we boys rounded the corner of the house, shoes, socks, blouses and skirts were flying off dripping girls. Green, Josh and Nate were draggin' behind.

At the fire, I said, "We got 'em cleaned up, Mrs. Nealy."

"Did you have to get that wet to do it?" Ma asked.

The boys appeared from behind us to the oohs of two mothers. Rance handed me a doughnut and I took a bite and offered the rest to Nate. He looked likely to throw up again. "Tucker Beavers, isn't it bad enough that you all are standing here soaking wet without you making your brother sick?" Ma scolded.

"Looks like more than these got wet," Mrs. Brown said as four bedraggled girls appeared on the front gallery wrapped in blankets and looking forlorn.

"My stars and stripes!" Mrs. Nealy exclaimed.

"Well, at least Parmelia is mature enough not to get dragged into *this* mischief," Ma said, hurryin' for the house. She shooed the girls back in the door and we heard her exclaim, *"Parmelia!"*

"Oooh!" Sue Brown's hand flew to her mouth, eyes wide. Parmelia being two years older than Rance was considered a young adult and "of courting age" and had been the center of bachelor attention during the course of the day. She had stayed in the house out of sight.

Rance had to giggle and I almost choked on my doughnut.

Our plan to keep the cooks busy failed. If any more bear sign was to be it would be up to Rance and me, so we set to cookin'. I rolled out dough and Rance plopped them into the oil. Our first batch was a little scrawny and overdone, but we got the hang of it — just as the dough ran out.

"Well, I guess that's that," Rance said.

"Yep, looks like it's up to you an' me t' finish." I reached for one of the doughnuts.

"Hold on, Tuck, we better make peace with those cooks." Rance picked up th' bowl and carried it to the house. We entered the front door to the tune of squeals as four girls in various degrees of dress disappeared into bedrooms.

Mrs. Brown stood hands on hips blocking our progress. "What kind of mischief are you up to *now,* Rance Brown?"

"We thought you ladies might enjoy the last doughnuts, so we cooked 'em for you," Rance said, handing the bowl to her.

"Why, thank you, Rance," Mrs. Nealy said, "we hardly had time to enjoy them ourselves, the demand was so high."

"Here's coffee t' go with them," I said, setting the pot on the stove.

"Well, how sweet of you," Ma said, "but don't think this will get you off the hook for this mess, and get outside, you're dripping all over the floor!" She didn't mention the puddles the girls had left or the pile of soggy clothes slowly feeding the puddle around them.

We went down to th' bunkhouse and dug out dry clothes. The men were all sitting around the porch, having watched the events from a safe distance.

"Better wear them boots 'til they dry or you'll never get into 'em again," Pete said.

"What did you get into, anyway?" Bob asked.

"Aww, the girls wanted t' go swimmin'

an' we had to act as lifesavers," Rance grunted as he pulled on a boot.

"Yore life *savin'* may turn into life *givin'* when those wimmen get ahold of ya," one of the hands drawled.

"Yeah, might be good for yore health t' strike out for th' hills afore they git done with those girls," someone else put in.

"How's come this got t' be our fault all of a sudden?" I asked. "All we were doin' was takin' care o' two pigs that ate too many sign an' got it all over 'em."

"Don't matter, son." Pa chuckled. "You two were th' instigators an' it's for sure those 'poor little girls' are filling their mothers' ears with how it's all *your* fault."

"An' knowin' wimmin as we do, it's just es sure they're believin' ever' word an' workin' up a good scoldin' mood," one of the boys said.

"If it was me, I'd a'ready been hightailin' it for tall timber!"

"Awww, you fellers are just funnin' us," Rance said. "How could a little dip in th' creek an' a few wet clothes be such a big thing?"

"Wait an' see, son, wait an' see," Mr. Brown said.

The talk drifted on to other subjects and Rance nudged me. "Think they're right?"

he whispered.

"Prob'bly, it's for sure Parmelia ain't gonna mention that she pushed you before you pulled her into th' water."

"Yeah, but why git all het up about it?"

"Wimmin."

"Yeah . . . I guess you're right." He sat there a moment. "You packed?"

"Mostly — got th' wagon loaded. All I need to do is hitch up an' go."

"Let's go," he said and slipped off the porch and around the corner, his boots makin' a squishin' noise as he walked.

Our departure from the porch, quiet as it was, didn't go unnoticed and just as I had the horses hitched, spares tied to the tailgate, Pete came around the house with the dogs. "Reckon you boys could take these dogs with you? They're pretty tired an' would like t' ride up th' mountain. I'll be along later."

"Sure, Pete, put 'em on," I said.

At a wave of his hand, and a word, Pie scrambled up the wheel and into th' bed. Sniffing around, he found Pete's bedroll and with three circles settled down on it with a sigh. Pete handed Duke up and he immediately pushed his way between Rance and I on the bench, and seated himself as if to say *let's git goin'.*

Rance grimaced and muttered, "Think I'll ride Ranger," and jumped down.

Duke acknowledged his departure and scooted over. With his ears pointed, he looked at me an' nodded as if to say *let's go!*

Just then we heard Rance's ma call, "Jim, do you know where Rance got off to?"

Rance clucked to Ranger.

"Don't know, but I'll look around for him," Jim Brown called back. I sat still until I heard the screen door at th' house slam, then slapped reins. By then, Rance had disappeared into the trees. Lookin' back, I saw Mr. Brown standin' at th' corner of the building. He was grinnin' and waved and turned back.

It was two miles up the trail before Rance stopped and waited for us to catch up. I say "us" for Duke was riding that seat like he had ridden on Pete's saddle and I was his driver. There he sat the whole trip. He even disdained lookin' at an occasional rabbit that ran at our approach, though if he had been on the ground, he would have given chase. Right then, nothing was more important than his ride.

We unloaded after dark and when I threw Pete's roll on his bunk, Duke took possession. No one could approach the bunk without a soft warning. Once I passed by too close for his comfort and got a sharp bark. Even Pie kept his distance, content to lie on the floor in front of the fireplace.

"Think I'll take this bunk over here," Rance said, "looks like Duke has that one."

"If you need me, I'll be under th' cedars," I said and retired to my customary sleepin' place.

I was vaguely aware of Pete puttin' his horse in the corral shortly before time to get up. Soon a fire was stoked up and breakfast was on. I drew a fresh bucket of water and went into the shack. Rance was still sacked out and I helped Pete fix breakfast. As we were ready to sit down, Pete said, "Fetch 'em," and the two dogs sprang into action. Duke hurled himself upon Rance and began pulling the covers down, shaking them furiously and growling loudly. Pie was pulling the blanket and it was more than Rance could do to keep it. Soon it was on the floor and Duke was barking loudly in Rance's ear.

"All right, all right, I'm up," he growled as he sat up, whereupon Pie wadded the blanket up to his satisfaction and lay down on it and Duke jumped down and strutted over to Pete for his strip of bacon.

"Get off my blanket, dog." Rance pulled on a corner and Pie's growl warned of a possible confrontation.

"Commere, Pie, an' git this bacon," Pete called and the dog reluctantly gave up his bed for food.

Rance stumbled around dressing. "These boots are too stiff," he complained.

"Thought I told ye t' wear them 'til they dried," Pete said through a bite of biscuit.

"I ain't wearin' boots t' bed."

Pete chuckled, "I did once, though she made me take my spurs off. Shore was glad, too, when her husband come home unexpectedly. Likely ran ten miles in my boots and bare-assed afore I felt it was safe enough t' stop an' put my pants on. Shore do miss them spurs." He shook his head sadly.

"That's hard t' believe," Rance said.

"Nex' time yo're up to Parsons' pharmacy in Tularosa, look an' see if they's a pair of Mexican silver-mounted spurs with little silver bells hangin' b'hind th' counter. Them's mine, but I don't aim t' claim 'em any time soon."

"I saw them," I said. "There's a sign that says *Lost Spurs, Not for Sale.*"

"Yep, ol' 'Saint Paul' Parsons is waitin' for th' rightful owner t' come in an' claim 'em. Won't happen s'long es *he's* above sod. I can't even trust myself t' go in there anymore, though I think I can draw afore he reaches that shotgun under th' counter."

"Fa-a-an-tastic," Rance said as he sat down.

We ate in silence and put away the dishes then sat on th' bench in the morning sun. "Pete, since you know our hands better than I do, why don't you tell us how this rodeo is gonna go down?" I asked.

He took a last draw from his pipe, tapped it out on his boot heel and sat back. The dogs sat in front of us expectantly as if they were listening to his every word. "We'll start at the bottom of th' Strip an' clean it as we come up toward th' pens. Me an' th' boys will be poppin' bresh an' you two grab th' stock as they come out. Big stuff will have to have both ropes on 'em if you keep 'em out of th' bresh. I don't think we will be able to hold 'em 'til we have a bunch, they're too wild fer that. Gather up all th' hobbles an' piggin' ropes ya got. We'll hobble 'em 'til we got a bunch then drive 'em to th' pen."

"It's gonna be slow, ain't it?" I said.

"Looks thataway."

"I should be the one in the brush with th' dogs," I said.

"We work t'gether an' *you* don' know signals t' give 'em, er whut they's sayin'," Pete said. "I won't be poppin' bresh too strong, jest directin' these boys as they work."

"I still don't feel good lettin' you do th' hard stuff like that."

"Cain't be he'ped, but don't worry, I been there afore an' these boys'll be doin' most o' th' work. Pick out your biggest hosses an' don't worry how fast they are. If'n one o' them critturs gits up a full head o' steam you ain't gonna catch 'im anyway. Usually they'll circle around an' head back into th' bresh. You can save a lot of runnin' if you just watch an' cut him off when he turns back."

We caught up our horses and headed down-pasture. Pete chose a small horse

64

from his bunch that looked like he had been in brush before from the scars on his forelegs and sides. One ear had a ragged edge and an odd droop to it. The dogs got excited when they saw Pete mount up on him and danced and yipped around the horse. The horse seemed excited too and nickered and snapped at them playfully a time or two.

Pete had t' hold them out of th' brush until we got to the end. "Sic 'em, boys," he said and the dogs sprang into action. He held back the horse to leave us with one last word, "Don't let any git back into th' bresh, those two git testy when they have t' run th' same critter out more'n onct."

With that, he was gone and th' sounds gave proof to th' phrase *brush poppin'*. We rode along with the sound of their progress. I heard a yip from Duke and a cow bawled. We could hear them gettin' closer until a black steer burst from the brush, Duke hangin' on to one ear and Pie nipping at the steer's heels. The steer shook his head and Duke dropped off and ran back into the brush. At that same moment, my loop settled over Mr. Steer's horns. With one last nip, Pie turned and followed Duke. Rance had t' throw twice t' grab the steer's back feet. We had him stretched out and I got hobbles on his front feet and back in the saddle just as a second steer broke out.

As if Duke knew we were not ready, he ran at the steer's head and when he lowered his horns to him, the dog grabbed his lower lip. With a roar, the cow lifted his head and shook as if to sling the dog off, but Duke held on until he saw the big loop settle over the steer's head. When he felt my pull, he dropped to the ground an' ran into the brush.

"Things go this fast, we'll be done by noon — or dead," I said as Rance shook out another loop.

"No kiddin'!"

The next cow to leave the brush was a mamma cow and she appeared hard on the heels of Pie who was hard on th' heels of a yearlin' calf. While Duke and Rance handled mamma, I caught her calf. With him hobbled, it wasn't necessary to hobble momma — we thought — but when we let th' calf up, mamma charged and it was just by a hair that my horse escaped her. As it was, her horn caught my pants leg and ripped it. My loop settled on her hind legs as she went by and she hit the ground hard. I was on her and had her hobbled before she could get her breath.

This continued all morning until we were

all soaked with sweat. All of a sudden, it seemed, we were out of rope and I hollered at Pete. He came out with the dogs who lay down in th' shade and panted. They were frothy and bloody about their mouths and I hoped it was mostly cow blood. Pete was as lathered as his horse and I could see a few thorns in his clothes and the horse's fore-legs.

"You boys hollerin *uncle* whin we're just gittin' started?" he asked.

"Looks like you an' th' dogs're nearer finished than we are," I said.

He grinned. "Let's git us a drink."

We let horses drink while the dogs waded out and lay down in the shallows, lapping water and lickin' their wounds. Pete pulled a pair of pliers from his bag and began de-thorning his horse and himself.

"Thought you wasn't gonna go hard in th' brush," Rance said.

"*I* wasn't, but this horse had other ideas. Spent most o' my time tryin' t' keep him down to a mere gallop, but it weren't gonna happen. He'll be more temperate tomor-rer."

"You'll ride him agin tomorrow?"

"Watch me try t' go without him."

When we counted up, we had twenty-seven head hobbled and scattered about.

That was not countin' three unhobbled young calves who stuck to their mammy's sides. They were all huddled as close to the brush as possible with the hobbles. Some were even tangled in the brush and had to be pulled free. We gathered them and it was a slow drive to the pens. After a bite to eat and change of horses, we spent the afternoon retrieving our hobbles and running the cattle into the holding pen. Duke and Pie didn't help much, just watched from the shade.

Sitting on the bench after supper, I said to the others, "We only have thirty head up, what do you think about roundin' up another dab afore we brand?"

"Me an' the boys are game," Pete said.

"If I can get outa bed in th' morning," Rance said.

I didn't say anything, but I felt a lot like Rance and I hadn't been hanging around a store getting soft like he had. Rance was always game. We turned in early.

A good night's sleep rejuvenated us and aside from an ache here and there we were good to go. We started at the lower end of the Strip again just in case some critter had moved into unoccupied territory, but it was clear except for one old mossyhorn we probably had missed th' day b'fore. He was some salty character and Pete came out to help us with him. Rance and I held him stretched out while Pete hobbled him side-lined, that is, forefoot to hind foot. Even with that, he was up in a flash, but when he started to run at Pete, his hobble tripped him and he landed on his nose. Another try or two convinced him that something was bad wrong and he quit. We had scrounged up all the piggins and hobbles we could and by noon we had thirty-five hobbled, not counting a half dozen calves by side.

The drive to the pens was slower than the day before due mostly to the slowness of the drivers. We could tell that the dogs and Pete's horse were more fagged out and it looked like a day's rest would be needed.

"Well, they're not th' only ones," Rance said as he got stiffly down from his horse. After lunch we retrieved hobbles and pre-pared our branding chute for the morrow.

We had just branded our first cow and calf when Rance said, "Here comes some side-saddle help."

Cindy rode by and waved as she continued on to the cabin. In a few minutes she returned astride one of the spare horses. With little talk, she took the tally book and helped Rance push the cows into the chute.

I could hear the two carrying on a lively conversation, but caught little of it. At noon, Rance said, "I didn't know Cindy had been helping you brand."

"Came up th' first day we branded an' did a good job," Pete said.

"Bet she couldn't be near as good sidesaddle." Rance grinned.

"If we had another sidesaddle, we could have a contest," Cindy quipped.

"Not none o' me," Rance began. "Them horns would ki . . ." He caught himself and turned red. There was an embarrassed quiet for a moment.

"Knew a girl onct could outride any man on her sidesaddle," Pete said. "Never saw her lose a race. Course that was due mostly t' that thoroughbred she rode. One day after a race, th' boys got t' raggin' her about that horse, so they swapped horses an' raced agin an' she *won* agin. That put an end t' that!"

It took 'til dark to finish brandin'. We made Cindy leave in time t' get home afore dark. When she heard we were poppin brush, she promised to be back.

Pete looked his "bresh horse" over and declared him rested and ready to go. The dogs were fit, so we set our sights on another

70

day or two of clearing the Nueces Strip of cattle.

It seemed the closer we got to the end of the Strip, the wilder th' cows were. "Not surprised at thet," Pete said. "Those wildest ones would keep th' most distance from all commotion."

"Do you think we'd have a chance o' runnin' 'em into th' wings without hobblin' if you ran 'em out th' end o' th' brush?" I asked.

"Yeah, if we were on both sides an' you an' th' dogs b'hind 'em, we might be able t' keep 'em bunched and running," Rance added.

"Might work," Pete said, "if we pushed 'em hard. I s'pect we would need t' have th' gate open an' haze 'em all th' way in."

"We'll have t' empty th' pen of what we got in there now b'fore we do that," I said. "Guess we'll be doin' some brandin' tomorrow."

"That's what Cindy's expectin' us t' do," Rance said. "She'll be here early in th' mornin'."

"That gal shouldn't be here when we try t' run cows," Pete allowed.

"We won't tell her what we're up to an' if we start early enough, she won't git here until th' fun's over with," I said.

Rance yawned and stood up. "Sounds like th' deal's set an' I'm headin' for bed. If I don't get up in th' morning, you can brand without me but be sure t' save me some fries."

"You sleep in an' some o' them fries'll be your own," Pete said.

Cindy did show up early and we put in a long day brandin'. These last cows were some of the worst for drivin' and a few of them we had to catch and throw just to get 'em branded. Cindy and Rance were on their third mounts for the day when that last steer took th' chute.

CHAPTER 5
THE SIDESADDLE VAQUERO

We had two classes of cow — wild unbranded and wild branded. Now came what we hoped would be our last run of wild unbranded cattle. Somehow, I would have t' tame 'em down b'fore turnin' them loose again, or they'd go right back into that brush. Gettin' rid of a bunch of those culled bulls and mossyhorn steers would help a whole lot and I guess truth is I would always have cattle in the brush. Only way out of that would be t' burn th' Neuces Strip, something I didn't want t' do. I might complain about brush, but that's good shelter for cattle in bad weather.

There was th' usual excitement among dogs and horses when we saddled up at three a.m. after a cup of coffee. For what we hoped was th' last time, we started at th' lower end of the Strip in case there were any critters backtracked on us. Sure enough, there were a few at th' very end and we picked up more as we moved north. Pete and those dogs didn't run any out and with me creek-side and Rance on th' other, we kept them ahead of us.

Our progress actually slowed as we got to the upper end, there were so many head that th' poppers had to range back and forth to keep cattle ahead of them. The creek was hard against a bluff on one side and brush on the other so I joined the poppers. With me on one end, dogs in th' middle and Pete on the other, we could hold the line pretty good and as we saw those first cows forced out into th' open, we pushed 'em hard.

I hit th' creek on th' run to get to my side and turn them in th' right direction while Pete and the dogs chased from behind. I could hear Rance chousin' them from his side and we kept 'em bunched and runnin'. He was up front turnin' them into th' left wing when a bunch behind him split and turned back. There was nothing we could do about it without losin' more and I had given them up when I heard a yell and saw Cindy riding straight at th' lead steer still sidesaddle! It seemed the world stopped moving and I stared at what was surely going to be a collision between horse and steer.

A black streak appeared and Duke, with a leap, caught that steer by his tail just above th' bushy end. He must have clamped down hard, for that steer bellered and whirled around in a circle several times trying to get at that demon that had ahold of his tail. The bunch following veered away and Pie was on them in a second, pushing them back into the rear of the run. As if on signal, Duke turned loose of the tail, hit the ground running and nipped the steer's heels back into the run, Cindy close behind.

I didn't have any time to think after I started breathing agin, as my side of that bunch had taken advantage of my momentary lapse and started for the unknown. I barely got them turned back inside the right wing. With them safely in the wings, we pulled back and as the space narrowed, those cows slowed down. Soon they were milling in front of th' gate and we gently hazed them in until they were all penned.

Cindy was mad as a hornet. "You started early so I wouldn't be here, didn't you?" she yelled. "I can do anything you . . ."

"Seems t' me you showed up jist in time," Pete cut in.

"Yeah and sidesaddle at that." Rance grinned.

"I can do anyth —"

"We *know* you can, Cindy, an' probably even sidesaddle, but if you had gotten hurt or worse herdin' wild cattle, theyed a-been two or three buryin's when my pa an' your pa got through with us."

Rance looked puzzled. "All I seen was Duke gettin' a merry-go-round ride on that steer's tail, what happened?"

"That bunch broke out ahind you an' Cindy was on a collision course with th' lead steer when Duke got there." Pete was grinning and scratchin' th' little dog between his ears. Duke panted happily.

"Cindy, you got here at just th' right moment an' got in on the most dangerous part o' th' drive, so I guess you could say you got in on it. It's sure you saved us a lot of work turnin' that bunch back an' we're grateful," I said.

That pleased her and she grinned a little. "And I did it sidesaddle!"

"My gosh, there must be seventy-five head!" I said, looking at the bunch.

"More like seventy, I should think," Pete said.

"Shore is a lot more'n *I* expected," Rance said.

We rested and pulled thorns out of horses, dogs and ourselves while we waited on our tally keeper t' get back. When we saw her coming, we pushed th' first two into our chute and were just finishin' brandin' and cuttin' when she came up behind two more head. When she saw the bucket for the fries, she said, a little too sweetly, I thought, "Tuck, your ma sent you up some clean clothes. I left them in th' shack."

What now, I said to myself.

Even quittin' early for dinner and restin' some then, we were all except Cindy pretty tired from th' early work and a little after mid afternoon we called it a day. There were still about half of the herd left to brand and we would be doing that again on the morrow.

"I swan, you must be the three laziest vaqueros I know," Cindy said.

"We been up since two thirty this mornin' an' we put in a good day's work afore you showed your face," Rance said defensively.

"Yeah, an' our day ain't done yet," I added.

"Pickin' splinters and thorns doesn't look like work to me!" she shot back.

"Got t' be done," I said.

"An' someone has t' cook fries." Rance grinned.

"O-o-oh yuck!" Cindy said and turned quickly and rode away.

"Got rid o' her!" Pete chuckled.

"Cindy! Tell Ma t' send me another shirt an' pants. I tore these t' rags in th' brush!" I called.

She waved her hand, not even turning or lookin' back.

"Don't you forget!"

Another wave of th' hand and she disappeared into the trees.

Ma's package just had underwear in it and a note on top that read "Change!!"

She peeked! Boy is she gonna get it!

We had Cindy a horse saddled and waiting at the pens and were all set up to brand while Cindy changed horses. Soon the air was filled with dust, smoke and smelled o' burning hair and we finished with th' last cow by mid afternoon.

"My next problem is t' get those culls out o' th' country," I said as we sat in th' shade and surveyed our work.

"Won't be easy," Rance said.

"We-l-l-l, it might not be as bad as you think," Pete said.

"How would you do it, Pete?" Rance asked.

"They's two ways t' do it, I guess. We could slit their eyelids so's they couldn't close their eyes but that's a pretty permanent thing t' do to a cow, or we could prop open their eyes with sticks. Either way, they won't pop brush if they can't close their eyes."

"I'd go for sticks. Buyers might not take lightly t' a bunch o' wild cows that could never close their eyes," I said.

"We got a total of two hundred sixty-three head and out of that there are fifteen bull culls and forty-two mossyhorn steers," Cindy said, consulting her tally book.

"That's fifty-seven times two, a hundred fourteen toothpicks," Rance said.

"Better git t' whittling," I said.

Cindy headed home early, vowing t' be back in th' morning and we spent a restful evening sittin' on the bench and cuttin' out little sticks for the animals' eyes.

It took us all morning to catch and attach eye openers to twenty-eight steers.

After noon, we let a couple of head out and they headed for the Strip as fast as they could. At th' very edge of the brush, they suddenly stopped and shook their heads from side to side. Again they tried to enter the brush, but stopped. After three or four more tries, they seemed to decide that they couldn't go there and turned back, bawling and after a while, they began t' graze.

"Turn out four or five more," Pete called.

It was a repeat of the first performance.

One of the second bunch pushed a little against th' brush, but he soon came back to the open and joined his companions. We slowly let the rest of the herd out and it wasn't long until the whole bunch was quietly grazing.

We drove them back into th' pen, which was easy enough. Next morning we finished installing props on the rest of the cattle and let them out a few at a time. When they were all settled down we began movin' 'em down to headquarters where we had a pen ready for them. They were pretty docile, to the surprise of all. The only trouble we had was gettin' them into the woods, I guess because they looked too much like brush the cows thought they couldn't go through.

Pa and Bob came down and watched as we stanchioned each cow and removed the eye openers. Soon the cows had filled up with water and were contentedly grazing or resting. Pa shook his head. "Those can't be the wild cows out of that pasture, you boys been strayin' over into th' big pasture?"

"No sir, the bulk of that bunch came out o' th' brush. Those eye props made 'em tame, an' I'll take that," I said.

"I seen wild ones tame down like this b'fore after wearin' those eye openers a while," Pete said. "Seems they either git t' seein' th' world different or they make up t' b'have so's they don't get *that* treatment agin, but I wouldn't throw away them props jist yet."

CHAPTER 6
WILD COW TRADING

My next thing to do was to find a market for the critters and quick. Pa had contacted a buyer for the Mescalero Reservation and a couple of days later he drove into the yard. One thing you could say about those cows was that they were sleek and fat — well, fat for an old longhorn at least — and the buyer liked that. "I'll take them in th' pen at eight cents to th' pound or delivered at ten cents," he said.

That eight cents sounded good. For sure I didn't want t' drive that bunch to th' reservation. "I'll take th' eight cents," I said.

The buyer rolled his cigar to the other side of his mouth and spat. He looked me straight an' said, "You sure about that, son?"

"I'm sure. I got a lot t' get done an' don't have time t' spare."

"OK." He shrugged, but I could tell he wasn't too happy about it. "Let's count 'em an' weigh, 'em out."

We set up to count and as he counted, he called out his weight of each cow. Now a good vaquero can guess th' weight of a cow to within a few pounds and it was very obvious even to a novice like me that he was underestimating the cows. Pete kept shakin' his head and mutterin' and I could tell by his posture that Pa was disturbed too.

The buyer hunkered down in th' shade against a fence and figured on his pad and called, "I got fifty-six cows at thirty-six thousand four hundred pounds and eight cents comes to two thousand nine hundred twelve dollars."

"Can't even git th' damned count right." Pete slapped his leg with his hat and stomped off.

"I counted fifty-seven head," I said, hunkering down beside him.

"Nope, there were fifty-six, son, don't do this as much as I do and miscount." He took the cigar out of his mouth when he spat this time. "That ten cents a pound still stands if you want t' make more on 'em."

I began t' suspect that his undercount and underestimated weights were for a reason other than pure dishonesty — though I would not have counted that out, either. "I wouldn't drive those cows up there for fifteen cents on th' pound."

The buyer lifted his hat and scratched his head. "Way too rich for me." Then after a minute, "I could go eleven cents."

"Make it fifty-*seven* head an' add a hundred pounds a head an' we might be able t' work out a deal," I said.

"You askin' me to pad my figures, boy?"

"No, but I expect you t' give me a fair estimate an' head count an' if you're so good at this, you know you have shorted me all around."

He got real red in the face and nearly bit his cigar in two. I suspect he was mad because he got caught by a kid he thought he could buffalo an' not because I accused him of cookin' th' books. He slammed his pad shut and stood up. "Don't look like we can come to an agreement, boy, hate it I wasted my time coming out here."

I was mad and I probably shouldn't have, but I said, "Maybe when you get a little more experience countin' an estimatin' weights, we can work some deals."

For a moment I thought he was gonna hit me, but he just turned on his heel and got in his buggy and drove off without a word.

I heard a snicker and turned to find the whole outfit standin' behind th' fence. "You yahoos been listenin' in on a private conversation?"

"Weren't so private whin yore talking 'bout them cows we sacrificed so much cloth, blood an' skin t' git," Pete said.

"I thought he was gonna hit you," Cindy said.

"I wonder if he was shortin' you for himself or because he didn't want t' drive them cows to th' reservation," Rance mused.

"I don't know," I said, "but we missed a cattle drive by one head, four cents a pound and fifty-seven hundred pounds."

"Well, I'm not so sure that fifteen cents a pound was enough t' entice me t' drive those cows *anywhere*," Rance said.

"Considerin' those cows, fifty-six head might be a good count after a drive," Pete added.

After dinner, Rance saddled up and rode to town. "Got t' get back to th' store where I can rest up an' heal," he called as he rode out of the yard. Pete rounded up Duke and Pie and left to take them back home and Nate and Green had to be kept from letting our dogs out of the corncrib too soon.

Bob was down in the meadow seeing to the hayin' crew, and Cindy was fillin' a water barrel on the back of a buggy when I stepped into the house to see Pa. He looked up from his books and said, "I thought you handled that buyer right well, son. Just remember that it's good not t' burn any bridges unless you have to. You may never know for sure what a feller's motives are when dealing with him an' you may want t' deal with him again someday."

"Yes, sir, but I still have those cows t' git rid of. Do you have any idea what to do now?"

"The butchers in town are always lookin' for a head or two an' there are three or four around Tularosa an' La Luz that might buy some. The army at Fort Stanton might take th' whole herd. Why don't you ride into town an' telegraph th' fort an' see if they are interested? You can check with th' butchers while you're there."

"Thanks, Pa. I'll do that this afternoon."

I stepped out on the porch and Cindy called, "Want to ride down to the hay meadow with me?"

"I have to go to town to see if I can sell some cattle," I replied.

"We could set this barrel off and drive on in."

I would have much rather ridden than to drive, but she had been so good to help with the roundup that I felt obliged to go with her. The smile on her face told me she was pleased. She insisted on driving and sat very close to me on that narrow seat. I think that right then and there was the first time I realized that she had grown into a young woman — and the thought was exciting and confusing.

I had a list from both mothers for things from the store an' Pa needed some salt blocks so we headed for the mercantile. Rance was sittin' on th' dock in his raggedy cow clothes, swingin' his legs an' talkin' "cowboy" to a couple of town girls when we drove up.

"Rance! Rance!" Cindy called. "Those blasted cows busted out of the pen and went right back into the Strip! We got to do it all over again!"

The two girls had turned to watch us and the look of dismay on Rance's face was a wonder. "Oooh . . . kay," his groan turned into bluster as the wide-eyed ladies turned back to him. "I'll hafta git a fresh horse, mine's played out." He rose somewhat stiffly as the girls set up a clammer to go with us.

"Too dang'rous," he said as he limped through th' door.

"Oh, Cindy, if you go, can we go with you?" they begged.

"Of course you can," she replied. To me she said, "Give me the lists and I will get the things and catch up with you at the telegraph office."

"I'll be there or at the butcher's down the street," I replied. "Think you can catch up with Rance afore he rides out, he was so anxious t' go?"

"I don't think that'll be hard to do," she laughed.

There were two ways t' get th' latest news those days, go by a telegraph office or sit in the barber shop a few minutes. If you wanted everyone's *opinion* of the news, you mostly got that at the saloon. The key was clickin' away as I walked up and I waited as the operator wrote furiously for a few seconds. "Wel-l-l, looks like the army's taken over the reservation again. I just got an order for th' law t' 'apprehend and arrest' th' agent if he shows up. Didn't say nothin' 'bout dead or alive, but it may be hard t' keep him alive around here if he's been stirring up Mescaleros again." He studied the message a moment, hollered "Message!" out the window, then turned to me. "What can I do for you, young man?"

At that moment a breathless and barefoot kid ten years old or so ran up to the window. "Here, Bo, take this to Deputy Simms on th' double; it's important." The boy hurried off, his bare feet squirting out little puffs of

88

dust at every step.

He smiled and shook his head. "Now then, what can I do for you?"

"I was just going t' telegraph the army t' see if they needed any beef, sounds like they might have a need for some now."

"It does at that. What say we address this to the Officer of the Day, an' he can get it to th' right authority." He was already writing out a message. "What do you want to say?"

"I have fifty-seven head of mixed cattle, will sell them range delivery at fifteen cents a pound."

"Army won't take things at an odd count, better t' say fifty head and deal with th' buyer when he comes," he said. "I'll ask him to reply as soon as possible, but it may be tomorrow before we hear from him." He finished writing the message and handed it to me. It read:

Officer of the Day, Fort Stanton, New Mexico stop
Have fifty head fat mixed cattle stop
Will sell range delivery at 15 cents per pound stop

I signed it and handed it back and paid the operator. "I'll be around town a couple of hours," I said. "If it comes in, I'd pay a boy a nickel t' bring it to me. It would be worth a meal an' two bits if he had t' bring it to th' ranch."

"Know just th' one t' do that." He grinned.

Jose Grijalva was the butcher Ma used when those times arose that we were out of fresh beef at the ranch or she wanted mutton or when Benito our bunkhouse cook wanted a goat quarter. His shop was just down the street and I walked over to see him.

"Buenos, Meester Tuck, how are you?" he greeted from the chopping block.

"Just fine, Jose, how are you and yours?"

"Wee all bee fine, Rosa ees een her — how you say — con-fine-ment and any time now will present me with a fine son!" Jose and Rosa had four daughters and were trying mightily to produce an heir to carry on the good Grijalva name.

"I have a few head of mixed cattle for sale. They are range fed and pretty slick, if you are in th' need for one. I'm sellin' them at ten cents a pound on th' hoof," I said.

"Sí, sí, Señor Tuck-er, I weel need one for thee shop and one for thee family when my muchacho is chr-r-r-istened."

"That sounds good, I will check with th'

other butchers and plan to drive them in tomorrow. You can have first pick."

"Gracias Tuck. I theenk Señor Johnson butcher a beef yesterday and it will not be soon that Ross and Raul weel butcher." The three shops kept track of what meat was available. In a limited market such as ours it would do them no good to have a surplus of meat on hand. That's not to say that the competition was not keen between them, for it was.

It turned out just as Jose said, Bill Johnson had plenty of beef available, but wanted a good beef for the next week. Jamie Ross needed a beef toward th' end of th' week. The Methodist Church had ordered a half for a barbecue Sunday evening. There was a corral at the wagon yard and I made reservations to use it for my little herd.

I found Cindy sittin' on th' dock by her purchases talking to a half dozen town girls. They were all atwitter as I walked up and there was a chorus of "Hello Tucker" in that coy singsong voice that made a fellow shudder to hear. You knew that something had, was or was gonna be afoot and it usually wasn't somethin' boys wanted to be a part of. I loaded the buggy as Cindy said her good-byes an' we got out of there as soon as I could, Cindy sitting close and waving until we passed from sight. She had caught up on all the town happenings and for the next half hour told me all that had been goin' on and not a little that was imagined had gone on. I listened but couldn't have told half of it th' next day. It began t' cool as th' sun receded and Cindy began to nod. About the third time she nodded off, she laid her head on my shoulder and was soon asleep, so soundly that I had to put my arm around her to keep her from falling.

I was surprised at how soft and smooth her arm felt and it was awfully warm and soft where she leaned on me. It was stirring things in me that I had not felt before. I had always thought of Cindy as pal and friend, but these feelings were different and I couldn't say that they were not pleasant and exciting. Something must have tickled her nose for she stirred and rubbed and instead of returning to her lap, her hand fell on my leg and remained there. That was how we rode into th' yard an' I was glad it was dark.

She didn't stir until we stopped and then she awoke with a start. "Oooh, are we home already? I must have slept the whole way!"

"All th' way from th' time you got me caught up on th' news," I said as I helped her down at her step. She helped me sort the packages going to her house and carry them to the stoop. She turned toward me and was so close we bumped together. "Oh," she said in surprise and something deep in my memory stirred. "At's hokay, 'Indy," I said in words I hadn't used in years, and I kissed her on the forehead just like Ma made me do when I was five and she was two.

Cindy stepped back a step and said, "Tucker Beavers, I'm not a little girl anymore, and you can stop that baby talk!" She whirled and the door was slamming closed before I could move. *Now what was that all about?* I led th' horses over to our porch and unloaded packages. By the time I had turned horses loose, Ma had picked up the packages.

"Have you eaten?" she asked, and not waiting for a reply went about setting a place and fishing dishes out of th' warming oven. I sat down and ate and caught her up on the happenings of the day. "Tomorrow I'm gonna take a few head of cattle to town for those butchers. Jose says that he will be a new father soon and wants a cow for his son's christening."

Ma laughed. "Jose is counting his sons before they hatch. He's expected a son four times without success and this time may be no different."

"He's sure countin' on it, Ma."

"The Good Lord will determine what he gets and I assure you that he will love his child whatever the gender will be."

"Thank you for supper, that was good," I said as I placed my dishes in th' wash pan.

"It would be good if you would take Nate and Green with you tomorrow." She was already washing up.

"Jehoshaphat, Ma, I can barely handle one herd of wild animals at a time, not *two*!"

"You watch your tongue, young man, you're not too old to be taken down a notch or two!"

"Sorry, Ma, you just caught me by surprise."

"Those boys have been riding long enough to be good at it and they need to begin to learn how to put their abilities to good use."

I suspect she could have added that our whole ranch could use a rest from their shenanigans. Now on top of herding wild stock, I was gonna have to keep two enthusiastic boys out of trouble. "But, Ma . . ."

"No buts, Tucker, you need to start teaching your brother — and Green — how to work and this is a good time to start!"

"Yes, ma'am." The discussion was over and the matter settled.

■ ■ ■ ■

When there was room, I slept in the bunkhouse because the men were up earlier and
breakfast was sooner than at the house. I
had just sat down to eat with the others
when the screen door behind me slammed.
I didn't look around until I saw smirks on
faces and someone kicked me under the
table. Even Bob Nealy was grinning. "You
weren't gonna eat b'fore your crew did were
you, Tuck?"

There they stood, too large sombreros sittin' on their ears, red paisley bandannas
around their necks, pants stuffed into boot
tops and outsized spurs attached in some
mysterious way to heels. I can look back at
that image and smile now, but at that first
moment I think I could have walked under
the table and not even had to duck my head.

"Come een, gen'lemen an' have thee
seat." Benito stood grinning at the kitchen
door, two steaming cups in his hand. The
two solemnly removed their hats and sat
down one on either side of me. Benito set
down the cups and I was relieved to see that
the concoction was more milk than coffee.
"Your plates will be right out," said the cook
who never filled any cowboy's cup or plate,

95

as he hurried off. He returned with two plates heaped with biscuits and thick'nin' gravy and one biscuit dripping with butter and honey — th' first time any of us knew honey had graced the bunkhouse table. We all dug in and the boys gallantly tried to do justice to the food before them. When we were finished and the dishes in the wash pan and a second round of coffee started, Bob laid out chores just like he did every day. He ended by saying, "Tucker and his crew are takin' a few head of those wild cows to town. Before you boys head out, help cut them out and get them on their way."

I was sure glad he said that, for I would have been half the day doing it by myself — with the help I had. Two ponies were tied to the rail and it suddenly dawned on me that I didn't just have two critters t' train, the number had just jumped to four.

We caught up and saddled and I was relieved to see that Bob had also saddled and taken the boys in hand. At least we wouldn't have to worry about them while we caught those cows. I told my helpers what I wanted and we soon had them bunched in a corner of the fence. When we tried t' move them, it was like bustin' a covey of quail. Cows went everywhere, mostly tryin' t' get back to the main bunch. By the time we got them back in the corner, everyone was in a lather. Even Bob and the boys had hazed in a couple.

There was only one thing to do and we set about doin' it. Soon there were three pairs of cows necked together, loose enough so they could walk but not run. We let number seven go and Nate and Green didn't have any trouble hazin' her out of the way.

The little bunch limped and bawled and scrambled through th' gate as Pete rode into the yard.

"Right on time, Pete, th' hard work's all done!" John Crider called. In keeping with the penchant to use nicknames, we called John Crider by the name *Cider* most of the time.

"He knowed that, Cider, been watchin' us from a corner o' th' barn," Bet Sommes called scornfully.

Just then one of th' pairs separated and departed for parts unknown. Pete caught th' hind legs of one of the steers while Cider busted the other. Examining th' rope trailin' from his steer's neck Pete said, "Looks like you boys need a refresher course on th' proper tying of knots."

"An' I guess yo're th' perfesser of knot

tyin'?" Bet asked.

"At your service," Pete said and proceeded with Lesson One until his "class" rode away full of derisive calls and insults. Pete grinned and shrugged. "Some people'll never learn. What are we up to, Tuck?"

"I've sold some of these cows to butchers in town an' we were just gettin' ready to drive 'em in."

"Looks like you got plenty o' help, but I think I'll ride along with you anyway, I need some things from th' store. Me an' these boys'll bring up th' drag an' you can take th' lead."

Well, there's not much "leading" to a bunch of mad wild cows tied to each other and I ended up ropin' th' horns of one pair and pullin' them where I wanted t' go. If they had ever figgered out that they could charge me together, we would have gotten t' town a lot faster. As it was, we fought most of th' way until they were so tired they quit an' just plodded along. Pete had boys ridin' flank and keepin' th' other two pair in line without ropin' them.

We got to that wagon yard with six fagged-out cows, three lathered horses and three tired cowboys. Pete helped me untie them while the boys watched from outside the pen. I took the boys to th' livery stable and

98

showed them how t' rub their ponies down after their work. We left them in the pen with feed and water and met Pete at Calico Cow for lunch. Four plates of steaks and vegetables and copious amounts of tea restored our vigor and we filled our dessert sides with lemon meringue pie.

The boys alternated between "cowboy cocky" and wide-eyed wonder. They were full of a thousand questions as if they had never been to town or eaten in a restaurant. But then I guess they had never been treated as an equal and eaten with "big folks," so they had reason t' feel cocky. They left to hunt up their buddies while Pete socialized in th' saloon. I hung around the mercantile a couple of hours talking to Rance and customers while the cattle had time to settle down and look presentable.

When the afternoon crowd thinned and Rance had a minute, he gave me th' high sign an' headed for their storeroom. I followed casually and by th' time I got there, Rance was rummaging b'hind feed sacks and pulled out a flour sack. Two bundles came out of the sack wrapped in more cloth. He unrolled the smaller one and out came a Colt Peacemaker .45. He opened the cylinder and handed it to me. The thing that made it smaller was the short barrel. "It's a

Shopkeeper's Model," Rance whispered. "I'm gonna keep it for myself an' put it under our cash box in th' store — after I practice up some."

As he unwrapped the second gun, I saw that the big difference was the barrel length. It was the classic Peacemaker .45 with the seven-and-one-half-inch barrel. Both guns were well used and this Peacemaker grips were a little beat up. "Look at the butt, Tuck," Rance whispered. I turned the gun up and there on one edge plain as day were two notches.

"Wow!" I said almost out loud.

"Shhhh! Ma doesn't know I have them. I thought you might want t' have this long gun."

"Shore, I do, how much?"

"Five dollars."

"Five? You didn't pay that much for *both* of 'em — an' it's used."

Rance grinned. "How about four?"

"I'd give you two on th' condition that it shoots well an' straight."

"Can't take two, but I'd go three fifty."

"I'll meet you at three if you throw in a box o' shells."

Rance ducked his head *as if* in thought and kicked at a sack of oats with his toe. I could see a smile tuggin' at th' corners of his mouth. I knew he would do it and that even at that price I probably had paid for both guns. The shells were nothin' to him, he would just take them off the shelf an' their store would pick up th' cost.

"I guess I could do that, Tuck, just for you." He held out his hand and we shook, the liar! I rolled the gun back up in the bag and went out the back door to put it in my saddlebag. When I went back into the store, there was a box of one hundred .45 shells on th' counter.

"Happy shooting," Rance whispered as I paid him.

"Don't shoot a payin' customer," I replied.

I went down to Jose's. "I have seen your cows, Tuck-er and they look good," Jose called from the back of the store. "I like the brindle cow, but alas, I shall not need beef for thee christening, wee will have goat instead." This was not a put-down for Jose's new daughter, the Mexican Americans love their barbecued kid, but the beef was reserved for that special occasion when Jose presented his son to the world. The curtain parted to the living quarters behind and Rosa entered with a tiny bundle in her arms. Two dark eyes peeked from behind her skirts as daughter number three followed her in. Rosa carefully parted the blanket and I saw a little button nose below tightly squeezed shut eyes and a head full of dark curly hair. Already she had lost her birth redness and her smooth olive skin fairly glowed.

"Eesn't she be-utiful?" Jose whispered. "Already she has stolen our hearts and she not two days old and without a name. Wee cannot use the chosen name. It is reserved for a later time, but wee will have to think of something beautiful before the christening."

Ma was right, I thought as I complimented Rosa and congratulated Jose. Being forewarned, I had bought a pink baby blanket to present to the new child from our family. "Here is a gift for the child from the Beavers family," I said, handing the package to Rosa, "and I have four suckers I need to get rid of if you know where they could go." A small brown hand appeared from behind Rosa's skirt. "Señora, there is some creature behind your skirt, do you know what it is?"

"Ahhh, Susana come out and say bueno to Señor Tuck-er," Jose called. The hand clutched a fold of Rosa's skirt and two brown eyes peeked around. "Say hello, Susana," Rosa whispered.

Susana smiled and her lips moved and

there was an unheard "hello." I held the four cinnamon suckers fanned out in my hand and she chose one, would have taken another one with the other hand save for a word from her mother. She turned to go and I called, "Tell your sisters I have something for them." Almost immediately, three heads popped through the curtains and the lure of three red suckers overcame their shyness. Each took one, the two older ones with a "gracias" and curtsey, the chubby two-year-old with an emphatic nod for a curtsey and saying an unintelligible thanks. All four disappeared behind the curtain with delighted giggles.

"So you only want one beef?" I asked Jose.

"Sí, I give my word for two, but now there is no need."

"That is all right, I understand," I said.

"Still, I must keep my word, but eet weell bee two, or three weeks be-fore I need heem."

"One of the steers is a little thin and should be fattened before he is butchered. How about you taking the brindle and the steer at today's weight and you can pay me eight cents on the pound for the steer when you butcher him?"

Jose rubbed his chin and thought a moment. "That is very generous, Tuck-er and I weel take them on these conditions."

I nodded. "We'll bring them down this afternoon."

Jamie Ross was standing in the door of his shop and called and waved me over when I stepped out of Jose's. I had barely made the middle of the street when he began talking. "You wouldn't have an extra head of beef in that bunch, would you? The church has decided they will need a whole carcass and that will leave me short for the orders I have."

Naturally I did and I gave him his pick on the first steer and reserved the next best for Bill Johnson. Bill seemed content with that, which made me glad. Actually, there wasn't more than fifty pounds difference between them and they both looked good — for what they were, overgrown longhorn steers and cows. That left me with a bull that had successfully dodged the knife four or five years in a row.

While the two butchers were there, I called Jose and gave each a piece of paper. "You three are probably the best estimators in town and I want you to estimate the weight of each cow sold. When you are through, I will use the average to get the cost." Without scales this was the fairest way I knew to get weights and make everyone happy. We set to estimating, sharing two pencils between the four of us. I estimated just to see if I came close to what the three got. The results were surprising, for there weren't fifty pounds' differences between the three butchers' estimates. Mine were a little off, but I learned a lot by listening to their comments. Next time I estimated, I expected to be better.

CHAPTER 7
THE TEXAS RAWHIDER

We settled up and I was counting my money when Pete walked up. He was grinning from ear to ear and I knew something was up. "Feller in th' bar took a likin' t' yore bull there an' wants t' buy him."

"Needs a beef?" I asked.

"N-o-o, more like he needs breedin' stock."

I know my mouth flew open and Pete almost laughed out loud. *"Breedin' stock?* Pete, you must have misunderstood!"

"Nope, 'pon my word, that's what he wants him for!"

I couldn't believe him. "No offense, Pete, but I have t' hear this for myself."

"Well, I think you should." Pete was laughing quietly.

As we approached the bar, a face disappeared from behind the batwings, and when our eyes got accustomed to th' gloom, Pete motioned me to a man standing midway down the bar. From a distance, he looked to be in his late fifties or early sixties. He wore bib overalls with the bib turned down over a wide strip of rawhide tied at his waist, the galluses making big arcs from back to bib. The left side of his shirttail was hanging out of his pants, while the right side had stayed tucked. There was a button missing where his shirttails parted company and a piece of cloth pulled through the buttonhole and pinned with a sharpened peg through the cloth. His ragged pants legs stopped above his bare ankles and I suspected he couldn't have hooked up his bib with the galluses let out full without cutting into his crotch. His feet were covered in the most remarkable pair of moccasins I have ever seen. They were sewn with the hair outside and held together with short strips of leather thong tied in knots so that the ends formed a fringe around the top of the foot. I seem to remember that it was the right foot that had the white fur and the left shoe was red. "Howdee," he said as we approached. "Name's Tom." He rubbed his hand on his pants and extended it to me. It was hard and rough and the grip was firm.

I returned his greeting and ordered a soda, a beer for Pete and a refill for the empty glass in front of Tom. He got right to business. "I shore tuk a likin' t' 'at 'ere bull o' yourn. 'Uld ye part w' 'im?"

It took me a moment t' translate that from his language into mine and I realized there was a wad of tobacco in his jaw that along with his clipped-off words made understanding him hard. He drank his beer with that wad in his mouth and I never did see him spit while he had anything in the glass.

"He's for sale, Tom. I've been getting eight to ten cents a pound."

"I ain't lookin' fer meat, I needs 'im fer servicing m' herd. Started out with one, but 'e bogged crossin' th' Pecos an' we broke his neck gittin' 'im out. Yore'n looks t' be es good es th' one I lost, mebbe a mite better. I ain't got no cash, but we might be able t' wuk out'n a trade if'n you w'nts."

"I'm sellin' cattle, not lookin t' trade," I said.

"I got horses we mought work sompin' out'n 'ith."

I could imagine th' kind of horses a Rawhide outfit would have after comin' halfway across Texas and New Mexico, but I sure wanted t' get rid of that bull and didn't care too much about what I got for it. Pete on the other side of Tom had been thoroughly enjoying the conversation, nodding and grinning into his glass so I said,

108

"Tell you what, Tom, I'll let you and Pete dicker over that bull and whatever he comes up with except more cattle will be good enough for me." Tom turned to look at Pete and it was my turn t' grin in my glass.

"Shore soun's good 'nough for me. 'Ow 'bout you, Pete?" Pete was having a coughing spell, but he managed t' nod his head. Tom turned back to me grinnin' and extendin' his hand. "It're a deal!"

My soda was finished and I left as quickly as I could. When I went through th' door, Tom was shouldering up to Pete and talking earnestly.

I found the boys at the ball field in a big argument. They couldn't find a pitcher for either side that could throw strikes and almost every pitch caused an argument. When it looked like the game was gonna end in violence, I stepped in. "I'll pitch for both sides and call balls, strikes and bases," I offered.

"Yeah an' you'll go easy on Nate," one of the opposition said.

"I won't go easy on Nate and one of you can get behind th' plate when he's up and see if I'm bein' fair."

After more heated discussion, it was decided that I could pitch and call so long as I was fair. At my suggestion, the game was started over and the ninth player was designated a rover since I would not field hits. All bunts had to pass the pitcher or they counted as a strike, no base stealing and we were only playing six innings. Even under those conditions, the game was hotly contested at times, but I did not allow any questionin' of my calls. We got to the top of the sixth as th' sun was settin' with th' game tied at ten all. Several people had drifted down from town and were watching, waiting for the game to end so they could haul tired ballplayers home to chores and supper. Nate's team was the visitors and three of the first four up got singles. The bases were loaded when the smallest kid on the field, batting ninth, came to bat with one out. He had such a small strike zone that I had walked him every time except once when he chose to swing. Our only bat was too big for him and he had struck out. Now th' game was on the line and his teammates were urgin' him on.

"Let him walk you, Peanut!"

First pitch; ball.

Second pitch; ball two.

"You'll win the game without even swingin'!"

Third pitch; strike.

"Don't swing, Peanut, don't swing!"

Fourth pitch; strike. Groans from the visitors.

Fifth pitch; very close, ump calls ball three.

"Three balls and two strikes, Peanut, watch it close!"

It got quiet as a cottage prayer meeting. I carefully wound and threw him a strike right in the middle of his strike zone. With a grunt, Peanut swung the heavy bat as hard as he could — and hit the ball! One bounce got it past the mound, and the rover picked it up. Peanut was almost halfway to first, short legs pumping, and a throw would get him easy, but the rover threw it home to get the force. Catcher dropped the ball, runner safe, but runner number two was too close to stop and go back and they ran him down, eleven to ten, two outs.

Nate came to bat and now the pressure was on me. Three players jostled to monitor the calls behind the plate. Nate was a lefty and I had a little trouble pitching to him. After two balls, the third pitch was right down the middle and he stroked it high into right field but — miracle of miracles — right field caught the ball for out three.

The home team came up just as the orb of the sun touched the top of the mountains.

Darkness would prevent any further innings. The heart of the lineup was up with the cleanup man batting first. On the fourth pitch, he doubled to center. Number five batter hit a first pitch single, runners first and third, no one out. The next batter struck out on three pitches and the seven hole batter singled in the run. It was one out, score tied at eleven, runners on first and second when Green came to bat. He had struggled all afternoon, walking a couple of times, flying out or striking out and had been on base only once. After three pitches, the count was two and one and I put one right down the middle. Green swung and hit a line drive on the first-base side of second. Nate, playing second base, gave a lunge to his left and knocked the ball down. He scrambled after the ball and picked it up just in time to tag out the runner from first. Meantime, the runner from second had rounded third and headed for home. Nate's throw home caught him by two steps.

"Out three, game over!" I called and walked off the field with eighteen boys calling for more even as dads, brothers and sisters were gathering them up and dragging them home.

In the mind of a kid, a tie is a loss and

there was many an argument and what-iffin' as the teams trudged home.

I could hear Rance talking to Nate, "Boy, Nate, if you'da been one step closer, you could have caught it and had an unassisted triple play!"

There was already one out, Rance, I said to myself.

Nate and Green argued for half an hour as we rode home in the gathering gloom. Pete joined us on the edge of town towing a ganted mare with a colt by her side. "Got rid of the bull." He grinned.

I didn't care what happened, so long as that bull didn't go back home with us. The mare didn't look like much, but the colt might have some possibilities. Even the mare might come out of it with some rest and good grazin'.

Even tired cowboys and ballplayers have to take care of their horses and it was a while before they could drag themselves off to a late supper and bed. Ma said Nate was still in bed when I stopped by the house after breakfast. She gave me a hug and thanked me for takin' them. I guess it turned out all right.

Pa was in his office goin' over something in his books and I went in to talk to him. He didn't like interruptions when he was at his books, so I just stuck my head in and said, "Pa, I want to pay Pete for his work, do you think forty dollars a month is enough?"

"I've already put him on th' payroll at forty a month, Tuck, and given him sixty dollars for a month and a half of work."

I had already counted out sixty dollars to give Pete, so I handed it to Pa. "I'll pay him so long as I have cash," I said.

"That's good, son, but why don't we keep him on the payroll here and you can pay me back when you have it?"

"Okay, Pa, thank you." He turned back to his books and I left.

Pete, th' Ganted Mare and colt, and I headed up to our cabin.

"Do you think that colt will make something?" I asked.

"Could." Pete nodded, then chuckled. "You should have seen thet rawhider camp. I almost got homesick — not thet me or my folks ever lived thataway, it jest reminded me o' my Texas home an' rawhiders thet lived around us.

"Rawhiders is a breed to theirselves. They live off th' land an' don't have a thing. If their cabin was made o' logs — which weren't often — it had no chinkin, if it had a roof, it leaked. O' course th' floor was dirt an' th' only tampin' it ever got was by bare feet walkin' on it.

"Most o' their horses looked like th' Ganted Mare, fact is, she looks better than th' general run. Ever'thing they had from th' wagon (if they had one) t' their clothes was held together with rawhide. They had rawhide buckets an' pans, hide beds an' covers, an' their chairs held together with rawhide an' had rawhide seats. If they decided t' go on a trip somewheres, th' first thing they did was go out, kill a cow an' skin it, an' don't think it was their cow. Most likely they didn't have a cow or a brand t' put on it — 'til they left th' country, that is. Then there wasn't a cow or calf in their path thet didn't 'take up an' foller' them. By the time they got t' th' Pecos, they'd have a herd an' most likely no three head would have th' same brand. If you challenged them, they'd say they didn't know nothin' 'bout how that cow with your brand on it got in their herd an' you was welcome to it, weren't nothin' t' fight over. They would make up for it in a day or two, anyway.

"John Chisum found it was good business t' pay a cowboy to escort a rawhider family through his ranch. Made them rawhiders awful sullen an' it got t' be known among them thet th' west side o' th' Pecos was starvin' time if they hadn't stocked up on beef b'fore they got there. It shore weren't a leisurely trip!" He slapped his leg and laughed. "I could tell you a hundred stories about thet breed an' most o' them would seem unbelievable. Never could figger how they got th' gumption t' get up an' move from where they came from to where they landed. Prob'bly got run off," he added.

CHAPTER 8
A ROUNDUP

A SEASON TO GATHER STONES

Usually we didn't talk much when we rode but I talked about my gun all th' way to th' cabin. I couldn't wait to try it out and after dinner, I got it out and showed it to Pete. He hefted it, tried its balance and looked it over closely.

"Let's go shoot it," I said digging out my box of shells.

"Not yet, boy," Pete said. "First thing is to clean this thing up. It's too dirty to shoot now." He went to his bunk and brought back the little box that held his gun-cleaning gear. "Take that gun apart and clean it good."

What I thought would take a few minutes took all afternoon. When I had it all apart, I was glad I hadn't shot it yet. It was as dirty a gun as I have ever seen. It looked like oil had gathered up all the dirt it could hold, then dried up and left th' parts covered with

117

a hard shell of gunk. What parts were not covered with gunk had a red coating of rust.

"Looks like she had a hard ride and was put up dirty," Pete said. He got a plate and covered th' bottom with oil and I soaked the parts and began scrubbing. Pete got out a little file and smoothed and shaped up a part here and there.

I got th' gun cleaned up and started putting it back together when Pete stopped me. "Son, you're gonna have t' make new grips for th' gun."

"I can sand these a little bit and they will do," I said.

"Might be so, but you don't want to keep those that have notches in them. It don't represent you an' might mislead someone into thinking they're yours. To some people it would be a challenge t' see if you could get another notch or they could add one to their collection. Those notches b'long t' someone else an' can't be transferred."

I thought about that for a minute and reluctantly agreed with him. I took the grips off to use for a pattern and on the inside of both of them were carved with initials TDH. Pete found a good seasoned chunk of walnut in the woodpile and helped me cut out two blanks. I spent most of four evenings carving out an' sandin' down good grips. Pete took each one and with a rattail file, knurled them for a better grip. On th' insides I carved my initials and put them on the gun. I had that gun five days without shooting it and I was eager t' see what it could do. I sat up a row of cans with a bank behind them and tried th' gun out from fifty feet. It shot good, but those cans were as safe as they were sitting on a shelf in the store.

Pete chuckled at my efforts. He had brought his gun out and with his four shots, four cans danced away. His stance was one I had never seen before. Standing square to the target and holding the gun in his right hand, he set th' butt in the palm of his left hand, arms extended, elbows bent slightly, and in a crouched position *sighted* his targets. It was a revelation to me.

"I always believed that a gunman shot from his hip with one hand and never missed his target."

"Tuck, thet's just a yellow paper Buntline dream. Th' most foolish thing a man can do is go into a fight with his gun in his pocket depending on his speed an' hip-shootin' to carry him through. A shotgun's the only thing I would shoot from th' hip with an' then not more than fifty feet from my target. I heard Wyatt Earp say he never got off th' first shot in a fight and he was never hit *and* he never missed with his first shot. He *aimed* his gun, Tuck, just like I do — maybe not in th' same fashion — but he used both hands and he didn't miss. Most of these so-called fast draws put their first shot into th' ground or their foot. A calm prepared man who aims with those two little sights on top of th' barrel seldom misses. Now *aim* like I showed you, take a deep breath, let it out and squeeze that trigger, don't jerk it. It's jest like firing a rifle if you do it right."

I tried his method and hit a can on my second shot. Right then I knew that learning to shoot a pistol was not going to be the breeze I had thought it would be.

Our days settled into a routine now that those cows were caught up. We left them in th' big pasture and rode out several times a day to be around them so that they would get used to us and not act silly when they saw us. Eventually they tamed down to where they hardly noticed us as we rode around and through them as they scattered out grazing. There were a few head that never did get used to us and ran every time they saw us. We quickly got rid of them in favor of the ones who didn't show run.

I still had those fifty head I wanted to get

rid of penned up at the house and it was a week before we heard from th' army. By then there were fifty-eight head counting the wild ones we culled from the pasture. Nate and Green appeared one afternoon with a telegraph from Fort Stanton saying a buyer would be by in two days to look at the cattle. I was glad t' hear that because that pen they were in was about grazed to dirt and Pa was getting antsy about it.

We rode in next afternoon, dragging two more wild ones as much to make it an even-numbered herd as anything. Green and Nate met us a ways out and I left them with Pete to drive in th' cattle. The boys were getting pretty good and their ponies showed real possibilities of becoming good cowponies. When they were close enough, I opened th' gate.

It was nearing noon before soldiers rode into our yard. There was a lieutenant and two privates with him and I wondered if he thought they would drive those cows back by themselves. If they tried, the Nueces Strip would be welcoming back some old tenants before they got off th' ranch. We just had time to look over my herd before Benito rang his bell and we went in to dinner.

The officer introduced himself as Lieutenant George Beckman and his men were Corporal Harper Ashburton and Private Leander Hardister. I could tell the lieutenant had never bought cattle and was nervous about it. We sat on th' stoop after dinner and talked a while.

Finally, the lieutenant got down to business and said, "I'm new to this cattle-buying business, and I hope I don't put you to a lot of trouble. We wouldn't come this far from the reservation to get cattle, but the ranchers around th' reservation have been warned by that Lincoln gang not to do business with us and for sure not to sell any of their cattle to us. The gang is mad because we caught the agent cheating and stealing and fired him. It cut them out of a lot of graft money. We have already missed one distribution and the Apaches are very restless about it. The only offer I am authorized to make is fifteen cents a pound delivered to the fort. We will take the sixty head and would gladly take a hundred more at that price. If they can be delivered in six days, there would be a bonus of a cent a pound."

I let that soak in a minute or two and said, "Six days would be mighty hard t' do unless we drove them hard and that would cause a lot of weight loss. I think we could fill th' herd out with a hundred more if you could ease up some on that six days, or weigh them out here at th' ranch."

"I don't have the option of changing the deal," he said. "Without contacting my commander and with the telegraph so unsecure as it is here, I can't risk using it and letting that Lincoln gang know what we are doing."

I sent Nate after Pa and he came down an' sat on the stoop with us. "What is th' deal, men," he said.

"The army wants a hundred sixty head at fifteen cents a pound and a bonus of one cent a pound if we can deliver them to th' fort in six days," I explained.

Pa shook his head. "Can't do Fort Stanton in six days with a herd, and we still have to gather more head first." He sat and it was awful quiet for a while.

"Nate, you and Green mount up and go find Bob. Tell him I need a hundred head gathered for trailing to the reservation. Want me to write a note?"

"No, sir!" came a duet from two fast receding forms.

"You say th' 'Paches have missed one distribution?" I asked, partly to let Pa know more of the story.

"Yes, and from what we can gather, the distributions before that were mighty sparse.

123

The women are fussing and the warriors are very restless and hostile."

"Lieutenant, we could make it to the reservation in six days if your commander would set up a distribution on the south side of the reservation," Pa said.

After a moment, the officer said, "I think that could be arranged if I had a way to contact him."

"It would have to be by messenger or the whole country would know about it an' there would be war," I said. In our country the Santa Fe Ring and their Lincoln County toadies were sincerely despised, though there were enough of them around here that they would know what was going on as soon as things got moving.

"You could send one of your men, but that would be obvious and might expose him to some danger," Tucker senior said.

"I can go an' no one'll see me 'til I walk into th' commander's office." It was Pete.

Pa looked up. "I don't doubt you could, Pete, you up for it?"

"Wouldn'a said nothin' if'n I weren't."

Pa turned to the officer. "Lieutenant Beckman, it's as good as done. Write your commander a note and tell him we will be at . . . Cienega Spring no later than six days from tomorrow morning. That should give him enough time to get things set up."

The lieutenant's hand moved as if to salute Pa but he caught it just in time and stammered, "Yes, sir."

There was a pad and pencil on the bunkhouse table for general use an' I showed it to the lieutenant. "That won't be necessary; I have official papers in my bags I will use so the colonel will know it is from me." He sat down and immediately began writing.

Pete and Pa had been busy and they came out of the barn with a little broomtail mustang saddled and leading another horse just like the first.

"Why you taking those?" I asked. "There's a lot faster horses than that!"

Pete frowned at my ignorance. "Ain't lookin' fer speed, lookin' fer *bottom,* Tuck." His voice said "Dummy" instead of Tuck. Sometimes back then my mouth ran ahead of my brain an' caused all kinds of embarrassements.

Eda and Sue Ellen came from th' house, Eda carrying Pa's Winchester .44-40 and a box of shells and Sue Ellen lugging his .44-40 pistol and holster.

"Here, Pete, I want you to take these with you," Pa said.

"Don't want 'em, Tucker — too much weight." It was th' only time I ever heard

Pete call Dad by his given name. Later, when I thought about it, I decided they must have known one another from times past. I have always suspicioned that Pete's appearance had not been happenstance, and that he had been on th' payroll longer than I knew but I never brought it up with either of them.

"Are you sure?"

"Got my defense right here." He patted the pistol tucked in his left side, butt forward. "I'll see you somewhere along th' way," he said taking the message and tucking it inside his shirt. He turned and headed for the mountaintop, going straight across country toward th' fort.

Pa watched him go and said, "I imagine that's about th' way this herd should go. Tuck, Bob's somewhere up Bluewater, go find him and tell him to come in and see me. You stay and help Cider and Bet round up those cows. I want all steers except you can throw in a cull cow or two if you run across them."

I had to catch up a fresh horse and it took a few minutes to get started. As I rode out, there sat Cindy waiting. We rode at a fast trot and located the crew by th' dust they stirred.

"Looks like they are already gathering,"

Cindy said. She rode so close that her sidesaddle knees occasionally rubbed against my leg. Once or twice, she kicked me and grinned, well, she used to grin, now it was the prettiest smile I had ever seen her make. Must have been practicin' in front of a mirror.

Bet and Cider were chousin' cows out of the brush down onto th' creek flat and Green and Nate were tryin'their best t' keep them and havin' a heck of a time doin' it. Their horses were in a lather and they were running helter-skelter after strays. Cindy found her pa and gave him th' message. Those cows were in a continual mill. It took me half an hour to get boys and cows settled down. I showed them how to keep a herd quiet and still keep strays in the herd. We spread them out so they could cool and I showed them how to loose herd the bunch, movin' them along slowly lettin' them graze as they went. As soon as all was quiet, I left Cindy in charge of boys and cows and rode to help Bet and Cider. By late afternoon we had our roundup and started drivin' them to th' ranch. It was almost pitch dark when that last steer was hazed into th' pen.

A Season to Refrain from Embracing

It was funny to see our faces in th' barn door light. Our skin had turned a dark reddish brown with dust and there were white streaks where sweat had made tracks down our faces. It looked like we were striped except in places where we had smeared sweat and dust into mud that caked and dried. Our clothes had taken on one color. The horses were no better off and we did our best to wipe them down even though they were more eager to break away and roll and drink water. I cleaned up Cindy's horse for her and she ran to the house. The boys raced to the creek and I heard two splashes. *Hope they took th' time t' take off their boots.* The two hands had finished and headed for th' bunkhouse. They hadn't eaten since breakfast and a little dust didn't bother them any. I forked down some more hay and drew more water. Benito had saved me supper and I ate two plates full before my hunger was satisfied. By that time, splashin' and laughin' at th' creek had quit and all was quiet except for cricket songs.

Even after washing up for supper, I still felt gritty and wandered down to th' creek to wash. I shucked out of my clothes and waded in. That water was plenty cool and felt good. I imagined the creek had just recovered from two muddy boys and here I was makin it muddy again.

Someone else came down to wash, probably Bet or Cider and I paid little attention until I heard a gasp and Cindy whispered, "Tucker is that you?"

I jumped like I had been shot. "It's me."

"You scared me near to death."

"You're safe, I ain't no alligator."

She splashed and washed her hair and I stood there neck deep and stark naked, not able to get by her and retreat to the bank for my clothes.

"There, that feels much, much better. I couldn't get clean at all without a bath and this is wonderful." She moved toward me an' I took a few steps backward, but th' bank was steep and I was runnin' out of water. I eased back to where the water was over her head and Cindy held on to my arm. I stood perfectly still, scared to death. She came closer and I felt her light gown against my legs. Suddenly she splashed water in my face and I instinctively pushed her head under. She grabbed me and pulled herself up, sputtering and giggling. I could feel her breasts against my side and her bare legs against mine and it sent chills all through my body. Something was happening to me down below and I turned away — a little.

Suddenly she gasped and whispered, "You're naked!"

"How else do you take a bath on a dark night in the creek?"

"I wear a chemise."

I touched her side and felt the thin cloth. "Mighty thin cloth."

"You could see through it in the light." She giggled, a little nervously, I thought.

"You should go," I whispered.

"Why?" she moved closer.

I turned away a little more.

"Tuck Beavers, I've changed enough boy diapers to know how boys are made and it doesn't bother me one bit." And she stepped in front of me and pulled herself close. "Oooo, *what's that?*" she stepped back in alarm.

"What do you think it is?" Obviously, she didn't know *everything* about "how boys are made." My face felt so hot I thought it must glow.

"I have to go!" She turned, then stepped back hard against me again and with both hands pulled my face down and kissed me full on the mouth. I listened to her splash across the creek and up the bank. I could see dimly a white form moving off toward her house and I heard the screen door slam.

Gradually, I relaxed and breathed again. I ducked under the cool water and imagined I could hear my ears sizzle as they went under. I stayed under until they quit burnin'. We boys had talked about sex before, but none of us had ever had any experience more than holding some girl's hand or givin' her a peck on th' cheek — and I had never even done that except to a sister or Cindy. This was my first encounter of an intimate nature and it had to be with Cindy in our own backyards. With Cindy! It was both comfortable and very disconcerting. She was my friend and companion, I had never thought of her in any other way until recently. All this change was confusing.

She hadn't seemed uncomfortable, it was me that got scared. It was me that would have run, but why? Was it because we were friends and I had never thought of her as a mature girl? I cherished my friend and companion, this new relationship was troubling and I was afraid something had passed away forever and I didn't like it at all.

In spite of my fatigue, I slept fitfully, my dreams alternating between pleasant dreams of her soft warm body touching mine in the pool, kissing me, and nightmares of Cindy going away forever, fading away like a soft

131

white mist. Four o'clock and people were moving around and I was glad to get up. This would be the first day of many busy days ahead and I was about to go on my first cattle drive.

CHAPTER 9
TRAIL HERD

Pa came down and ate breakfast with us. After we ate and had our second cups of coffee, he told us his plans for the next few days. "We have agreed to sell the army a hundred sixty head of cattle for the Apache reservation. In doing so, we will have the wrath of the Lincoln County gang come down on us. It is probable that they will do everything they can to stop us. They feel no compunction in letting men, women and children starve if they can profit by it. They have no problem inciting the Indians to rise up and rebel and kill innocent people and destroy property so long as it isn't them and theirs. We are going to drive this herd over the mountains directly to the reservation and hopefully away from prying eyes. Lieutenant Beckman has sent word to the army to meet us at Cienega Spring six days from today. He will ride with us and he and his men will help protect the herd from whatever comes against us. Bob will stay here and look after the ranch, the rest of us will go.

"Those cattle from the back pasture are pretty wild and we will have all we can do to keep them together. We will need to neck a few together to convince them to go along with us, so take all the rope you can find. I want every man to have extra horses in his string, we'll need them. There won't be a wagon with us, it's too rough, so Benito will take what he needs on packhorses, and we may have to tighten our belts before we get there. What bedrolls you take will have to fit behind your saddle. Take your guns and keep them close. We can hope we don't have to use them, but it's best to be prepared. We need a head count when they come out of the gate, Bob. I want to take more than a hundred sixty head but not more than ten over.

"Nate and Green are going to take care of the cavvy daytimes. We'll have to take care of them at night." I couldn't believe my ears, but when I looked around, there they stood, all decked out and grinnin'. I didn't know what Pa and Bob were thinking to let those two boys go in the face of potentially dangerous animals — the two-legged kind.

"We'll climb up above the head of Bluewater Creek and follow the ridge around to the Rim Trail above Dog Canyon. From there on, we aren't likely to run into prying eyes. Any Indians we meet should be glad to see us and they may be of help to us.

"As the cows come out of the gate, we'll keep them bunched and moving right on to the divide. I want to push them a little bit, enough to keep them moving without time to think up mischief. Benito and Bob and the boys will start right away with the cavvy. Let's go, look sharp, we'll have our hands full."

Hands full was an understatement. Time and again, we almost lost control of things. It was like a wild cow scramble to keep those cows together. Any time you could look up and see a couple of cows down or being necked together. It got to where we could tell which ones would need necking before he got full through the gate and usually someone was there t' throw a rope on him and find him a partner. Their antics kept our herd stirred until they gradually fell back to drag with the other rebels.

Midmorning, Bob brought a change of horses for each of us and it was none too soon. We could only change horses one man at a time and then hardly had time to saddle up before some emergency demanded our attention. I never noticed when Bob left but he sure was a welcome sight when he reappeared mid afternoon with another remount and a big olla of water.

"How are the boys doing with the horses?" I asked as I threw my saddle across a fresh horse.

"Pretty good, Tuck. They stay busy, but the horses are used to the trail and they know near as much as the boys do."

"I didn't think about the lack of water up here on the ridge, we'll have a time if this bunch doesn't get some soon."

"Probably th' first won't be until you get to Penasco Creek sometime tomorrow," Bob said. "There's a seep at the old Rogers place but it will only take care of the horses. I imagine that's where you'll spend the night."

"You gonna stay with us a while?"

"I'll head back tomorrow morning, I suppose," he said.

I heard a shout as I mounted up and looking back down the trail I saw two vaqueros approaching, each with one remount. They turned out to be Newton Mills and Napoleon Witt from the Rafter JD.

"Heard you boys was movin' a herd an' we come t' help," Newt said as he rode up.

"Truth is, ol' Zenas seen gravels rollin'

down into th' river an he said, 'You boys git up there an' tell those yahoos t' git off'n that ridge afore they send th' hull mountain down on us an make a lake out o' this ranch.'" Nap grinned.

"We could shore use your help," Bob said. "Just pitch in where you see a need. I'll take your remounts to th' cavvy."

We turned toward the herd and it wasn't a minute before all three of us were busy. I didn't see more than a glimpse of either one until we bedded the herd. Nap was attackin' a plate of frijoles and saltback when I got to the fire and dished up my meal.

"I know where you got those . . . mossy-horns; in that . . . infernal back pasture where you sent . . . cows t' grow wild," he said between bites.

"That's almost forty-percent right," I replied.

"Do yuh reckon th' 'Paches'll git wilder eatin' that wild meat?"

"Don't see how they could get much wilder."

"Yuh shoulda been 'round here afore they tamed down," Nap said just before he filled his mouth with biscuit.

We ate hurriedly and rode back to th' bed ground to let a couple more go in and eat. Most of the cattle had laid down, but there were several who stood sullenly looking at us.

"Woulda shot any ranny on the trail that looked like that, they're nothin' but trouble," Newt spat. "Too durn many o' them here fer that."

"Can we do anything about it?" I asked.

He spat again, rolling his quid around. "We could hobble them, but it would stir up the whole herd jist gittin' to 'em."

"I shore hate to leave them. They're a wreck waitin' t' happen," Bet said.

Just then one of the steers started out of th' herd intent on Cider riding by. Pretending t' ignore the animal, Cider rode on until the steer was clear of the herd, then man and horse turned away from the herd and after a few steps loped off down the hill followed by that steer. Soon they were out of sight and we heard a commotion. Presently, through a cloud of dust, the cross-hobbled steer reappeared with Cider drivin' him from behind.

"Now, thet's a trick!" Nap said. "Wish they all did that, we could keep 'em out of th' herd and all *could* be hunky-dory."

"Yeah, but not likely," I said.

"Drive thet critter back down th' trail a ways an' we'll bed him separate from th' herd," Nap said. "Let's see if ol' Cider kin lure any o' th' rest o' them troublemakers out."

I took up where Cider left off with the steer and drove him back until he couldn't see th' herd. He was restless for a while, then lay down. As I rode back toward the herd, I met Newt chousin' another mossy-horn my way. "Derned if he didn't git another one." He turned back while I drove idiot number two to his mate. This one refused to lie down and stood facing me every place I was making a low moaning sound in his throat.

"You're th' first one I'd shoot," I warned him, but he just kept up his hate song. I got close enough to him, he thought, and he lunged with his hind legs, thinking to charge me full speed but his hobbled front leg came up short and he tumbled over on his nose, not hard enough to really hurt himself, but enough t' get his attention. The air went out of him with a huff and he had a time gettin' to his feet. By then the mad was out of him and he looked around a moment, grunted and lay down. It took most of the rest of daylight t' lure out four more troublemakers leavin' four out in the middle who never offered to charge. As it got darker, they lay down one by one and by full dark, all was quiet.

"Wouldn't bet fifty cents against a hundred dollars they'll stay that way," Bob said.

Pa divided us up and we all went to our duties. Nap and I were given th' job of covering the cavvy while the two so-called nighthawks were put under Benito's wing. He took them well into the woods to bed down where no runaway cow was liable to go.

"Where's he gonna get second watch t' take over for us, Nap?"

"Didn't hear about no second watch and not a word about sleepin'," he replied. "Looks like we're gonna do away with that little luxury fur a while."

It sure looked that way. I was a little put out being put in the rockin' chair this way, but a little after midnight by my guess, Cider rode up and sent us back to the herd while he and Newt watched the horses. Six of us rode herd on those cows all night, with an occasional peek at those mavericks back down th' trail. To our great surprise and greater joy, the whole bunch behaved all night.

I don't believe I have ever seen so many stars in my life as I saw that night. Up there on that ridge it felt like we were so close we could touch them. I could hold out my sombrero and cast a shadow on my horse's neck. The only place there wasn't a star was inside the crescent moon. The many stars around it showed the outline of the dark side.

The smell of wood smoke mingled with coffee told us that breakfast was soon. Cider and Newt presently rode out on fresh horses and we ate and changed horses by turns. The gray was beginnin' t' turn red when Benito and the boys moved the cavvy out and we brought our outlaw steers up. The Tularosa Basin was still purple black and sunlight was just beginning to creep down the San Andres on the far side when we moved out. We let the herd graze slowly up th' trail until we judged that our cavvy was well out of the way. So far, the herd had behaved pretty well, but as soon as we picked up the pace, they began to act up and we were very busy the rest of the way. As we approached the Penasco Canyon, the cows smelled water and forgot their orneriness. A little over a mile down the river another canyon comes in from the right. There was more water there and the side canyon was a good place to keep the cattle for the night since it was too steep for them to get out the sides or upper end. After they had their fill of water, we drove them up th' side canyon, releasing those that were hobbled or necked together.

"Maybe sore necks and legs will calm them down some," Bet said as he coiled the last hobble up and hung it over his saddle horn.

"They's unrepented devils, Bet, an' don't you git yore hopes up too high, th' fall might hurt." Cider was still smarting over the torn pant leg and skin one of the steers had given him earlier. A long bloody scratch down his horse's flank showed just how close they had come to a goring.

"Someone tell Benito I'll be takin' my supper in bed tonight. If I'm sleepin', he kin jist leave th' tray on th' nightstand an' I'll find it when I wake up — some time next week," Newt said through a yawn.

"Ain't you heard, man? All beds has been confiscated and sleep has been postponed 'til this herd is delivered," Nap said as he rode up from the camp. He handed me a plate of frijoles and biscuits and said, "Big Tucker said you and I was first watch an' I brung your supper. Spoon fell off by thet juniper, fellers, if'n one o' you would pick it up as you go by."

"How am I supposed to eat without tools?" I asked.

"Oh, you'll manage." Nap hardly broke stride as he rode by and spurred after a mossyhorn set on going the wrong way down the canyon.

I turned around and tried to sop up beans with a biscuit half as I rode. "Feller ought t' at least have a spoon an' get t' eat on th' ground," I muttered.

"Hey, Tuck, here's your spoon," Bet called as he rode up. "It's clean, I licked it."

"Thanks, Bet, you know I'd do th' same for you."

"Don't mention it, pal."

Nap had hazed that stray back to the herd and was busy stringin' rope across th' mouth of the canyon. I balanced the plate on my horn and tried to eat with one hand. "Git down an' pull up to th' table t' eat, Tuck."

"If I got down, I couldn't get back up unless this hoss laid down an' I doubt he would get up, either." I finished hurriedly and helped Nap string rope from tree to bush across the canyon. He produced a piece of white cloth and we tore it into strips and tied it along the rope. It wasn't much, but it might deter a cow from escape — unless he was determined.

Cows started grazin' up th' canyon an' we squatted in th' shade of a juniper and let our horses graze. After a while, Nate brought me a fresh mount and took mine

143

back to the cavvy. He was tired and dusty, but his grin told me he was havin' the time of his life. Ever' time I got still, I caught myself noddin' off, so I walked up and down that rope, like a guard on post. Near the branch at the bottom of the canyon, I saw something white in the gravel an' when I dug it out, it turned out to be a spear point. I washed it off in a pool and admired it until dark gathered and I couldn't see it too well.

Nap was rolling a cigarette as I walked up. "Look what I found down by th' branch."

"Let's see," he said lighting his smoke and holding his match over my hand.

"It's a spear blade, ain't it?"

"No," he said, hefting the point carefully, "I think it's a knife blade, see th' notches are on th' side of th' hilt? Those are called tangs and this is called a corner tanged knife."

That sure surprised me. "I didn't know you were so knowledgeable about these things."

"Got stuck in a line camp with nothin' but some perfessor's books he'd left there an' that was all there was t' read. I thought that snow would *never* melt and let me outa there."

"How'd th' handle fit on it?"

"Don't know, book didn't know, either,

but it had lots of theories." He took his last draw on the cigarette and heeled it out. "If we get th' chance, we'll try out some of those ways."

We continued to guard the canyon, though the cows had grazed so far up we couldn't hear them. "Probably bedded down restin' an' plottin' mischief they're gonna do tomorrow," Nap grumbled.

The big dipper had rotated around th' north star a little more than a quarter of th' way from where it was at sunset when we heard horses makin' their way down. When they got close enough, Nap called out soft, "Who goes there? Stand forth and be recognized." Must have been more of that professor's reading material.

"Th' password's 'sleep' and it's Cider an' Bet come t' relieve you."

"About an hour late, I figger," I said grumpily.

"Naw, sir, we's right on time by my calculations," Bet corrected.

"It's all yours. The herd's moved up th' canyon, probably huntin' a way out, but bein' quiet about it," Nap said. We heard them get down a ways away. "That rope across th' canyon is a few feet in front of you," Nap called as he mounted.

"I saw a nice soft rock up th' side here an'

me an' hoss are gonna go up there an' bed down," I said. "Anything happens, don't let nothin' run over us."

"Jest don't go t' snorin' too loud an' spook our horses," one of them muttered.

I already had my blanket around me to ward off the chill and it didn't take me long to find two boulders I had in mind and squeeze between them. I felt the warmth they had stored up from the day and I was soon asleep.

The sound of horses approaching and the position of the dipper told me dawn was near and I jumped up and saddled the horse and rode back down to the branch. Everyone was gathered around Pa and he was giving instructions. "I want a head count as they come out of the canyon, so Bet and Tuck will go up and move th' herd this way. We'll open the rope here and I will count. The rest of you string out along th' rope and pick up the herd as they come out. Nate and Green are waiting at the top and they will haze them up th' Rim Trail. Keep them moving slow and when they're all caught up, we will move them a little faster."

Bet and I made our way up the side canyon as high up one side as we could get and we got by the herd. "I'll go up on top and rustle out any I find while you mosey th' rest out," Bet said.

I turned and followed my bunch already moving down the canyon. Only two or three tried to climb th slopes until they couldn't go any higher and slid back down to th' bottom in a shower of dust and gravel. One got behind me. Bet would have to pick him up. The steer stayed close behind me, but wouldn't come closer until I rode up the opposite side, then he trotted back into the herd. I kept just enough pressure to keep them moving through the gap.

Bet came down behind two old mossy-horns and called, "We'll have to neck them, Tuck."

I shook out my loop and we roped them almost at the same time. When they were necked together, they got the privilege to be last through the gap. Bet started rolling up the downstream rope and I took the upstream line down and coiled it over my horn. I guess their count was good, Pa and Bet were already riding up th' valley behind the herd and I hurried to catch up.

CHAPTER 10
TROUBLE ON THE RIM TRAIL

A SEASON TO PLANT

The chow was all packed when we rode into camp, but Benito handed each of us a tortilla roll full of beans and salt pork and a mug of coffee — my second meal horseback. Guided by knee pressure, my horse followed the herd and stopped only when I drank coffee. He kept looking back until I gave him my last bite of tortilla and beans, then he loped on as if to say *now's the time for business.*

We had passed the trail up from Dog Canyon and expected to begin seein' Indians. We didn't for a while because when they heard us comin', they disappeared into the brush. After we passed, they would follow a ways behind and the drag got glimpses of them from time to time. There must have been more than a dozen of them when Pa rode back and told Benito to pick out a steer from the drag to butcher. Only the boss had seniority over the cook in picking out his meat and Pa generally let the cook decide.

"When we get to that spring at Cox Canyon, butcher him and we will invite our followers to be our guests. I'm hopeful we can plant a few seeds of good will. I want to talk to them and get them to help us or at least not delay us in any way."

"Sí, Señor Tuck-er," Benito said and crossed himself when Pa turned away. Nothing scares a Mexican American more than an Indian, be he Apache, Navajo or th' tamer Yaqui. Every time I saw him that morning, he was keeping the cavvy between himself and those Indians.

In a few minutes, Green rode up an' said, "Mr. Tucker said he would help drive th' cavvy and I could help with th' cattle." He grinned.

"OK, Green, you take th' drag and keep them moving as close to th' rest of th' herd as possible. Watch Benito, he's so scared of the 'Paches, he's liable to try to get in th' herd."

I left him and rode up th' rim side of the herd t' guard against runaways goin over th' bluff. In a few miles the trail veered away from the rim and we had a little more breathing room to work — and so did those cows. Pa kept our horses close to the drag

149

and sometimes I couldn't tell if Benito was in drag or cavvy. I don't think either bothered him much. A time or two when I caught a glimpse of Nate, it looked like he had someone riding behind him, but I couldn't be sure because of the dust.

We stopped the herd just past Cox Canyon and when I got back to the drag, Benito had made his kill and was bleeding it out in a pan. Pa and Nate had ridden back down the trail a ways and I could see for sure that a kid was riding behind Nate.

This was a favorite camping place on the trail and a lot of firewood was stacked around the fire pit. Benito had Green breakin' sticks and throwin' them into the pit. Presently, they caught from the coals left buried under the ashes. Green piled more fuel on the fire. Every pan the Old Woman had was out and waiting for service. Green was working hard t' keep up with the orders barked at him. I felt it was my duty to keep th' cavvy rounded up and as I was changing my saddle over to a fresh mount, Bet rode up for the same purpose.

"What's yore pa doin' back down the trail, Tuck? Is that another critter ridin' with Nate?"

"To answer your first question, Dad's inviting our trail mates to dinner, an' yes, that's some sort of critter ridin' with Nate, but I don't know who."

"No wonder Benito's in such a frenzy, I'm gonna give him plenty room t' work," he said and he made a wide detour around camp.

Mounted again, I could see that Pa and a couple of Indians were squatting in the dirt talking. Presently they rose and one Indian looked back down the trail and waved. In a moment several figures appeared in the trail walking our way. They stopped to confer a few moments and several of the women detached themselves and hurried ahead toward the camp. Benito had partially skinned the carcass and was busy making son-of-a-gun stew when they arrived. They immediately resumed skinning and cutting up the meat. Cookie warily helped and guided the new cooks in preparing the meat.

There were about twenty people who had been following us and a pitiful lot they were. Some had been to the western reservations visiting friends and relatives and some had been in the Basin hunting and gathering — mostly fruitlessly. All of them looked drawn and tired and there was no question but that they were hungry — had been for some time. I looked back down the trail and saw a man doing something extraordinary. He was carrying a papoose and a young woman clung to his arm. Almost before I realized, I was riding toward them. I stopped in front of them and got down, signaling for the woman to mount my horse. She couldn't. The man handed the papoose to me and helped his wife into the saddle. Taking the reins, he headed toward camp leaving me behind carrying the baby. I peeked through the blanket and uncovered a curly head. Two big black eyes blinked at me in the sunlight. At the camp the woman was helped down and without taking a step sank to the ground. Another woman took the baby. Pointing to her breast and to the mother, she said, "No leche." The mother had no milk to feed the baby.

"Well, I know just how we kin fix that!" Nap's voice came in my ear and I jumped, not knowin' anyone was near. He grabbed a jelly pail Cookie had set out and headed for his horse ignorin' Benito's fussing at him. "Come on, Tuck, you kin help."

"Got a cow in th' herd fixin t' come fresh an' her bag's a-swellin. We'll catch some of her milk fer th' baby," he explained as we rode.

"Sure," I said, "we'll just call her out of th' herd an' tell her what we need an' she'll just let us fill that bucket to th' rim!"

"Somethin' like thet — hey, Newt, com-mere, we need yore help. Whur's thet cow 'bout t' drop, we need some milk fer th' babies in camp."

"Whut babies?"

"Apaches come t' camp starvin', Benito's butcherin' an' cookin' fer 'em."

"Well, I'll be . . ."

"Don't jist sit there 'I'll bein', find thet cow, man."

"She's over in th' shade layin' down," said Bet, who had ridden up an' listened.

"Think we can catch 'er layin' down?" Nap asked.

"I doubt it, but we can try," Bet replied.

We cautiously rode over and looked at th' situation. She was layin' on her side, legs stretched out, an' I thought she would give birth any minute.

"Mighty ripe, ain't she," Bet said.

"If'n two o' you could git close enough to her, you could jump on her hips an' hold her down 'til we got a couple ropes on her legs an' we could milk her right where she lays," Newt whispered.

We drew straws and Newt and I lost. "If you kin git to her afore she knows it, y'can jump on her hips an' she won't be able t' git up," Bet whispered.

"How d'you know?" I asked.

"Done it afore." He nodded emphatically.

"You ain't never, Bet Sommes, I knowed you since we were both pups an' you ain't never done nothin' like thet!" Newt spat.

"I done it, too."

"Ain't never . . ."

"Quit yer fussin' an' git busy," Nap hissed. He started shakin' out his loop and Bet followed suit while Newt an' I crawled toward that cow. Somethin' must have warned her, for she suddenly rolled up on her belly and started pullin her hind legs in to stand. We both stood and ran to jump on her hips, but we were too late, she was already on her way up. I made a dive for her hips, but she shied toward me and I overshot, turning a flip over her and landing on my back. Almost before I had hit, she was turning to gore me. Her horn ran up my leg and under my belt. With a beller that must have alerted the whole herd, she lifted me up then tried to shake me off her horn.

"Unbuckle your belt, Tuck," someone hollered.

That was th' *last* thing I was gonna do. If I turned loose now, she'd have me cut to ribbons before I hit the ground. She started buckin' an' kickin' an' I held on as best I could. All of a sudden she went down, someone had roped her hind legs. I felt a rope hit me and I hooked the loop over the tip of her horn sticking out from under my belt. A yank pulled her over on her side with me on top. I ended up with my left knee on her head and my right foot on the ground, almost standing up. *Now* I unbuckled my belt and retreated.

"Good work, boys," Nap yelled. He was already on the ground with his bucket while his horse kept the rope tight. Kneeling, he pulled her udder from under her top leg and cleaned off a teat. A few squeezes brought a little milk, but not much. "She's not lettin' her milk down," Nap said. "Tuck, hit her right there like a suckin' calf'd do."

I hit her with my fist.

"Harder."

A little harder.

"Agin."

I hit her again and she let her milk down. Nap milked furiously and soon had that pail full from just the front two teats. "Good work, boys, you can let 'er up," he called as he ran to his horse.

"Wait'll I'm outta here," I yelled, runnin' for my horse. By th' time I got mounted, Bet and Newt had shaken the ropes loose and ol' bossy jumped up on th' prod. She looked around for a target, but only saw mounted horses. As if she knew she

155

wouldn't win, she lowered her head and shook it, clattering her horns against the gravels.

"Don't think I want to milk any more wild cows," I said.

"Ya looked pretty good ridin' that horn." Bet chuckled.

All was bustle around two fires going. The women had built a spit over each and a hindquarter was on one and ribs on the other. Nap had a crowd of little ones around him and he was dipping cups of milk for them. Even the weak mother was drinking some while the woman holding the baby dipped a cloth in the warm milk and let th' baby suck.

Even though there was obvious food getting ready for them, there was a sense of urgency in the people. Even the braves watched and occasionally lent a hand, something remarkable in the Indian culture. *Dear Lord, what must it be like on the reservation?* I thought.

A little naked boy who looked to be three or four years old stood with distended belly watching the meat.

"Looks like he's been eatin' good," I said.

"Yore belly swells when you ain't had any nourishment, Tuck," Cider said.

I think every one of us were around that

fire helping those people. Benito was cookin' everything he had and as soon as it was ready, it was eaten. I noticed that the men didn't eat much, but made sure that women and children were fed first. Their traditional role in their culture was to provide the meat and food for the tribe and they must have felt they had failed. It was extraordinary to see, for in normal times, the man was served first and all others fed last.

Like ghosts, people kept appearing around the fires and our crowd had more than doubled by the time Benito began slicing off chunks of roast. As soon as one spit was emptied, it was refilled with fresh meat and it looked like that steer wasn't gonna last much longer.

Pa had been squatting in the dust with Lieutenant Beckman talking to a group of warriors gathered around them and when they had finished, he stood and motioned for us to follow him. We hadn't seen much of the soldiers; they had stayed ahead of us, watching the trail for trouble that so far had not appeared. When we were away from the fires a ways, Pa stopped and we gathered around him as close as our horses would let. "Boys, we're losing time sitting here and the Indians tell me the reservation is like a keg of powder with th' fuse lit. Th' army is going t' stay with the Indians for a while. Nate, I want you and Green to drive th' horses up to th' meadows on top of the mountain and hold them there. We will gather the herd and follow. Benito will stay with the fires until the food is gone and then come on. We won't need him b'cause our food will be all gone by then. We'll drive th' herd as late as we can and hopefully we can get to Cienega Spring late day after tomorrow."

One of the things I will never understand is how and why that herd didn't scatter all over the mountain, but it didn't. There must have been angels herdin' 'em They're th' only ones who could have overcome th' devil in those cows!

A little riding got them bunched and movin' an' th' devil came out in 'em again. By the time we got to that meadow, our horses were done in and so were we. "It's still an hour 'til sunset," Pa called. "If we push them on, we'll have a downhill run tomorrow and most of th' way to th' spring the next day."

"Got t' have fresh horses, boss," Bet called. Pa nodded. We changed mounts two at a time. "Hey, Nate, did I see you with a passenger while ago?" I asked.

"Yup, you did." Nate grinned.

"Well, you gonna keep it a secret?"

"Aw-w-w he was just one o' those 'Paches needin' a lift. I got him up an' he wouldn't leave 'til th' herd stopped an' he smelled food cookin'."

We moved on with fresher horses until it was almost black and those *cows* decided it was time t' rest. After a little mill they scattered out on a bed ground and settled for the night. "Well, I'll be switchered if them bullheaded cows know when t' quit better'n us!" Bet said.

"Shows who's smarter," said I and headed to find a bed. Pa had Green and Nate in tow and called, "Tuck, watch those horses, I'm putting these boys up for th' night." He must have forgotten me, for it was after midnight when I finally gave up an' found a sleeping body, kicked it and said, "Watch th' horses." Whoever it was grunted and I handed him my reins. I don't remember laying down, but I woke up in th' gray of dawn wrapped in someone's blanket.

"Am I dreaming or do I smell coffee?" a lump nearby that turned out to be Cider muttered.

It had been so natural to wake to the aroma of coffee that I hadn't thought that there wouldn't be any today, but it was there sure as shootin'.

We were drawn to the fire and there squatted Benito, stirring a pot of S.O.B. stew on th' fire next to a big coffeepot. "Thee A-Paches were indignant that I had *cooked* the stew and would not eet it!" He grinned.

"Does that mean they filled up on other stuff?" I asked.

"I theenk maybe yes, maybe no," Benito said. "They are able to come on behind us, now and I theenk they weell all live."

A TIME TO HATE

We took time for a cup of stew and left, riding with our cups full of coffee. Those cows surely didn't know what they were headed for, b'cause they seemed eager to move an' we directed their route. I could see the dust of the cavvy ahead of us as we dropped off the hill. I was riding left flank when the herd suddenly stopped. Looking ahead, I saw the cavvy had scattered and there were a bunch of riders gathered around Pa. As I rode up, one of the strangers was saying, ". . . we're gonna cut th' herd to see if they are all your'n an' if they's any disease in 'em."

"On whose authority are you doing this?"

The man looked pained. "By th' 'thority o' th' sheriff o' Lincoln County."

"We're not in Lincoln County and we are

160

not going to Lincoln County and *you* have no jurisdiction in Otero County!" Pa said. His temperature was rising.

Someone in their crowd snickered. By then we had all gathered and we quietly pushed our way into the crowd so that the strangers were separated an' Pa wasn't cut off by himself. They were a dirty, slovenly lot, reeking of whisky and tobacco and dirty bodies. My hand was inside my coat resting on my gun.

Nate and Green were behind Pa a ways and I saw that Green's face was swelled on one side and he was spittin' blood. The crimson print of a hand was plain. The man on my right noticed my gaze and sneered, "I don't 'bide smart-mouthed kids back-talkin' their betters. Had t' apply a little discipline to 'im." He was still snickering when the barrel of my pistol backhanded him across the bridge of his nose with a loud crack. Everyone jumped and looked our way. I heard guns cock like crickets. The man slumped forward and I kicked him out of the saddle and slapped his horse away. I swung around and aimed at the head of th' man on my left.

"If you bullies think you can ride in here and slap around little kids at your pleasure, you're sadly mistaken." My voice was shak-

161

ing with anger, but my hand was steady and the barrel bumped hard against the man's skull just behind his ear.

I guess my finger was tightening on the trigger, for Nap said quietly, "E-e-e-ase up there a little, Tuck."

I shudder now to think what a bloodbath I could have caused right there, but at the time I didn't think, I reacted. That mob who thought they had the upper hand was caught off guard and my act caused them to lose what advantage they had.

"Looks like your inspection duties are over here, fellers," Pa said. In the distraction he had drawn his pistol. "Cider, you start on that side and Nap you start on your side and see how many guns you can collect from these fellows."

"You can't do that, I'm a deputy . . ."

"You are just a man trying to steal my herd in this county!" Pa interrupted.

The man on the ground groaned and I swung down and pushed him back down. The bridge of his nose had disappeared and his eyes were already swelling shut. His breath came in wheezes through his mouth and when he tried to breathe through his nose it just made a whistling sound.

With my boot planted not too gently on his chest, I called, "Nate, come over here and get this man's guns."

Both boys got down and came over. Green pulled the revolver out of his holster. "Take his belt and holster too, he owes it to you."

He unbuckled the belt and Nate kicked him in the ribs to get him to roll over. Both boys grabbed the belt and jerked it out from under him.

"Is that all you can find?" I asked.

All they could find in his pockets were a folding knife, some coins and a twist of tobacco. Green kicked his ribs again and the man rolled over groaning. Patting his pockets, Nate found something and pulled out a whiskey bottle more than half empty.

"That was his breakfast, boys," Nap said. "Probably s'posed t' be his dinner too."

"Might as well have it now while he's restin'," Green said and poured the remaining in his face. The boys started to return to their horses and I asked, "What about his legs and boots?"

"We forgot."

They patted his legs and found a nasty-looking little revolver strapped to the inside of his left leg. When they pulled off his boots, a knife in its scabbard fell out.

"Here, Nate, let's empty that little hidey gun." Nap took the gun and carefully removed the cylinder. He shook the bullets out and held up four large-caliber shells. "Looks like those things are forty-fives! Barrel ain't two inches long! I'm gonna keep this cylinder, Nate, that gun's too dang'rous fer you t' shoot," Nap said, handing the gun back to the boy.

"That's OK, Mr. Nap, I got his knife," the boy said as he grinned.

"Ain't right, teachin' boys t' rob a injured man," Deputy said.

"It ain't robbery when they disarm a dangerous hoodlum who attacks harmless boys," Bet put in.

"I *tole* him t' leave them boys be," the man who had been next to me muttered. He was rubbing a spot behind his right ear.

"He could'a done a lot less damage t' hisself takin' this whole herd 'stead o' molestin' them boys, I reckon," Newt drawled.

"You fellows need to move out of the way, there's gonna be a herd come through here in a few minutes," Pa said.

"You can't take our guns, they's Injuns out here," one of the men whined.

"Might be mad Injuns after we tell 'em you was tryin' t' steal their meat," I said.

"You cain't do that to white men!"

"We won't be," I yelled at him.

Pa turned toward the herd. "Men, let's get that herd moving!"

And that's just what we did. The mob — there might have been ten of them — moved away reluctantly, the boy-slapper hanging on to a stirrup for guidance, since by now he was so swollen he couldn't see.

I helped gather th' cavvy, poor Green trying valiantly to help with one good eye. Somehow, Benito came up with a fistful of snow wrapped in a rag. "Place thees on your face, Green, eet weel take out some of thee swolens."

Green gingerly touched his face with the ice and flinched. After three tries, he could keep it on his face, "Fanks, 'Nito," he slurred through swollen lips.

"Tuck, I will stay with thee boys an' you can bee free to help weeth thee cows," Benito said.

"If you run into problems, fire a shot an' we'll come a-runnin'," I said.

"Next time we just might take care of it ourselves." Nate had fire in his eyes.

"Don't be too hasty, Nate, you might shoot th' wrong ones, just point that hidey-gun at 'em an' holler bang." At that moment, a big steer broke and headed for the cavvy and I ran to cut him off and send him back where he belonged. From then on, I was busy with the cows and didn't think about the boys until late in the day.

We got to the little lake below the spring the next day later than we had expected and there were a couple of soldiers there waiting. Lieutenant Beckman had a conversation with them then came over to tell us that the army had set up camp at th' junction of Silver Springs Canyon and Elk Canyon where there was more water.

Pa looked at the dwindling light. "Well, boys what do you say, camp here for th' night or push 'em on down-canyon in th' dark?"

"They's water all th' way down, boss, we could push 'em as far as they will go an' be that much closer in th' mornin'," Cider said.

"T'ain't like we has all that much t' eat here," Newt said.

"I say let 'em go 'til they stop fer th' night like they did afore," said Bet.

"All right, men, let's move them on down the canyon. I'm sure the sides are steep enough t' keep them close. When they start to mill, we'll let them settle down for the night. Lieutenant, you can tell your people at th' forks we will be there at first light." That would be the sixth day.

Beckman nodded and taking Corporal Ashburton and Private Hardester and leaving the other two soldiers with us, rode down-canyon to report to his commander.

Those cows had filled on water and we moved down the valley at an easy pace. After the steepest part was passed, the canyon began to spread out and the slope wasn't as steep. We didn't go far until th' herd began t' mill an' we let them bed.

Benito's stew was gone, but he had a fire going and coffee on. With only two on watch with the herd, the rest of us gathered around and filled our cups.

Green's face looked worse, the prints of the fingers were long blue streaks that radiated out of the red circle of the palm print. His eye could open just a slit and it watered a lot. It hadn't swollen much more that I could tell.

"Shoulda kilt 'im," Bet gritted.

"Naw, Bet, Tuck give him some o' his own an' he'll suffer most as much as Green an' on top o' that, those boys with him'll give him hell fer gittin' caught unawares like that," Nap said.

"I thought Tuck hed started a war there fer a minute," Cider said.

"Me too," Pa said. "If those men had been fully sober they would have reacted quicker and we might have had real trouble."

"I'm sorry, Pa, but that man was braggin' he did it an' I lost my temper."

"I probably would have done th' same

thing," Pa said and the rest nodded in agreement. He set watches and we turned in for the night. He gave Nap and me last watch. "When your relief comes out, they'll bring you fresh mounts and you cut out eight or ten head and herd them ahead to the forks. That will give th' army something to start butcherin' 'til we get there with the whole herd."

"We'll git 'er done, Mr. Beavers," Nap said as he rolled up in his blanket.

I really don't remember my head hitting my saddle-pillow and I swear it had barely touched down when someone was kickin' my boots. "Rise an' shine, Tuck."

The way things go on the trail, last watch is longest b'cause all the rest have fudged a little on their time and this watch was no different. An empty stomach and little sleep made time drag even more and it seemed like a week before we saw Nate and Bet bringing out our mounts. From back of the herd, Nap rode around one side and I rode around t'other, picking up early risers around th' edges. When we got to th' front, we had a dozen or more head and we hazed them on down th' valley. They left their herd reluctantly and I heard a beller or two from behind. When I looked, Lead Steer was up, head high, and catchin' up fast. The rest of th' herd was scrambling t' follow. "Looks like th' boys are gonna leave afore breakfast," I called to Nap.

"Cows is th' most frustratin' critter they is, first you cain't git them t' trail, then ya caint git 'em t' stop!" he called.

Ol' Lead Steer caught up with us and shouldered his way through our bunch to lead. By th' time we had gone a mile that whole herd had found their usual positions and were all strung out movin' down th' valley.

Our pals were hurrying t' catch up. "Boss didn't say t' take th' whole dern herd, Tuck," Bet called grumpily.

"They come uninvited," said I.

"I'll bet. You was just put out at havin' last watch an' took it out on th' rest of us."

I had been eyeing a bunch of riders off to th' side and as I got closer, I could see Pete holdin' a rifle on th' deputy an' his bunch.

Newt was close to me and he and I rode over to see what th' trouble was.

"Howdy, Pete," Newt called. "Drive's over an' you kin come out of hidin' now."

"We're s'posed t' be herdin' cows an' not outlaws," I added.

"Found these fellers shakin' out their yeller slickers an' had a time convincin' 'em it weren't gonna rain," Pete replied. "Funny

169

thing, they's out here in Injun territory without a single gun in th' bunch."

Looking around, I didn't see the scoundrel I had hit.

"Oh, they donated their guns to us so we could protect our herd from thieves an' Injuns," Newt said.

"How nice, fellers," Pete addressed the mob, "ya never know what might happen on th' trail an' on th' reservation an' it's always good t' go well-armed."

Lieutenant Beckman and a detachment of soldiers rode up with another officer who I learned was a captain and Beckman's commanding officer. "Who are these men, Pete?" the captain asked.

"These are my friends from th' ranch," Pete replied, indicating me and Newt, "and these are fellers who can't tell weather too well, they was shakin' out their slickers thinkin' it was gonna rain any minute." He grinned.

"These men tried to stop our herd yesterday an' we ran them off," I added.

"Do you men know where you are?" the captain asked the gang. There was no answer. "You are trespassing on the Mescalero Apache Indian Reservation. And if my nose serves me right, you have introduced whiskey to the reservation on top of attempting to interfere with army operations. You are now under arrest. Dismount! Sergeant, disarm and take these men to the camp and hold them there until I determine how and when we take them back to the fort."

After the McSween fight in the Lincoln County War, Colonel Dudley had been replaced as commander and new officers came in who had very different attitudes about the whites and Indians. All the country outside of Lincoln County except the Santa Fe Ring was happy about it. Now I have to say here that not everyone in Lincoln County was in cahoots with the Ring. There always were more good people living there in difficult circumstances among the few bad.

The sergeant and his men got busy separating men and horses and searchin' for weapons. Only knives were found.

"We can give you the guns these men were carrying yesterday," I said. I knew Pa wanted to get rid of them somehow and this was a good way.

"Bring them to the camp and I will gladly take care of them," the captain said.

The soldiers soon had the mob lined up two by two and they marched them off down the valley. We saw nothing more of them and I'm glad.

The cattle were delivered and Pa got a receipt for them. The army fed us a great meal and we drove the cavvy off to the side and watched the goings-on.

There was a stir among the Indians and I looked up our back trail to see the large group we had fed comin' down th' hill. Several mounted warriors, including one who must have been a leader or chief among them, rode out to meet these newcomers and there were shouts of greeting and much talk. After a few moments, the chief and two of his men rode over to us and stopped in front of Pa. Speaking in Spanish, he said, "You have been kind to my people and without the food and milk some of them may have not lived much longer. For that, the Dine' are grateful and we will remember that you are our friend."

"It is good to remember that most white people do not wish harm to the Red Man, but there are bad men among us that would do harm to both red and white men for their own selfish gains," Pa said. "We do not wish to see women and children starved and only did what we could to help."

"Because of this time, men of the Beavers will always be welcome in the land of the Dine'," the chief said. "I would buy the

172

Mexican cook Benito if he is for sale," he said. With a smile, and with a handshake he left to attend to business among the Apache.

"What ya think 'bout that, Benito? Th' Buck wants yuh t' cook fer him," Cider said.

Benito crossed himself and rolled his eyes. "Not eeven eef Señor Tuck-er asked mee, would I go!"

It must have been a monumental thing to the Mescalero, because more than once I have seen cowhide shields made with the beaver brand from those cattle — and it may be that *some* of those shields came from cattle not born back then!

Since that time, any man riding a horse with a Beaver brand has always been welcome wherever an Apache was met.

CHAPTER 11
BACK TO THE RANCH

When General Carlton and Kit Carson had first rounded up the Mescaleros, they had given the Indians their meat allowance on the hoof. Problem was that the distribution was not uniform and some families were going hungry while others had more than enough. On top of that, the warriors slaughtered the cattle in the same fashion as they did the buffalo, by running them down and shooting them. This led to much waste and the agent for the tribe soon established a fair distribution procedure where the agency slaughtered the cattle and distributed the butchered meat evenly.

"Heiskell Jones and his son Jim were among th' first if not *the* first butchers for the distribution," said Pa. "They slaughtered and distributed the meat fairly and the 'Paches respected them for it. That was before the war, don't know when they quit. The war Pa referred to around this corner of New Mexico back then is the Lincoln County War.

"They lived over at Seven Rivers," Pa continued, "and some of th' boys have a place up Rocky Arroyo, rough around th' edges, but they're good folks. I still hear old-timers speak favorably of Heiskell's wife. Everyone called her Ma'am Jones."

Even with such a short notice, there were already Indians camped around the bottoms. It wasn't the normal distribution day, but Captain Needham Hale, acting agent, ordered the distribution to begin at sunrise the next morning. Already the soldiers were slaughtering and cutting up the carcasses. On an upturned wagon box, they piled the meat in portions for each family. Just like the contents of son-of-a-gun stew, the Indians ate everything but the hide, hooves, horns and holler. Hide and horns were laid aside and the women took of them what they needed. Soon, hides were stretched and drying and the horns that were taken were set aside for carving into spoons and dippers and other things at a later time.

"I guess sooner or later they'll find a use for the hooves," Pete said, "but they ain't gonna be able t' use th' holler!" That started a running conversation among the whole bunch.

"They shore make some folks look wasteful," Newt observed.

"D'ya reckon they could teach those Rawhide Texians anything?"

"Ain't too much separatin' them two breeds, now. If they ever got t'gether, it'd go bad for white folks."

"Rawhiders *is* white folks!"

"Ain't seen a white one yit!"

"Ya haveta scrub off a couple o' years o'dirt, Bet, they're under there."

"That may be somethin' th' Injuns could teach. They're cleaner than rawhiders."

"Smell better too."

"Injuns got a peculiar odor, I kin smell one a mile away."

"*I say*, Injuns smell better."

"Don't start no argyments, boys, save 'em fer th' judge."

"Whut judge?"

"The one you gotta 'splain why you busted up th' saloon to."

"Ain't busted no saloon — an' got caught for it."

Pa had heard enough banter. "Tuck and I have got to go to Fort Stanton, men. Bet, you and Cider and Pete take the cavvy and the boys back with Benito. Newton and Nap, here is pay for th' days you helped us. I'll thank Zenas when I see him, but tell

176

him how much we all appreciate your help. We couldn't have done it without you."

"Zenas told us t' tell you we would be on Rafter payroll an' not to pay us nothin'," Nap said.

"Nevertheless, I want you t' take this, you earned double pay for what you did."

They took the money hesitantly and I heard Newt whisper as they left, "Don't tell Zee an' we'll double up."

"The army mess will feed us another meal and I have bought enough food for your return trip, so you won't starve on th' way home. Sooner you get goin', th' better, I expect this place will be full t' bustin' by tonight an' I had just as soon not have our horses near."

We got a good meal at the mess and said our good-byes. At the last minute, Pa, noticing Green's face, decided to take him to the fort to see a doctor there. Of course, that meant Nate was goin' with us, bein's they were practically joined at the hips. We said our good-byes and went on our separate ways.

It took us two days to reach Fort Stanton and by that time, Green's swelling had gone down quite a bit, but the whole side of his face was green and blue. You could still see the handprint. I wonder that his head wasn't knocked clear off, but being small and wiry, all he got was knocked out of the saddle.

"That was probably good," Pa said. "He only took one blow thataway."

None of us could look at the boy without getting angry and I regretted at times I didn't do what Bet said and kill that piece of trash and I said so.

"Killing's awful final, Tuck, and you never know what will come of a man down th' road. One thing I am sure of is that he'll think again next time he wants to molest a kid like that," Pa said.

At the fort, we got paid — without the bonus — and the doctor looked at Green's face. He looked in his mouth and saw that his teeth had cut his cheek inside, but it was healing all right. He prescribed that Green wash his mouth out several times a day with warm salt water and we bought a supply of salt to use on our trip home.

While we waited on the doctor, his orderly told us about a man that had come in with a broken nose and his eyes swelled almost shut. Doc had to pack his nose to open th' passages and that involved a lot of pain for the man. He had stayed around th' fort a couple of days then disappeared. Nate started t' tell him what had happened, but I stopped him in time. Less said, the better.

While we were there, John Chisum's Jinglebob outfit drove in a herd for the agency and they sure looked scrawny. Old John Chisum was selling his culls off for beef for the Indians. I was amused t' see that our culls were in better shape than his culls. I asked one of the vaqueros if they had any bulls that would improve the breed, but he said that John had so many longhorns that he wasn't interested in improving the herd yet. By that, I took it that I would have to get any bulls for improvement somewhere else, maybe El Paso or shipped in from the east somewhere.

We left by the road to Capitan then cut cross-country to the Ruidoso road and on down to Tularosa. Pa wanted to get out of Lincoln County quickly to avoid possible trouble with what passed for law in that country. We rested a day at Tularosa and let th' boys do some tradin'. Pa told them to trade the pistols in for something less dangerous to them and with a little work they talked the clerk into trading two Stevens .22 single-shot boys' rifles for the guns, holster and belt full of shells. We made saddle loops and left town with both guns proudly dangling from saddle horns. Breaks and layovers were taken up with shooting lessons and target practices. By the time we got to La Luz, they had both shot up two boxes of shorts. Pa bought them three more boxes apiece and kept four in his saddlebags.

By the time we got to Lee's ranch at Dog Canyon, they were in a sweat to shoot some more. Mr. Oliver Lee was at home and he took the boys out and let them shoot a Winchester and talked to them some time about guns and gun handling. They were all eyes and ears, for Mr. Lee was somewhat of a legend in the country.

We got to the ranch late in the afternoon and there was quite a welcome to the boys. They were full of talk about the trip and the things they had done and Green got lots of sympathy from mothers. His face seemed to be much better, but it was still vividly colored.

"Why didn't you paint t'other side, Green?" little Josh asked.

"Cause it hurt too much," Nate put in.

A SEASON TO LOVE

Cindy didn't pay me too much attention, but poured sympathy and affection all over Green. I thought her face was rather pink and my ears burned. We avoided each other by unspoken mutual consent and I soon left for the cabin. Pete had been there several days and I wanted t'see him, but mostly I

180

think I just wanted t' get away from all th' fuss and soak up some quiet. Pete seemed of th' same mind and we spent the next few days ridin' among th' stock and watchin'. I was down by the lower end of the Nueces Strip beating the brush t' see what came out when I looked up and there came Cindy sidesaddle in a pretty dress. She blushed some and I could only grin, but my face felt warm.

She came close and laid her hand on my arm. "I want to thank you for taking up for Green, it was very brave of you."

"I hardly thought about it." I shrugged. "No one should get by treating a kid that way."

"I'll bet he doesn't do it again."

"Maybe." We rode in silence, just the creak of leather and the clop of the horses' hooves in the dust.

After a while, she asked coyly, "Have you had a bath lately?"

"Most every night here, but no one interrupts me."

She laughed and nothing was said for a while until I told her that Pete and I were going down to Las Cruces and possibly even El Paso to look for gentlemen cows for the herd.

"I know you call them bulls, Tuck, and it

181

doesn't bother me when it's between you and me." She was blushing again, but not so much this time.

"Well, I'll still call 'em 'gentlemen' in front of you," I said.

"When do you plan to go?"

"Probably early next week, there's a sale at Las Cruces and they might have some good stock there. If not, we're going t' look at going on down to El Paso or thereabouts."

"Thereabouts?"

"Some of the ranches may have improved stock they would be willing to sell."

"I've never been to El Paso."

"Me neither. Pete says it can be pretty rough there."

"I left some things at the shack for you. Your mother said to be careful and not break the bowl and bring it back Saturday."

"OK, if Pete gets there before we do, you might be able to take it back today."

"I won't be going back there, I have to get back before dark."

"You're not going t' wait 'til I take a bath?" I asked and she slapped my shoulder. I caught her hand and held it. It was warm and soft and I could smell lavender perfume. *What is this?* I thought. *Here's my pal and buddy and I'm getting silly and giddy just touching her.* It was all unsettling to me. I was losing Cindy my pal and seeing her as a desireable young woman. Part of me was excited at the change and part of me was sad it wasn't still the way it had been for as long as we could remember. Sadly or happily, life never stands still, it has to keep moving.

"Ride with me to the ridge, Tuck." And we rode up the hillside, stirring grasshoppers out of the way and listening to crickets sing their evening song. We stopped under the trees and she leaned over to me and it seemed just the natural thing t' do to kiss her. "Will you be coming down Saturday?"

"Maybe Friday night if we get things done in time," I replied.

"I'll see you then. Rance said to tell you there's a game up Saturday afternoon with the La Luz team. Good-bye, Tuck." And she turned and cantered off down the path.

Pete and I did go to El Paso looking for breeding stock. The best we could find was half Durhams and we brought six back to the ranch. When the time was right, Pa put four of them with our main herd and took out all the Longhorn bulls. I put two Durhams in the Far Pasture and the spring crop of calves showed the difference. It was a year before we found pure Durham stock. Their introduction really improved the looks of the herd and we went for some time with the Durham-Longhorn cross, gradually weeding out the old Longhorns.

Pa made Bob Nealy full partner in the ranch and I was glad. Bob had poured as much work into the place as any of us and he deserved to be included. I can't say that I courted Cindy, we just sorta fell into that kind of relationship and everyone was aware of it. Rance paid her a lot of attention as if he didn't know how we were and I was jealous part of the time.

1883

In the fall of the third year of my management of the Far Pasture, Pete was penning up some stock when one of those big Durham bulls knocked a five-hundred pound calf into him and broke some ribs and his thighbone on the same side. When he came home from the doctor's, we laid him up at the bunkhouse and he got fairly spoiled by th' women. That marked the end of his riding and he stayed on with us working around the place and running the fencing crew when we had one.

Nate and Green took a shine to the cabin and spent a lot of time up there. They had graduated from the .22s and both had

Winchester .44s. Sue Ellen inherited one of the boys' rifles, and the other was reserved for Joshua when he was old enough. Later on, they were continually competing to see who was the best shot. I think Sue Ellen eventually became the best, but Josh was a very close second.

One day after they had been to town, Green and Nate appeared with revolvers on their hips. Both mothers lit into them. They lost the guns until Dad and Bob could mollify the women. Both boys became pretty good ballplayers, Nate pitching near as good as Riley Giddens.

Speaking of Giddens, we all wondered how the Lincoln gang learned about our drive to the reservation so fast until we heard that John R., Riley's pa, had learned about it somehow and had sent Riley to telegraph Jim Dolan at Lincoln. Giddens Mercantile bought wholesale from the Murphy-Dolan Company and I would say by that and what John R. did, that he was a part of the Santa Fe Ring. First time I saw Riley after that I gave him a good lickin' and we were not friends anymore. The Browns' store benefitted by the incident, for several people who had traded with Giddens took their business to Brown's. Our animosity toward Riley caused him to leave town and John R. let it out that he had gone east to get his education, but we knew he had only gone to Lincoln where he worked in the mercantile store.

CHAPTER 12
THE ROCK SALT SALE

1884

The old owner of Browns' store had been buying wholesale from the Murphy-Dolan Company and when the company signed an agreement with Giddens to sell wholesale to him and no one else in Pinetop, the store went on the market. When Jim Brown bought the store, John R. Giddens offered to go into partnership with him and just have one store in town. Mr. Brown considered it, but there were too many unanswered questions and conditions. They never could come to an agreement, so the two stores continued to compete.

Most of the Rio Grande valley south of Socorro bought their wholesale supplies from El Paso, and Jim Brown secured agreements with them to stock his store and by doing so squelched John R.'s plan to eliminate his competition in the town. Competition between the two stores was strong, sometimes heated, but there had never been any violence between them. Rance and Riley got along fine until the trail drive and attack on Green and Riley's whipping.

With Murphy-Dolan it was a different story. They viewed Pinetop as their exclusive territory and the El Paso suppliers as invaders in the same light that they had viewed John Henry Tunstall. Problem was they couldn't kill off the competition as easy as they had in Lincoln County. The Santa Fe Ring interfered in the situation by passing laws taxing any merchandise bought out of Texas. The only thing that did was turn a lot of people in the south of th' state into smugglers and no one in that region thought of it as being dishonest. Some famous European philosopher once said, "Some fool will make a stupid law and some other fool will obey it." Well, maybe he didn't say "stupid" but you get the gist. Folks of th' south valley were not stupid and they eventually got enough political strength to get those laws repealed.

There was some scattered violence when the laws were in effect. Th' Santa Fe Ring even sent "state deputies" down the valley to patrol the roads looking for what they called contraband. When they were laughed at and kicked out of the country, Dolan sent the very same men back to rob and other-wise harass the merchants. That, too, came to an end when a few new oblong shaped mounds appeared along the river road and a couple of tarred and feathered figures were dumped off the train at Carrizozo. The Coe boys told that by th' time they got t' Lincoln, th' feathers had either been picked off or buried in tar. They said the men complained that the tar was too hot. Kerosene got rid of a lot of the stuff, but you could still pick them out of a crowd.

Riley Giddens was gone a little more than a year and when he came back it was clear that he had learned a lot from his schooling in the east. Riley's new form of competition took on a shady and destructive nature and feelings became so heated that Pat Garrett sent Deputy George Ryles to stay in Pinetop until things could be cooled down some. Even then trouble was still bubbling underneath and a smoldering fire is bound to break out sooner or later.

Rance's mom, Sue, was th' store's stay-at-home bookkeeper and she began to notice discrepancies in the quantity of items bought and items sold so it was decided to inventory the entire store. When finished, it was apparent that various items had been disappearing from the stock. The Browns took steps to improve security especially in the storage room, adding a bar across the doors and fastening windows tightly. Still, things were missed and careful observations showed that things had been moved around that Jim and Rance knew they hadn't done.

"Looks like we'll have to guard the place night and day," Jim said to Rance.

"I can start sleeping down here for a while, Dad, if you think that will help."

"I don't want to hire someone to guard th' place, so we will take turns staying here and see what happens," Jim told Rance.

So it was decided that, a week at a time, each would sleep in the store and keep watch, all this being done in secret. Rance's first week went quietly. He didn't sleep well in the strange environment between waking several times a night and getting accustomed to the sounds old buildings make in the quiet gloom.

Mr. Brown's first two tours of duty were just as uneventful and they were beginning to wonder if the guarding was worthwhile.

It was on Tuesday night of Rance's third night duty that all the boredom and watching paid off. He had just dropped off to sleep on his cot behind the counter after his first inspection tour when he became aware of a new sound in the room. Without moving, he listened for a moment to the soft metallic clicking sound. It was coming from the front of th' store and he hazarded a glance over the counter. In the soft light from the Town Hall light across the street, he could see the shadow of someone at the front door. He was picking the door lock.

So that's how he gets in! His dad had forbidden Rance to carry the shotgun loaded with buckshot.

"A few things lost in a burglary aren't justification for killing, Rance," he had said.

So Rance had loaded the gun with rock salt. If needed, his pistol would be sufficient in close quarters.

He heard the bolt slide back in the lock and ducked behind the counter. The door opened with a small squeak. Even though the blinds were pulled, he could still make out the silhouette of a man moving across the floor, his feet making hardly a sound. *He's barefoot,* Rance thought.

In the stockroom, the man lit a candle and rustled around in the boxes of goods. Meantime, Rance found the toys and opening several packages, quietly scattered jacks across the floor on the path to the front door, sure the sounds he made would not be heard in the stockroom. He then resumed his vigil behind the counter, his cocked shotgun laying on top of the counter pointed at the front door.

Presently, the light went out and the burgular crept out of the back room with his arms full of boxes. As he neared the door his heel encountered a jack and he stumbled picking up another jack in the ball of his other foot. A box or two spilled from his arms as he tried to hurry on uninjured toe and heel across the floor. He had just reached the door when Rance called, "Halt there!"

Punctured feet forgotten, the man tossed the boxes high and opened the door as the first barrel of the shotgun went off. The man dove across the sidewalk amid boxes and broken glass and was fast disappearing down the street by th' time Rance reached the door and discharged his second barrel.

He barely had time to light a lamp before Jim Brown came in from the house, shirtless, pants partially buttoned, one gallus hanging and his old Navy Colt in his hand. "What happened, son?" he called.

"We had a visitor and I sent him home with salt in his pants."

"Looks like you two had quite a party."

"It was mighty short for all th' mess it made," Rance replied looking at the glass and window shades shot to pieces and all

192

the boxes that were in the way peppered with holes.

Sue Brown appeared at the door. She had taken more time to dress than her husband. Several others appeared at the door including Deputy George and John R. Giddens. His face was pale and he appeared shaken.

"You played jacks?" the deputy asked. "Didn't you have any cards?"

"We were playing for boxes an' I think he made off with a couple of my jacks," Rance replied.

Someone from the sidewalk called, "There's a pair of boots out here."

The boots were set neatly together by the door and one look at them told Rance who had been wearing them. He dared not look at John R. "Bring 'em in here, we'll hang 'em up so th' rightful owner can claim them."

"Fat chance, that," Deputy George grinned.

"I surely hope you scared him off for good," John R. said. "We've had a couple of break-ins ourselves." He had regained his composure somewhat.

Rance avoided eye contact with him. "I'll get a broom, Dad, and we can board up the windows until tomorrow."

Jim Brown was pulling on a jack impaled

in the sole of his slipper. "All right, we can use some of those box slats for now."

The crowd began to move off to inform anxious wives of the event. "Better get your key," the deputy said, pulling it out of the door. It was the skeleton style and had been filed down to work in the store door.

"So that's how he did it," Jim said. "We'll be getting a better lock, that's sure!"

"You may need more rock salt too." Deputy George was picking out rocks imbedded in the door frame.

"I had to persuade Rance not to use lead."

"Lead might have been my choice too, Mr. Brown, you never know what these sneaks will do. I would be careful where I went and what I turned my back on for a while was I you, Rance."

"You can be sure of that!"

By the time the place was cleaned up and made secure, it was three a.m. and the two men went to the house to await their four o'clock breakfast time. Sue Brown was waiting their return and set about fixing their meal while Rance dozed in an overstuffed chair.

At breakfast, Jim asked, "What are we going do with the shot-up clothes in those boxes?"

"If they are not in too bad a shape, I guess

we could sell 'em at a discount," replied Rance.

"Some of 'em are gonna be full of salt rocks."

"Well, George did say that we might have t' buy more — how about leaving them in th' boxes an' sellin' blemished clothes at a five-percent or ten-percent discount, plus a penny for each salt crystal found in the garment?"

"Why would you make light of a thing like this?" Sue asked. "You could have been killed, Rance."

"But I wasn't harmed, Ma, and what else do you want t' do with all that stuff, burn it?"

"Making light of it might send a message that we are not intimidated by burglars and thieves," Jim said.

"I'll make some signs and we'll have a sale Friday and Saturday, Pa."

"Sounds good, son, let's get to the store. I think we have some small panes of glass, but I'll bet we have to order those tall panes for th' doors. Hope El Paso or Albuquerque has some."

Wednesday, hand-painted signs appeared in the windows of the Brown establishment. The signs read:

SALE SALE
THIS FRIDAY AND SATURDAY
DUE TO AN INCIDENT LAST TUESDAY
NIGHT
SEVERAL CARTONS OF DRY GOODS
WERE
DAMAGED
These goods will be Sold From the
Cartons at a 10% Discount,
First Come First Served.
IN ADDITION,
A further penny will be discounted for
each salt crystal found
In the garment!

Another sign beside the first listed the
items for sale:

Ladies' Summer Union Suits
Were $0.42 Now $0.38!
Teamster's Double Breasted
Blue Twill Shirts
Were $0.96 Now $0.86!
Buffalo California Heavy
Made Flannel Overshirts
Were $1.92 Now $1.73!
Men's and Boys'
Genuine Muskrat Fur Caps
Were $2.83 Now $2.55!

Handbills were tacked up over town announcing the special sale, and the sale was a huge success. They sold out of the stock. Sue spent Friday and Saturday morning selling the Ladies' Union Suits discretely to the lady customers.

Every garment was shaken out to reveal any salt crystals and it was great fun. Jim had added salt to the garments and by mid-afternoon Saturday, there was a pint jar on the counter half full of rock salt, much more than one shotgun shell would hold. Men around town wore their shirts and caps with the holes either showing or prominently repaired and they came to be called Rock Salt Shirts or Rock Salt Caps. Of course, ladies' union suits did not share the light of day except on the clotheslines, and the men had fun asking their lady friends if they were wearing their Rock Salt Unions.

It eventuated in that area that for years after that event, any garment that was worn with hole or patch was called a Rock Salt garment, whether it be pants, shoes, hats or shirts. Anyone who broke a window would order replacement by asking for a glass of the required dimensions "to replace a Rock Salt Glass."

Of course you know who had worn those shoes as well as Rance did. In addition to a couple of punctures in the bottoms of his feet, Riley had cut his feet on the shattered glass and was not seen *walking* around town for some time after the break-in. His relationship with Rance remained just below the boiling point and everyone had the opinion that it could break out at any time. The shoes hung from a nail high on the shelves of the store until . . . but I'm getting ahead of myself.

CHAPTER 13
THE KILLING RAID

A SEASON TO MOURN

We had always lost a few head of cattle along, usually just a calf or steer. We marked that up to a hungry Indian or pilgrim family and let it go. Occasionally five or six would disappear at once and we would track them, sometimes getting them back and making it hot for the thieves who mostly stole them to sell to a butcher somewhere who didn't pay attention to brands.

The boys and I were way up at the top of the range in 1884 moving cattle down for the fall when Sue Ellen appeared at the far end of the pasture we were in and fired her gun in the air. That meant we were needed pronto and we trotted down to her. As we neared, she was screaming, "Hurry, hurry!" Her face was streaked with dirt and tears and scratches and her dress torn where she had run through the trees and brush and her horse was covered with sweat and foam and all done in.

"There's been a fight and Pa and Bob and Pete are shot up. We can't find Bet and Cider anywhere." She turned in her panic and would have run that horse to death back down the mountain if I hadn't caught her.

"Stand still, Sue, take a deep breath an' tell us what happened," I said, setting her down and seeing to the horse. She was so upset that I had to shake her to get her attention. I held her sobbing until she could get ahold of herself enough to talk. Meantime, Nate had unsaddled her horse and Green had thrown a rope over a limb and they had hauled saddle and bridle up in the tree. They turned the poor horse loose and I put Sue in my saddle and got up behind. "Now, Sue, tell us what has happened as we ride."

Between her sobs and our trotting we gradually got part of the story. Cider had found where a bunch of cattle, two hundred or more, had been gathered and driven up toward the Far Pasture so Pa and Bob, Bet, Cider and Pete had ridden up to see what was going on. After noon, Pete rode in all bloody and said they had been shot up at the cabin. Eda was there visiting with her new baby and she took care of Pete while the two moms and Cindy went to the cabin in the wagon, Josh went to town for the doctor and Sue Ellen rode to find us.

We changed our route and rode for the ridge where we met Cindy driving the wagon with the two men laid out in the bed, the wives beside them. Pa was dead, I could tell it. Bob didn't look much better. Mom was stricken and pale. She just stared at Pa and barely acknowledged us. Both women had been crying and Cindy could barely see for her tears. We were all affected greatly and after a moment or two I got down and climbed on the seat beside Cindy and drove. Nate had to lead Sue's horse she was so upset and we proceeded down to the ranch house.

Doc had Pete in the bunkhouse treating him and he came out to look at the other two. One look at Pa and he shook his head. I could barely see what he did with Bob and I couldn't hear a word anyone was saying. Someone put his arm around me and led me away and I saw others lifting Bob onto a door and carrying him to the bunkhouse. Others were lifting Pa and carrying him to the house. When I looked around, the yard was full of people, wagons and horses. Women were tending to Ma and Bob's wife, Presilla, and the others while the men helped with Pa and Bob. The horses were stabled and cared for by others.

Rance had his arm around my shoulders and was saying something, but I could only hear a ringing in my ears. I shook myself and a world of sounds, of Rance and other people talking in low voices, harness jangling and people weeping, met me, and then faded away again. I don't know how much later it was when I found myself sitting on the bunkhouse stoop in the dark and Doc Hutto was above me addressing the crowd, "Pete and Bob are going to be OK. They both are shot up some, but nothing that could be fatal, all things being normal."

His voice faded away and the next thing I heard was the sheriff say, "And if you are volunteering, step over here and I will swear you in. There was a bunch of moving around me and soon nearly every man mounted up and rode out behind the sheriff.

I saw the sun come up and all was quiet. Someone was moving around in the bunk-house and I got up and looked. A lady I didn't know was tending to Bob. Pete slept on another bunk. Presilla lay asleep on another. Holding her finger to her lips, the woman handed me a steaming cup of coffee. I took a sip and looked at the cup in surprise. There was more than coffee in it. "Something to calm your nerves," she whispered. Taking me by the shoulders, she pushed me to a rocking chair on the porch and I sat and sipped my drink. The door creaked and Benito crept out with the coffeepot. He was pale and his eyes red. "Ees ver-r-ry bad, Tuck, ver-ry bad," he whispered and went back inside.

The sun was casting a golden glow on the house and the shadows of the trees were creeping across the dusty yard, letting the daylight in. The cup was empty and I set it on the floor and walked across the yard to the house. All was quiet in the big room. There were people sitting around talking quietly. Dishes rattled softly in the kitchen. The people stood when I walked in. No one spoke, but my old Sunday school teacher took my arm and we walked over to where Pa was laid out. He was washed and clean, his thinning hair combed neatly — not its normal condition and I reached and touseled it. "Now time has stopped for you, Pa, and you will be forever fifty-three."

The posse came back two days later with Bet's body. They had found him on the trail to th' Jornado beside his dead horse. Both had been shot. There was no sign of John

203

Crider anywhere. When the herd crossed the border into Texas, the posse turned back.

At first, I thought to bury Dad on the place, but if we had, it would have been a constant reminder to us, especially Mom. She was taken with her grief and I talked it over with the rest of the family. We got a large plot in the town cemetery and buried Dad there with Bet beside him. Eda's husband, Joe Meeker, took care of all the arrangements and the whole country came to their funeral. The church was overflowing and crowds stood outside around windows to hear the service. I don't remember a word the parson said, only remember that they were comforting at the time.

I don't know why, I only know from many occasions that there's something of a relief when the burial is done. Maybe it signals the end of a chapter of life. It's those that don't realize that a new chapter has to now begin that don't get over a loss. Anyway, that's how I feel, I don't know what others feel. It was as if a dark time had been lifted from my vision and I saw the sunshine and the good people around me.

There was a meal at the church for the family and friends and near everyone stayed. It was a comfort to hear people talk about

Dad and Bet, the things they had done in their lives. With all the hugs and handshakes and good words, reunions with people from afar, I could feel some healing and saw it in the rest of the family. Mom didn't stay too long, she and Cindy went back to the ranch to be with Bob and Presilla. Pete had insisted on coming to the funeral and one of the C-B boys brought him down. I had made him sit with the family and it was a comfort to see him up, even though he was still awful weak and pale. He went back with th' women.

Most of th' men were standing or sitting around the yard smokin' and visitin' and I wandered over among them. Oliver Lee was over in the shade of a cottonwood and motioned for me when he caught my eye. He rose and shook my hand. "Sorry about this, Tuck. It's a bad deal." Zenas Meeker moved near and laid his hand on my shoulder.

"Joe sure has been a help and comfort for us, Zenas. He's a good friend," I said.

"It's good to know, Tuck, I imagine if he had been anythin' less, his ma would have gotten into him pretty good." He grinned.

We sat on our heels and Mr. Lee had a stick in his hand drawing in the dust. "Zenas and I have been looking over the range some and have learned some things about those rustlers that you should know before you go after them. They got away with so many cattle by scattering men all over the range and easing small bunches together. We found where they had joined and that's where Crider found their tracks."

"Best we can determine, there were ten t' twelve of them on unshod horses," Zenas said, "an' we can identify at least six horses by their tracks. They went south an' cut th' Rio Sacramento an' followed it t' th' sink."

"The boys say from there they went straight across the Jornada to the state line in the Cornudas Mountains." Mr. Lee was drawing a map of the route as they talked. "I don't think those cows had much time to rest or graze until they crossed over. In my time, borders and lines didn't make much matter, but these boys today have telegraph and telephone and they've gotten lazy. They'd rather call someone else to 'keep on the lookout for' than do it themselves."

"An' some fat-assed deputy in Texas'll 'keep a lookout for' as far as he can see out th' window between th' toes of his boots," Zenas put in. "By now, they are in Mexico, probably headin' for th' Beaver Ranch t' upgrade their stock."

"Son, we looked at the area around the

line shack and this is how we make out how things went down," Mr. Lee said. "Tucker and the boys found the herd in the pasture alone. Leaving Bet with the herd, they rode up toward the shack looking for the thieves. Some of them were hid out in the woods and after they passed, opened fire on them. Those at the cabin opened up and they had the boys in a crossfire.

"Looks like Pete and your dad charged the woods and Bob and Cider charged the cabin. They never made it to the woods, both horses going down within twenty yards of each other. They forted up behind the carcasses and fought for some time. Pete got a good groove down the side of his head and was out of it and Tucker took several shots in the body from the cabin.

"Cider made it to the cabin and Bob made it too, but he was afoot by then. They made it hot for the boys in there. We found blood in several places, a lot at one of them and I'm pretty sure that man didn't make it. They must have taken his body with them or buried him where we haven't looked yet. By the takin' of the bodies, we don't think they were Mexican or American." Mr. Lee looked at me. "Meanin' they must have been Indian or mostly Indian." He had drawn a map of the battle as they had talked.

"Tuck, they was just too many holes knocked in the chinkin for anyone outside to be safe and they eventually stopped both of them. Somehow, Crider rode away through the woods and headed back to the herd. I imagine if you could follow their trail you could find two or three graves out there," Zee said.

"I'll go with you when you go, Tuck," said an unfamiliar voice and I looked up to find a ring of men standing around us. I hadn't even thought about it, but these men, pioneers and sons of pioneers, had known a thing like this could not be ignored. They knew what they would do and knew that I would do the same.

"Thanks," I said.

"Now, don't you go off half-cocked," Mr. Meeker said. "I have sent some Mexican Americans down t' spy out th' lay of th' land an' they will be back in time an' we'll know a lot more about what t' do."

Oliver Lee tapped my knee with his stick and looked straight into my eyes. "The law here is weak and polluted and there is *no* law in Mexico. You will have to be your own law and when the time comes, do what you have to do and go on."

There it was, the old law of the range. The old-timers had to stand and live or die by it or leave. These were the survivors, the ones who stayed, talking to me — grizzled and scarred — but still here by the strength of their own resolve. That law was alive when they talked to me that day, and still is today, for a man has to be strong enough to protect himself and his own. The best the law can do is investigate the crime and chase the perpetrators, hand them over to the courts, which, in most cases, slaps wrists and lets the criminal go to commit more crimes. I wonder when the time comes that the easy judges and lax juries stand before the final Judge if they will find on their hands the blood of innocent people harmed by the criminals they should not have turned loose. It takes strength and resolve to do the right thing. Many cases are decided in the judge's chambers. All that is left then is to hem in the jury with rules and limits so they will come to the desired conclusions. Too many courts practice law and not justice and it seems nothing ever gets finished.

Late that afternoon I walked with some of the family to the graves. Not much was said as we watched the golden light of the sunset silhouette the Organ Mountains. That day they looked like tombstones.

CHAPTER 14
PECOS PETE GETS HIS SPURS

CHAPTER 14
PECOS PETE GETS HIS SPURS

I knew that handling two hundred head of cattle in the Far Pasture was pretty easy compared to a range with four thousand or more head on it, but I didn't know just how much work it was until I had to take over th' job. We had the fall roundup coming up and all the other ranches were working cattle. The only hired help we could get could not work for us full-time. Green and Nate and I were the most experienced hands in the family able to work — and it wasn't until we began that I realized how little experience that was. Nothing against th' boys, they were just getting started, but I should have known more and taken more responsibility when Pa and Bob were working the range.

Joe and Eda B. came to stay with Mom and were welcome. That gave us six hands, counting the two boys, Joe and me with Cindy and Sue Ellen. Eda took over the

210

daily running of the household, leaving Mom and Presilla to tend the invalids and Benito to do his thing in the bunk kitchen. Most of the nurses' work was in keeping the two warriors still and quiet enough to heal. It didn't keep either of them from giving advice, most of which was welcome.

Considering the lightweight help we had, Joe and I decided to build a pinch chute for our brandin' and cuttin'. The week after that we began the fall roundup. It complicated things to have to drive the cattle to the chute instead of workin' on the range, but that was th' only thing we could do. Sue Ellen kept the tally book and the rest of us rode. Our first job was to round up Far Pasture and process those cows. When we were done there, we threw them out and drove our other cattle to the pens at th' ranch house. We made Josh permanent brander and the rest of us, boys an' men, took turns working on th' ground. Cindy rode all th' time and almost wore herself out doin' it.

It took our crew longer to get the job done and snow was flyin' before we were through. The cattle were all movin' out into the Basin and I know we missed a lot of calves that stayed in that lower range. Spring roundup would be heavy again, if we could keep rustlers from appropriatin' our unbranded stock. Sure enough, there was a lot of two legged activity on the range that winter, more than usual and I must have used up a couple of boxes of ammunition runnin' off would-be ranchers. I fired near misses so much that I got to wonderin' if I could ever hit a target again. Joe and I didn't bother riders passin' through so long as we didn't see a ring or buckle that had turned blue and black from too many heatings.

If we ever saw smoke or dust, we would investigate and most often we found a rope-and-ring man ready to do his artistry on a calf's rump and ear. It was almost a weekly occurrence, so much so that we got adept at lettin' the brand artist get the calf tied down before we ran him off. We could then brand the calf right and let him go. We had so many piggin' strings by spring that we were givin' 'em away. Luckily, none of our rustlers showed fight, though a few returned our fire halfheartedly, just to let us know they weren't happy. It was sad commentary that there were people in the Basin who were ready to take advantage of someone's misfortune like that, but I found that it's th' same 'most everywhere. It got so bad that I got belligerent with anyone riding through the range, even though there were several other herds workin' the Basin.

A SEASON TO HEAL

Pete didn't heal too well. It seemed that he lost a lot of his get-up and go an' all of us noticed that he had aged a lot since the fight. He was up when we got back from that first roundup after the fight, but still couldn't do much. Doc recommended that he go over to Hot Springs and take the baths and Bob paid him his wages plus six months more with th' promise that he had a job when he got back.

We were makin' plans t' take him to the Springs when Polly Ann Brown rode into the yard. "Here is a package for Pete, we thought it might be important, so I brought it out right away," she said.

Pete was sunnin' himself on th' bunkhouse stoop and Polly laid th' package in his lap.

"Wonder who that's frum," Pete muttered. It was addressed, To: Mr. Pete Kidd, Mountain Beaver Ranch, Pinetop, New Mexico, in a neat female hand. It was postmarked Tularosa and there was no return address. Fishin' for his knife, Pete cut strings and unwrapped th' brown paper. Inside was a package wrapped in Christmas paper and tied with a pink ribbon. The package jingled musically as he turned it. By now a crowd

213

had gathered and a chorus of voices urged, "Open it, Pete!"

Pete grinned and sat with the unopened box in his lap. "Got a idee who this is from and what it is, boys," he said and if it could have, his grin broadened.

"Why don't you just wait 'til Christmas t' open it, then?" said an impatient Green. "If'n you know what it is an' it won't spoil."

"Patience is a virtue — you ain't learned yit, have you, boy?" Pete grinned at him.

"Please, please, *please*! Uncle Pete, open it now!" Polly Ann begged.

"Yuh think I should?"

"I don't care if ya ever open it!" Green was disgusted.

Carefully, Pete unwrapped the package saving the wrapping for Sue Ellen and ribbon for Polly Ann. He lifted the lid and removed the tissue-wrapped contents. It was a single Mexican spur, trimmed with newly polished silver and tiny silver bells.

"Where's the other spur?" Cindy asked.

"Got an idee I'll have t' go git it myself." Pete grinned.

I struggled to keep from laughing out loud. "Looks like your plans have changed a little there, Pete."

"Shore 'nough, they have." He handed the empty box to me. Placed neatly in the bottom was a two-month-old page from the *Tularosa Valley Tribune*. The circled headline of a front page article read: "Paul Parsons, Long-time Resident, Dies." I put the lid on the box and set it up on a shelf over the washstand.

"Why would someone send you only one spur?"

"Who sent it?"

"What you gonna do with it?"

The crowd was full of questions. I sat myself on the stoop to listen to Pete squirm his way out of this.

"This here is one o' my spurs I lost a long time ago," Pete began, "an' th' feller that found 'em held a grudge agin me. All these years, I knowed whur they were, but t' try t' git 'em would have spilt blood an' they was a good chance some of it would hev been mine. I guess by sendin' me this one, he is buryin' th' hatchet, so to speak."

"Yeah an' mebbe he's baitin' you an' when ya go to get that other spur, he'll bury th' hatchet in your head," said Nate.

Pete nodded. "Could be, but somehow I don't think so."

Sue Ellen stepped behind Pete, reached up and took the box down. "There wasn't any note with it, Pete?" She opened the box and seeing the newspaper, read the article a moment. I could almost see gears in her brain turnin'. "Paul Parsons the pharmacy man at Tularosa died." Her mouth opened as if t' say somethin' then closed as she looked down to read more. ". . . two weeks ago . . ." — more reading — "had a heart attack . . . wife will run the store . . ."

"S-a-a-y ain't that th' store that had that fancy set of spurs hangin' behind th' counter for so long?" Green asked.

"It was, *it was,*" Nate shouted. He picked up th' spur and examined it closer. "Sure 'nough, Pete, this is one of 'em."

Eda B.'s eyes widened and her hand flew to her mouth as she gasped, then blushed and began laughin'.

Sue Ellen looked up in surprise, then thinking about what had been said and lookin' at Eda, some idea of what she was laughin' about came to her and she began to blush and giggle. "Pete, I think I know where you lost those spurs," she said between giggles.

Now it was Pete turning red and his grin got bigger. Sue Ellen laughed, I couldn't hold back any longer and soon all of us who were aware of the old gossip stories were laughing.

Nate, Polly Ann, Joshua and Green were mystified at the hilarity. "What's so funny?"

Nate asked.

Polly stomped her foot. "Tell us, too!" she demanded.

Eda wiped tears from her eyes and said, "The funny part is *where* th' spurs were found, Polly."

"Where!" the girl demanded.

Sue Ellen stooped and whispered in her ear between giggles. Polly's eyes got big and bigger an' pink began to climb up her neck until her face turned crimson and she turned and ran away.

Sue Ellen fanned herself with the box lid, and broke out in laughter again. "Pete, you scoundrel!" she called.

"What in thunderation is so danged funny about all that?" Nate shouted. "Are you gonna keep it all to yourselves?"

"If Polly can know th' story, why can't we?" Josh added.

"Tell 'em, Eda," Joe demanded.

"I . . . no, no, no!" Eda began laughin', fannin' herself and blushin' all over again.

"Ain't you gonna tell 'em, Eda?" Joe teased.

Eda B. turned and ran back to the house, Sue Ellen close behind.

"*You* tell us, Joe," three boys demanded.

Pete had been quietly rockin' and holdin' the spur in his hands. "Th' thing they found

217

so funny, boys, is that gossip has it thet Saint Paul Parsons found those spurs in his bedroom an' th' window was wide open, curtains flappin' outside th' sill."

"An' I s'pose Miz Parsons wus in th' bed?" Nate grinned.

Pete nodded. "That's th' story, all right, but I ain't confirmin' or denyin' anythin'. That's how gossip starts an' ruins many a good man or woman's reputation."

"That *is* a little funny, but I don't see it bein' all *that* funny," Nate said.

"That tale's been around for years, Nate, but today is th' first time anyone has known who th' runaway was," I said. It was really the second time, since Pete had told Rance and me about it at the line shack.

"Who it *might* have been," Pete interjected.

"Well why did those girls think it was so funny?"

"Because they had known the gossip a long time an' here they discovered it was true and who that runaway was an' that widow Parsons was sending Pete a message that the coast was clear for him t' come an' claim his other spur. You don't often talk about those things in mixed company."

"*I* see. Pete was gittin' some strange stuff, almost got caught an' lost his fancy spurs in

218

th' bargain," Green said mischieviously.

"It *might* have been Pete," Pete corrected. "Gonna be hard livin' 'round here, now," he muttered.

"Looks t' me you have a decision t' make about where t' go," Joe said.

"Which has more healin' power, Pete?" I asked.

"Guess I'll hafta d'cide." Pete grinned, but we all knew what his decision was.

It was well before daylight next mornin' when Pete, Green and Nate rode out for Tularosa. A disgusted Nate and Green came back that night leadin' Pete's horse. The ride down the mountain had been so rough on him that Pete took a train from Paxton siding and our boys missed their chance t' see the city without adult supervision.

About a year later a card came to the ranch announcing the marriage of Pete Kidd to the widow Parsons.

All four of us boys worked the spring general roundup, takin' what was ours home every Saturday evening and back at the rodeo late Sunday evening. There wasn't a lot of relaxin' time.

To our surprise, we didn't have too many cows left barren by calves with a different brand. That made us feel like the hard winter's work was worth it but we vowed that missing so many calves would not happen again. By common consent of the ranchers, any calf found with a different last name than his mammy got rechristened and there were no arguments about it, though some wranglers with unregistered brands looked awful wistful at times.

One of the young Stone boys, Bud, had been courting Sue Ellen and there was a June wedding at the ranch. With Nate living in the bunkhouse, Ma was left alone in the big house and she insisted on Joe and Eda B. movin' in permanent with her. At the same time we made some substantial improvements on the Nealy house. It now looked more like a ranch owner's place.

Our fall roundup started earlier and we had the advantage of Bob being back to work. It was obvious he wasn't up to full speed, but he knew what needed to be done and kept us on target. The whole crew made sure no calves got bypassed and we threw the cows on the lower range with confidence they would mostly all be back in the spring with the right brands on their rumps.

Cindy had been a great help and comfort to Ma, sometimes helping with the house chores when Ma had one of her spells of melancholy. As long as she was busy Ma was all right, but idleness was her bane. The tragedy we all went through had drawn Cindy and I closer. It was generally accepted that we were sweethearts and we endured a lot of teasing from our brothers and sisters. My tomboy playmate had matured into a young woman and I looked back on those tomboy times with less regret at losing a pal and more gratitude for gaining a companion who knew me better than anyone else. Yes, there was passion, but never the intimacy that comes in marriage. There wasn't th' time and certainly not the place for it in those two households.

Green and Nate took over the Far Pasture and lived up there most of the year except through th' winter. We never let cattle go wild there again.

CHAPTER 15
THE BEST LAID PLANS

The second winter after the fight was th' coldest in memory. There was much snow even in th' Basin. At times the sands couldn't be found because all the ground was white. It was a good harbinger of a bountiful grass crop and most ranches added cattle. We knew normal times would return and bought a few feeder calves for the summer, plannin' to harvest extra hay against dryer years.

I was sweepin' th' last offerin' from th' skies off our bunkhouse porch early one afternoon in January when Napoleon Witt rode in from the Rafter JD.

"Howdy, Nap, light an' come in an' warm yourself with some coffee," I called.

"Thankee kindly, Tuck, believe I will."

I stuck my head in the bunkhouse door an' called, "Benito, hungry cowboy comin' in. Green, would you take Nap's horse to the barn? Feed him a little corn, too."

"Oh, that horse don't know what t' do with corn, Green, jist a little hay'll do him," Nap called.

It was always a welcome sight t' see visitors come in an' we all gathered 'round th' stove after Nap had eaten t' hear th' latest news. We hadn't been visitin' long when Eda B. came down and chastised Joe for not bringin' Nap up to th' house.

"Oh my, where are my manners, Miz Eda, I have a note for you and one for your ma, Miz Mary, from Miz Meeker an' plumb forgot it!" Nap said. "I'll bring 'em right up." He shrugged on his coat, patted his pocket to be sure th' notes were still there and headed across to the house with Joe.

"Well, we'll be gittin' the news from th' wimmin for th' next week," Nate grumbled.

"Yeah, but there'll be a lot more of it after it's been filtered through a female head," I said.

Green came across the porch stompin' off snow and banged through th' door. "Whur's Nap?"

"Up to th' house gittin' th' news expanded through th' wimmin," Nate mumbled as he whittled kindlin'.

"We'll get news from Nap an' th' girls'll interpret it for us th' whole next week," I said.

223

Green grunted his boots off an' propped his feet against th' stove rail. In a moment, his socks began steamin' and he moved. "Don't take long t' get warm there!"

"Haul out th' checkerboard, Green, an' I'll teach you how t' play," said I.

"Gimme two kings an' I'll eat your whole army!"

"In your dreams."

"Ain't there anything interestin' t' do around here 'stead o' playin' checkers an' dominoes?" Nate asked. "I'm goin' huntin'."

"Saw elk tracks in th' back pasture the other day," Green said.

"All you'd see up there now is their bellies draggin' snow," Nate said. "Better t' hunt elk down in th' foothills."

"I'm not too hungry for elk meat, but I shore would like a little venison roast with taters an' gravy," I said.

"Well, don't jist sit there slobberin' all over your shirt, git yer gun an' let's go!"

"We got company, Green. Let's visit a while an' when he heads back we'll go with him an' git us a deer."

He got his rifle down and started cleaning it. "I'll be more than ready fer that!"

It was nearly an hour before Joe an' Nap came back across the porch. Nate an' I were playin' off a checkers tie for the rights t' clean out barn stalls. When Nate looked up, I skipped a space an' double jumped a king and checker.

"Whoa there, feller, put those back an' git back where you was. Yuh think I don't know where ever'thing is? Can't fool me that-away."

"He at it agin?" Joe asked.

"He's tryin' but can't git 'er done," Nate said, movin' in on my only king.

Nap chuckled, "Looks t' me like cabin fever's spreadin'. Hope I didn't bring it to yuh."

"This bunch hears th' screen door slammin' an' they start gripin'." Joe laughed.

"They're talkin' up a deer hunt, Nap, want t' go with us?" I asked.

"Shore 'nough, I would, that last Mountain Beaver steer we et was awful rangy."

"Eet may bee you should not eat thee meat t'night eef you want to tell Señor Zee you have not been eating thee Rafter beef." Benito waved his fork from th' kitchen door.

"I'll take your advice to heart an' think on it, 'Nito." Nap laughed. He drew a piece of paper from his shirt pocket and handed it to me. "Zenas wrote you a note, Tuck."

"Thanks, Nap, have a seat here an' finish this boy off for me while I read it."

"Oh, no you don't, I won't take a ringer

for you when I got you on th' ropes. We'll just wait 'til you have digested all that an' finish up," Nate growled.

"Any big words in that, Tuck? Ya want I should read it to ya?" Joe asked.

"I can navigate this right well, but you might want t' answer Zee about how his no-good son is gittin' along."

Zenas had written almost a ledger page full. This is what he wrote:

Friend Tucker. My two men have come back from "Spying Out The Land" and this is some of what they found. The Thieves crossed the Rio Grande south of Socorro Mission and drove the herd into a valley on the south side of the Los Medanos Hills just southwest of El Paso where they stayed a few days. The boys caught up with them there, and the gang was made up of Indians and Halfbreeds. They left two graves there. From there they moved west to the Foothills of the Sierra Madre where there is a Ranch. According to my men, their range is at least 30,000 acres and at least half the Cows they saw wore the beaver brand. The ranch is run by a Mormon from Arizona and he has no problem with appropriating Gentile Property and there were at least four New Mexico brands and a half dozen Arizona brands in the herd. They claim his market is north of there in Navajo and Utah Territory.

They say he goes up Skeleton Canyon and down the San Simon valley to the Gila and on to the Indian Reservations. After that, they are pretty much Home Free, as no one is gonna ask any questions. This is a fantastic claim and I can't see how it is done without some People looking the other way as They pass by. The rancher claims he often goes as far north as Lee's Ferry and sells his remaining herd to the Lee and Darrow clan. From there, I would guess the herd is distributed among the Saints. You know how I feel about Mormons and that's all I will say about that. The ranch has about 50 hands, a lot of them Hardcases, but some just Vaqueros who are not likely to put up a fight for Anyone. Grass starts greening there in Feb. and that's when they start north. If I was 20 years younger, I would be riding with you. Might just do it anyway.

Your Friend, Zenas M.

So that is what it is, Indians stealing American cattle, a ranch in Mexico selling them to Indians and disreputable ranchers in northern Arizona and Utah. It answered a question for us because we could not figure why someone would steal cattle and take them to Mexico where there is no market for them. Joe read the letter and looked at me as he handed it to Green. "What do you think we should do, Tuck?"

"I don't know, but I'm gonna do some deep thinkin' on it."

Green looked up from the letter. "Let's go wipe out th' whole bunch of 'em."

"Thieves are like roaches, Green, where you find one, you'll find a dozen. I'm not sure I want to do that much killin'."

"You know how Pa feels about Mormons," Joe said. "He knew the Fanchers and Bakers very well and has never gotten over that happened to them at Mountain Meadows. I suppose a lot of that has rubbed off on me and I would love t' mix it up with 'em — for Pa if for nothin' else."

Fear, dislike and downright hatred for the Mormons was very prevalent back then and isn't much easier nowadays. "They could be Baptists, Methodists or Catholics for all I care, and if they kill my family and steal my property, I'm gonna go after 'em," I said.

"I reckon you're right there, what does their religion have t' do with it if they are murderers and thieves?" Nate scratched his leg with his toe.

"We need to think this out and we *don't* need to let wimmin know a thing about this," I said. "They don't need added worry about what we might or might not do an' we don't need their conditions put on whatever we plan t' do." I looked Josh, Green and Nate in th' eye an' all three of them nodded.

"Mum's th' word, boys," Joe added.

I did a lot of thinking the next few days and so did the others. We discussed a lot of possibilities, but none of them would hold up under close examination. Some o' my thoughts I kept to myself, such as who should go. Certainly, Nate could not if I went (and I was surely goin' t' go) because he would have t' carry on th' family name should something happen to me. That meant that his twin brother Green could not go either — and that was a good thing too. Josh was out of th' question, being too young. Joe would be welcome t' go, but Ma needed a man's help an' input right now and that was up to me or Joe. Bein' married less than two years didn't help his case much either. I couldn't ask Rance t' go as the Browns were having trouble enough with the Giddens and Dolans of Santa Fe Ring fame.

As time passed and we could not come up with any plan of action, it became more and more apparent that we needed t' know more about the situation and that would involve some spyin' around. Naturally, I took up that responsibility an' the others reluctantly agreed. It was set up that at the end of spring roundup I would just ride away without comin' back to th' ranch. That way, our wimmin would not know anything about it until the deed was done.

Roundup was a lot of dust, runnin', bawlin', brandin', spills and thrills — same as always. We enjoyed mixin' with other outfits an' watchin' or participatin' in pranks an' fun that naturally go along with a roundup. Josh came with us a couple of times, but a week at a time was about all he could endure at his age.

We were south of th' sink of the Sacramento River one Friday and we had only eight head of Beaver cows t' drive home. By that, we knew only one man was needed to "rep" the rest of th' roundup and naturally that would be me. Back home, I packed a very small bag of gear, mostly food and ammunition, an' hid it down the trail a ways. Spring cleaning was just windin' up in th' two ranch houses. They had even invaded our bunkhouse and "straightened up things" there. It was all topsy-turvy. We couldn't find anything. Nate wandered in late Saturday night and sat down in the dark an' missed his bunk. He forgot those wimmin had moved it. The rest of th' week end was uneventful. We spent our spare time catchin' up on chores around th' place an' Joe an' th' boys loaded up a wagon with fence posts and wire for a project they would start early Monday morning. Chores caught up, Cindy traipsed off t' town Sunday to spend the night with a friend. I spent a little extra time with Ma, but not too much as to rouse suspicions.

CHAPTER 16
THE PARTING

A TIME TO EMBRACE

1886

Mid afternoon, I loaded my packhorse and saddled up. A couple of miles down th' trail, I stopped t' pick up my plunder. When I dug under the brush, that sack wasn't there! I looked and looked until I was sure it was gone. I had thrashed around and spoiled any sign that might have been there, so there was nothin' t' do but move on. An hour later, I came up on my empty sack layin' beside the trail. When I picked it up, there was an arrow drawn in the sand under it pointin' into the brush toward th' river.

This gave me pause, it could be one of th' boys, but they were all there when I rode out and I doubted they could have outrun me without bein' detected. *Or* it could be an Apache who found my gear an' now wanted more. Usin' th' Pecos Pete philosophy of self-protection, I drew my gun and carefully crept through the brush. There was no way to do that quietly with two horses in tow but I wasn't about t' let them out of my sight. Tracks showed where a horse had crossed the river and I could see wet sand and tracks where he had waded out on the other side and into the brush. I mounted up, pulled my rifle out of its boot and sat there a full ten minutes watchin' bushes along the far bank. Once committed to that river I would be a pretty sitting duck for anyone layin' up waitin'.

A soft snort from my packhorse, and my horse's pricked ears told me they had scented the other horse. Brush stirred and I saw a horse over my gunsights push her head through. It was Cindy's mare! Now I really was in a quandary. Was she in trouble, or was this one of her tricks? Even so, I still hesitated to expose myself crossin' th' river.

"Cindy!" I called. In a moment, she stepped out of the willows and I lowered my gun. "What in the world are you doing out here?"

"Waiting on you, dummy. Are you gonna shoot me?"

"I just might!" We waded across, both horses wanting to drink. "What are you up to stealin' my plunder and hidin' out like this?"

"What are *you* up to, sneakin' around and hiding gear in the woods?" she retorted.

She ran into my arms as I got down and we both nearly fell down. Laughing, she said, "Don't you know by now that you can't keep secrets from me? I know just what you are up to, you're going to Mexico and not the roundup." She said this in her matter-of-fact way, and I couldn't tell if it was with approval or disapproval.

"Who told you?" I asked.

Slapping my chest soundly, she said, "No one, *I said* I know you!"

"You couldn't tell by lookin' at me."

"Couldn't I? How long have we known each other, how long have I loved you and known everything — well almost everything — about you?" she giggled. The breeze riffled th' river, sending up a thousand drops of sunlight and the tender willow leaves shook gently. It was pleasant holding her near, smelling her hair and feeling her warmth and love for me.

"Come on, I have made us a camp."

"Made *us* a camp?" *What is she up to,* I wondered, and visions of many things passed through my mind, including th' idea that she entertained thoughts of goin' with me. "You can't go with me, Cindy," I said softly.

"I know," she whispered, "but I can be with you and hold you one more time before you go. See, I have set up a camp and brought a roast and vegetables and even some tea for our supper."

And she had, even to th' point that there was a little firewood beside the fire pit. I unpacked the horses and led them down to drink. Back at th' trail, I brushed out all sign that we had left and our tracks on both sides of th' river, then picketed all three of the horses back in th' willow bushes where they wouldn't be seen.

"Well, lady, our hideout is complete, what now?"

"Start us a fire and I will get the roast cooking."

We busied ourselves with the little things of making camp just like we had done dozens of times, only now it was just her an' me, and it seemed like the first time. Her hair was pulled back loosely, her cheeks a soft pink and her nose showin' a first glimmer of tan and freckles she got in th' summer. Her hands were quick and sure as she prepared our meal. I found a piece of log washed up in some flood years ago and wrestled it into camp for a seat and sat and watched her cook.

We talked of many things, the roundup,

spring cleanin', Eda B.'s approaching confinement, the boys and how they had grown. It was one of the most pleasant times we had ever spent together and every detail is still etched in my memory. She sat on the log and I sat on the ground by her knees, the log my backrest, as we ate and talked.

She always got chilly after activity around th' fire and eating and she slipped down beside me with a little shiver and snuggled under my arm. We sat there watchin' our fire die and a red sky slowly turn purple. Overhead, the first stars twinkled into view.

"Remember the first time I kissed you?" she asked.

"You mean th' first time you trapped me naked in th' creek?"

"Yes," she laughed, "and it was the first time *I* realized I didn't know everything about boys!"

"It was so funny, wasn't it? I still laugh at how naive I was."

"About me, or about s-e-x," she spelled, "or about us?"

"About all of it, I still wanted my pal I had grown up with, but she had changed — was goin' away — and even though I liked th' change, I missed my pal. I still dream of you touching me then running away, your white gown floating across the yard."

"We're not so naive now, are we?"

"No, I suppose eighteen and twenty-one years are *much* more mature than fourteen and seventeen," I laughed.

"I really do, Tuck. You have done a man's work since you were fourteen and I have become a woman. Most of our friends our age, especially the girls are married."

"Are you ready to marry now?"

She poked me sharply in th' ribs. "I've been ready for some time."

"To tell you the truth, so have I, but th' last two or three years haven't been accomodatin' for us. I would like to be a little richer than flat broke an' I'd like t' have a decent place for you t' live."

"The cabin under the bluff would be a castle for me."

"You deserve better."

"I *desire* you."

I pulled her over on my lap and she lay her head on my shoulder and I gently undid her hair and smoothed it over her shoulders. "Are you sure you are ready to marry me tonight?" I whispered.

"I'm very, very sure," she whispered.

We sat there like that a long time, gently rocking and holding each other tight. Her lips were warm and her body firm just like the time in the creek. With her hand on my chest she pushed herself up and I unrolled my bedroll under the shelter of that log. I heard her scramble under the covers and I couldn't get my boots and clothes off soon enough. When she came to me, there was no gown between us.

Never was a night so sweet. Never was a night so short. We woke with a light dew on th' covers and a chill in the air. Cindy raised her head and the cold air rushed under the covers. She shivered and snuggled close to me.

"Aren't you gonna light the fire, woman?"

"Don't do a man's job — when a man is around."

"Think I'll wait 'til it warms a little."

"What are you gonna do until then?"

"I can think of a thing or two."

The sun was high when we finally got up. She stood on the bed and dressed and I watched her every move. I had never seen her naked before and she was as beautiful as I had imagined. When I got up to dress, she giggled and giggled.

"What's so funny?"

"Now I know all about boys, especially big boys!" Fumbling with the buttons of her blouse, she came to me and pressed her bare breasts to my bare chest. My arms went around her bare back with skin so soft and we stood there a long time. I felt a tear run down my chest.

"We'd better get going, your girlfriend is gonna wonder."

"Oh, I'm not supposed to get there until today," she said ever so sweetly.

"You are a schemer!"

"Yes, and don't you love it?"

"Yes, but not as much as I love you."

Her lip trembled and she turned away. "Get the fire going, man." It was her best gruff woman voice, but there was a little tremble in it.

We ate the remainder of the cold roast and drank hot coffee and the small talk slowly faded into a sad silence. When it was unbearable for us both and we were nearly in tears, I rose and pulled her up to me and said, "It's time to go, Cindy girl."

"I know." She turned to pick up camp and I went for horses. While they were waterin', she came down and we washed the camp dishes together. "I'll put everything in your sack and the leftovers on top for your lunch," she said as she stood.

She took the mare's lead and turned for camp. The sight of her leaving almost overcame me and for two cents I would have stayed, but for the images of three men in their graves and two more shot nearly to rags. Those men cannot be left and forgotten, all their sweat, blood and life breath taken by thieves who would kill for a few insignificant head of cattle. Were it cattle alone, we wouldn't be here so secretly, but in a home of our own, living and loving openly. Pa and Bet and Cider would still be riding the range and Bob and Pete would not be shackled with the pain of their wounds. It made me so angry my hands trembled and I gripped the leads so tight it hurt. I stood there until it passed. This was not a time for anger. And Cindy needed all the tenderness my being could muster.

She stood in the middle of our little clearing looking around, her horse saddled and ready to go.

"The dishes are done and the house is straightened up, what are you going to do the rest of your day, woman?" I asked trying to be light but failed. The words seemed hollow and my voice far off.

"I'm going to go visiting friends and pretend to be happy and excited and answer all their questions about you and when we will have our wedding and where we plan to live and a thousand other things, and I have to do it without a tear." She stood there rigid, her fists beating softly against her sides and great tears running down her face, her hair in disarray.

"I can't leave you this way, Cindy."

She turned to me and I folded her into my arms, her fists on my chest. "You *have* to go, you *have* to make them pay, you *have* to stop their raids on us, you *have to stop the killing, Tucker, stop the killing!*" She sobbed a moment, then stood back and looked me in the eyes. "I have loved you from my first memories, Tuck, you are as much a part of me as . . . as these hands. Our hearts beat together and if yours stops, mine will break . . . Go, Tucker Beavers, go and avenge the blood that cries from the ground, but come back to me . . . come back, Tuck." She ended in a whisper.

"When I come back, we'll build us a home under that bluff." I kissed her one last time and set her on her horse. "It's hokay, Indy."

"Tuck . . ." She smiled.

"Go, lady, have your hen party, but wash your face before you get there!"

I heard her splash across the river and soon followed her. She turned right to the turnoff to town. I turned left and rode on down th' river.

Sue Brown watched through drawn shades as Cindy Nealy rode into town past closed and shuttered doors. She saw her look of

241

concern when she saw the black ribbon on the door to Giddens' store. Only the saloon and the deputy's office were open and there was a crowd in the saloon, unusual for this time of day.

As Cindy rode up to the Stark house, Sue overheard Kizzie Stark say, "Cindy, have you heard, Riley Giddens was killed last night!"

CHAPTER 17
A MURDER SO FOUL

A SEASON TO KEEP SILENCE

Mrs. Brown sighed. *These young believe they are immortal and the loss of one of their generation comes as a mighty shock, for then every individual is forced to face the fact that they too are only mortal and it could happen to them as well as it has happened to the unfortunate one. This is especially true in a small community such as Pinetop where the young people know each other well. The absence of one of them will be noticed almost daily.*

As time passed, I noticed that those who liked Riley Giddens genuinely mourned his passing and those who had not been as close to him mourned and suffered the qualms of conscience. Everyone felt regret — regret for not being friendlier, for things said and unsaid while they had the opportunity. Within the whole community people grew closer and shared thoughts and feelings more freely and openly. It was a tender time wrought by tragedy.

All we knew about the incident was that Riley had been seen in front of our store arguing with another person. The argument suddenly turned violent and the two men fought. Riley was knocked to the ground and as the other person jumped on him, Riley fired his gun — and apparently missed. The unknown man wrenched the gun from his hand and beat him senseless with it.

Three men were witness to the fight, a cowboy fresh from the range and quite drunk, "Doc" Shull who was notoriously nearsighted, and Bill Evans, who, hearing the shot, had ridden up only in time to see a figure disappear around the corner of Town Hall. The Town Hall light shone on the fight, but the witnesses could only see the figures in silhouette and not details of their faces. They could only agree that the two combatants were about the same size and from their actions, age. The sound of the shot drew a crowd and they gathered around the still form of Riley, in the process eliminating any sign that might have aided in tracking or identifying the runaway. John R. and his wife were called and it was some time before they could be calmed enough to let the men move Riley to the doctor's office. Rance came from the store with a door and they gently lay Riley on it and took him to Doc Hutto's. Riley never gained consciousness and passed away at 2:17 a.m.

Deputy Ryles took statements from the three witnesses and everyone who had something to add to the story. In a couple of days, Pat Garrett arrived to help investigate. Because of past troubles between them and their similar sizes, my son, Rance, was suspected as the killer. He was questioned sternly, but nothing came of it. Pat and Deputy George then began questioning anyone who looked remotely likely, even to the point that they rode out to the roundup and questioned the men there.

That was when they discovered that Tucker Beavers was missing. They determined that he had ridden out from the Beavers Ranch Sunday afternoon and hadn't been seen since. I know Tucker Beavers well and find it hard to believe that he would do such a thing.

Well, you know, dear reader, that Cindy could vouch for Tuck's whereabouts that night, but because of the stigma of what they had done, she kept quiet. If the time ever came, she would speak up and bear the shame to save her lover.

Time went by with no further developments in the investigation and the suspicions stayed with Tucker. Sheriff Garrett even went so far as to put out a bulletin describing Tuck as one wanted for questioning in a murder. Tensions gradually relaxed and it was accepted that Tuck was the prime suspect. Tucker, unaware of the happening, went on his way to Mexico.

CHAPTER 18
HERMANAS

A SEASON TO SEEK

The horses and I got a late start and it was noon when we watered at th' last pool of th' Sacramento River and turned toward Turquoise Siding thirty miles across the Basin. It was after dark when we got there and the horses were a little tired. After waterin' at the tank, we moved across th' tracks and I found a spot of gramma grass for the horses to feed on, rolled up in my bedroll and slept. I awoke with the passing of the three a.m. train from El Paso puffin' through to the discomfort of my horses. The train didn't stop for water and after it passed, I got up, made a pot of coffee and ate. Another watering, then the long ride to San Augustin Pass.

I camped that night by Organ Tank with two broke cowboys headin' east after a round of Las Cruces nightlife. I rode south on th' flats between th' Organs and Las

247

Cruces to th' Rio Grande below Mesquite. The road from there to El Paso was busy and the travelers interesting in their variety. I rode partway with a cowboy headed to the city for some needed recreation. He knew the country west of El Paso and advised me to take that trail along the border where water was available about every day's ride. I took his recommended trail and heeded his warnings about the Apaches and their possible presence in the area. We did the bulk of our traveling at night laying up during daylight hours. Five days later we arrived at Hermanas' store after traveling all night and most of the day.

There was only one building and a small corral, nothing else. The building was well fortified, with gun slots around the walls and in the wall above the flat roof. At least five trails met at the building. The sign over the door read: *Groceries, Hardware, Tack, Beer, Whiskey and Billiards.* Some wag had written *when in stock* after Tack and *always in stock* after Whiskey, and I found that to be exactly the case. Beneath that, the sign read: *Tito Jimenec, Prop.*

The shelves behind the counter were bare save for a few forlorn and dusty items no one would buy, but the bar was shiny and there was no dust on the bottles behind the bar. As I passed through th' door, a man I took to be Tito reached into an olla hanging from a beam and brought out a bottle of beer, opened it and set it on the bar.

"Buenas, señor, welcome to Hermanas."

"Buenas." I took a long drink from the bottle. It was pleasantly cool and I was unpleasantly dry. The beer was pretty green. The label said it was from Chihuahua, Mexico. Pieces of what had once been a large mirror behind the bar were fitted together like a puzzle on the wall, with only enough space between pieces for the nails that held them in place. The uneven adobe wall gave each piece a different angle so that each held its own image. It was very confusing to look at and I could imagine what eight or ten beers would do to an observer. There was a wadded blanket and pillow without case sprawled across the billiard table.

"Ees hot, thee weather, no?"

"Sí, very hot," I replied. It had to be over a hundred degrees and this was only the first of April. I wondered what it would be in August.

As if he read my thoughts, Tito said, "Thee summer is thee wet season here and we are cooler then."

"Much rain?"

"Sí, much thunder storm, much light-en-ing." He rolled his eyes and shrugged.

I laid a fifty-cent piece on the bar for the beer and he took it. There was no change coming. "Where could a feller get water for his horses?"

"Ees a well behind store, señor, eef there ees agua in eet." He shrugged. I took it that he didn't drink the stuff. "You can camp by thee house, iss only shade near."

"Gracias." I finished my beer and looked out his back door at th' well. There was water in it and I drew the trough full for the horses. They drank gratefully and I staked them on some sparse grass nearby. With my bedroll spread in the shade of the building, I lay and watched night crawl up the eastern sky. When it was fully dark, I picked up and moved out a hundred yards or so, beside a large clump of prickly pear.

I was awakened by th' thunder of hooves and shouts of several men calling for Tito to open up, which he must have done, for soon it was quiet except for an occasional shout from inside the building. They were still goin' next morning when I went in. Tito's bedding was thrown in a corner and the four men had a hot game of billiards going, playing by rules only they knew. The propri-etor was nodding in a leather-bottomed chair propped against the wall on two legs. One of the front legs was missin'. Seeing me fishing in the empty olla for a beer, he shrugged and shook his head. "Iss eempty an' I cannot keep eet filled."

"Tito is a le-e-e-tle bit short of ambition," a vaquero leaning against the wall said with a grin, his hands spread a yard apart to show how much a "le-e-e-tle bit" was. He wore the dress of a typical ranch hand, though a little more rundown than what we wore around the Basin. "Tito, how about some breakfast? We're gittin' awful hungry workin' on this game," the man said.

"Sí, sí, eet ees come-ing, Señor Con." He tipped the chair carefully on its three legs and moseyed to the stove where a pot simmered. I supposed it contained the universal frijoles and it did. With a nod, Tito cut a couple of jalapeno peppers and an onion into the pot and stirred them in. "Ees ready soon." Wipin' off the stove top, he plopped several tortillas on it and warmed them. He ladled out six bowls of frijoles and I was pleased to see there were chunks of meat in them. From beneath the bar came a bottle of salsa an' six warm beers. "Fill that olla with th' rest of them beers," a lanky cowboy drawled.

"Sí, Señor Beel, ees time to eat now, no?"

"I swear yo're th' laziest barkeep I ever seen," the shortest of the men said.

"You got thet right, Shorty," Bill said.

Con, who seemed the most ambitioius of the quartet, introduced himself and the others to me. "I'm Conly, an' this here is Shorty, th' tall one there is Bill but we call him Slim, an' th' last one down there is Gabby. We call him that 'cause he talks so much." Gabby just nodded an' grinned. In truth he seldom spoke. "We're th' entire staff o' The Ranch of the Carrizalillo Hills."

"You can call me Tuck," I said.

We set to the task of eating, and nothing else was said until the meal ended.

Slim sopped the last of his bean juice out of his bowl and looked into th' pot. He fished around for a moment and said more to himself than anyone else, "Not a bean left. Tito, the frijoles is gone!"

"Sí, Señor Sleem, they go in your third bowl."

"Well, what air we gonna have for dinner?"

Tito shrugged. "More frijoles, but thee goat, she ees gone."

"They's more kinds o' meat 'sides goat, Tito. If'n they was one in th' country, I'd run you in a cow."

Tito shrugged. "I no got no cows or goats," he said as he left the room.

"That man is lazy enough t' be a good fiddler," Slim observed.

"I noticed an absence of cattle in the area as I rode in, what happened to them?"

"That Apache outfit drove through here an' ever' cow thet seen 'em jist joined up with th' crowd an' left. Wiped us clean." Con spat. "We're workin' up a plan t' git our cows back — an' a little boot t' go with 'em."

"Did they have a brand that looked like this?" I asked, drawing a beaver in the dust on the floor.

"Yup," Shorty said.

"And some of them had 2 in the beaver's tail?"

"Yup, shore did."

"Those are our brands. They raided our ranch in the Sacramentos two years ago and killed my pa and two of our hands, shot up two more men an' left with th' herd."

"Two year, you say?" Slim asked. "Then why did it take 'em so long t' move through th' country, they took our herd four months ago."

"More like six, seven months ago, Slim," Con said.

"Eight months an' two weeks," Gabby said. That was the first time I heard him speak.

"Gabby don't miss th' passage o' time," Shorty said.

"Maybe they were hidin' th' herd from their ranch so they couldn't git caught with 'em," Con said. "We know they have a spread over by th' Sierra Madre, been run off'n it three times."

"I'm on my way there to scout th' place out. We're gonna get our cows back an' some measure o' satisfaction. They have been stealin' from us for several years, don't even bother t' change th' brands."

"I allus thought that was their brand." Slim rubbed his chin doubtfully.

"I guess they could feel safe claiming it as theirs way down there so far from our ranch," I said. "I have the New Mexico Brand Book in my gear and you can find our brands in it."

"Seen 'em both in there," Gabby said.

"If'n Gabby says it, Gabby seen it," Shorty averred.

Con nodded slowly, deep in thought. "I s'pose you air gonna go 'spy out th' land' like th' Hebrew children?"

"Somethin' like that. I don't know anything about th' range or the people. If I can figure a good way t' get our cattle back, I'll go back home an' gather enough men t' do th' job."

"Take an army," said Slim.

"Might not, Slim, if'n things was jist right," Con said. "Boys, this feller's gonna need a guide if'n he does what he wants t' do an' live through it. I suggest we be those guides since we don't have any brandin' an' doctoring t' do with our big herd."

"*Our big herd's* gittin' fat on Beaver range an' we sit here day after day hopin' they'll come back to us on their own. Never seen it happen an' never expect to. It's time t' *do* somethin'," Shorty said.

"Tuck, reckon you could put up with four broke vaqueros taggin' along with you?"

"Wouldn't hurt a thing an' we might be able t' do somethin' t' get this thing straightened out," I replied.

"I'll telephone th' ranch an' have th' houseboy bring in our bedrolls an' extry mounts an some grub fer th' trip," Shorty said.

"Better yet, why don't me an' you go t' thet cottonwood you call a house an' retrieve our bedrolls an' catch up some horses t' pack it all on. We'll catch our grub on th' hoof where we find it." Slim slapped dust off his sombrero on Shorty's leg.

"Was that from your pants or Slim's hat?" Con asked.

We stepped out of the cool adobe house

into the glare of mornin' in time t' see Gabby ridin' off southward.

"I'm damned if that feller ain't a man of few words an' fast action!" Shorty exclaimed as he grabbed up his reins an' loped after.

"We are gonna need more grub for the trip," I said. "I only planned enough coffee an' grub t' get me goin'."

"Closest store with anythin' in it is Hachita an' it's fifty miles th' wrong direction. Those boys'll git our grub, what little there is of it, an' it should keep us goin 'til we git t' Alamo Hueco or Antelope Wells," Con said. He squatted in th' shade an' rolled a cigarette.

An hour later, Gabby and Shorty rode into the yard with four spare mounts, four bedrolls and a gunny sack with a little food in it. I surmised rightly that this composed th' entire estate of El Rancho de Carrizalillo Hills.

It must have been a week after the five rode out of Hermanas that Pat Garrett got a telegram from the Luna County sheriff at Deming. It read:

A man calling himself Tuck and matching your description passed through Hermanas last week about Tuesday or Wednes-

256

day. He was last seen traveling south with four rustlers of local fame. They were traced to the Mexican border.

Pat read the telegram and laid it on his desk. It had been assumed by the locals at Pinetop that Tuck was the killer, the sheriff had doubts, but why was he on the run? Rustler was a term used a little too freely and the good sheriff was well aware of that, having worn the title himself a time or two. He stared at the telegram, tapping his pencil on the desktop. "He's goin' after his cattle! Good boy!"

CHAPTER 19
ANTELOPE WELLS

I was used t' travelin' dry country, but this Sonoran Desert was somethin' new. It was drier, hotter, and sparsely populated with plants. I noticed how carefully th' boys filled their canteens and how they made sure their horses were well-watered, and I followed their example. With a whoop and holler we left Hermanas b'hind.

The rule all over th' southwest was then and still is that there were two enemies when traveling, 'Paches an' desert. Around the Basin, our chief worry was desert. Indians from the reservation were more likely t' take stock an' what they could pilfer than they were t' kill, though they loved takin' potshots occasionally. Here in the south country, that priority was reversed. Bronco 'Paches would pop up anywhere anytime, and we were all wary.

Boundaries and borders are lines on maps that mostly arbitrarily divide people and philosophies, sometimes languages and cultures. The lines are seldom seen on the ground unless they divide differences in wealth and well-being.

In those days, there weren't any of those differences between the US and Mexico. Thus it was that we didn't know when we entered or when we left Mexico when we cut across the corner of that country to Arizona. We followed the valley between the Carrizalillo Hills and the Sierra Rica Hills, staying north of a large dry lake, but unable to avoid the choking alkali dust. We rode abreast with several yards between to keep the dust to a minimum and still our own tracks stirred dust enough t' coat us all with a thick layer of alkali.

It wasn't long until we had a serious thirst and I noticed as I sipped my water that the others drank deep. *It must be the liquor,* and I thought nothin' more about it. I guess every hour or so I took a small sip of my water, but it didn't seem t' give any relief from heat or dryness. The others didn't drink for over two hours after that first time and then they drank deep again. *If they keep this up, they'll be dry an' sufferin' before we find more water,* I said to myself. No shade. And we didn't stop at noon except t' wash out our horses' mouths and nostrils. It seemed t' refresh them an' we moved on at a walk. Even though I kept on sippin' water, I was really dry and sufferin'. It must have been a hundred ten degrees or more, and I quit sweatin'. Mid afternoon, we turned toward a little group of hills to the west of our track and hard against them, we found an overhanging ledge that gave us all ample shade. Shorty turned his canteen up and drank the last of his water, and the others cleaned theirs out to th' last drop. I shook my can and it felt half full. Now, I was the only one with any water and th' way I felt, I wasn't in any mood t' share.

"How much water ya got left, Tuck?" Slim asked, grinnin'.

"Oh, just a little bit," I lied.

Shorty jerked the canteen out of my hand and I came near to drawin' on him. "Hold on there, Tuck," Conly said menacingly.

"Th' thing's half full!" Shorty exclaimed.

"Let's see," Con said and shook th' canteen.

"Hell's bells, Tuck, what are ya thinkin' here?" Conly asked. "I thought you was frum dry country."

"I did too 'til you dragged me out on this desert," I croaked. "That Tularosa Basin looks like a Garden of Eden compared t' this." I kept my hand close to my gun. If they were gonna take my water, they were gonna have some extra ventilation holes t' hold so's it wouldn't run right through.

"I'll be damned if th' boy don't know how t' survive dry country travel," Shorty said. "Did ya notice how we drank our water?"

"I thought it was th' liquor."

"Nope, wasn't that, Tuck, why thet leetle bit o' drinkin' jist quenched our thirst," Slim said. "Us Gila Monsters an' Horney Toads has learned thet you don't sip an' nurse yore water out here, ya take big drinks ever' time th' thirst hits ya hard enough an' you'll keep your pores watered an' your kidneys wetted. Little sips jist make you more thirsty."

I looked from one to the other an' realized they were not jokin'. My head hurt an' my mouth was dry as dirt. It felt awful full of tongue. "Here, Tuck, take a long drink of this and slosh a little on your hanky an' put it on th' back o' yore neck," Conly said, handin' me my water.

It was just against my judgment t' waste water thataway, an' I hesitated.

"Go ahead an' drink," Slim urged.

Shorty took my water an' opened the lid. He poured some over my neckerchief around my neck. Shoving the can back into my hands he demanded, "Now, *drink.*"

Reluctantly, I lifted the water to my lips an' began t' sip. Gabby reached from behind and tipped th' can up perpendicular and I nearly choked.

"Damnation, Tuck, drink it," Conly demanded, and I drank.

"Now, he's done an' gone t'other way," Shorty said as Gabby pulled the canteen down and capped it. "Enough for now," he muttered and handed it back to me.

"We'll rest here fer 'bout an hour, Tuck, an' just afore we leave you drain thet tank dry, an' thet's a order." Shorty grinned.

We stripped saddles off our horses and moved deeper into the shelter.

"Don't sound right, do it?" Slim asked. "Out here you have t' know where you are an' where water is an' you have t' build up a mighty lot of faith that water'll be there when *you* get there. Gen'erly, if you still have water in your tank, you've wasted it an' let yourself suffer unnecessary. Don't matter anythin' if ya save water an' th' well's dry, you'll still get farther with water in yore gut than in yore can."

I have to admit it tasted great an' I felt better. With little more talk, we all lay back on the cooler sand an' napped. When I woke up I was sweating again. I drank th' rest of my water and saddled up.

"How ya feel now, Tuck?" Conly called as we rode out into the sun.

"Purty good," I answered. I maybe was a little sullen. I should have known t' follow th' others an' I wouldn't have gotten into trouble like I did.

"It's OK, Tuck, lots o' folks make th' same mistake, only some o' them don't have someone around t' teach 'em how t' git along out here, an' they gen'erly don't make it," Slim called. After that, there wasn't any more talkin'.

At evening, Con led us down the western bank of the dry lake to a seep that provided water that wasn't too strongly alkali.

"One thing about this gyp water, you won't drink it an' stay constipated," Slim said, returning from a trip behind a clump of prickly pear.

"Don't matter how much gyp water you drink, *you* still come back from th' bushes full of it," Shorty observed.

"This coming from a feller who could talk ears off a brass billygoat," Slim remarked to no one in particular. "Ain't them beans cooked yet?"

"No, but if you et them now, you could git twice th' use out'n 'em," Con said.

"How's that?"

"Eat 'em raw now, drink water for breakfast an' swell all day long!"

"With this alkali water, things won't have time t' swell much."

"Yuh got thet right, Tuck."

Gabby had walked over to an oblong pile of rocks an' straightened up th' octillo cross at th' head. Graves reminded me of th' ones I had left behind and I walked over. "Someone you knew, Gabby?"

"No, just someone we buried," he replied.

"Me an' Gabby rode up here one evenin' an' found two saddled horses drinkin' at th' seep," Shorty said as we sat down an' waited for coffee t' boil. "We backtracked th' horses an' 'bout a quarter mile away found a dead man. His canteen was half full o' water. Movin' farther on, we couldn't find anything of his pardner, so we canceled our search an' slept at th' seep. Next mornin', we followed their trail an' it was two hours, 'way out there on that lake bed we found Number Two. He had been shot an' th' canteen he had was empty. Funny thing was, th' initials on th' canteen was th' same as was on that other man's belt buckle. From that, we figgered one o' th' boys was a drinker an' one was a sipper. When one canteen was empty, ol' Number One won th' argyment 'bout whose water was left. We've augered an' augered 'bout which was th' sipper an' which was th' drinker an' never come to a reasonable answer."

"Wouldn't yuh think Number One was th' sipper since he still had water when you found 'im?" Slim asked.

"If thet's so, why was his empty canteen with Number Two?" Conly asked.

"Did they have th' same initials," I said.

"Nope, not by th' things we found in their possibles," said Shorty.

"Anythin' t' tell yuh whose horse was whose?"

"Nope," Gabby said.

"Wish you'd quit hoggin' th' conversation like that," Slim grumbled.

"Maybe ol' One took a likin' t' Two's belt buckle an' took it," I offered.

"He wouldn't 'ave gone to th' trouble t' put his on a corpse, would he?"

Gabby cleared his throat and said, "I'll bet if you go out there an' check out that canteen hangin on Two's grave, you'll find that it had a leak an' ol' One, th' sipper, bein' conservin' as he was, poured his water in Two's tank an' came on sippin 'cross th' lake."

"Pore feller must be exhausted after that speech," Slim muttered.

"That sounds most reasonable t' me," I

265

said, "but we'll never get t' th' bottom of it 'til we meet 'em at th' Judgment."

"For sure, *some of us* is likely t' meet at least one of 'em whichever place we end up," Slim said.

"It oughta be worth a sip o' water fer ya if you send word up what ya found out," Shorty offered.

"How you so certain our residences won't be *re*versed?" Slim asked. "Course, I'd be just es glad t' buy th' information from you for a sip o' *my* water."

"Wouldn't surprise me none if you two end up bein' neighbors arguin' over which one got that sip o' water first," Conly said as he poured himself a cup of coffee.

There was no grass to speak of an' we kept our horses tethered close after dark. Frijoles and coffee for breakfast and we set our sights on Little Flat Top Butte, passing a couple of miles south of it and over th' pass below Pierce Peak. Th' spring at Alamo Hueco was sweet and we took th' opportunity t' wash off dust, even though it was a temporary thing. Four hours later we were just as dusty as before.

Marshes on Willow Creek was a summer camp for the shepherds from Antelope Wells. It had good grass and we decided t' camp there t' give our animals time to graze a bit since they had been without for a while. There was a gathering of jacals under the trees around shallow "wells" — really no more than deep holes that filled with water. It seemed the male population, all six of them, had an aversion to labor and a distinct skill in producing progeny. Puberty marked the time children began wearing clothes and there was no age demarking th' time t' begin wearing shoes. We bought half a goat t' go with our beans and the children gathered around watching us.

"I think we should stay here a couple o' days an' rest th' horses," Shorty said eying a couple of girls long past th' dressing age.

"Seen their ma. Weighs two thirty an' not forty years old," said Gabby.

"I'm not talkin' 'bout a permanent arrangement, here," Shorty retorted.

"Her ma is," Gabby replied.

After supper, Shorty wandered off an' when we got up next mornin' his bed was still rolled up where he had thrown it.

We left Willow Creek early the second day on horses well fed and Shorty whistlin' a tune no one could identify.

An hour later, Shorty was still whistlin' an' our ears were gittin' awful tired. I tried t' get more distance from him, but th' next

267

man on my side was Gabby an' he wouldn't move or trade places with me. I began lookin' around as if I had lost somethin'. It wasn't in my pockets or my saddlebags or any other place I looked on me an' my horse, so I rode over beside Shorty an' started searchin' his things. He stopped his whistlin'. "Here, Tuck, what you doin'?"

"Just lookin'."

"Well what for?" he asked grumpily. "I ain't got it, whatever . . ."

"I know you ain't *got* it, but I thought it might be around here sommers."

He pulled up an' the rest gathered 'round. "Well, what in tarnation is it an' I'll help you find it!"

"It's that dadblasted tune you been tryin' t' find th' last two days or more."

Shorty pushed his hat back and his mouth flew open but he was at a loss for words.

"Been lookin' fer it over on my side for a while, an' it ain't over here, neither," Slim noted.

"More'n likely, he lost it at Willow Creek," Con allowed.

"Why don't you stow that whistle away an' tonight when you unpack, that tune might roll out from sommers?" Gabby spoke again!

Antelope Wells was a little more estab-

268

lished than the houses at Willow Creek. Most of the shepherds were out on th' Playas with their herds.

"We'll camp here a couple o' days an' scout south t' th' ranch. Mebbe we'll see sumpin' helpful," Con said.

"This isn't 'sposed t' be where that ranch is," I said.

Conly pointed southwest. "Yuh see them hills over there? Well th' range we're lookin' for is on th' west side o' them."

"We were always told they were a hundred miles or more on west from here."

"Jist what them polecats wanted yuh t' b'lieve," Slim said. "Nothin' better'n havin' you lookin' for 'em sommers they ain't."

It sure is fortunate I found these fellows or I would have bypassed this place and gone on another hundred miles and spent a lot of time lookin' for something that wasn't there. Quite possibly, I would have given up and gone back home to try again another time and missed th' opportunity t' learn something while I was there. Conly had hunkered down an' was drawin' in th' sand.

"We're up here" — he poked a dot for Antelope Wells — "an' this is th' range o' hills we're lookin' at. They run north an' south." South of th' hills he drew a line wigglin' northeast. "This here's th' Rio Casas

Grandes an' it runs into th' Laguna Guzman here." He drew a line running north and south ending in a lake. "Th' Beaver range runs from about that river north to th' States between El Medio and the San Luis Mountains. Headquarters is here, 'bout midway o' their range over on th' western slope of El Medio. They's a string o' line shacks runnin' north an' south from headquarters agin th' foothills of El Medio an' they're manned by one er two men all th' time."

"Most of 'em is Mex — tough Mex — with jist enough Anglos sprinkled in t' keep 'em lined out an' honest," Shorty said.

"Yuh mean honest to th' Anglos, they's on their own with ever'one else," Slim corrected.

"They aren't too neighborly like I said," Con added. "I been run off quite promptlike whenever I tried t' make a friendly visit."

"They claim th' ridgeline o' th' hills for their eastern line, but this time of year when grass is good, they'll let their cattle wander around th' ends of El Medio onto sheep range. I don't know what they claim for their western boundary, probably up on th' San Luis hills a ways," Conly added.

270

"How many men do you think they have?"
I asked.

"At least half a hundred, prob'ly more,"
Slim said. "We hear they have a line of
shacks on th' west side same as on th' east."

"Does that mean another fifty men over
there?" I asked.

Shorty rubbed his chin. "Prob'ly not, but
I wouldn't bank on that."

"Seems you fellers are quite acquainted
with these people, what kind o' chance
d'you think I'd have just ridin' in to th'
ranch like I was passin' through, do you
think they'd run me off?"

"If'n you's Mormon, they'd welcome yuh
with open arms," Slim said.

"It'd be awful hard t' make a Mormon
outa Old Hardrock Baptist stock." I
grinned.

"Maybe not," Gabby spoke for th' first
time. He got up and dug around in his possibles bag an' came back with a book in his
hand.

"Th' Book o' Mormon, well I'll be!" Slim
exclaimed.

"Useta be one," Gabby said, "saw th' light
when one o' th' 'postles came t' marry a
twelve-year-old girl for his tenth wife. Shot
th' 'postle's cojones off an' took my little
sister an' left."

271

"Bet that made nine wimmin mad . . . n-o-o-o, mighta made most of 'em happy," Shorty chuckled.

"If you gonna be a Mormon Baptist, you better learn how first, Tuck. Suppose you attend th' Gabby School o' Mormonism an' th' rest of us will scout around a little bit?" Conly asked.

I looked at Gabby an' he nodded.

"OK by me, see if you can find a way for me t' get to th' ranch house without bein' stopped by a guard."

"We're all set, then. Best t' let our horses rest a day afore we go, they're liable t' get a good workin'," Conly said.

We spent the afternoon and next day relaxin' around an' visitin' with th' locals at what passed as their cantina on th' plaza. Some of our time was spent lookin' for Shorty's tune, but we never found it. Once or twice we heard him whistlin' below his breath an' someone would call out, "No, that ain't it, either, Shorty!"

Late afternoon, Shorty, Slim an' Conly rode out towards th' San Luis foothills an' Gabby started tutorin' me t' be a Mormon. He had me read certain portions of the book an' I'll have t' say that it read like a fairy tale in King James's language. Far from it t' call me a Bible scholar, but I'll stick with it an' good ol' time religion. At the end of two an' a half days, Gabby declared me a proselyte but said, "They's no way you kin pass off es anythin' higher."

"If it gets me by, I'll be satisfied."

"Just remember and don't cuss an' if you slip up, get real embarrassed an' apologize all over."

Three tired horses came draggin' in three dusty riders evenin' o' th' third day an' we went to th' cantina for tamales an' chili.

"They shore got a spread an' it's well guarded," Shorty said as we lit our after-dinner cigars. "I didn't see any way t' git t' th' ranch house without bein' seen."

"Your best bet is t' come in from th' north like you was come from Arizona er Utah an' wave that Mormon Bible at 'em. Even th' Mixicins would know you was a brother an' git you t' headquarters," Conly said.

"I taught him th' secret handshake — if he gits near enough t' use it," Gabby said.

"Didja teach him not t' cuss?" Slim asked.

"Don't think you could *teach* that, but I tole him 'bout it."

Con took a long pull on his cigar and said through a blue cloud of smoke, "If we could git 'im t' marry a couple o' these señoritas, he'd have it made."

"Made with th' Mormons, hell with th'

señoritas," Shorty said.

"An' you're th' one t' know that, I reckon." Gabby grinned.

"Hush up!"

"Looks like they got our cattle hid out on th' west side of th' range," Conly said, "it might be that we could drive 'em over into th' Rio Bavispe valley, but we never could git plum away with it — would have t' fight our way an' we are *mighty* undermanned fer that."

"That'd be away from where we want t' end up," Slim pointed out, "an' that's 'Pache land. Best drive 'em down th' Grandes an' cut north from there."

"I might see somethin' when I've had a chance t' look around a bit," I said. "I wish we had a way t' communicate with each other while I'm there."

"No telegraph or tell-a-phones in this country, Tuck," Shorty allowed.

"An' it's not likely that we could get close enough t' see any signals ya might put up, lessen it ud be smoke signals," said Conly.

"Take a big fire from there," Slim said from under his hat.

"Best not t' send any messages either direction," Gabby put in.

Conly rubbed his cigar out on his boot heel. "Right, Gabby, communication is too risky t' try. It would be best t' go in an' look around an' git out as easy as you can. Do you think you could get a good idea of th' layout in four or five days?"

"If they're hidin' our cattle, it may take some time t' ferret 'em out. When we leave here, I want t' have th' whole Beaver herd, not just th' ones they stole last. Then there's th' blood debt someone there owes me an' my family. I don't expect you t' participate in that, but I want th' killers of my pa and our men."

"Ya have a point there, Tuck, if we only git our cattle back, they're still there an' we jist might not git back t' th' home range afore those scalawags steal 'em back an' take four or five scalps. I don't see how we gain anythin' until we convince them thet it's not profitable t' steal our cattle."

"Well, Gen'ral Robert E. Conly, sir, jist how do you propose t' do thet? Seems t' me five agin fifty or a hundred is kinda long odds," Shorty said with a salute.

Gabby had been scratchin' in th' dirt an' now he spoke up, "Seems like a waste o' time t' send Tuck in there an' wait t' see if he lives long enough t' git out when we want t' put an end t' th' whole operation. For shore we can't take on all th' ranch at once, but we can take on a few at a time when odds er in our favor."

Slim brushed his sombrero off an' sat up wide-eyed. "That *was* Gabby! I didn't know he had breath nor words t' talk that long!" He began fanning Gabby with his hat, "Don't overheat there, boy."

Shorty, who was kind of a spokesman for Gabby at times, looked at his drawin' in th' dirt. "I see what you're thinkin', Gab, if we take them on one line shack at a time, we might be able t' make some real headway afore they catch on t' what's happenin'."

Conly scratched his chin. "If we didn't bother th' cattle an' jist concentrated on people, those cows'd be there in th' end an' we could have 'em all without havin' a runnin' battle plumb across th' country."

"I ain't into a lot o' indiscriminate killin', how can we convince some o' those boys t' leave off without lead poisonin'?" Slim asked.

"Yo're right there, Slim, a bloody range war would attract a lot of attention — an' feudin' after," Shorty allowed.

"I think if we done things right, we could scare off a bunch of superstitious people an' we may can convince some o' th' others t' join us. We could do it real quiet like at first so as t' not gather much attention to ourselves an' by th' time someone notices an' gets concerned, we might have knocked odds down t' where we could handle it," I said.

"What you-all er talkin' about is gonna take a lot o' spyin' out an' plannin'. We don't know nothin' about this bunch an' how they operate an' we're gonna havta know all that stuff afore we do anything at all!" Shorty said.

Conly looked around. "Anyone got a plan?" he asked.

"Tuck's gonna have t' spy out th' headquarters, an' we need t' ride 'round th' whole range an' git a idee o' what we're up agin. Me an' Shorty'll go to th' north end with Tuck an' run him onto th' ranch then scout around th' west side o' their range. Slim, you an' Conly scout out th' east side an' meet us at th' river junction southeast of El Medio. Tuck'll be in a hurry t' leave th' ranch t' stay away from those two bandits that chased him an' after a day or two o' rest he'll be ready t' git on south outa reach." All th' while he was talkin' Gabby was drawin' on his map showin' what an' where things had t' be done.

Slim just stared agape at Gabby, for once, speechless.

Conly slapped his knee. "That's a plan!"

"Let's talk t' th' locals here first an' see if

they know anythin' thet can help us," I suggested.

"I done been talkin' some," Conly said. "An' they's plenty they can tell us. Seems that headquarters was home to several o' them an' th' ranchers 'bought' th' place from them real cheap an' run 'em off. We might even get some assistance from them."

"A-sis-tan . . . whur'd ya git thet word, an' how much did yuh pay fer it?" Shorty demanded.

"They don't allow jest anyone in there t' buy 'em, just them as kin handle 'em. You couldn't git past th' four-letter division," Conly scorned.

"Huh, I hed bought up th' *five*-letter section afore you could even talk . . ."

Gabby punched me an' whispered, "Let's go into th' cantina an' talk."

Chapter 20
A Plan Is Born

A Season to Gather Stones

We slipped quietly away leavin' those three t' auger "all things trivial." In th' cantina, we found several gathered over their beers watchin' th' sun set. Gabby sat and I bought a couple of bottles for ourselves and fresh drinks all around. While the women talked of things women talk about, men talked of man things — sheep and cattle, water and grass, and things of th' past. Someone lit a candle, and the women faded away to their homes with a word here and there to husbands.

Gabby passed out cigars and we all enjoyed a smoke. "I was telling my friend here about the Beaver Ranch and how the Anglos had taken it from you. How long ago was that?" he spoke in Spanish.

"It was twelve summers ago, Señor Gabby, and there were six families there with over two thousand head of sheep on that range,"

279

said an old man with one good eye. "These men you call Mor-mans came in and stayed a while, then one day they came to us at the placita and said they would buy it all for silver. We said 'no, we do not wish to sell,' but the men insisted. When we refused their offer, they left. A few nights later, bandits attacked one of our herds and killed many sheep and the shepherd, Julio's nephew. There was much fear among the people and we brought our herds into the folds, but the grass was grazed down and the herds had to travel far to get to feed each day. It was no good, so we spread them back on the range. That very night another herd was attacked and the men beaten. We knew it was Anglos and the Mor-mans were the only ones around. We couldn't keep our sheep and men on the range so we moved over here where there were more people and good range. The plaza was almost deserted and the Mor-mans came back and bought all the houses for a pittance. All was lost." The old man shrugged sadly.

"It is as he said," a man with a large gray mustache spoke up. "We were robbed of our homes, our sheep and our range — and there is no one to right this great wrong!" He banged his fist on the table angrily.

"Why don't you take the placita back?" I asked.

"What good are shepherd's staffs against guns, señor? We have few guns and not many of us to overcome so many men on the rancho."

"It may be that we could help you," Gabby said. "They have stolen our cattle and we want to get them back. If we worked together, we might both get a little justice."

There was a moment of silence as we savored the smokes. "This is possible, señor, but for now our young men are all out with the sheep and will not come back until just before the rains start. Then there will be many of us and perhaps we can rid our valley of these men."

"We are going to spy the range out and by the time of the rains will know how things are over there. Perhaps by then your men will be back and we can make plans to get our possessions back," I said.

"They watch the skies and will try to be here before the rains start," the one-eyed man said.

"How old is your placita?" I asked. "Has it had a long life?"

"Many years ago our grandfathers built the placita, but the Indians — the Apaches — got so bad many were killed and they

281

had to leave. It is only in the last generation that we, the grandsons, have come back to claim our land and sadly the threat of the Indian is still with us," a man with a long scar down his cheek said. "The Indians and their half-breed Mexicans gather sheep and cattle for the ranch and the Mormans pay them for what they steal. It is a good arrangement for them, but very bad for us," he concluded.

"How many guns do you have here?" I asked.

"Only four or five, and they are very old."

I took it that the guns would be of the muzzle-loading variety and therefore of little or no use to us. We would need men with modern repeating weapons to be effective in a fight. It was becoming very apparent that our battle would have to be one of attrition, not an overwhelming assault on the ranch. Still, more men to help would be very good.

"Subtiley an' piecemeal, subtiley and piecemeal," Gabby muttered as to himself.

"Sí, that is the way it has to be," the man with the mustache said, "you will have to be very treacherous to rid us of these men."

The more I thought of it, the more complicated the problem became. With three cultures intermingled, one approach would not be effective. Ghosts and superstition might be effective against the Mexicans, possibly a little with the Indians, but hardly any with the Americans. Mysterious death would be effective with the Indians and probably with the Mexicans, but not with the Americans. The threat of deadly disease might send them scattering, but after the threat was gone, they would most likely return. Still the Americans would remain and they would likely be our most dangerous foe.

"Where do they get their supplies?" Gabby asked.

"They go to Tucson mostly but sometimes they go to Chihuahua," the one-eyed man called Carlos said.

"It is so, but they do not buy much in Chihuahua because the cost is too high," said Felipe Francisco, he of the gray mustache.

"That's a long way to go for supplies, is it not?" Gabby relit his cigar.

The man with the scar spoke, "I am Raul Garcia, who was once a soldier of the Republic. I received this token when a French saber kissed my cheek long ago. We were a poor underfed and under-armed army, but the hope of freedom burned deep in our souls and we fought like devils. The French dogs could not prevail against such ardor. Early we learned to deprive him of his provisions which fed and armed us. Little ammunition and no food made our enemy discouraged and weak. Soon many Frenchmen were defecting and deserting the Emperor and the forces of freedom prevailed. It appears that we are much in the same situation here, my friends, perhaps the same methods will prevail again, no?"

"Perhaps they might," I said, "but it will take much time."

"Is not time the thing we have the most of?" chuckled Carlos Diaz.

"Ahh, time is an unknown quantity for each, but with many, there *is* much time," said Raul.

"Sí, sí, but with the Anglos, time must be spent quickly, my friend," Carlos chuckled.

"They have too much to do, these Americans," said Felipe.

"I suspect that this is one time we will be forced to have more patience, don't you?" Gabby asked. The pungent cigar smoke surrounded his head like a wreath.

"I think you are all right. If we are to wage such a war, we will have to become invisible from both you and the enemy," I said. "We would not endanger you by being visible here, but it would be a good thing if you could be our eyes and ears around the range. You could keep us advised about the things going on and we could make our plans based on your information."

Far into the night we talked. Conly came looking for us and sat and listened and planned with us and when the cocks crowed at midnight, we had bones of a plan made. It only remained for us to flesh it out and most of that could only happen as events occurred.

"Wisdom of elders and acts of sons," Gabby said as we turned in and I guess that is just what it was.

Over breakfast we informed Slim and Shorty of our night's work and they were able t' add some refinements. "If we are t' be invisible, th' proselyte don't need t' make his appearance at th' Placita," Slim said.

"May be that these men at th' Wells can help us there," I said. After breakfast I got pencil and paper from my bags and we went up to the cantina. It was early and not many were about, so we sat in th' shade of th' ramada an' waited.

"How can these people git anythin' done sleepin' half a mornin' an' half an' afternoon?" Shorty chaffed.

"This is th' land o' *poco tiempo,* my friend," Slim said. "Maybe we could learn a little from them."

"Yeah, an' git nothin' done. We're up afore daylight an' goin' 'til dark an' still there's lots undone."

"I think it may be a matter o' vision. Our southern neighbors don't see or look much beyond today an' we are always lookin' out further — sometimes years further. We are driven by our visions an' they are only concerned about today — a little *mañana*, hardly ever *pasado mañana*," I said. "Besides that, I think siesta may be a good way t' pass the heat o' th' day, don't you?"

"We-l-l, it's shore th' way t' extend th' day into night. Think I'll try it nex' time we git t' El Paso," Slim allowed.

"Better put El Paso an' siestas out'n yore mind fer a while," Shorty muttered as he kicked a cat away from his feet.

"Aww, Shorty don't be ugly t' th' cat. She just tho't she recognized th' hide them boots was made out of."

"Wasn't that, Slim, she knowed there's somethin' dead *in* thet boot," Conly corrected.

"I'll show you somethin' dead, you scamp, ain't nothin' wrong with my feet."

"Nothin' a good scrubbin' with lye soap an' a wire brush won't fix, anyhow," Conly shot back. "I swear I ain't never smelled anythin' like it, 'cept in a charnel house."

"When you ever been in a charnal house?" Slim asked.

"Salt River Cave, Superstition Mountains, eighteen seventy-two battle, seventy-six Apaches killed," Gabby quoted.

"What was that?" I asked.

"General Crook's soldiers trapped the Apache chief Nanni-chaddi and his people in their cave ranchiera. It was halfway up a cliff an' no one could get to it if it was defended. They taunted th' soldiers until they started firing into the roof of th' cave an' killin' Indians with ricochets and boulders thrown from the top."

"I swear, Gabby, yo're a wealth o' knowledge," Shorty said in admiration.

"Virtual en-cyclo-*pedia,*" Conly pronounced.

"You speak of the skull cave at Salt River, do you not?" It was Felipe Fransisco, who had quietly slipped in during our conversation.

"Sí, Señor Felipe, Gabby here was jist givin' us our daily history lesson an' confirmin' Conly had been to a charnal house."

"Charnel indeed," he said. "My nephew was captured by Nanni-chaddi and lived with the Indians until the massacre. He was in the cave and crawled under a slab of rock when the shooting started. The scout Sieber

287

found him and returned him to his mother. He could no longer speak the Mother Tongue, but now he has become a man rich in land and sheep."

"Well I'll be," Slim said. "We shore live in a small world, don't we?"

"Sometimes small and terrible," Felipe replied in Spanish. It was the language we customarily used with the people of the village.

"Señor Felipe, I have brought pencil and paper in the hope that you could draw a picture of the placita for us," I said.

"I certainly can," he replied and taking the pencil drew a very good plan of the community, explaining where the main house was, the bunkhouses and other buildings and their current uses.

Eventually Raul, Carlos and a couple others showed up and the boys got them busy drawing a map of th' whole range and filling it in with locations of springs, line shacks, arroyos and hills. By th' time Raul and Carlos were through, the map was full of valuable information and Shorty and the others felt confident that they could easily navigate through the range by it.

"This is the line of the peaks of the mountains where our ranges meet," Carlos was saying. "Even now the ranchers are pushing their cattle over on our range eating grass our sheep need."

Shorty pushed his sombrero back on his head an' said, "Well now that might just be th' place t' begin this waltz. Let's just chouse those critters back onto their own range."

"That might cause trouble for these people," Shorty said.

"I don't think so," I replied. "There's not a horse in th' whole town an' for sure not a shod horse. We could move th' cattle over an' then hunt a hideout to disappear into."

"The upper San Luis hills are rugged with many hiding places and there is grass enough for the horses," Julio Horrera advised.

"That sounds very good, Julio, but you must not know anything about who and where we are. It is for your own safety as well as ours," I said.

"We will need a way to contact you. If you see a candle in the south window of the chapel some night it means we have news for you. There will be a shepherd with a flock moving south and he will have a message for you. A candle in two windows means the message is urgent and you should send someone to the chapel at once," Raul the soldier said.

"That is good," Conly said. "When you arise from your siesta, we will be gone an' you can truthfully tell anyone who asks that you do not know where we went. After that, we will look at the chapel windows every other night starting two nights from tonight."

"It will be safest if you four are the only ones in the village who know about this. Choose your spies carefully. Be sure they are loyal to you and not to the ranchero," I added.

"It will be as you say, I will see to it," Raul said.

"If you know when a supply wagon is on the road, going or coming let us know and we will appropriate it for our supplies. We will get to you whatever weapons and ammunition become available. Be sure the ones who get them know how to use them effectively."

"Sí Señor Tuck. That will be most important."

"Sa-a-y, I'm going to be wearing a green sash on my Sunday pleasure rides, just in case I run across some of your boys out target practicing," Shorty said.

"You got enough green sashes for all of us?" Slim asked.

"I will provide you with them," Carlos said

and hurried off to his house.

"The clouds have been gathering each afternoon and I think it will not be too long until the rains start," Felipe said, "then we will all be here waiting for your return."

We made small talk while we waited for Carlos. Loud excited female talk from his house indicated he had encountered trouble and when he appeared, it was obvious that green was not to be our sash color. Instead, he held out five sashes of blue calico and said sheepishly, "I am sorry señores, but the green sashes are not available."

We all laughed and Slim said, "That's good, Carlos, no one else is liable to have the same sash, it will be unique to us."

And that's how we became known is some circles as the Calico Gang!

CHAPTER 21
THE MONASTERY

It was close to noon when we finished our conference so we ate a hearty meal of goat tamales an' frijoles with the olla-cooled green beer to wash it all down. Before Julio left for his siesta, I bought a bag of beans and the fore quarters of the goat he had butchered. It might be monotonous food, but it would be nourishment enough.

Soon, all was quiet in the little settlement and we quietly left, picked up our camp and rode due south. When we hit solid ground, we muffled th' horses' hooves and turned west. Almost immediately we saw cattle scattered over the range. This was strange land to them and it wasn't hard t' get them headed for the safe confines of their home range. It was five angry men who gathered on th' shady side of a little potato hill.

"I feel right at home, chousin' my cows about."

"Me too. Tuck, knowed several o' them by

name," Shorty spat. Our mood had turned grim.

Conly had his binoculars out an' scanned the area for several minutes. "Don't see any bodies messin' around, but I'll bet they're there sommers."

"I'm s'posin' they are gonna want t'git to their shack afore dark, so they should be movin' soon," Shorty surmised.

"We could start moseyin' thataway an' see if yore prognostications is right," Conly replied.

"There you go agin, now I *know* you stole that word, 'cause you never gradiated beyond th' fith or sixth letter section," Slim said accusingly. "P-r-o-g-n . . ." He rolled his eyes upward and counted on his fingers. "They's at least seventeen letters in that word . . ."

"Exactly sixteen," Gabby pronounced.

". . . sixteen letters an' fer a fact you stole it, you jist ain't qualified t' use it," Shorty declared.

"Now Shorty, I jist cain't he'p it if'n you are unliterate an' don't know proper words o' th' King's English an' their meanin's. Best you can do is stick close t' me er Gabby an' we might interpret fer you if'n you don't git too obnoxious . . ."

We left th' two of them augerin' and

293

moved across the plain north of El Medio where it was a little quieter. We hadn't gone a quarter mile before Slim on the far north of our line hazed a cow out of the brush an' sent her our way. From then on, we flushed out and moved cattle until we had nearly a hundred head. We were nervous about being seen but it seems Shorty was right about any watchers shagging down-range t' home.

When we neared th' San Luis foothills we pushed those cows into a lope right on south. When they hit a downhill slope, they just kept runnin' and we could hear them for a long ways.

"We better hurry or we won't have light enough t' find us a hidey-hole."

"I got you covered there, Slim. Julio said there's a ledge up there we can creep under an' no one will see us from down here," I answered.

"Jist be sure you kin find it in th' dark an' not walk us off th' top of it."

"I saw where it was, what say I go an' start a cookin' fire an' I'll put out a light t' show you-all th' way home?" I volunteered.

"No-o siree bob, not when we got th' hungrys, you ain't gonna git by with that," Conly said. "B'sides, I've had enough o' yore cookin' fer a while. You'd probably burn th' water afore you even got beans in th' pan."

"Well, I didn't know you had a yen fer beans, Conly. I guess th' rest of us could get around these tamales I got from Julio an' you could wait fer yer beans t' cook."

"You ain't got tamales."

"Shore do, but you can cook beans if'n you want to."

We had reached the top of a hill and turned south, riding single file along a path that wound along the slope. When I judged we were far enough, I turned west down th' hill out of sight of th' range. It was pitch black and we had a hard time finding the shelter. A little fire, some hot coffee and warm tamales and we were rolled up asleep. The eastern sky had a little streak of light along th' horizon when I stirred up th' fire and started coffee boilin'. One by one th' others woke up and filled their cups. It was pleasant watchin' shadows creep down th' high mountains, sippin' hot coffee an' no one sayin' much, just enjoyin' the moment. When th' orb o' th' sun popped free of th' horizon promisin' another hot day, we began t' pick up camp. We were rolling up our beds when th' air turned blue with Shorty's curses.

"What's th' matter, Shorty, find a snake under your bed?" Slim asked.

"Worse than that," he spat. "I rolled out on top of a damned fresh cow pile."

"Did it make th' bed softer?"

"Bet it was warmer."

"It weren't softer an' it weren't warmer, thank you," Shorty gritted. He had a stick trying to scrape the dung off his tarp.

"I smelled somethin', but just thought it was your feet," said Slim.

"Tonight we can roll out while you can still see," I said. "While we're this far north, let's find us a hideout up here an' then we should go on south an' find another place t' hide."

"Good idea, Tuck, an' maybe we can get a third place in those east side draws comin' out o' th' mountain," Conly said.

We struck out south, not fearing t' be seen because of hills between us an' th' plain below. Gabby, Slim and Conly made Shorty ride last in line, pretending his bedroll was stinkin'.

"Well, at least anyone trailin' us'll think we're jist cows when they smell Shorty's bed," Slim observed.

"Tuck, there's th' ruins o' some kind o' monastary up here somewhere thet Mexicans think is haunted," Gabby said. "It would be a good place t' hide out, at least th' Mexicans an' Indians will give it a wide berth."

"If they lived there, it must have water nearby. Let's find it."

We found the ruins at the third green spot we came across, tucked down under cottonwood and elm trees a little ways below a nice spring that bubbled up, ran a ways past the ruins and sank into the sands. There was no sign of human activity anywhere near. Even the presence of water could not induce shepherds or Indians to visit the place. Rock and mud walls rose some places over six feet above the floor of the building and it would be a good place to shelter ourselves and our stock. We determined to spend the rest of the day there and prepare it for occupation, cook our beans and meat and let the horses graze. Salvaged timbers and limbs from the fallen roof made a lean-to against one of the walls that was set into the bank of the gully. With a little work, it made a shelter that would shed water and the bank would be good insulation against the cold when it came. A fireplace and partial chimney in one corner under the lean-to made a good fire for warming and cooking.

Slim surveyed the arrangement. "A right cozy little place, I would say."

"I was born in somethin' not much more than this back in Kansas," Gabby said, "was three years old afore Pa could afford lumber for a house in front o' that dugout."

"That was where your biggest danger was a cow gittin' on th' roof an' fallin' through," Slim observed.

"We had a log house in th' Ozarks, a slantin' rain'd wash chinkin' out an' th' thatch roof would leak after a year or two. I spent half my childhood cuttin' more cane an' thatch fer thet house," Shorty said. "Better tend to them beans, they're boilin' pretty good."

"Be sure you cook th' goat smell outa thet meat."

"You jist tend t' your knittin' an' let me worry 'bout thet meat, Mr. Bossy."

"Anyone complains about th' chow can cook," I declared.

"Right on, Tuck, thet should quieten 'em down," Shorty waved his spoon at th' others.

The other room became our stall. A couple of bars over the door kept the horses secure. No one slept under the shelter with the weather being as nice as it was. Shorty was banished to the downwind of the other beds, though there wasn't any odor left on his tarp.

■ ■ ■ ■

A monastery in these hills was a surprise to me and I eventually found out that the San Bernardino valley where John Slaughter had his ranch was named after a mission built there by the Jesuits. Most likely this place we were in was not a monastery, but an outpost where priests trying to win the Indians stayed. When th' Spaniards expelled the Jesuits from the country, they told their proselytes to keep the fire going in the mission so it would guide them back. The legend is that the Indians kept the fire going for some time but when the priests failed to return, they abandoned the mission and it fell into ruin. By th' time Texas John bought th' grant, the mission was just a pile of clay and old adobe bricks.

Legend also told that the priests buried their gold and church treasures in th' plaza. Many years later persons unknown left th' impression and rust of a steel box in th' bottom of a hole in front of the old church and disappeared with it. No one knows what was in the box.

With everything secure as we could make it, we cached some food nearby and moved south among the hills early the next morning, keeping a line of foothills between us and the plain. A dam across th' foot of a draw an' smoke rising told us that there was a line camp or shack there. We marked the spot for further investigation and continued on.

The slopes of those mountains are very rough and traveling parallel to the crest is like riding a huge corrugated roof. It was either up or down and around the brushy timber, never an even or level patch of land to be seen. We spent the whole day going what would have been fifteen miles on the plain below. Late in the afternoon we watered at a spring trickling down one of the draws an' staked our tired horses t' rest and graze.

"Forty miles o' ridin' an' still in sight o' where we started," Shorty said as he lay back under a stunted oak and pulled his sombrero over his eyes."

"Me an' my horse would be happy if we never saw another draw t' cross in our lives. I counted a hundred draws afore I run out of stick t' notch an' quit," Conly said.

"Figger that got us halfway here," I said.

Gabby had a little fire under a cedar tree. While the coffee boiled, he roasted a leg of goat and gnawed the meat off. "Where we gonna hide down here?" he asked between bites.

"Well, what ya say we follows this here river t' th' top an' see what lies above," Slim drawled. "Give me a hunk o' thet goat, I'm starvin'."

"Git yer own hunk, it's ever' man fer hisself, cook's off tonight," Gabby replied.

We went to bed with the sun and didn't rise 'til ol' sol came around again. A breakfast of coffee and a can of tomatos and we climbed the draw until we came to a wall of solid rock that rose more than a hundred feet above us. Water trickled from a hole under the cliff and it was plain to see that much more water had gushed forth in times past.

"Well here we are at th' end o' th' ride 'less these cayuses can walk vertical," Shorty drawled.

"There might be a place here along th' bluff we could fort up in if we had to," I said, "let's split up an' go each way an' see what we can find."

"Since this idee is yours, you should git th' pick o' which way you go, Tuck, an' that way looks easiest. I'll go with you," Conly said as he started left along the wall t' hoots from th' other three.

"Hope you fall in a hole, you sluggard,"

Slim called.

With horses secured, we walked th' wall on foot. Conly and I walked over two miles along the base of the cliff without finding anything that would work as a shelter. Our progress was cut off by a deep gully where the cliff had fallen away and it looked like th' whole side of th' mountain had followed. It was a hole a good sixty feet deep, th' end of the rock ledge we stood on every bit as vertical as the cliff above us. When we got back to th' spring, Gabby, Shorty and Slim were lounging in the shade. "Found our hidey-hole," Slim called.

"Whut's it look like?" Conly asked before he stuck his face back under springwater.

"Purty good, got a little seep where we could drink an' a tight squeeze gittin' in it that could be protected by one man," Shorty said.

"Well, soon's we catch our breath, I want t' look at this place an' see if it's any better than th' one we found," I said.

"Yeah, you'd hafta go some t' beat th' place we found," added Conly.

Three grins told us something was up. They acted unconcerned and Shorty said, "We're so tired from lookin' we're jist gonna sit here an' rest while you two go 'round an' see th' fort. It's behind a big rock thet's fallen off'n th' cliff. There's a little crack you kin squeeze through an' it opens up into a good space fer a ways then th' back is filled up with rocks an' dirt a goat couldn't climb. It looks like a huge piece o' th' bluff broke off an' slid a ways t' make th' crack — jist right for a home away from home."

"Don't worry, you can't miss it." Gabby couldn't hide th' smirk on his face.

"Well, Slim, I guess we should look at this place, but it would have t' be somethin' t' beat our hole."

"Shore would, but I guess we should at least give these boys th' courtesy o' lookin' at it." We both got up and started along the bluff. It curved back to the left so that after fifty yards or so, the boys at the spring couldn't be seen. Another fifty yards and our way was blocked by a huge rock as big as a good-sized barn.

Conly swore, "Them yahoos didn't go a quarter mile along this trail!"

There was a path two yards wide between the cliff and the rock and just a few feet along the path was a crack in the cliff that ran at a sharp angle back from the face of the rock. As it climbed the rock, the crack narrowed until it touched the cliff overhead. From a distance, the crevice could not even be seen. Still muttering, Conly squeezed

303

through the crack and I followed. We scraped through only a few feet when the crack widened into a narrow space that could be made comfortable for a shelter. "Them so-and-sos didn't go a foot beyond this."

"Yeah, an' they let us go on when a little hoot would have stopped us from all that walkin'," I said. "They need some come-uppance."

"Shore as th' world."

"We should tell them about th' place we found."

"Yeah, I'm sure it's a lot better than this."

"Well, we can't build it up too high or they'll suspect us, Conly."

"Right, we'll jist tease 'em along 'til they can't help but go see fer theirselves."

The sound of water dripping somewhere back in the dark recesses of the crack told us that we would have water and looking around in th' dim light, we could see that this place could make a satisfactory hide-away. "Let's bait our hooks an' go back," I said.

"Shore thing," and we scrambled out of the cave. Back at the spring, Conly raved at the boys, "You rascals coulda hollered us back t' look at that cave b'fore we walked our boots off lookin' fer another place."

I pulled a can of tomatos out of my possibles and began t' open it. "I guess that's right, Conly, but we wouldn't have found th' place we did."

"Guess so, but still, they could hev let us see it afore we left an' we might not have had t' come back t' take them back with us."

All was quiet for a few minutes as Conly and I ate our tomatoes. We were splitting a can of peaches when Shorty said, "You couldn't have found a place as good as thet." It was really a question.

"What you think, Conly, is our hole as good as theirs?" I asked.

"M-mm, I guess at least as good. It may not be as well hid, but it's shore roomier."

"Th' water's warm, but there's more of it, you could even take a shower under that little falls." I popped a peach half into my mouth an' couldn't answer Slim's questions. By th' time I had swallowed, the questions were old and I didn't bother t' answer.

Conly finished his peaches, drank th' syrup an' laid back with his hat over his eyes. "Siesta time."

"You ain't gonna let us see this hotel with hot runnin' water you found?" Shorty asked.

"Nah, we got time, I'm gonna rest some."

"Tuck, you gonna take us t' see it?" Slim asked.

"Why? You could find it yourself just by walkin' around th' bluff. B'sides, you done found a good place here 'thout wearin' your feet out walkin' in those boots."

"Does seem a little close t' th' spring here, don't it?" Conly's voice came from under the sombrero.

I rubbed my chin. "Well, the fact th' water doesn't run out of that cave would be an advantage, no one would look in there if there wasn't any water." I pulled my boots off and began rubbing my feet.

"By th' by," Conly lifted his hat a little, "we could see th' placita an' make out a line shack or two along th' other side." He lay back down.

Shorty nudged Gabby. "Think they're tellin' th' truth?" he muttered. Gabby shrugged.

Slim shifted his weight a little an' stood up. Casually, he said, "Guess I'll go see this palace."

"What's yore hurry, it's siesta time," I said and lay against my saddle, my hat over my eyes.

"I'm comin' too," Gabby grunted.

There was gravel crunching and th' three started off. "It's over a mile around there,"

306

I called by way of warning, but got no answer. I couldn't discern their mutterings. I could hear Conly snickering. "Shhhh, Conly."

"They cain't hear me," he laughed. "We got 'em!"

For a while we could hear mutterings and sounds coming from them. Once it sounded like one of them fell. "I guess that crack is th' best we could find, but what are we gonna do with our horses?" I asked.

"We need t' look at that, don't we? Might es well do that while they're gone, we might hafta hole up in th' cave t' save our hides," he laughed.

The outer edge of the big block that had broken off overhung th' edge of the bench and we had t' scramble around it mostly on our hands and feet. At the north end of the block, we came up against a stone wall that ran from the block along the edge of the bench. Another two hundred feet of scramble and there was a corner of the wall. Up on th' level bench, we stood and surveyed a large corral nearly an acre in size surrounded on two sides by solid rock and two sides by stone wall over chest high where it hadn't fallen down. In the middle of the fence was a gap that had once had a pole gate.

"Well, I'll be," said Conly, "and there's th' front door to our cave!"

The big block was over ten feet from the cliff face and there were remains of a roof made out of poles and cross thatch leaning from th' top of the boulder to the cliff.

"A right comfortable home," I said, "and they had their corral right in th' front door."

"That crack those boys found was their refuge an' water supply."

"Right, Conly, they didn't live in that crack, this was their home. I guess they kept sheep in here and grazed them along th' bench an' mountainside."

"There's room t' bring horses through th' shelter t' th' corral. Why don't we do thet an' let them boys find us?" And that's just what we did. A half hour's work and the whole camp was moved. We spent the rest of the afternoon repairing that rock wall and finding poles t' close th' gap with. It was getting pretty cool and we had a fire going and frijoles boilin' when we heard th' boys comin' through th' passage.

"Did ya find our cave?" I called.

"No, th' mountain had fallen off an' we couldn't git there," Shorty spat as he plopped by his saddle an' rubbed his achin' feet.

"An' it was more like *two* miles 'stead o'

308

one," Slim said.

"Two miles an' . . . ten yards," Gabby corrected as he grunted his boots off.

"If you fellers weren't so all-fired set on boots too small for your feet, you'd get by better when you have to walk," I said.

"I 'spose yo're a lot better," Slim retorted.

"At least my boots fit an' they're not a size too small."

"Only *one* size?" Gabby seemed surprised.

"Go out front there an' look at our corral," invited Conly.

Slim stretched his neck an' gave a glance at the fenced corral. "Looks good from here."

"Me an' Tuck built that fence while you were gone, guess it wouldn't be askin' too much of you-all t' tend th' cookin' fer say th' next week t'even chores out."

"Why, shore, Con, an' just t' make it more 'even' I'll make your bed ever' mornin'," Shorty replied.

"Thankee."

After we ate, we climbed up on top of the block of rock and watched th' valley below. The afternoon sun showed features of the western side of El Medio clearly. "There's headquarters." Conly nodded toward a group of buildings about midway down the range.

"I see two line shacks south of the placita," Slim said.

"Three," Gabby grunted.

"Just where d'yuh see three?"

"One" — Gabby pointed — "two . . . and three." He pointed halfway across th' range between th' mountains.

"That's just a brush pile, Gabby, I swear . . ."

"Brush *arbor*." Gabby's talk was finished.

"Cain't argue with Gabby, Slim," Shorty said gently.

We couldn't find any shacks north of headquarters, but they had to be there, and probably another arbor halfway across the plain on that end. As night fell, lights came on at the placita and fire flickered at the arbor. We thought we could see three lights against the hills north of headquarters, but we couldn't see the plain where we suspected the north arbor would be.

"Question is, how many are on this side," I said.

"Yeah, there could be one right under our noses an' we wouldn't see it from here," Conly said. "We need to make a scout an' find out."

"Do you really think we need another hidey-hole?" Shorty asked.

"We should have something over on

310

t'other side in case some emergency comes up an' we need t' duck in a while."

"I think you're right, Tuck," said Conly. "Something really secure an' fairly close to the placita."

"Well, we're whilin' away too much time here, we need t' start actin' if we're ever gonna git things done. I have a bunch t' do afore I git too old an' time's a-wastin'," Slim said. "We need a plan."

"Tomorrow, you, Shorty an' Conly ride around th' south end o' th' range an' find us a hideaway over on th' Medio. Leave a stash there an' find somethin' on th' north end t' hide us too. Tuck an' I will scout th' east side o' th' San Luis an' cause some distraction so no one will be gazin' at th' mountains an' spy you. We'll meet at th' monastery two nights from tonight."

"Here, Gabby, there's a half cup o' coffee you can drink. Maybe it'll wet yer throat enough 'til you git down an' find water, after thet speech," Slim said sympathetically.

"I'm goin' t' bed." Gabby got up an' scrambled down th' rock.

"Couple o' big days ahead t' git all thet done," Conly said and climbed after Gabby.

"Throw my bedroll up here, Con, an' I'll sleep up here an' keep a little watch."

"Shore thing, Tuck."

It was cold on top of that rock exposed to the breeze an' layin' on solid rock. I didn't sleep well an' got down before anyone else awoke. Th' smell o' coffee an' bacon brought them around soon enough and we set about our two chores for th' day. Finding our way down off that bench was a job. First we had t' find a place where th' bench side wasn't too steep for the horses, then we had to find our way over that corrugated ground to the south end of the range. Gabby and I stopped in the brush a little south of the brush arbor about mid afternoon. The rest would continue on south in order to be out of sight of the arbor when they crossed th' plain. After they left, Gabby said, "We'll wait an' jist ride up th' middle o' th' range in th' dark an' see if we kin find any guard camps." With that, he lay down against his saddle and slept. I was glad for that opportunity after th' restless night I had. As I drifted off, I heard th' rumble of thunder. It sounded like it was far to the south of us.

We woke late an' when we finished th' last meat an' beans, it was pitch black.

"Time t' go," Gabby said quietly and put on a pair of mocassins. I hung my boots over th' saddle horn and padded after him in mocassins of my own.

"We need more nourishment than this," I whispered to his back as we led the horses and walked out on open range. People talk about how much light th' stars give out here at this high altitude, but they don't talk about how *far* you can see by that light an' believe me, it ain't far. We angled for the middle keeping as far from that arbor as we could. Gabby stopped and we surveyed the foothills. He grunted and pointed to a pinpoint of light that wasn't a quarter mile north of where we struck th' plain.

"Reckon they saw us?" I asked.

"Doubtful, ain't heard any shootin'."

Here, we mounted and rode at a walk right up the middle of th' range. From what we saw, there were at least four camps on the west side of the range, placed at about equal distances apart. A gap in the line made us think that there was one camp we couldn't see and riding over closer we caught th' gleam of a rising moon on adobe of the fifth camp. From there, we hustled back to mid-range and walked between our horses hoping we wouldn't be seen.

The last camp interested us because there was a large fenced pasture in front of it and we walked over to the fence to see what it was about. A couple of snorts from our horses told us that this was the horse pasture. Naturally, our brains began t' crank out plans and by th' time we were in the brush, we had hatched out a way to retire those horses from th' range. It was good to get to the monastery and have a hot cup, set beans t' cookin' an' fall asleep.

CHAPTER 22
A CHANGE OF PLANS

A SEASON TO PLUCK

We like to claim that the Tularosa Basin is
the last frontier of the west and if so, then
the land from the Animas Valley westward
to the Sierra Nevada is the last of the *wild*
west. That vast range from south of the
boarder to Canada is the favorite haunt of
the Long Riders. I can count a half dozen
robber's roosts strung along the back range
of the Rockies and that's not counting Hole
in the Wall, Brown's Park and a bunch of
ranches strung out where a man could
exchange his tired horse for a fresh one
without any questions. It's told that Butch
Cassidy once established an alibi after rob-
bing a train in Montana Territory by appearing in western New Mexico a little
more than two days later. My four companions seemed t' have an intimate knowledge
of this wild country, though I never ventured
to question them about it. They were good

company, hard workin' when there was work, loyal and dependable, but I was pretty sure they didn't want to be seen in public north of the border the time I knew them.

When Conly, Slim and Shorty heard about the horse pasture, they knew just who they could contact to dispose of the horses quickly at a decent price. Slim rode north th' next morning and came back on a different horse the morning after that. "All's set," was all he said and the rest were satisfied. I didn't say anything.

The only question was how we were going to get that herd out of the pasture. A little observin' of th' operation revealed that th' cavvy was looked over by two young boys and that their main responsibility was to see that they were well watered each evening and keep a watch over them by day. This consisted of one boy riding over the range some time around noon and locating the herd. Our plan was to capture the boys and drive the cavvyard north after dark. Just as we were putting our plan into action, Shorty saw a dust out on the plain and it was headed for the horse pasture. As we watched a couple of boys drove twenty or thirty horses into the corral at the shack and after they had eaten, the four boys retired for the night.

"Well, we have a decision t' make," Conly said. "Do we take th' herd now with all th' horses here and have to handle four boys or do we wait until tomorrow night after they have taken thirty head of fresh horses out of th' pasture?"

"I'm sure not anxious t' tackle four boys when I can tackle two," Shorty said.

Slim thought a moment then said, "If we go tonight, headquarters'll know a lot quicker what has happened and will naturally take out after us a lot sooner than we planned."

"But *not* with fresh horses," Gabby added. "We hold th' boys long enough t' get th' herd movin', then let 'em go."

"Yeah, an' I want t' see them hotfootin' it across thet open range with half wild cows roamin'." I said. "The more horses we run off, th' less horses they have t' chase us, I say we go now." To that we all agreed and with a little refinement of our plans we went into action.

Shorty and I were given th' task o' entertaining herders an' sendin' out any corraled horses. While he entered th' line shack, I let down bars and shoo'd th' horses north. That done, I hurried to the shack t' help Shorty. As I approached, I heard such a commotion that I drew my gun and crept around back.

317

Through a window, I saw that Shorty was barely able to hold four panicked young men at bay. They seemed on the verge of rushing him when I called out in Spanish, "Hold there, you're covered both ways!"

That only seemed t' make them more agitated, but th' fact of bein' target in a crossfire fight caused them to pause long enough for Shorty to speak, "Tuck, they's so wrought up b'cause they say th' boss'll kill them if th' herd gets stolen, an' they mean that literally."

"Sí, señor, the segundo is a bad man. If we fail him, he will kill us. We are as good as dead now," one of the boys said.

I stepped through the window and said, "We can't let that happen, you men sit down an' let's talk this over." That seemed to calm them some and they sat on the floor.

"We have t' *move,*" Shorty said urgently.

"You are right, but we have a problem here. We don't want to leave these boys here to be killed, what can we do with them?" I spoke in Spanish for the prisoners' sake.

"Take us with you or give us horses and we will run away."

The other boys nodded in agreement.

Shorty gave a short shake of his head.

"You can't go with us. Where would you go from here?" I asked.

"We would go south," one said.

"No, you can't go south, you would rouse the whole range and get yourself killed to' boot," Shorty put in.

"You can only go north at least a good ways before you turn east or west. Remember, the ranch hands will be hot on our trail for a while and we all will have to do some hard riding." I looked at their strained faces.

"I will ride with you and the herd," one who looked to be the oldest said.

"No, you can't," Shorty said.

I looked at Shorty. "Do you believe them?"

"From what I know of this place, they are right about the boss killing them."

"If we take you to the trail over San Luis Pass would you go over and disappear and never come back?" The chorus of "sí!" settled the issue and we herded them out the door. Their haste was so much that we had to hustle to keep up with them. Their fear was genuine and I felt better about our intentions. As we caught up with the herd, all four boys caught horses and mounted.

Shorty called out, "Let 'em go, boys, they're leavin' with us!" I saw someone to my right lower his rifle. The boys crowded around me and the spokesman said, "We will stay with you, señor, until we reach the trail." There was nothing t' do but agree with them and that is how I got t' be drag — again.

My partners moved the herd with practiced efficiency and we pushed north at a lope. When the herd knew th' wire was down on th' fence, they surged through and we were on our way. The four boys helped keep our herd together as much as they could and keep sight of me. An hour at a lope tired th' foals and they began to lag, the mothers staying with them and as they reached us in the drag, we pushed them away and left them behind.

We reached the San Luis Pass trail just before dawn. With the low light, dust and tracks of th' herd, I almost missed it. My prisoners, if you could call them that, gathered around me and I pointed out th' trail, which I'm sure they knew well. "There is your trail. It is too dangerous for you to go south to Bavispe, take the trail north to Tucson, go with God and do not return." Each boy gave me his hand and I gave them two pesos each — probably more money than they had ever seen. I watched until they were only dots on the side of the mountain, then rejoined the herd.

We skirted Lake Cloverdale to the west and by mid afternoon, the clouds over the mountains had built high and began to drift over the plain, bringing rain and lightning and thunder to the south of us. The herd seemed to recognize the danger and needed no encouragement to keep moving north away from the storm.

Late in the afternoon we found water at Double Adobe Creek below Animas Peak and the horses rested for an hour. With fresh horses at dusk, we moved the herd up Adobe, over the divide and down what the boys called Gillespie Creek. Crossing the Playas Valley in the dark, we passed between the Big Hatchet and Little Hatchet ranges and into the Hachita Valley where we made camp at the upper end of the marshes. The cavvy spread out some and grazed. Behind us, the thunderhead spread its anvil high over the sky, illuminated by the occasional flash of lightning that lit up the lower parts of the cloud. It looked like kernels of popcorn with lights inside.

"I think thet thing came all th' way up over Cloverdale," Conly said.

"At least it washed out some of our trail, as if we were goin' any way but north." Slim's grin flashed in the firelight.

"All we need now is a good storm t' build over Animas an' wash out our tracks where we turned," Shorty wished.

Gabby looked over his cup. "With lots of luck."

"All we got to do is hold 'em 'til mornin' an' it'll be someone else's problem," Slim said as he stood up stiffly. "These knees ain't what they used t' be."

"Jist needs some oilin', I heard 'em creak from here," Shorty remarked.

They still joked some, but there was a change in all of us. We were more wary and observant of our surroundings and there was an air of serious purpose in all our work. The fire put out, we rode loose herd on the horses, but they were too tired and hungry to move about much. We probably lost a dozen or more mares with foal. They would most likely drift back to familiar range or be picked up by our pursuers who were sure to come.

Just at daylight a group of riders approached from the north and Conly and Slim rode to meet them. They talked for a few minutes then moved toward the cavvy.

"Time to go," Conly called and I followed him as he headed south down the valley. I didn't get too much of a look at the men who took the horses, but generally, they were of th' type you wanted on your side or didn't want to meet up with "on the prairie."

I heard Slim behind me call something to

the other two and in a few minutes, the three drove up ten head of horses.

"Got us some spares, Tuck," Shorty called.

The new owners of the cavvy were already rounding up the herd and heading them north. Three men detached themselves from the group and followed us. They turned right and headed up th' trail between the two Hatchets and Slim said, "Bet no one comes through that pass for a while."

Our pace slowed some and we felt relief from the stress of the last three days. Around mid afternoon, the clouds over Big Hatchet began their rumble and we rode up one of the draws for shelter. I had a chance to look at our spare mounts and found four of them had Beaver brands. One of them was John Crider's horse.

My feelings must have shown for Slim said, "What's wrong, Tuck?"

"That's the horse John Crider was riding when they raided us. We never saw him again."

"He took th' last long ride for th' brand," Shorty said softly.

"And I intend to send someone after him or go myself," I answered.

It rained buckets and we sat under our slickers in a futile attempt to keep our saddles and ourselves dry. The horses stood together, rumps to the wind and heads down while the lightning flashed and the thunder rolled over our heads. The weather fit my mood and the others left me to my thoughts.

I suppose that subconsciously I had hoped John was still alive somewhere and I would find him. The appearance of his horse in the rogue ranch's herd made me face the hard fact that he was gone. Pa, Bet and now Cider gone, Pecos Pete all stove up and Bob Nealy feelin' every change in the weather for th' rest of his life, all over a few head of cows. That price is too high and demands more reckoning. As I sat there, my resolve grew. I would not go home to get help, I would demand the books be balanced now.

It was still raining when we left th' draw. Hopefully it would rain enough to wash out our tracks some more. I rode one of our Beaver horses an' it seemed that all four horses knew me. Cider's horse ran beside me, just like he had done when his master was astride him. It haunted me. More than once as we rode that night, I looked over t' see if Cider was still awake. When th' risin' sun shone on Hat Top Mountain, we turned into a cove in the hills and let th' cavvy rest. Our intent was to spend the day here and time our departure to reach Antelope Wells after dark.

The summer rains are spotty at best and you can be choking on dust one minute and hock deep in mud the next. Here, it was still dry and we soon had a fire going, coffee boiling. There was a little saltback left and we shared it with a pot of frijoles set on the fire for supper.

"Someone's gonna have t' watch th' horses," Conly said, "I'll take first watch."

"No," I said, "I'll take it, I couldn't sleep anyway."

Conly looked at me, then slowly nodded, "OK, Tuck, wake me about noon an' don't let th' beans boil dry." Without another word, four beds rolled out under four cedars an' soon were held down by sleeping men. I walked around a bit, made a circle of the cavvy and sat in th' shade of a cedar up on the slope a ways.

My mind was on those three lost companions and I must have relived every moment I had spent with them. Bet and Cider were there at the ranch before I was born and they were as much a part of our lives as the rest of th' family. It made me think about th' life of a cowhand and how they came to feel they belonged to th' land as much as any man who had th' deed and paid taxes on it. They knew every nook and cranny of their range, knew th' cows — most of them by name — and where they could likely be found. Year after year, through all seasons, they rode and looked after cattle and horses, mended fences, cleaned out water holes, pulled cows out of bogs until the flow of th' seasons was ingrained into their minds and bodies; until they went about the work of running a ranch without a word of instruction. No wonder so many of them "rode for the brand" and had little patience for the itinerant vaquero who didn't feel th' same way. Their loyalty wasn't to a man or a particular brand so much as it was to the land, to their range, to an institution. Time after time as owners came and went, many a hand "came with the ranch." It was their place in the world and the seasons. I suppose Solomon could have been just as right if he had written, For every*one* there is a season and a time for every *man* under heaven.

Only God knows when those seasons end and I suppose that is rightly so. Now the seasons had ended for Pa and Cider and Bet. They are frozen in our minds just as we had last seen them in their lives. We wouldn't see them grow older, watch Pa with his grandchildren or Bet and Cider with wives and children and probably ranches of their own. They are gone, laid beneath the soil somewhere, to become a part of the land they loved. I suppose it is only right that they be so.

I thought about my family, Ma, Eda and Joe — they had a second child by now — Sue Ellen and Bud, Nate, Bob and Presilla, Green, Josh, and most of all Cindy. What were they doing? I could almost tell, for the flow of the seasons on that range was in me as much as my blood and bones. What did they think of me now that I was four months gone?

A whiff of smoke reminded me of the fire and frijoles and I hurried over to check on them. They were on the verge of scorching and I added water to them and wood to th' fire. A thought came to me and I rummaged around and found hobbles and put them on each horse except for the one I saddled and staked near the camp. The sun was past zenith when I finally felt fatigue, so I ate and woke Conly. I didn't even roll out my own bed, just lay on his and slept.

We were in th' shadow of th' mountains when I finally awoke, stiff and sore. Conly had a different horse saddled and staked and he was dishing out beans and coffee for the rest of us. Almost nothing was said as we ate, saddled and removed hobbles. The cavvy moved off with reluctance, but soon they seemed to sense they were heading for the home range and went willingly.

The moon had risen over Antelope Wells and there were two candles burning in the chapel windows. The sheepfold was full and there was a single candle guttering in the cantina. Without a word, Slim, Gabby and Shorty posted themselves, rifles ready, about th' plaza while Conly and I entered the cantina. I looked around and eventually, the huge muzzle of a shotgun laying across the bar came into focus.

"It's Conly and Tucker, Julio," I whispered.

Slowly a figure rose from behind the bar. "Hola, Tuck-er, I was not sure." His voice sounded muffled and slurred and when we were close enough, we could see that he had been badly beaten.

"What has happened, Julio?" Conly asked.

"The Beaver men came looking for horses. They were sure we had stolen them and they beat us to confess. Felipe is near death and they have taken the young men away."

"We saw the fold full, who tends the sheep?"

"The children and young girls, Tuck. We do not know what they have done to the young men. They took them to the placita. We are being watched. Oh, what can we do?" he almost wept.

Conly put a hand on his shoulder. "We must go get them, my friend," he said gently.

"I will go tell the others," I said, "and see about Felipe."

"Tell the boys to come here and you hurry back too, Felipe can wait."

I rounded up the guards and we met under the ramada in front of the cantina. Julio limped out and gave us each a bottle of beer. There followed a tense discussion of what and where and how and we decided that some of us would distract as many of the people at headquarters away and some of us would attempt a rescue.

"I can cause a distraction if I had some help and you three could be the rescuing heroes," Gabby said.

"There are some boys here that could be of use to you, Gabby. I will get them." Julio limped off into the darkness.

"Real saints we're dealing with here. Any idiot can see that these people could not have anything t' do with their horses. It would be deadly for them," Shorty said.

"It may yet be if we don't act soon," Conly said.

Soon boys began to approach and Julio

limped back with the last one. "These four are our most able ones left."

They were young, all right, the ages we could not tell in the dark, but only one had reached what should be his full stature. Two lugged guns that when set down were taller than they were.

"We don't need guns, men, but we do need fuel and powder," said Gabby.

With that, the two gunmen proffered powder horns and Shorty muttered, "Oh no, muzzle loaders!"

"Is there more powder?"

"I have about half a keg," Julio said, "but it is very old."

Julio turned to one of the boys. "Nava, the keg is in the storage room under the box of dynamite."

"Dynamite?" four voices exclaimed.

"Bring it too!"

"I should get the dynamite," Julio said hastily.

He moved toward the cantina and Gabby followed. When he returned, he was walking carefully with a crate held away from his body. "It's weeping, the sawdust is wet." He whispered as though speaking aloud would cause a catastrophe.

"Lordy," Shorty whispered.

"How can we move it?" Slim asked.

"You can wrap each stick in cloth and keep it out of that box," I advised.

Julio produced a large rag and we tore it into squares. Gabby carefully set the box on the floor and handed each of us a stick as we got ready for them. They were all wet to some extent, the bottom sticks the wettest. "That's one short," Gabby whispered as he stored the wrapped dynamite in a flour bag.

"I'm keeping one," Slim whispered. "Give me a couple of coils of that fuse and two caps."

"Don't nobody kick this box of sawdust." As a second thought, Gabby sat the box on a table. "Now, me and the muchachos . . ."

"Uno muchacha," a voice from behind said. We turned to see another figure standing there. She was dressed in the pants and blouse of a man with a blue calico sash tied around an obviously slim waist. "I *will* go with you," she said with the determination that precluded any objections.

"*Ir de mal en peor,*" one of the boys muttered. I imagined his eyes rolling upward as he spoke.

"Not 'bad to worse,' she may go with us," Gabby said.

There were four soft groans and Julio chuckled, "She says she can do . . ."

". . . anything you can!" I could almost

331

hear Cindy's voice, and I smiled.

We parted and the girl moved into the circle.

"The muchachos and muchacha will ride with me to the north of the range. You three get as close to the placita as you can and try to determine where the men are being held. You will know when the diversion begins and you can go to work. It will be after dark tomorrow night," Gabby added.

"There is a trail over El Medio to the plaza, but it is not good for horses," Julio said.

"I know the trail!" one of the boys said. He was short but stockily built.

"You should take Sergio with you, then," said Julio. "You should go now, there is much to do and a long walk. I shall be the only one here who knows what you do and where you go, it is safer that way."

"We must take our water," Sergio said, and we watered the horses and filled our canteens before we left. Sergio rode in front of me and led us to the trailhead. Gabby rode north with the other four, driving the spares with them.

"We see flashes of light in the mornings from that peak and know someone is watching us through the glasses," Sergio said.

"Where can we hide the horses?" I asked.

"There is a place of much shade in the cove where the trail starts up the hills and it is good to keep the horses in, but there is no water there."

"It will have to do, may be that they won't have to stay there long," Conly said.

"Is the trail plain enough for Gringos to find, Sergio?" I asked.

"Sí, you can find it."

"Will you stay and care for the horses while we are gone?"

There was a long pause and a disappointed boy repied, "Sí, I can do that."

"Sergio, everything we do now is important and your job is just as important as ours. We must depend on the horses to save us and the young men when we come back. To have them here and safe may be the most important part of our mission," I said.

Shorty dug into his saddlebag and brought something to Sergio. "Take this gun and here are some more shells. When we return, we will whistle and you won't shoot us then, will you?"

"No, Señor Shorty, I will look before I shoot you. The trail begins there under the pillar of rock. It passes under the peak where the watchers are, so you must be careful there. After that the trail is plain."

CHAPTER 23
FIRE AND THE HOLE

A SEASON TO KILL

Sergio led us to the trail under the pillar and from there it was easy to follow even for Gringos in the dark. Soon we caught the smell of smoke and moved much more cautiously. "I don't like th' idee of leavin' folks with guns b'hind me when I goes out a-larkin'," Shorty said.

"Me, neither," Slim said.

"Let's you an' me pay whoever's up there a little visit an' explain our feelins."

"Shore 'nough, Shorty, that's jist what I was a-thinkin'."

At a likely-looking place, they slipped through the brush up the hill and Conly and I moved on at a slower pace waiting their return. Turning a bend in the canyon we climbed, we heard a soft whistle ahead of us and ducked into the brush. The whistle came again and Conly motioned to me. "That's the boys," he said, and we moved on up either side of the trail in the shadow of the brush.

"Pssst, we're over here," Slim called and they stepped out on the trail. Both men were loaded with extra equipment that clattered softly as they set it down.

"Weren't no need o' both of us goin' 'cept t' haul all this plunder," Shorty said. "They's only two of 'em."

"We'd better find a place t' stash that stuff er you'll be announcin' our presence afore we git t' th' placita," Conly allowed.

"We thought it might come in handy if we have t' make a hasty exit an' if not, th' men we rescue would use it."

In a soft first light we found a pocket behind a boulder a few feet off the trail and stowed rifles, guns, bandoleers and water. Shorty stuck a pistol in his waist and handed me another. "Don't hurt t' have a little extra firepower around."

I checked th' load and stuck the gun under my belt in th' small of my back. It chaffed a little, but it was reassuring t' have it. The sun came up and we climbed with it up the mountainside. It was hot and we stopped often to drink and rest. The men feigned exaggerated concern about my welfare and makin' sure I drank enough. It was easy to get out of breath at the altitude of the mountain and our pace slowed accordingly. The sun was past zenith when we reached th' divide and looked down into the valley below. The buildings were all under the shoulder of the mountain and out of sight. Slim used his recently appropriated glasses t' scan the valley.

"Don't see a soul stirrin'."

"Must be siesta," I said dryly.

"Looks mostly downhill from here an' I'm sure glad of that," said Shorty.

"You just be sure of your brakes, 'cause if you don't, yo're liable t' be halfway across th' valley afore you git stopped," Conly said as he led the way downward.

The sun was peeking under th' brims of our hats before we reached th' foothills. We climbed one of the last hills to look over the situation. The trail came onto the plain a few hundred yards south of an adobe-walled corral and we worked our way north to the hill above the buildings. We spread apart along the ridge and took inventory of things below. Several well-armed men lounged around and it was plain they were not where they were by accident. One of the houses seemed to receive special attention, the door on our side was barred from the outside and I surmised that was the place where the Antelope Wells men were held. As I looked, there was movement below the parapet on the roof of the tallest house and a lookout stood and surveyed the valley.

We gathered in the gloaming and made plans. "Gabby went north, so it's sure he will do somethin' on th' north boundary o' th' range. We are gonna need t' be high enough t' see thet an' still be a lot closer t' th' plaza t'act quickly," Conly said.

"Looks like there's enough cover for us on that slope right above th' houses," I said. "Maybe we could just watch that lookout on th' roof an' know what's goin' on."

"I can stay higher up and watch, then I will shoot the lookout and anyone else who shows his head!" a voice from the brush said.

"What the . . ." We all spun around guns drawn.

"It is I, Sergio," and he stepped out of the brush, a bandoleer over his shoulder and one of our confiscated rifles in his hand.

"You damn near got four new holes punctuating your body, boy. What are you doing here?" Conly demanded.

"There is a secret passage from the majordomo's house to the hills I forgot to tell you about. If you didn't know, they could get behind you and trap you. It may be that we could use it to our benefit," the boy said, his teeth showing white in the fading light.

"*We* could use . . . to *our* benefit? Since when were you included in this here rodeo?" Shorty asked.

"It has always been so, señor, since we were run from this place of my birth and home," the boy said. "Do you wish to see the entrance to the passage now?"

"Not yet, Sergio, our plans are not complete and we need to think more since you have informed us of this new opportunity," I said.

"Where's Gabby when we need more planning?" Slim asked.

"I'm thinking that he is planning something that will draw people from here, aren't you?" I asked. "So when he does his thing, we should wait to see how many are drawn off before we act. When they are gone, we can try to open up the prison and let the men out. What then?"

"We should split up, some coming up the trail and some riding and driving their horses south away from the enemy," Conly said.

"Will they have presence of mind to do as we say?" I asked.

"That we will have to see when the time comes, I reckon. Some of this here plan will have to be spur of the moment," Slim opined.

"I think so too. Best we can do in the end is plan so we don't get in each other's way and don't end up shooting at each other. Sergio, you go up there on that rock and build yourself up a fort to shoot from and get the lookout and any others you can. Don't shoot anywhere else unless you have a sure shot that won't hit any of us. When you can, go and cover the door or whatever it is to that passage and don't let anyone out of it. Can you shoot?" The boy grinned and nodded.

"Slim, Conly and I will go to the jail and open it. Shorty, move down close and empty the corral when the dance starts. Be ready to direct the men when they come that way. Take a couple of them and run those horses around the end of the mountain. We'll try to meet you where our horses are hid or at the Wells. After those prisoners are released, we will cover you and then hustle up the trail and guard the retreat. Sergio, when you think the game is over, hightail it to the trail. Don't dawdle, we do not want to shoot you in the darkness."

"Sí, if I do not come soon enough, I will return over the mountain by myself. I know trails others don't."

"Good, see to your guns and we will wait under your rock. Don't shoot until I call you, then count to ten five times slowly before you shoot."

"Good plan, *Gabby*," Shorty whispered, and he crept off on his assigned mission.

It got dark and we waited. We could see a long way up the valley and a light flared in the middle. It grew until it was a huge fire. "North arbor's burnin'," the lookout called below. "Someone's gonna be cuttin' an' haulin' brush tomorrow." There was a casual comment or two made back and forth and quiet returned as the fire flared and died down. The lookout started to say something when there was a sudden flash like lightning and an orange mushroom-like cloud rose over the northernmost line shack on the west side of the range. A few seconds later, the sound boomed across the valley, echoing back and forth between the two mountain ranges. Men appeared from everywhere and we could hear shouts and running feet. Just as calm was restored and the men crowded around some authority giving instructions, a second flash and boom and a cloud arose over the former location of the second line shack.

"Start counting, Sergio," I called softly and moved down toward the plaza as the men of the ranch ran for their mounts. They had thundered out of the plaza heading north only a minute or two when I heard a shot and saw the lookout throw up his hands and fall.

"Counted too fast," I muttered.

"Don't think he could count above five, Tuck," Conly chuckled. He raised his rifle and fired and I heard a gun clatter to the paved alley.

Gunfire came from the direction of the corral, and Sergio fired again. I heard someone cry out. Then fire came from a window toward Sergio's fort. The bullets ricocheted away and I thought about shrapnel hitting the boy.

In his excitement, the defender in the window had forgotten to douse the lights in the room and when his silhouette appeared, two rifles spoke and there was no more firing from the window. I ran to the corner of the building fronting the plaza. Horses were returning from the north and when the first horse appeared I shot it, then fired at the rider. Three more quick shots stopped the riders crowding behind and they made a hasty retreat.

Slim reached the jail door and threw off the bar. Conly's rifle was speaking a regular tattoo to the south of the jail and I moved away from the corner out in the plaza. Fire began to pour from the entrance to the plaza and from over the dead horses there. I knelt behind the well curb and returned fire. A figure emerged from the corner I had just vacated and his rifle was raised when I saw him. I made a desperate dive to the ground, realized I had put myself in a crossfire and was scrambling around the well when a shot rang out and the man fell. "Thanks, Sergio," I muttered. I popped three quick shots in the direction of the dead horses, waited until the spate of return fire quit and ran diagonally across the plaza for the corner of the jail. It had emptied and Slim was tossing a lighted fuse into the room. "Run, Tuck," he called and sprinted for the corrals with me close behind. As he cleared the corner, two shots rang out and I saw him stumble then run on. Another shot and I rounded the corner gun raised and shot almost point-blank into the body of a man standing there. He was so close, I grabbed the barrel of his gun and jerked it from his unresisting hands as he fell.

Firing from the plaza told me that the men there had flanked my old position and were advancing. I turned and pumped a couple of shots into the dark and the jailhouse erupted into a ball of fire and dust.

"An' that was only a half stick," I heard Slim near and found him lying by the corral gate. "I'm bad hit, Tuck, you go on an' I'll cover you."

"No way, mister!" And as I stooped to lift him, something slammed into my hip like a mad steer and sent me rolling. My right side went numb and I thought I had lost my leg.

"Where'd they hit you, Tuck?"

"Think they shot my leg off," I gritted. I felt down my hip to my leg. "Nope, it's still there," but my hand got hot blood when I passed it over my hip. "Got me in the hip."

I crawled to Slim and he ran his hand over my hip and found the source of the blood and stuffed something into the hole. "No butts about it," he chuckled — even in his own pain.

We crawled and slid into the corral and somehow got the heavy solid doors shut. There was a bar for the inside latch and it took us both to slide it into place.

I got very dizzy and lay down. The numbness was wearing off and pain washed over me and down my leg. Something struck the back of my head and I blacked out and must have passed completely out. Someone was calling me from far, far away and I tried to answer. Finally, after a long time, it seemed,

I spoke and a moment later I could see again.

"Thought you had left me," Slim said.

"Guess I did for a minute," I managed to reply. Bullets spattering against the door had found a crack between timbers and a splinter or bullet had hit me. Th' back of my shirt felt wet and when I felt of my collar it was sticky and wet. I lightly ran my fingers up my neck and into my hair until something stuck me. It was the sharp end of a splinter that had entered my scalp a couple of inches above, run along my scull until it tried to exit and got stuck with the end exposed. It was a long splinter as big as my little finger and some of it was sticking out of both holes in my scalp.

We looked for holes t' shoot out of. Slim fired his pistol through a crack and we heard a scream. A body fell against the door. "Sissy, I just shot your leg," Slim called. He was answered by a string of curses. "Got t' remember some of those, amigo, mind repeatin' that last one?" The man didn't repeat, but added another string of original curses, going several generations in both directions from Slim's birth. "Beautiful," Slim's voice trailed away and I knew he was sinking. He had two gut shots, one that smashed th' bottom of his rib cage and one below that.

"Hang in there, Slim, we'll get outta this somehow." I reloaded all three rifles and our pistols. Slim was breathing real shallow and I put one of his pistols in his hand. He muttered something I couldn't understand and lay still.

A sound above my head caught my attention and I smelled wood in the dust falling on me. "They're tryin' t' saw through th' bar, Slim." With the aid of one of the rifles, I slid up the door until the thrust of the saw brushed my hat. My shot through the crack below the bar set the sawyer's shirt on fire and he fell with a sigh. I pulled the saw through as far as I could and with all the strength in me, bent it flush against th' door.

"We gotta git outa here, Slim." I kept talkin' to him even though I knew he would never hear again. Digging sounds coming in the wall told me there were footholds being dug for climbing. It was futile to try and stop them with bullets and my fogged mind took a few moments to remember Slim's half stick of dynamite. I retrieved it and the fuse and cap from his body and dug furiously at the adobe down low on the wall. I packed the dynamite in the hole as much as I could, lit a short fuse and crawled away. "Look out, Slim, that wall's gonna blow!" I had barely gotten snug against the wall when the stick blew and the whole wall fell.

As the dust settled, there rose a gentle groaning that grew and the door on that side fell in almost covering Slim's body. It lay at a slant on some of the fallen bricks and I saw a chance t' hide under it. Bullets were flying through the breech at a furious rate, but no one was volunteering t' charge the corral with the chance that there might be more explosions. Desperate to move quickly and unable to, I shoved all my weapons under the edge of the door at Slim's feet, then backed under th' door and fainted. I must have been out only a few seconds for the bullets were still flying. Reaching out to plug my hole with a brick, I was startled to see the plain tracks where I had dragged myself. There was no way I could erase them. I was as good as caught — and dead — until I saw Slim's boots. Very carefully I reached out and rerouted the ruts of my drag to the upturned heels of Slim's boots. Hopefully no one would look close enough to discern that they were not genuine. I dug out dirt with my knife and plugged th' hole, pushing bricks around to make room for myself and prayed, "Don't move the door, don't move the door . . ."

CHAPTER 24
SERGIO'S WAR

A TIME FOR WAR

Later when Tucker first got to Bavispe, Sergio told his part of the fight that night. We insert it here so the reader can better follow the story in its proper order. — Ed.

I am to start the war! I, Sergio Hernandes, shepherd of Antelope Wells, will start the war that is to regain our placita and range from the hated Gringos! What an honor and responsibility! I must not fail.

On top of the big rock, I quietly built me a rock wall with holes I could shoot through. "Start counting, Sergio," I heard Tuck call and I began counting, 1-2-3-4-5-6 . . . 10. 1-2-3-4-5 . . . 10 . . . 1-2-3 . . . the lookout unexpectedly turned our way, had he seen something? Could he have heard me counting? What did he see . . ? he just as suddenly turned back and was leaning over the parapet to say or call out to somebody when I shot.

I heard Tuck say, "Counted too fast." But what was I to do? The lookout was about to sound the alarm and without my shot to start them, my companions would be caught unprepared. Conly fired the second shot of the war and I heard a gun clatter on the pavement somewhere. They were running on their way when a shot hit my fort and splattered shards of sharp rock in my face. I ran my hand over my face and winced as it scraped a rock sticking out of my cheek. When I pulled it out, I bled a little.

Tuck-er was shooting across the plaza at the men who were riding back from their start for the north. A horse was down at the corners and someone was firing from behind it. I could see his boots as he lay there. I sighted the boots and moved up the legs until my shot would barely clear the horse's body and fired — and missed the man. Again I sighted and fired. This time the man rolled over, writhing in pain and I got a third shot. He didn't move again.

When I looked back at Tuck, he was still firing at the men across the plaza and he didn't see the man creeping up on him from behind! My sights were on him instantly, but I could not fire for fear of hitting my friend. Tuck jumped up and ran and I fired.

The men at the corner began firing wildly several bullets hitting my fort and I shot back at them until my rifle was empty. They disappeared behind the buildings as I reloaded and I thought of the secret tunnel. Jumping down from the rock, I crept as quietly as I could toward the gully where the tunnel opened. The heavy door was open and I froze in my place. Carefully, I scanned the gully and hillside, but there was no movement. I must have watched only a few moments, but it felt like an hour. I jumped into the gully and as I landed, fired two quick shots high into the passage then whirled and fired up the gully even as I dove to the ground. Nothing happened. I lay still longer. Nothing happened. I began to crawl toward the door and when I had gained the darkness just inside the door, I waited again. A drop of sweat dripped off my nose and I heard it plop in the leaves at my feet as I reloaded.

I had become accustomed to the dark, but the darkness of the tunnel was as my father had said: "darker than the bowels of hell." I could see nothing — and I had gotten into a fix. Any movement now would show me in the light of the doorway if there was anyone waiting there to see.

The sounds of many guns echoed in the passage and it made me angry that I was missing the war, trapped by my own imaginings in this hole. As I turned to go, someone called softly, "Please, señor."

I slammed myself against the wall so hard I banged my head on the rock. "Who's there?"

"Please, señor, do not shoot!"

"Who are you?"

"I am a servant of the Señor McClusky."

"What are you doing here?"

"When the shooting started, I hid in here." There was a pause. "Who are you?"

"I am Sergio Hernandes come to take my home back from McClusky."

"I would run away from here if I could."

"What is your name?"

"My people call me Small Yellow Bird. I am of the Deer Water Clan of the Dine'. Here I am called Maria."

A Navajo! I thought. *What's a Navajo doing way down here?* Then it dawned on me that this was a Navajo slave, probably captured by the Peublos and sold to this man McClusky. A door at the other end of the passage opened and a gruff voice called, "Maria, come out of there — now!"

"I must go!"

"But which way will you go?"

350

There was a long pause, then, "I will go with you."

"Who is in here with you, Maria? Get in here now or get a whippin'."

I heard her stir and footsteps running my way. As she passed, I fired three quick shots at the silhouette at the end of the passage. It was a long shot for a pistol and I missed, but the door slammed with a curse and we were left alone.

The girl ran straight up the gully where any shots coming from the tunnel would surely get her. I slammed the door shut and propped a big rock out of the bank against it and turned to follow the girl.

"Maria, where are you?" There was no answer. "Maria!" a little louder. Still no answer. "Maria answer me! Where are you?"

"Here, sir." Her answer was barely audible and I moved toward the sound. I had actually passed her when she reached out and touched my leg. "Here I am."

I didn't let her know how much that startled me, just said, "Follow me and stay close," and headed for the sounds of firing. The sounds kept moving away as we chased them and I realized that they were moving over the trail through the mountains. It was no use fighting through this brush, we could never get there but if we struck straight up the mountain, we would soon hit a trail that more or less paralleled the other trail until they intersected high on the hill. We crashed through the brush until we found the trail and hurried up it.

"Señor . . ." She was out of breath and so was I and we stopped to rest a moment.

"Can you go now?" I asked and she answered, "Yes."

"We do not want to shoot you in the dark," Tuck had said and as we neared the other trail, I stopped and listened. To our right from down the trail came several shots and presently I heard gravels rattle under someone's feet. Pushing Maria down flat on the ground, I cocked my pistol and aimed at the tall shadowy figure. "Conly?" I called low.

Instantly the figure sprang out of sight and in a moment called low, "Who is it?"

"It is I, Sergio and a companion."

After a pause, "Send your companion out in the trail and have him stand very still, then you come out very slow and stand beside him. Hurry!" he hissed.

I tried to push the girl out in the trail, but she clung to me saying, "No, no, no."

"She won't go alone, Conly. We are both in the trail."

"*She?* Well git up the trail, Sergio, and be

352

quick about it!"

We moved up the trail as fast as I could push the girl ahead of me until Conly called, "Find a hiding place in those rocks to the left and I will hide in these here. They're gaining on us and we'll have to slow them down a bit."

Now, Maria pulled me into a hollow between the boulders and I made myself comfortable and reloaded. Conly fired and shots replied, the bullets ricocheting off rocks with a whine. I watched and held my fire until I saw a figure emerge from the brush. My shot brought a cry and a half dozen shots my way. Now, Conly fired and I heard a body fall on the trail — very close to us. "Watch out, Sergio, they're sneaky."

"Sí," I growled back as I fired at another shadow and ducked.

Maria gasped, "Look up!"

I looked and fired at almost the same instant. My second shot hit a flying figure coming over the top of the rock and he fell among us. He didn't move and we scrambled around the boulders to another spot. Two shots came simultaneously from Conly's position and I heard him grunt.

"Are you OK, Conly?" There was no answer. "Conly!" Still no answer. "Conly's hurt, Maria, you stay here and I'll go look."

"No, I will come with you."

"*No! You stay here.* Take my gun and be sure you don't shoot us." She took it and I heard it cock. Well at least she knew how to get ready to shoot.

I crawled back down the trail and into the spot where Conly had hidden. "Got one in the shoulder, Sergio — the right one."

"It doesn't seem to be bleeding much and it went clear through, get up the trail and I'll cover you. Give me your gun."

"Here's one, I'll keep the other," and he was gone as I blind-fired down the trail.

"Go with him, Maria," I called. I heard them move up the trail and fired again. There was no reply and I was about to retreat up the trail when I heard steps and fired almost point-blank at a figure rushing at me. The flash of my shot lit his face for a second and he fell, his gun clattering before him. I grabbed it as I ran up the hill.

"Here, Sergio," Conly hissed and I fell behind another boulder.

Maria was tying Conly's right arm across his stomach with his sash and I suddenly realized there was light enough to see a little. It was darker below and I heard someone moving on the trail and fired two shots blindly. The sounds stopped for a moment and when they began again, I aimed at a shadow and fired. The shadow fell and rolled back down the hill a ways.

"You're a regular killing machine," Conly whispered. "Take the girl and run to the top of the ridge. I'll cover you from here."

"With your left hand?"

"I'm good with either, now go."

We ran while he fired down the hill. I turned at the top and Conly started up the hill. Just as he got to the top, a shot from below felled him like a tree. Maria's shots startled me a moment then I was out and dragging Conly over the ridge.

"Take care of him, Maria." I peeked over the ridge and found the trail empty. There were sounds of running fading down the hill. As I watched our backs, Maria carried on a running commentary, "He is still breathing . . . has lost a piece of his ear and I can see his jawbone . . . there is so much blood . . ." I heard the sounds of cloth ripping. "I must stop the blood . . . the ear bleeds more than the jaw . . . There . . . the ear is stopped bleeding and I have tied up his jaw, can we be moving now, señor?"

"Sí, as soon as he wakes up, unless you can carry him."

"I cannot do that."

"I know, Maria, we'll just have to wait until he wakes up."

We waited and waited some more until I finally said, "Shake him, Maria, and see if you can wake him."

"Señor, señor, wake up it is time to go, wake up, we must go."

"Conly, wake up, amigo, we must go." Conly groaned and the girl talked to him softly until he sat up. His head was swathed in rags ripped from the hem of Maria's skirt. Already, the blood had soaked through them. Maria's blouse was covered in blood. "Conly, you have to get going. We need to be out of the mountains and you need help. Maria, lead him down the trail and wait for me in the canyon. I will guard our backs and be there as soon as I can. Hurry, already the cloud is building and this afternoon it will rain."

Conly stood and Maria led him slowly down the trail. I watched down the back trail, but nothing moved — hadn't moved for the last hour. *Are they gone?* I asked myself. The first boulders down the back trail were only about fifty feet away and I gathered myself and ran to them, keeping low as possible. No one fired at the target I had given them. Now hidden in the rocks, I wondered what next to do. No one had showed themselves, but there could be someone on the other side of this very rock and I would not know it. I stopped sweating and my head swam. The sun was high overhead, but the growing cloud hid it and the shade was welcome. I heard a soft rumble high above me, felt the warm breeze rising from the valley. The rain comes soon, and I must be off the mountain. Gathering myself, I raced zigging up the hill and over the ridge, still no shots came and I turned and peeked over the rocks. Nothing moved. I ran down the hill a hundred yards and slid behind some bushes. Still no movement from behind us and thunder rumbled louder. The hot wind was blowing up the mountain from this side also. It would meet the wind from the other side and together they would shoot into the sky, feeding the clouds just like they have always done.

I glimpsed Con and Maria as they disappeared behind a hill far down the mountainside. It seemed Conly was moving better. With one last look up the trail, I turned and ran down the hill. I only looked back a couple of times on my way down, the flashes of lightning and roaring thunder drawing my attention away from any thoughts of danger from mere men. It began to hail and I ate the ice as I ran. It got bigger and made thumping sounds as it hit the dirt. When it hit the rocks, the ice shattered like an explosion. I had to find shelter and await the rain. It came, sweeping away the hail with a whoosh and suddenly it was very, very dark. I had intended to continue running down the mountain in the rain, but this was not like any I had ever seen and I could not see the ground, so I stayed under the shelter of the ledge soaked to the skin and shivering.

It seemed the lightning was searching for me, striking the rocks and flashing as if to see me in the light. Time and again it struck the mountain. When my hair began to crawl over my head, I ducked and listened to the fire sizzle into the booms of the thunder, then all would be still for the shortest of moments and the fire would come searching again. *"Dios mio!"* I prayed. *"Por Dios, save me and I will never climb your mountains in the storms again!"*

I don't know how long I laid there, I might have even slept, I don't know. Gradually, the storm moved out on the plain and the afternoon sun made rainbows on the back of the rain as it moved away. Now the cloud only grumbled, because it had not found me and I moved on down the trail.

I found Conly and Maria at the bottom of the mountain by the gully that still ran from the downpour. The horses were gone. Maria held in her skirt a large quantity of hail and Conly's shoulder and jaw were packed in ice. Even wet, bedraggled and ragged, I could see how pretty she was. She had very nice legs . . .

That night I ran to Antelope Wells and found it empty as I had expected. In the pens a donkey brayed and I loaded him with what food and supplies I could find and by sunrise we were back at the canyon. We gave Conly whiskey until he was happy then Maria poured some on his wounds and gave him more to drink. When he had relaxed some, she sewed up his jaw and shoulder. She was very pale when she finished and I gave her a strong drink of the whiskey. Her color came back and the two of them rested and slept while I watched.

Again the storm rose above the mountain but this time it chose another path and moved away from us with only a little sprinkle of rain. Toward evening we loaded Conly on the donkey and crossed the plain to Bavispe.

SHORTY GETS STAMPEDED

I'll never forget their faces when I took down the bar and pushed the jailhouse door open. "Don't just sit there staring, it's me, Conly, get up and run!" They were still for another moment and another round of shots rang out and they were like stam- pedin' cattle. I turned and ran to the corner to cover their retreat and the bunch turned the corner heading after the horses.

I heard Shorty's whistle and the horses thundering out of the corral and away. He shooed them south and they were loping off when the crowd caught up with them.

I started taking fire and Slim appeared from the plaza. "Go on, Con, I'll cover you. Tuck's right behind me." He turned and fired at a figure darting for cover. I turned and found myself pulling drag duty to those ex-prisoners. Now I pride myself on my foot speed, even in my boots, but those boys took their foot in their hand and *ran*.

"Where will we go?" they called to each other.

I yelled, "Up the mountain trail." When they turned up the mountain trail, I stopped to cover their backs.

Someone grunted behind and I whirled and almost plugged Shorty. "Where'd you come from?"

"Never mind, what *I* want to know is why you let your herd stampede into my herd and stampede it?"

"Cain't stop a stampede that easy, Shorty. You let your herd dawdle along all th' time knowin' I had a bunch of nervous rannies behind you in a hurry t' git somewheres."

Shorty looked behind me and said, "Looks like th' boys have stymied th' crowd a little, let's set up and help them when they come." We set up our ambush, Shorty to the left of the trail behind some rocks and I crawled under brush at the intersection of the mountain trail with the path we were on.

"I was doin' fine with th' horses when that bunch caught up to us — an' I'll be durned if they didn't just sweep me along with them and stampede those horses! I tried to get out of the way, but they would have nothing of that and just pushed me on. I got lucky and ran past the trail an' they turned up it. Took me a quarter mile just t' stop."

There was a sudden boom and the jailhouse dissolved into dust. "There goes Slim's dynamite," I said.

"They're comin'," Shorty said low. "Why don't you slip up th' trail a ways an' I'll direct th' boys your way an' cover their backs."

"OK, Shorty, tell those boys t' hurry," and I moved up the trail a hundred feet or so. I didn't want to get too far from Shorty in the dark. Presently, a figure came running down the path and Shorty stood up and said, "Up th' trail there, Tuck."

The man Shorty took for Tuck hesitated

an instant and as he approached Shorty shot him square in the chest. He was so close I saw Shorty's face in the flash of his gun. The killer hardly broke his pace as he fired and turned the corner. I let him get nearly to me before I shot him just like he shot Shorty. His face in the flash showed complete surprise then he fell into a heap on the trail. I raced down to where Shorty lay. He was still breathing softly, the hole in his chest gurgling with foamy blood.

"Shorty can you hear me?" He took a shuddering breath, squeezed my hand and lay still. Slim was kneeling beside me and he said, "Go cover the boys up th' hill, Con, I'll take care of Shorty. Tucker's safe an' won't be comin' this way."

I turned and ran up the trail a long ways before I caught up with the tail of the stampede. Two men jumped out with clubs and I called out just in time to avoid being poleaxed. We found the cached guns and covered the back trail until the main body was well down the mountain.

CHAPTER 25
REFUGE

A SEASON OF HEALING

I awoke under the door to a startling silence that sent my buttocks and leg into spasms. My head ached and every time I moved I got real dizzy. I felt like throwing up, but there was nothing there and pain shot through my head like someone had hit me. Dim light was filtering through cracks above me and it took me a few moments to remember where I was. Slim's body was gone. I reached out to touch the place where he lay and my fingers felt a strap buried in the dust. Absently, thinking about Slim, I pulled the strap until it would move no more. Sleep came and I woke myself pulling on the strap. For some unknown reason, I had to free the strap and I pulled until I was too tired to pull more. Again, I woke myself, this time, I was digging out the dirt down the strap. It ended in a snap on a metal ring and I could not pull more. I began digging around the ring and suddenly realized that it was attached to Slim's canteen. Water! That was it, I was desperately thirsty and there it was. It took me some time to dig out the canteen. When I lifted, it felt heavy and I prayed it was full . . . Shorty handed me the water.

I fumbled the cap off and took a sip. "Go ahead and drink, Tuck," Slim said. "Us Gila Monsters an' Horney Toads has learned thet you don't sip an' nurse yore water out here, you take big drinks ever' time th' thirst hits ya hard enough an' you'll keep your pores watered an' your kidneys wetted. Little sips jist make you more thirsty."

I took another sip and Gabby's hand came from behind and tipped the can up.

"Now *drink,*" Shorty demanded, and I drank. A thought came to me through my fog and I jumped as if I had been shot again. "You too, Shorty . . . an' Gabby?"

"Us too, Tuck, but we taken *some* with us an' th' Antelolpe Wells boys got away plumb clean."

"Except for those two who stayed with Conly an' shot up a couple o' those 'breeds there at the end," Gabby added.

"Don't go lookin' for our rifles, Tuck, they's all broke up an' what parts is left is all bloody with Comanche blood." Shorty chuckled.

"You hafta be quiet, fellers," I whispered. "No one knows we're under here," but they were gone. The boards above me got warm and I slept.

The next time I woke, there were no light rays coming through the cracks and I could hear voices coming nearer. ". . . wall will have to be built back."

"Yes, sir, we will start making bricks right away." Someone in hard boots walked up on the door. "We will have to move the door . . ."

"No, no," came an impatient voice above me, "leave it right where it fell and we will lift it when the wall is strong enough to hold it. Build a pole fence across here and use the gap as a gate until we are ready to restore the wall and we'll think about this door then."

"Yes, sir." There was silence for a moment then the second voice asked, "Do you think this is the end of it, sir?"

"Only God knows the workings of the Devil and his minions, but we will stand firm. He upholds the righteous and we will prevail."

"We must avenge our fallen."

"In due time, the arm of God is strong and his anger is terrible. I am the arm of

God." After a few moments, he continued, "Have the men bring the horses here and prop the pole fence up until morning. We will fix things more permanently in the light."

Another pause and the boots turned and stomped off the door. I heard him say as they left, "God's hand will uphold us. Only God can remove us from this place."

The hand of God does not uphold thieves and murderers, I thought. I took another long drink and slept again. The thunder of horses approaching awoke me and I heard voices. A horse took a few steps up on the door and someone hollered, "Git off that door, you spavined piece of horse meat." With a snap of leather on horsehide and a grunt the horse moved off the door.

"Hold them in there until we get these poles in place." I recognized the voice as the one who had been with the "Man of God." There was much bustle and moving around. People walked over the door like it was a floor and the dust nearly choked me. I was glad it was so strong. It never moved.

Things quietened and someone asked, "Are you gonna set a guard here, boss?"

The foreman answered in a lowered voice, "And who would you suggest that is fresh and will not sleep on the watch."

"Not me," came a chorus of voices.

"Just as I thought. We will depend on the lookout on the roof to keep us safe while we sleep the rest of the laborers." And the sounds of the men faded into the darkness.

It got quiet with only the sounds of the horses moving around the corral. I partially dug out the hole I had crawled in and felt the cool air wash in. A horse snuffled the opening, snorted and moved away. When I saw moonlight, I knew it was after midnight and bundled my gear and quietly dug out of the hole. The horses stirred slightly and moved away from the smell of blood as I stood. For a moment, I was so dizzy I thought I would fall. When that passed, I thought of my tracks and tried to wipe away any sign that I had been under the door. I limped to the fence and lay the poles down. The horses immediately showed interest and I moved into the shadow of the wall and waited.

Cautiously, they moved toward the gap, snorting and blowing. A mare braver than the others moved up to the gap and stepped out, looking back as if to say *so far, so good.* Others moved closer and gradually the whole bunch approached the hole. As a small gelding neared, I laid my canteen strap over his neck and he stood still as if I had lassoed him. With my gear strapped to my back and the strap snapped to the horse's headstall, I led him to the high end of the door and somehow climbed on.

Once out of the corral, the cavvy moved with purpose and me laying on the back of that little horse. It was as if they knew the back wall of the corral would shield their movements from the lookout. At least, no alarm was raised and the horses moved casually on to the plain, grazing as they went. I was in more of a hurry and when I thought it was safe to do so, guided the horse across the plain for our hideout on the San Luis.

We made a meandering walk across the plain so our tracks would not raise suspicions. Half of the time I was too sick and dizzy to sit up, but when we got to the first foothills, I was forced to sit up without regard to the pain and guide the horse. Behind the first hills we turned south to look for the way up to the bench and the corral. It took us three tries to get up the slope and onto the bench. From there it was easy traveling and I lay down and must have slept. Somewhere deep in my unconsciousness I felt a change in our motion and the snort of the horse brought me full awake. His progress along the bench had been stopped by the corral fence and he looked back at me for instructions.

I guided him down the wall through the gap and dismounted — if you can call sliding off his side into an unconscious pile on the ground a dismount.

"Well, I guess you know whut a little bullet makin' a small hole in yore body can do t' you." Slim's voice came to me in the darkness.

"It shore do hurt, Slim, an' you got two."

"Two in th' gut, an' I'm th' one thet plugged you," I heard his chuckle.

"You?"

"Yeah, I plugged yore bullet hole with my tobacco sack," he chuckled again and said more to himself, "Laughin' don't even hurt my ribs."

"It don't hurt 'cause you're dead."

"Must be it, Tuck. Look t' yoreself that you don't come this way just yet, you still got things t' do . . ." His voice faded away and I woke with a start.

It was fully dark, black as the insides of a cat. There was a gentle rumble of thunder off to the east and the grass around me was wet. I could hear a horse cropping grass nearby. After a long time, I sat up and by scooting backwards across the ground on my good hip found the wall and climbed it until I could stand on my good leg. It was several minutes before I remembered where the gap was and I worked my way to it and the poles that closed it off. With the poles in place I considered my situation.

It would take me days t' walk around that wall to get to the shelter, not to mention th' damage I would do to the wall, I had caused enough just standin' up. As if to answer my dilemma, that little horse walked up and nuzzled my arm.

"So you want to help, do you? How about if I hang on to you and we walk to the shelter?" We proceeded straight across the corral with my arm over his neck and the bum leg between us. Presently, he stopped and I reached out and felt solid rock. "It's to the right there, little pony," and turned him. We felt our way until the rock cornered. He nickered and I said, "You smell water, don't you? Need a drink, little feller? Follow me."

I reached the cliff face and followed it to the crack, the horse close behind. When I slipped into the crack, he would have followed if it had been wide enough. With his shoulders wedged into the hole, he snorted until I returned with my hat full of water. It took three trips before he was satisfied and backed out of the crack. I followed and at the fireplace lay down exhausted. I awoke in the dawn cold, damp and shiverin'. It took a lot of scootin' and cussin' t' get a fire started, but when it was going good, I warmed and slept some more. When I awoke, the sun was straight overhead and I was wet with sweat. I made my way back into the crack to our cache and retrieved the sack of food. A can of tomatoes restored me somewhat and with a pot of beans boiling on the fire, I ate a whole can of peaches.

The sudden flash of lightning and simultaneous crackle of thunder warned us of impending rain. The pony trotted into the shelter, ears flattened and I thought he was going to walk right through the fire. I managed to calm him and we stood facin' the opening and watched the rain. Fortunately, the cloud grumbled off the mountain and across the valley before we were too wet. The horse grunted and moved back to his grazing.

I added a stick to the fire and dozed off leaning against the cliff wall. Light was fading and the beans were done when I woke and I ate the whole pot. This was not going to be another cold night with the fire going. More fuel and I curled up for a nice sleep. A wet nose on my ear woke me up shivering and I stirred the fire and added wood.

The horse gave a satisfied snort and turned his rump to the fire. I thought the opposite side of the fire would be safer for me, crawled around there and returned to my nap.

I lost track of the number of days and weeks that all I did was eat and sleep and haul water for the horse. When he had grazed the pen for a while, I opened the gap and he grazed along the bench. I had thought that he would wander on back to his range, but he stayed. It may have been that he didn't know how to get off that bench by himself. I didn't object to his company.

Rains on the mountain fed the seep in the cave and it became a regular stream. When I couldn't stand th' stink any longer, I took a shower under the falls. First with my clothes on so I could wash them, then without them so I could get my body clean. I near froze, but no longer smelled and the horse seemed to appreciate that. I know my nose did.

My hair had been caked with dried blood and with it clean it was time to see about removing that splinter. It felt like the best thing to do was to try to pull it out th' way it had gone in. A tug or two felt like th' whole back of my scalp was comin' off and

I rested a minute. A little trickle of blood ran down my neck and under my collar. I dipped the end of one of my washed socks into the boiling coffeepot and held it against my head. It stopped the pain a little and I kept bathing it with that hot coffee until I thought th' splinter was loose. It gave a little at the top when I pulled on it, but it felt like it was gonna pull th' bottom hole through the top one. Some more coffee soaking seemed to help and this time when I pulled on the splinter, it gave a little — and hurt like thunder. The splinter was still stuck to my scalp inside and no amount of soaking was gonna loosen that. Turning the splinter a little made it bleed and sting. I turned it back the other way with the same results. By twisting it back and forth, I could feel the scalp loosening from the splinter. I gave a strong pull and it moved a little, but it hurt so much I thought I would wet my pants. I rested a few minutes and as if to fool myself grabbed the splinter and jerked it out. I was so surprised I dropped the thing down my collar. After the bleeding stopped I fished the splinter out of my shirttail. It was as thick as my little finger and about an inch longer. Soaking in blood had turned it a deep brown, almost black and I threw it in the fire.

Whether it was by accident or on purpose, Slim's tobacco pouch plug in my hip turned out to be a blessing because the tobacco acted like a cleanser and kept the wound from festering. I don't remember doing it, but I had removed it and placed it flat over the wound and held it in place with a big strip of shirttail and my pants. If I didn't move much, it would stay in place.

Gradually I improved and my strength came back. It just didn't stay as long as I thought it should and I was still handicapped by that. The nights grew colder and the days grew shorter. Leaves turned brown and fell and the rains stopped. The firewood we had stacked was gone as was most of the firewood I picked up along th' bench. With the food down to the last, I knew I had to move on or do something t' maintain my estate. As soon as I was able, I began climbing up on the top of the rock and watching the range. There didn't seem t' be a whole lot of human activity except around the plaza where it looked like they were restoring the ruined building and corral. I wished I had Slim's glasses. One night it snowed and I knew it was time to seek a lower and warmer altitude.

One option was to raid one of the line shacks for what food they might have and make a run for Bavispe or Tucson. Two was to try for the monastery stash. The line shacks presented the most problems because I would have to find a time when they were not occupied and I wasn't sure I could make the trip to either town. The problem with the monastery was the rough terrain we would have t' cross t' get there — and after our dustup, I couldn't be assured that our presence there had not been discovered. I studied on it for a couple of days and it came down to a coin toss. Pony called tails an' won. He chose the monastery route and before we got there, he was regretting his choice. Both of us gave out and we spent a couple of nights on the road, so to speak, and got to our destination late on the third day. It didn't look like anyone had been there since we had left. I found our cache and figured that the food would last a month or two if I were careful. Fortunately, Pony didn't eat beans and there was plenty of grass about.

I continued my regimen of healing, though I felt useless in doing so. There wasn't much else I could do here by myself. Slim and Gabby and Shorty were all dead if my delusions were right and I had no idea where Conly was. He could be dead too, for all I knew. There didn't seem to be much else to do but try to get out of the country alive and live to see another day when I could return for my cattle.

CHAPTER 26
BAVISPE

A SEASON FOR PEACE

It was noticeably warmer at the lower altitude of the monastery and I felt much better there. Pony enjoyed his new quarters and there was plenty of dried grass to feed on. We were closer to the plain and I expected him to return to his companions, but he didn't. I enjoyed his companionship and we had many a conversation around the fire at night and when the cold northers blew down and kept us close in the shelter.

I tried keeping track of the passage of time, but the best I could do was mark off the days. I lost track those first days after I was shot and now I didn't even know what day of the week it was, as if that mattered to me, each day being the repeat of the day before except for minor occurrences. The days warmed and the leaves popped out on the bushes. I watched the snow retreat up El Medio until there were only patches here and there. It seemed the grasses of the valley got greener every day as they were fed by the runoff from the snow and I could tell the cattle were scouring with the fresh food.

Down below th' spring the old monks had built a garden and dug little trenches t' irrigate it. In my boredom, I rebuilt the dam, cleaned out the old ditches and let the water run through them. One day as I was toying around with my ditches, I noticed greenery poking up through the dead leaves and wiping them away discovered onion greens poking their spears through the dirt. Other places in the little plot showed signs of new life and I watched closely as some sort of greens poked their leaves out. I couldn't believe the variety of plants that responded to the watering, but it wasn't long until I had onions and leeks and some kind of greens t' eat. As spring advanced, beans began t' sprout and send up their vines and that little garden came back to life. It occupied a lot of my time and attention until one day I realized with a jolt that I had the energy to be doing a lot of things besides sitting around watching beans and strawberries grow.

It was time to move on, but where and what to do? Antelope Wells would be abandoned and probably occupied by the enemy, so it would not do to go there. I couldn't go home without seeing how my Mexican friends had fared and then there was Conly, I had to find out what happened to him.

They had talked about the valley of the Rio Bavispe and their kin at the town of Bavispe, had Carlo and Felipe, and that would be the most logical place they could go easily. The people would travel down the east side of El Medio, cross the plain at night and be in the canyon to the pass by daylight, over the pass and down the Bavispe to the town the next day.

The sheep would be another story. Most likely, they would drive them over San Luis Pass into the valley of the Rio Bate Pito and down that river to the Bavispe. They would keep them where there was room amongst the herds already there and would still be near their families at Bavispe. That would be the first place I would look. Even if there were none of my friends there, I would be able to reprovision for whatever would come next.

Pony was sleek and restless and after I had cleaned up around the monastery and cached two of the rifles and some ammunition, I mounted his bare back late in the evening and rode out on the plain in the dark. We checked out the corral at the horse pasture and found horses in the pen and saddles hanging on the fence. I threw the best-feeling saddle over Pony, took down the pole gate and let the horses out without waking the sleepers in the line shack. The stirrups were too short and I had to ride a ways with them before I stopped and adjusted them. We drifted south veering toward the middle of the range and when the horses showed reluctance to go farther, I roped one of them and took him with us. We skirted the brush arbor and by th' time light was showing in the east we were well into the canyon and climbing toward the pass. We took a long nooning, crossed the pass and rode into th' outskirts of Bavispe in the evening shadows of the Sierra Madre. Siesta had been over some time and people were moving around, the smells of suppers cooking reminding me that I hadn't eaten in over twenty-four hours — and that mostly onions an' greens, the frijoles being long gone. As I rode up to a likely-looking cantina, a familiar voice called, "Where you go there, Gr-r-r-ringo?" and there stood Raul Garcia the soldier.

"I have come to find my friends of the Antelope Wells," I replied. "Do you know of them?"

380

"Sí, sí, señor," he reverted to Spanish. "They come soon. Come down and have a drink and speak of life and times with me." He called for beer through the door.

I got down carefully and tried my bum leg a step or two. It was stiff and I limped to the teraza where Raul stood and shook the hand of the first human I had spoken to in months and months. A young boy padded out with two bottles of that green beer clinking in his hand and I was glad to accept a long drink from one. The lump in my throat was not because I was overly dry.

"Here you are, my friend, as one from the dead, you must tell me of your adventures since last we met — but wait — if you tell me now, you will be telling it again and again through the night." He motioned and the boy set a chair behind me and I gladly sat down while Raul pulled up a table and sat next to me in the second chair the boy brought. My hip and my head hurt something awful. Even the green beer tasted good and by the second bottle, the pain had eased some and I eagerly attacked the steaming plate a portly señora set before me. She stood by me without a word, her hand on my shoulder.

A crowd was gathering in the gloaming and the señora called to a tall figure approaching, "Come quickly, see Señor Tucker, he has risen as from the dead!"

"Don't you try flumoxin' me, Eliticia, I know when yo're funnin' an' that ain't funny talkin' 'bout th' dead thataway," the familiar voice retorted.

I started to rise, but the hand on my shoulder restrained me. "Be still, muchacho, this is your welcoming day."

Conly Hicks stepped up on the teraza, leaned close and stared at my face. "Sure looks like Tuck, even smells some like him, but a little past ripe to me, Eliticia. We need to peel a layer or two of that hair and dirt off his face and ears and I'll tell you for sure who this saddle bum is."

"Saddle bum? The pot calls the kettle black!" she sniffed and flipped Conly sharply with her towel.

"Bring me a light, boy, an' let me git a good look at this feller. I want t' know if I'll have t' shoot him fer im-per-son-atin' a saintly man," this in English.

The light came and Conly placed it on the table between us and stared at me intently. In turn, I could now see him plainly and his looks had changed somewhat. There was a long red scar along his jaw that ended where his left earlobe had been. The scar had been stitched, the needle

382

holes still visible. "Done it myself t' keep th' flies out an' my jawbone in." I could see where a bullet had passed through his right shoulder close to his neck. It must have broken his collarbone.

He spoke in Spanish, "I'm damned if you don't *look* like Tuck of the Two Beavers, but I cannot tell for sure through all that hair. Eledina, run get my shaving gear and tell that clerk at the store to get over here as you go by. Anybody heard this creature speak?"

A slim and very feminine figure hurried away. "Is that Eledina, El Muchacha?" I asked.

"Ahhh, he does speak and with the voice of Tucker . . . still . . . You don't worry yourself about that muchacha, she wears my brand and I won't stand for any rustling."

There was now a big circle of smiling faces around the table. Felipe elbowed his way through the crowd. "Do not be frightened of Señor Conly, Tuck-er. He has been *un poquitin* loco since the Battle of the Placita."

"*Muy loco!*" one of the younger boys whispered.

The crowd chuckled while Conly glared. "Eliticia, it's time to celebrate! Bring drinks for all and whip us up a feast!"

"But Señor Conly, you do not know . . ."

"Oh, but I do not yet know if we are celebrating the return of a lost son or the last meal of an imposter, but we *are* celebrating!" he called loudly. "Someone find the fiddle and the accordion!"

The crowd laughed and dispersed to pick up their drinks and sample the food lading the tables around us.

Conly sat down across from me. "Sure is good t' see you, Tuck, I been awful lonesome since th' four of you left me alone t' herd these people."

"I'm glad t' see you're still among the living, Con, wish I could say th' same of th' rest."

"They're gone, all three of 'em." Conly said with a catch in his voice, "When things settle here a bit we'll put our heads together an' round up th' whole story. Are you well? Slim said you were OK and would be safe eventually, told me he had plugged you . . ."

"But Slim died in th' . . ."

Conly waved his hand. "I know, I know. Did he really shoot you?"

"No, he plugged th' bullet hole in me with his tobacco sack."

Conly's eyes narrowed and he grinned. "That scoundrel, always jokin'. Where'd you git hit?"

"In th' hip."

"Th' butt!" he exclaimed loudly. "You got shot in the butt!" he said again in Spanish. It was suddenly quiet and some female giggled.

"The *hip*!" I said firmly.

"Let me see the scar and I'll tell you if it's the hip or the butt," he said loudly. Slowly I stood up and the crowd got quiet. I pulled up my jacket and a murmur went through the room. I made to unbutton my pants and the girls tittered. Then I turned my side and showed him the bullet hole in my pants.

"Unless you were scrunched around in your pants, that looks an awful lot like the butt to me. That hole over the hole in your skin?"

"Yes, and I think the bullet hit my hip bone and crippled me some."

"Must have bent after it hit your ass."

"Conly, it didn't hit my . . ."

"Hold on, there, stranger, here comes the store clerk and right behind is the shaving equipment. Now, the moment of truth comes. Here, Humberto, take the size of this feller and get him some good clothes. We're trying to clean up the town and this is the first big step toward getting fresh air in the place."

"Please stand for me, Señor Tuck," Humberto said. He took the measure of me with his eye and said, "I can fix him up, Señor Conlee."

"From the skin out, now, and put it on my chip, if you would. Soon as I get this razor stropped and working, I'll be able to tell you if it's going to be working clothes or burying clothes. If it's burying, we'll need a tie."

Humberto leaned closer and whispered, "Señor Conlee, sir, I am so sorry, but your chip is full."

I reached in my pocket and pulled out a few pesos. "Will this buy the clothes?"

"Sí, señor, and more."

"Apply what is left over to Señor Conly's chip — and add a pair of socks to my clothes."

Conly made for my face with scissors and razor and I held up my hand. "This ain't the place for haircuts and shaves, let's get away from this food and somewhere private."

"Come with me, señores, I have things ready for you on the patio," Eliticia motioned.

She led us through the cantina and kitchen to a small patio which gave entrance to the living quarters for the family. Motioning me to a chair, she took the scissors from Eledina and began clipping my hair. It was plain that she was proficient at the task and I was relieved. I had seen the products of Conly's haircutting. She exclaimed when her fingers found the scars on the back of my head and I had to explain them.

Soon, several boys appeared with steaming buckets of water and filled a tub standing there. A small tyke stood by with towels and soap waiting for Eliticia to finish her task. She wielded the razor just as efficiently and soon several months' worth of hair was littering the floor. El Muchacha looked at me closely and exclaimed, "It is the one you call Tuck-er, Conlee, *it is,*" and she would have hugged me except for the dirt and hair clinging to my clothes.

"I was pretty sure of it, but these days you can't be too careful," the tall cowboy drawled. "Get yourself out of those clothes and into this water. Too bad it ain't still boilin', the dirt would come off faster."

I began to slowly undress as the women retreated. The water was hot and it felt very good. I think if it had been boiling, it would only have felt better. The bath was just like a warm bed and I could have slept if Conly hadn't been chatterin' to me all the while. As I washed, the water turned turbid, then gray and th' soap suds faded away. Last of all, I washed my hair and when I stood up, Conly poured a bucket of hot water over my head and body. The air was cold and I got chilled as I put on my new clothes. To my surprise and satisfaction, they fit well and I must admit I felt and smelled much, much better. Eliticia and El Muchacha returned and surveyed the results with satisfaction as if they had done it all. A few more snips with the scissors and a good brushin' and they declared me fit for company and shooed us back to the cantina where everyone had gathered as the cold night air made the warmer room more inviting.

I was ushered to a table in th' middle of th' room, a fresh beer thrust into my hand and a heaping plate set before me. I didn't hesitate, but set myself to th' task of findin' the bottoms of both containers. A fresh bottle was set on the table and the empties removed. Conly stood up and with th' voice of a bull called in Spanish, "All right, my friends, now is the time to hear this man's testimony about his activities the last seven months. Make yourselves comfortable and we will begin."

"Wait a minute," I said. "What day is this?"

"It is miercoles," someone called.

"No, it is martes," another answered.

"Miercoles!" came a chorus of replies.

"So it is miercoles, but what month is it?" I asked.

"This is Wednesday, April the twentieth, eighteen eighty-seven, Tuck," Conly said quietly.

I was stunned. April the twentieth? That meant that I had spent the whole winter in hiding and healing in the mountains. "That can't be, you're fooling with me again."

"No, Tuck, I'm not fooling with you about that." Conly's face was sober.

Eledina who was sitting between us put her hand on my arm and patted softly. "It is true, Tuck-er, you have been gone a long time."

I sat in thought, how could that be? Had I slept days at a time to lose track of the passage of time that way? Was I totally out of my head? I didn't understand, couldn't make sense of it.

"Just put it away for now, Tuck, you'll dope it out sooner or later," Conly advised. "Now," he hurried on, "tell us what happened after we split up at the placita that night."

Even though the night was etched into my mind, I had to think back to the start and go from there to the time Conly asked about. "Sergio started the dance too soon." I looked at Conly and he nodded. "Then we ran toward the jailhouse — you shot someone in the alleyway, then ran past the jail. I held off the gang returning from their start toward the blown-up line shacks while Slim opened the doors to the jail . . ."

"And those lads galloping out of the door just swept Shorty up and he rode the crest of that wave past the entrance to the trail over the mountain. If they hadn't known about that trail and turned, I suppose he would still be riding that wave — across Equador about now," Conly chuckled.

"As Slim passed the corner of the jail, he took two shots from someone behind the building. I turned the corner and got the shooter. I found Slim lying by the corral wall. He was hit bad by both shots and couldn't walk. As I stooped to help him up, I got hit and went down. That was the end of our running and we crawled into the corral and closed those big doors. We fought until I got that splinter in my head and Slim died. When I heard someone digging footholds in the wall beside the door, I stuffed the last half stick of dynamite into the wall there and blew him a good toehold, but I don't think he was able to take advantage of it.

"The door on that side stood a moment or two then fell in on top of the broken wall leaving a hollow place and I crawled under it and covered up the hole with dirt and bricks and passed out. When I woke up, Slim's body was gone and it was getting daylight. I found Slim's canteen and drank." I paused and whispered to Conly, "That's when Slim and Gabby and Shorty came to me and gave me their lesson on the proper way to drink water in the desert. That's how I knew they were gone."

Conly nodded. "I set up at the head of the trail and kept the gunnys from running up the backs of our friends. Shorty got outrun by the horses stampeding and came back to help. He got murdered where the trail over the mountain starts. He thought it was you, Tuck, running down the path and stood up to direct you up the trail. A dirty sneaking coward let him think it was you and shot Shorty as he ran by. When he turned up the trail, I gave him a dose of the same medicine. Shorty was still breathing when I got to him, but he only lasted a moment more. There was nothing I could do, Tuck, and I had to leave him there with Slim. He told me you were OK and to go

391

on," he whispered. His voice was low and husky and the room was very still, the only sound a single cricket singing outside the window.

"I retreated as the men climbed the mountain. Two of the boys came back to help. They retrieved the cached weapons and fought beside me. They fought fiercely and neither one made it to the top. Sergio and Maria and I got in those boulders at the top of the pass and held them off until they quit. By the time we got to the bottom of the trail, I was pretty well done in. Sergio found Antelope Wells abandoned and brought back a donkey load of gear. We holed up in a canyon at the end of El Medio until it was dark enough for us to cross the plain safely. Rain washed away all our tracks and I suppose the rancher didn't bother to find out where we went. He hasn't come here looking and we haven't visited him, either."

I wondered who Maria was then decided I would find out sooner or later.

Sergio came out of the crowd and grinned at me. "How did you get away from the placita, amigo?"

"By the way," Conly interrupted, "I have now taught that muchacho how to count past ten. Where are we now, up to fifty?"

I laughed, "Don't worry about it, Sergio,

you started the dance and fought a good fight, saved my bacon at least once."

Sergio smiled.

"Tell us how long you stayed under the door and how you got away," someone urged.

"I am still confused about time, if this is April — abril — I am not sure just how long I stayed there. I thought it was only one day and two nights, but could it have been two days and three nights? I don't know . . . At any rate, the rancher came out and stood on the door just above me and gave his instructions to his segundo about fencing off the gap and putting horses back in the corral. I remember he said that only God could run them off that place. I slept a lot. Guess I had lost a lot of blood and my head and hip really hurt. Toward morning of the second night — I guess — I crawled out, covered the hole back up and let the horses out of the corral. I caught that little pony and we rode to the shelter on the bench. We stayed there until the food was about gone and it was too cold to stay longer, then we made our way down to the monastery and stayed there until two nights ago when we headed for Bavispe. You know the rest."

There was a long quiet spell, each of us lost in our thoughts of that day and time.

Finally, I asked, "What happened to Gabby?"

"I can tell you!" Eledina, El Muchacha said. "When we rode to the north, Gabby made two bombs and showed us where to put them by the two northern line shacks. We rode to the arbor and I lured the men to us in the rocks and the others killed them." She blushed to a lovely peach tone while the audience laughed and hooted. "He sent two of us to each shack with instructions to light the fuses and run when we saw the fire take the arbor. Then after dark, he set the arbor afire and hid in the rocks again. The first adobe blew up and we could hear things falling on the plain a long time. A few minutes later the second house blew up. For a long time we waited for the ranchers to come, but they didn't. When no one came near, we rode toward Antelope Wells and met the men coming with the sheep. We helped them up the San Luis Pass where some of the ranch hands caught up with us. We held them off a long time until the storm came and they caught up to us. Gabby told us to run and he would hold them off. That was the last we saw of him alive. After the storm and all was quiet we crept back in the dark and found him in the rocks. There was a man lying across his body and both were dead. There were three others among the rocks, all dead." All was quiet for a moment and she wiped a tear from her cheek.

"Heroes all," Conly said, "now let's drink to their memory and to this one who has returned as from the dead!"

And that we did until the beer was warm and we had too much. It was a wake and a celebration and I slept well on the floor until pain woke me in the middle of the morning. I don't know which hurt worse, my hip from sleeping on the floor or my head from green ale.

CHAPTER 27
THE BAB-TEEST WEDDING

A SEASON TO DANCE

Bavispe was a pleasant little town and I enjoyed my stay there. Many of the people were from Antelope Wells or kin to them and everywhere I went there was always someone telling me how grateful they were for rescuing the captured men. I stayed with Conly, who stayed in a little shack close to the river not far from where Eledina lived with her grandmother, who watched the poor girl like a mother hen, determined that Conly's courtship should be according to the proper Spanish traditions until the priest should come and marry them. It was only when Eledina could escape detection that she and Conly could be at ease together. I thought Conly was being very patient with the old folks.

This was the first time that I felt that I could reasonably expect that mail could reach home and I wrote a letter to Mom, one to Bob Nealy and one to Cindy. I planned to send them to Tombstone with the next ones to make that trip.

I had been there only a couple of days when Sergio came into the cantina with a grin from ear to ear. "What's making you so happy, there, Sergio?" Conly asked.

"I have decided to take Maria to her people. And Papa has given me an eighth of our sheep to take as a gift for them."

"That is very good, Sergio, will you be going right after the priest arrives?" I asked.

"No, señor, we will leave right away."

"Right away? Without the Church's blessing? What do your folks say?"

"Madre is very upset, Papa just shrugs and grins and Maria says we are married already."

It might have been the two or four beers I had already had, or maybe it was out of sympathy for the saintly Madre, but I opened my mouth and started digging a hole I couldn't climb out. "What would the Madre think of a Baptist wedding instead of a Catholic wedding?"

"Oh, it must be Catholic, Señor Tuck, we do not know what the Bab-teest wedding is."

"It is very similar to the Catholic ceremony only it is not in Latin and everyone can understand what is said — and it is just as legal and binding in the United States as the Catholic marriage." That was the second shovel full.

Sergio mulled that over his beer and right in the middle of our discussion of the merits of a certain horse set to race the Bavispe champion, he said, "I think I will ask Madre."

"Ask Madre what?" Conly asked.

"If the Bab-teest wedding would be good enough."

"Sergio, we are in the middle of a serious discussion about something very important to the people of this town and you want to talk about —"

"Tell your madre I would be happy to perform the Baptist wedding ceremony for my friends," I interrupted.

"I will ask her . . . but not tonight!" And we resumed our conference on the merits of such-and-such horse and such-and-such racetrack.

Well, naturally, I had forgotten the whole episode until a day later, Sergio came in all grins and shook my hand. "Madre thinks the Bab-teest wedding will be good! She wants to talk to you about it."

Conly looked at me with a big grin. "Is this Bab-teest wedding something like a shot . . ." I kicked him under the table with my good foot. From here on, my main concern was for Sergio and Maria and Mama's peace of mind, so I began digging again. "I will be glad to talk to your madre about this."

She was a sweet little lady, grown stout from her child-bearing years, and I could tell she was quite devout. She was very concerned about the propriety of a "Bab-teest" wedding and I assured her that the Territory of New Mexico recognizes the Baptist ceremony as legal and binding. I'm not sure that she was comfortable with the idea that a mere layman of the Baptist Church could perform the ceremony, but in view of the alternative, it would have to do.

"Ohhh, what have I done?" I groaned to Conly.

"I knew you were in trouble when you started talkin' over your beer. Never do business in your cups, Tuck."

"You gotta help me outa this."

"Son, they ain't no 'outa this.' You gotta produce now."

"She wants the wedding in the church, but I can't do that."

"Makes th' sin worser if you do it in the church-house?"

"You know it don't an' you know I can't

imply the blessing of the Catholic Church on a Baptist ceremony."

After a few moments of deep thought, "Tuck, where was Adam an' Eve married?"

"It for sure wasn't in a church, was it? I doubt that they even lived in a house."

"That's right, an' who performed th' ceremony?"

"Why God did if there was any — ceremony, that is. How'd you get t' be such a theologian?"

"Served a couple o' terms in a Methodist Sunday School. Why don't you have your weddin' in th' same place Adam an' Eve had theirs?"

"You mean outside?"

"Yeah, outside *in a garden.*"

"Now all we have t' do is find a garden."

"If you've been down by th' acequia, you surely noticed the gardens. Sergio's ma has th' prettiest flower garden behind her house an' it has th' prettiest path t' th' back gate thet would be a perfect aisle for th' bride t' walk down."

"How do you know all this from walkin' along that acequia in th' dark with El Muchacha?"

"I also looks where I'm a-goin'."

"So now I have t' convince Madre t' have a wedding in her flower garden with people

400

tramplin' around an' such."

"Look it over an' see for yourself."

So I looked it over and saw the possibilities and convinced Sergio that this was the place for the wedding. Maria was happy with the idea and the couple talked to Mama and Papa. Mama was adamant that the wedding had to be in the church just as the priest required until Papa spoke in his wisdom, "Mama, is not God higher than the priest, is not He even over the Holy Papa? If he blessed Adam and Eve in the Garden, would not our wedding in the garden be a picture of that? What could be better?"

That won Madre over and thence she worked tirelessly to blend the garden ceremony with the church ceremony. The date was set for the afternoon of Sunday, April twenty-fourth, and all were busy making preparations for the event. The change of location and 'priest' caused all kinds of discussions about weddings and places for them and such, but the veins of these people ran more with native blood than Castilian, and their bent was more toward the practical than the Canon of the Church. In the end, the garden ceremony was accepted, though with reservations in some households.

Conly and I labored diligently over the words of the ceremony and we got mighty close to the whole thing. I practiced and practiced and rehearsed with Madre and the couple until they were happy with all of it. The day rushed upon me, just as much as it must have dragged for the happy couple. I bought a tie and borrowed a dressy coat for the occasion and at the appointed time the ceremony began under the rose arbor at the foot of the garden. I certainly don't remember much of it, but at the end the couple and the Madre were beaming and happy. We retired to the patio where a meal was served and the mariachis played. A good time was had by all. El Muchacha and I think three other brides-to-be approached me about performing the ceremony for them.

Lupe, one of Gabby's muchachos, announced he would go along with the couple and help herd the sheep. Apparently, our little war had spawned a thirst for adventure in the four young men — a thirst that had not experienced the high cost adventure sometimes demanded.

I gave my letters to Maria with the request that they be given to the Slaughters at the San Bernardino Ranch. They would find their way to the mails from there. Sergio's father gave him one eighth of their flock and early on Monday morning, they began their slow drive north up the valley of the Rio Bate Pito. Conly and I rode out the first evening and took some items that the boys had forgotten and a load of tamales from one mom. They were on the move at dawn and we returned to Bavispe.

As we rode, we discussed our future. "I don't think we will ever get enough men together t' rid this country o' those people, Conly."

"I don't, either, and we've already paid too a high price with nothin' t' show for it."

"You can't say that, we never got t' put our plans into action, but we had t' rescue those men an' that cost us a lot. I would bet that if we could ask Shorty or Slim or Gabby, they would still say go."

We rode a long ways before Conly nodded and said, "You know, I think you're right about thet. Still, if we could have seen th' consequences we might have done things differently."

"Maybe so, but you can't see th' end o' any play an' th' results might have been th' same — or worse. As it is now, you an' I know that five or six or sixty men aren't likely t' rid th' country o' that outfit, that much we've learned out of this. What th' rancher said about God bein' th' only one that could remove him from that place might be right."

"I'm not even sure it is worth it now."

"No, I expect you wouldn't now that you have El Muchacha to look after. A woman sure changes a man's outlook on life, don't she?" I laughed.

"Taint nothin' I don't want t' do, Tuck."

"I know."

We rode in silence for a few minutes.

"Conly, I think I'll be goin' home soon. I suppose you will have t' hang around here at least 'til th' priest cycles through, but if you ever need a job, there's one waitin' for you at the Two Beavers."

"Thanks, Tuck, an' I . . . we . . . jist might take you up on thet. Eledina would like t' see some more o' th' world an' th' Basin would be a good place t' start. Doubt thet I'll stay around here in sheep country — ain't no place for a vaquero."

CHAPTER 28
THE BIG SHAKE-UP OF 1887

A SEASON TO BREAK DOWN

I was yearning to get home after being gone more than a year and made preparations to leave. I couldn't take all the Beaver horses we had found so I gave most of them to Conly with a bill of sale and kept four including Pony for myself. I paid off Conly's "chips" at the store and cantina and had money left over for the trip home. My intention was to leave Sunday night the first of May but our good-bye celebration left me in no shape to travel. Instead, I left quietly during siesta Monday afternoon and traveled across the south end of the Beaver range all night. The temptation was really great to fire the south arbor, but it was several miles north of my path and I didn't want to stir up that wasp nest.

Antelope Wells was totally abandoned so with apologies to Felipe's wife, I housed the horses in their house before daylight and retired to the coolness of the cantina ramada and slept in Julio's hammock. Late in the afternoon, I let the horses out to graze in the big sheepfold that had grown up in the greenest grass.

Tuesday began th' strangest day of my life. The deep blue sky was especially clear and still, even for this land of blue skies. When I went for th' horses, they were in a panic to get out of the house an' I near lost them — would have if I hadn't hopped on one of them and rounded th' others up. I couldn't find anything in the room that might have panicked them. *Maybe it was th' spirit of Felipe's wife chasin' them with a broom.* Though they were some calmer outside, they were still agitated and I was barely able to keep them from stampeding again. It was futile to try to load up or saddle and I spent the morning going from one to the other trying t' calm them. We were all exhausted by noon and I took the precaution of hobbling them before retirin' to Julio's hammock.

Someone shook my bed and I awoke in a panic, my gun in my hand. There was no one there and I lay back, my heart still pounding. As I calmed down and my mind relaxed from the scare, I became aware of the strangest sounds of moaning and groaning coming from somewhere outside. My bed shook again, this time harder — it was an earthquake! I raced for my horses. They were standing with heads lowered, hooves spread as widely as those hobbles would let them and it was then that I realized that they were the ones making the groaning sounds — a sound I had never heard from a horse before. The hair of my neck stood up and my hands and arms felt cold and tingled like they were asleep.

I had reached the rock wall of the pen when a loud boomin' sound rang across the plain from th' west. It sounded a little like thunder but underground. I looked across the plain and saw dust rising high above the mountains. It looked like a line of smoke from a grass fire advancing toward us at a fantastic speed. Before I could move it struck and th' ground under me rose several feet and I was thrown down violently. The rock wall fell with me and as I tried to rise a second wave hit and I heard timbers crack and walls collapse and amidst it all the screams of the horses.

Everything went black for a moment and I vomited. The ground still shook, but not as violently as before. When I stood, it was like ridin' on a boat that softly swayed on the waves. The air was thick with dust and I could barely make out the outline of the mountains. Here and there, columns of smoke arose along the mountain sides and even at this distance, I could distinctly hear rocks and bluffs collapsing sending up more dust clouds. It seemed that their fall sparked fires and there must have been a dozen within sight.

Th' horses were all flat on the ground. Some didn't move and some were strugglin' against the hobbles tryin' to get up. As quickly as I could, I released the hobbles and the animals that struggled stood. Instead of running as I expected, they just stood in one place, feet widespread, head down. Even after releasing a couple of them, they lay still a while, then eventually stood, heads down and backs to the west. Suddenly they all moaned and another shock struck, not as violent as the first.

I stood in the midst of total destruction. Not one wall stood and the roof timbers were strewn in all kinds of positions. When I looked, the wells were all dry, not a drop of water to be found. The ground still trembled and shook periodically and the horses seemed to know when another quake was about to happen.

Without water, we were in trouble and as

soon as I had rescued what equipment I could, I loaded my packs on the now-docile horses, and tying them head to tail, we headed back to Bavispe — or what was left of it.

Not trustin' myself to the saddle, I walked leadin' the train. When they balked, I knew another shake was coming and they never gave a false alarm. Sometimes I would sit until the shakin' stopped, sometimes I stood with legs spread wide. Never once did I avoid findin' myself on all fours or lyin' on the ground. As darkness fell, lights from many fires winked on the mountainsides, some of them were pretty bright. There was still no wind, as though nature was awed by its own violence and held its breath.

All night we walked, pausin' with the shakes and continuing on toward the south-west. At El Medio, we suddenly ran into water. It was three or four inches deep and seemed to be running somewhere down the foot of the hills. All of us drank. It was warm water, but tasted sweet and never more welcome.

Continuing south along the foothills, we found many places where new springs had come to the surface and I no longer worried about water. We cut straight across the foot of the mountain. The rising sun revealed the brush arbor collapsed flat. The four corner posts leaned at crazy angles and the timbers had all fallen. Something caught my eye and when I moved the brush, I found a body under one of the heavier log beams. This was the first of many I would be seeing in the days to come. Footprints going north told me two had escaped the destruction.

The Rio Casas Grandes flowed full almost to the top of the pass but the west side of the pass was as dry as ever. We stayed on the flats, and the shoulder of the mountain kept me from seein' town. Dust and smoke were thick and I became disoriented because I could see no sign of the town with its tall church tower. I realized that bell tower was no more and the broken rubble I was seeing was the remains of the town of Bavispe.

There were cracks and fissures all along the river bottom and we had to pick our way around them. The river was hardly flowing, I suppose because the fissures were taking in the water. Some of them were very deep and when I tossed stones in them, I could hear them striking the walls of the crevice for a long time. It was spooky and I hurried across to enter a new and strange world. It was quiet in the town — deadly quiet. Not a soul was to be found. Most streets had been covered by debris and I had to pick my way carefully. Some of the four-foot-thick walls were still standing and it looked like the fallen timbers of the roofs had done much damage. I climbed to the top of a wall and looked around. It seemed that to the south on the plain I could see shapes that looked like tents and there were thin columns of smoke like the ones a campfire would make. As I returned to the horses, I saw a body under some timbers and bricks and when I drew closer I heard soft cries. I dug away the rubbish and lifted a timber off the woman, but when I touched her, I knew she was dead. The sounds were coming from beneath the body and I had to dig it out and move her to find an infant lying in a cast-iron kettle that the woman had covered with her own body. Though wet and smelly, the child was unharmed.

It was twice as hard to get back to the horses with a baby in my arms and I devised a sling and tied the baby to my back to free my hands for climbing. I had to rest at the river and I gave the child water and some bread soaked in water. He ate in a frenzy and protested loudly when I had no more to give. His wails disturbed the already-jumpy horses, and we hurried on south toward what I hoped was a tent town. The baby announced our arrival loudly and I was met by a half dozen women who took him away leaving me to fend for myself. There was a picket line with a few horses tied and I knew by the knots that Conly was around somewhere. I found him under a tarp nearby with his head swathed in a bloody bandage and one arm tied to his torso. Eledina was resting against his side with her head pillowed by his good arm. I stood there a moment and she opened her eyes. "Don't tell me he broke something again," I whispered.

"It's only the other collarbone, Ghost-of-Tucker," he said without even opening his eyes. "El Muchacha has sprained her ankle an' it made her easier t' catch. Now, she can't run away."

I sat down on the ground, suddenly very tired. "How are the people?"

"Scared to death and sad and hurt and crying," Eledina said with a sob.

"I found a baby in the town. He was in an iron kettle under a woman's body."

"There are surely others, but the people are too afraid to look," Conly said. He still hadn't opened his eyes and I knew he was hurting.

"Can I do something for you?"

"No but these people need a leader. You need to take over, Tuck."

"Where is the alcalde?"

"Under his roof."

I sat there a moment. "Then I guess we should call a meeting and get organized, there is much to be done."

"Go and we'll wait right here."

"He is in much pain, Tuck."

I patted her shoulder. "I know, I will send you both some help as soon as I can."

I walked through the camp speaking to this one and that and surveying our situation. They were battered and scattered and scared. All were anxious about the sheep camps and their people there. Little food was visible and there were almost no pots or pans for cooking. The clothes on their backs and what sheets and blankets they could grab were all they had.

There were a lot of bumps and bruises and not a few broken bones. The people had done what they could for the hurting, but many of them would need skilled medical attention — and there was none available. At my suggestion, the women set up a hospital and gathered all the injured there.

I found the merchant Humberto sitting by a fire, his head wrapped in cloth and an ugly welt across his cheek. Together, we

413

made a list of the things most needed. It was little use to set priorities because all were urgently needed.

In spite of the periodic shakes, I called for all the able-bodied to meet in the middle of the camp. When they gathered, we talked about getting the things we needed while Humberto went through the crowd taking a census of who was there and who was missing. In a small town, and especially a Mexican town where the people are close and there is much kinship, it is surprisingly easy to account for all the people and within a few hours of questioning, he had a very complete census of the townspeople. In the following weeks, Humberto stayed busy keeping a daily diary and record of the activities of the community. I understand that even after the emergency, he continued the diary and it is a remarkable history of the quake, its damages and the rebuilding of Bavispe.

I appointed the most responsible and healthy men to be captains of teams to do specific jobs such as gathering firewood, getting clean water, finding food and setting up a commissary where it could be distributed. We made a systematic search of the ruins, each team given specific areas to cover. If anyone was found alive, all crews gathered to help free the victim. We rescued five from the ruins the first three days of searching. After that, there were only bodies to be found.

Each team that went into the ruins carried white rags to be tied on sticks and set near any bodies they found. The man who served as the town's undertaker set up a morgue by the cemetery and all the bodies that could be recovered including three who had died in the camp were identified and laid out there. The undertaker's team recovered the bodies they could get to. They needed help where much debris had to be moved. We buried forty-three bodies with very little ceremony. That could be accomplished when the priest came and held a memorial mass.

Another crew was set to making tents and shelters. We sent two of the older boys north to check on the sheep herds and to bring back enough sheep to serve as food for several days. When the boys returned with a herd of sheep they had fantastic tales to tell of the events along the Rios Bavispe and Bate Pito. They told of dried wells and springs and new springs, a lake over a mile wide and two miles long, but only four to six inches deep. A huge gap could be seen high on the mountains and it ran from

415

south of the Rio Colonia Morales almost to the Arizona border. Later we learned that this fissure was between thirty and thirty-five miles long. It didn't reach the border, but there was much damage in Arizona. John Slaughter's buildings at San Bernardino Ranch were destroyed.

The quakes continued but after May fourth, 1887, they were much less violent and the interval between events gradually widened until they ceased sometime in late 1888. It became apparent that land west of the great fissure had subsided, including Bavispe and the surrounding valley. Many mountainsides and cliffs collapsed and rivers were dammed making temporary lakes until the rivers carved out new channels and the lakes drained. The fissures in the valley and river bottoms gradually began filling and the rivers settled down in their sometimes new channels. Fires set by the collapsing rocks gradually burned themselves out.

Conly recovered from his injuries and was a welcome help. He took a great interest in the damage the quakes had caused and spent a lot of time exploring the valley.

"How deep do you think those fissures are?" I asked him one day.

"Well, some ain't very deep, maybe from

a foot to ten feet. Some are as much as thirty feet deep and then some of them don't seem t' have a bottom. I estimate that they may be deeper than the Fiddler's Green, which is five miles deeper than hell."

"You seem t' know an awful lot about fiddlers," I laughed.

"My pa was one an' a sorrier man you never met. I've collected a lot of sayin's about fiddlers an' as far as I can determine, they's all true and may not go far enough t' reach th' whole truth."

In late May very welcome help came in the person of Doctor George Goodfellow from Tombstone and his caravan of supplies and medical equipment. He quickly had a large tent set up and Bavispe had a hospital. The twenty-nine severely injured were treated, put to bed to convalesce and the walking wounded treated. Just as soon as the good doctor had the hospital in hand, he turned his attention to the results of the quake, some of which he felt every day.

Conly became his guide and together with C. S. Fly, the photographer, the three explored and recorded the effects of the quakes. Their search for a reported volcano proved futile but the doctor's report of the quake was well received in the States. He was preparing to return to Tombstone when

I stopped by one evening to thank him for all he had done.

"It was my pleasure to be of use, Tucker, and I will resupply and return later in the summer."

"We will look forward to that, Doc."

He cocked his head to one side and looked at me. "I've noticed your limp. Did you get injured in the quake?"

"No sir, we had a little set-to last year over in the next valley an' I got shot in the hip."

"In the butt?" he exclaimed and I cringed.

"No, Doc, in the hip, right here."

"Pull your pants down and let's take a look."

I dropped my pants and he examined the scar. "Healed good," and he turned me around and looked me over. "No exit wound."

"No, the bullet is still in there somewhere."

He felt all around on my right cheek and grunted, "Found it. It doesn't feel like it's too deep. When I come back, I'll get that out for you. If it stayed, it would eventually give you lead poisoning. That puts a new light on the saying 'get the lead out of your ass,' " he laughed.

I had to grin. "Doc, if I ever get shot again, I hope it isn't in th' hip."

"There are better places to get shot, I suppose, but none of them are good."

He left in a day or two and we didn't see him again until the last of July or first of August. Some government officials in Washington commissioned him to come back and investigate the quake and write on it. He and Conly were off again after he cut the bullet out of my backsides. It wasn't too bad, but I sat on one hip for a while. The aggravating thing about it is that I could not go exploring with them.

It was early October and the town was on its way to recovery. Streets had been cleared and old bricks were being salvaged while an industry down by the river was busily making new ones. Three or four houses would soon be complete and it was a pretty sure thing that everyone would have adequate shelter for the winter.

When they came back, Con was in a dither to go up to the Beaver headquarters and see what had happened there. "From what we can tell, Tuck, the place oughta be jist as flat as this place. I wonder how people got along up there."

Well, he didn't have t' ask twice before I was ready t' go. Con had t' help Doc with his notes a couple of days and when he came to th' make-do cantina th' second night, our horses were saddled and waiting. All we had t' do was load our packhorse, drink a beer and go. We got over the pass an' camped on th' headwaters of Cassas Grandes. It was good t' be in th' open again and I slept very well — until thoughts of what we would find on the range woke me early in the morning and sleep left me. Eventually, I gave up and started a pot of coffee. Conly woke grumpily and didn't speak until his second cup. "S'pose since we're up, we may es well saddle up," he grunted, and that's just what we did.

Sunup found us picking our way down the valley and when we reached th' plain we watered again and headed straight for the placita. We had almost reached the ruins of the southern arbor when I noticed a dust on the trail behind us. "Someone's comin' up b'hind us, Con."

He turned and looked a long time, fished his binoculars out of his pack and studied some more. "They's three of 'em."

"Can see that with my bare eyes. Can you make out who they are?"

"I know one of them for sure an' she's gonna get a earful when she gets here."

"Eledina!" I laughed. "You have anythin' t' say t' that girl, you hafta go through me."

"Huh" was all he said, but he couldn't help grinnin'.

We rode on at a slower pace and the trio caught up with us about halfway across the plain. It was Nava and Benito and of course, Eledina, El Muchacha.

Conly looked at her and asked, "Did you bring your gun?"

"Yes, I did, and I will be glad to use it if I have to," she responded, her eyes flashing.

Nava looked at Conly. "She was going alone and we could not let that happen," he said apologetically with a shrug.

"Humph." The girl looked scornful.

"I thank you for that, Nava, an' you too, Benito. Soon, she will learn what I do with rebellious women."

"Ha, Conly Hicks, I already *know* that," the girl smiled coyly and now Conly blushed.

"Come on, let's go." He turned and led the way, El Muchacha riding knee to knee beside him.

Benito held his sombrero in front of his face and stifled a laugh. Nava and I chuckled until we could hold it no longer and the three of us laughed and laughed.

CHAPTER 29
GOD REMOVES

A SEASON TO BUILD UP

We could tell well before we got there that the buildings of the little community were all destroyed and there was no sign of human life anywhere around the range. There were cattle scattered all over the plain and they gave us a wary eye as we passed. I could see several calves and as far as I could tell none of them were branded.

Conly studied the placita with his glasses and said, "I see smoke coming from one of th' ruins, there must be someone there."

We moved on cautiously until we got behind the remains of the corral wall where we stopped and discussed in hushed tones what to do.

"We don't know how many there are," I said. "One of us should try to get close enough to see before we do anything else."

"I should go," Benito said. "I am the quietest one here because of my Apache training."

"I didn't know you were with the Apaches," I said. It was obvious that he did not have Apache blood.

"As a child I was taken from my mother and adopted by an Indian family who treated me as their son. I left them after living with them for twelve winters."

"OK, Benito, go find how many are there and come back here," Conly said, and we waited, impatient for his return. The minutes dragged into an hour, and the next hour was half over when the scout reappeared.

"There is only one at the fire and none other in the town, but there are bedrolls for four. I see dust way out on the plain toward the northwest so the rest must be there," Benito reported. "These are not Anglos. I think there are none here."

"Well, it looks as if we are having good luck so far," I said, "let's go a-visiting. Benito, cover the one from behind and we will ride around and get his attention from the west side of the camp. We will give you a few minutes to get in place."

"Sí, I go now."

After a few more dragging minutes, we circled around and clattered into the plaza from the west.

"Hallo-o-o-o the camp," Conly called loudly.

We saw a head and a rifle barrel appear over the partial wall of one of the houses. Some word from Benito behind him and the rifle disappeared.

"We come as friends," Conly called as he dismounted and helped Eledina down. Benito stood up on the wall, rifle casually held in his arm.

"Welcome, to your home," the stranger called after the Spanish custom, and we walked around the wall into the remains of the house. Though our eyes were on our host, I glanced around the cleaned-out room, noticing the four bedrolls, the salvaged furniture and the repaired fireplace in one corner where the man had been cooking.

The young man looked at me and exclaimed, "Señor Tuck-er, the horse thief!"

Startled, I looked at him more closely and thought he was familiar. "The vaquero from the horse camp?"

"Sí, it is I, Natividad who you captured in the horse camp not too long ago." He looked at me, a mixture of emotions showing in his expression.

"Ah-h-h, it is you from the horse camp," I said. "You have nothing to fear from us this time. We come in peace."

"It is just as well, we have no horses." He shrugged, and we all laughed.

"That is a long story, my friend, and we will talk of it over our supper," I replied. "Come down, Benito, all is well."

"I will stay until the ones coming have arrived," he replied. "They draw near."

Natividad stepped to the doorway as three horses clattered into the plaza and stopped. "It is well," he called, "only Tuck-er the horse thief and his friends."

We all walked to the door to see three riders, guns in hand, watching us. "We come in peace, amigos." I stepped forward, holding up both hands.

"I see that you are telling the truth, Natividad. Did you tell him we have no horses save the ones we ride?" one of them called, and we all laughed.

"We do not come to steal horses, amigos, we come to see what remains here," Conly called.

They conferred in low tones for a moment and then cautiously dismounted, one at a time. "I recognize you now," I said, "please do not be afraid. I have much to tell you and you will understand why we became horse thieves and didn't kill you that night. Come in, we have brought food." Still, they were wary and I could not blame them. Nava and Conly unpacked the horse and brought the packs to Eledina by the fire where she and Natividad began unpacking and cooking the food we had brought. The four were plainly hungry, probably having only meat to eat for some time and when we ate, they devoured the tortillas and beans, hardly touching the steaks Natividad had been cooking. We, on the other hand, devoured the meat with relish, not having anything more than mutton, goat and venison.

"Conly, I sure do like th' flavor of this Ranch of the Carrizalillo Hills beef, you must have improved your herd over plain longhorns," I said.

"My constitution will not allow me to eat my own beef, so this must yours. Tastes a lot like beaver tail to me," he said with a grin.

Our Mexican friends exchanged questioning glances and Nava shrugged. "We do not know what the two gr . . . Anglos are saying, either."

"You must explain yourselves to the men," El Muchacha said as she ladled the last of the beans into four empty plates.

"I think you are right, Eledina," I said. I rummaged through my packs and brought

426

out two branding irons, my Lazy Beaver Two and Pa's Mountain Beaver brand and handed them to the boys. We could tell their curiosity was aroused and when Conly produced the brand for his ranch there were exclamations of surprise.

"These are the brands of our range," the one called Ricardo said.

"No, my friend, these are the brands of *our* ranches far to the east of here," Conly said. "The cattle of your range were stolen from us."

There was a long silence and Jacobo said to his friends, "I think these men are right, the herds the Indians brought were always branded and these were not the only brands they brought."

"Do you say that our Beaver cattle were stolen from you, Señor Tuck?" one of them asked.

"Yes, my *papa* was named Tucker Beavers and he registered the beaver brand in New Mexico. He gave me some cattle and I branded them with the 2 inside the beaver tail brand." I showed them the brand book with the registered brands in it. They were fascinated with the book listing all the brands and looked through it eagerly, identifying several as ones they had seen on the cattle of the range.

"What did McClusky say about the cattle the Apaches brought to him?" Conly asked.

"They were not Apache, señor, they were Kiowa and Commanche," Angel replied. That sure was a revelation to us. Conly asked, "Are you sure about that?"

"Sí, sí," came a chorus from the four.

"Señor McClusky said many times that the Indians brought him cattle that he had gotten at a good price," Natividad said. "He laughed when he said it and it always puzzled us."

"Now you know why," I said. "Some of those cattle came at the cost of the lifeblood of those who owned them. The Indians or McClusky did not buy them, they stole them."

The four looked at each other in anxious realization. "We did not know, Señor Tuck," Angel said.

"I am sure you didn't, Angel, and I do not hold this against you."

"He did this thing for many years!" Jacobo exclaimed.

"Do you not remember how he said that stealing from the Gentiles was no wrong? How he paid us very little of the wages he had promised us?" Ricardo said angrily. "How I wish I had known before, I would

428

have . . ." He drew his knife across his throat.

"Ah-h-h but his end came at the hand of God, Ricardo, it is better than to have his blood on yours."

"What happened to him?" Conly and I said almost in unison.

"First, we must tell you what happened to *us*," Natividad said. "We did not go to Tucson as you said, Tuck-er . . ."

"We only got to the place you call Tomb-stone." Angel shuddered.

"I can only imagine an Angel in Tomb-stone," I laughed.

"It is a place that needs many workers and we could have had three or four jobs before we got to Allen Street, that is why we did not go to Tucson, señor," Ricardo said apologetically.

"It was not a requirement that you go to Tucson, Ricardo, just that you go *north!*" The boys looked relieved. Why would they think that they had to obey the letter of my word?

Jacobo started, "We worked in the mines and made very good moneys . . ."

"Until the ground shook and we got very sick under the ground," Angel concluded.

Jacobo began again, "The dust and dirt and rocks fell and we thought we would die . . ."

"And we led the others out of the mine and never will we go back underground until they lay us under for good," Ricardo finished.

Conly laughed. "We just need one of you telling the story so our feeble minds don't get confused."

There was some little discussion among them until Ricardo said, "*I* will tell the story because I am the oldest and know it all best."

After a feeble protest or two, he began and he told the story with whispered promptings from his three compatriots. "So it was that we found ourselves above ground, but without work. There was much excitement in the town and we heard many stories of women fainting, things falling on people, and things dancing off the shelves. A vaquero came from Charles-town and said that the saloon walls did the two-step and the floor did the shimmy. We did not know that these were dances until someone explained to us —"

"Tell him about the sheriff," Jacobo interjected.

"Sheriff John Slaughter's whole ranch at San Bernardino fell flat, but no one was killed there. We did not hear of anyone killed in Arizona —"

"Or New Mexico," whispered Angel.

"Or New Mexico" — this with a scowl at the whisperer — "but there was much damage all around us —"

"The Mormons," prompted Jacobo.

"One day —"

"Four days," Natividad corrected.

"Four days," Ricardo continued, "after the hardest shake, which was the first one, the Anglos from the ranch came through town on their way to Utah, they said. We saw them in time to hide and they only stayed one night before moving on. There were no Mexicans with them. We were glad they had not stayed, for they would have surely found us and that would have been very bad —"

"Doctor Goodfellow," came yet another interruption from Natividad.

"For several days we did little but help clean up the damage of the shakes then we heard that Doctor Goodfellow was going to the quake area and we volunteered to go with him. At San Luis Pass, he released us to come here to find our homes. When we got to the range, we found all the people gone —"

"Except for . . . ," Angel whispered again

". . . the ones that did not survive . . . ," Ricardo said.

"Now you must come with us and see." Jacobo could hold still no longer.

They led us to a hill some ways north of the placita where the community cemetery was. There we saw a row of fresh graves, four in all, only one marked by a cross. The writing on it read:

Marthann McClusky
d. Mayo 3rd 1887

"The others had left in such a panic that they did not delay to bury the dead which we found when we arrived. Señor McClusky was under the wall and timbers of the house where he lived and we did not find the others until we started cleaning up or the coyotes and wolves showed us where they were. They had already found Señor McClusky and much of him that was not buried was gone." Ricardo shuddered.

"The wolves left when we buried the last body so we do not think there are any more in the placita," Natividad added.

The next day we found the scattered remains of Gabby and Shorty and buried the two together in the little cemetery not far from Slim's grave. We stood there a moment contemplating the events of the last few months then returned to camp sad, tired and sleepy.

The smell of my coffee boiling woke the others and they gathered around the fire in the cool air and warmed their insides with the scalding drink. I had not slept well, my mind goin' over all kinds of ideas and by the time stars started fading, I had worked out a plan in my mind.

To tell you of how we worked my ideas into a plan for the range and cattle would be better saved for another time. I have talked too much and you haven't told your story and how you came here, so let me just say that the end result was that Conly became the foreman of the Mexican Beaver Ranch. The original natives returned, rebuilt the placita and Antelope Wells. They have grown prosperous under Conly's management and all the range around El Medio became the range of their sheep and our cattle.

Almost before I knew it, spring of 1888 was upon us and I had been gone from home going on two years. Those three letters I sent with Maria and Sergio was their only communication from me. We made some final arrangements and early one morning I rode out alone for home, the hoots of the vaqueros echoing in my ears for dodging spring roundup.

At El Paso, I sold my horses and took the train to Socorro. Two days later I rode into the last camp of the Basin's spring roundup.

"Howdy, stranger, lite an' have a cup, supper'll be ready directly," a man I didn't know called. I tied my horse to a wheel of the bed wagon and went to the fire. Benito Garcia our camp cook was pouring a cup of coffee and when he turned to hand it to me, his eyes grew wide with surprise and he dropped the cup. "*Madre de Dios!* Eet iss Tuck-er or hees ghost!" He crossed himself and turned a shade paler.

"I'm no ghost, Benito," I said, both puzzled and aggravated at his reaction.

"You are Tucker Beavers?" the cowboy asked.

"Yes, an' I ain't dead."

Benito had overcome his shock and grabbed me in a big bear hug. "You are back and alive!" he exclaimed over and over. While he retrieved the cup and poured more coffee, the stranger offered his hand and said, "I'm Jim Hardy from the Rafter JD. Haven't been in th' country long, but I've heard you mentioned from time to time. The word got out around here that you were killed down in Mexico. Some say you were shot an' some say th' earthquake got you.

That's why Benito was so surprised."

"Sí, Señor Tuck, please forgeeve me for my seely scare. It is verrry good to see you alive and well."

I laughed, "That is OK, Benito. I might have been just as scared if I saw your ghost." I took the cup and squatted by a wheel of the chuck wagon.

"Sí, sí, Señor Jeem, that iss thee favorite place for Tuck-er to seet in thee camp!"

Jim Hardy refilled his cup and squatted near. "Your brother Nate and Green Nealy are reppin' for th' Mountain Beaver outfit, they should be in soon. Tomorrow should be our last day of this rodeo an' I'm sure glad t' be goin' home."

We talked of small things, the weather, cattle business and such until the crew rode in on a cloud of dust. I watched, but didn't see Nate or Green until a tall man who looked a lot like Bob Nealy in a scraggly beard walked up and poured himself a cup of coffee. "Howdy, Green," I stood and said.

His back was to me and he turned so fast his coffee sloshed. "Tucker? Tucker Beavers? Is that you?"

"It's me."

He stepped toward me, cup in one hand and coffeepot in the other, spread his arms and looked perturbed at his hands.

"Here, Green, let me take that afore you spill th' whole thing," Jim Hardy laughed.

With hands empty, Green hugged me and shook me by the shoulders. "We was told you was dead! You're gonna hafta do a lot of explainin' t' git outta that!"

"Ain't my fault you got misinformed. Didn't you get my letters?"

"Right now's th' first time we seen hide or letter from you."

"I wrote over a year ago . . ." The thought came to me that my letters would have gotten to San Bernardino a day or two before the quake. Most likely, my letters are still there under a few tons of adobe and timbers. I was a little stunned.

Green was talking, ". . . out riding herd, you ough t' ride out an' see him."

"Nate?"

"Yeah, git your horse an' let's ride out."

We rode to the herd and saw Nate on the other side of the Beaver bunch and waited for him to come around to where we sat. I pulled my sombrero low over my face and pretended to draw in the sand.

"What you doin' back so soon, Green, you ain't had time . . ."

"Git down off'n thet horse an' keep yore hands where I can see them," I ordered in a disguised voice.

"What?"

"Better do as he says, Nate, he's trouble," Green said.

I heard him dismount and stand there. Still hidin' my face from him, I strode to him and started to say, "I'll jist take this gun . . ." then I grabbed him in a bear hug of my own.

"What the . . ."

"Gottcha," I laughed and let go.

"Tuck? Is that you, Tuck?"

"In th' flesh," Green hollered. "In th' flesh, Nate!"

It was his turn to grab me and we all laughed. Our tears were not all from mirth.

"You're s'posed to be dead! Josh is sure gonna be mad when you kick him outta your bunk."

"Is that all you can think of t' say?" Green laughed.

"No — no not at all," Nate stammered.

A rider had ridden up and now he said, "Nate, Jim wants you three at th' wagons. I'll ride herd here 'til you get back."

We mounted and rode back to the fire. Most of the rest of the crew had come and were sitting around eating. They all rose and greeted me, familiar and new faces I hadn't seen before. It seemed to me that some of my old friends were a little reserved and I was puzzled.

After the meal, Jim Hardy said, "Now, Tucker, we *all* want t' hear your story, tell us what you've been doin' these last two years."

So we sat and I told them all the happenings of the past two years. They listened closely, askin' a question or two here an' there and I heard someone ask, "Shot in th' ass?" when I told about our fight. It was quiet for a moment when I finished.

"Sounds like you had a time of it," Hardy said. "Guess it's time t' turn in, boys."

One of the boys that had been around a long time, I don't even remember who, asked, "Y' heard any news from 'round here while you were gone?"

"Not a word. It was like I was in another world down there."

"Guess you didn't hear 'bout Riley Giddens, then."

"No-o-o, somethin' happen to him?"

"He was killed, beat t' death."

I guess all that I had been through had toughened me some and the feeling of immortality no longer ruled in my life. "I'm sorry to hear about that."

"They ain't caught th' killer yit," someone else said.

Nate stood up, hand hooked in his gun

belt. "Some say it was you done it," he said lookin' at th' crowd.

"Me?"

"Yeah, it happened th' night you left."

I noticed Green standing in the shadows across the crowd. "I had nothing t' do with it," I said to the men. "I was on my way to Mexico." It didn't sound very convincing, because I suddenly remembered I had been in the arms of my lover instead of on th' trail.

"Well, I guess that's up to th' law t' find out. *Nothing's gonna happen here,* but I suppose you are fairly warned about what some people think happened that night," Jim Hardy said. "Get t' bed, men, I expect tomorrow's gonna be our last day at this an' the thing with Tucker here will take care of itself. There's no need for us t' do a thing tonight," he said with the meanin' of his words plain t' read.

I was really stunned. Some of these men, friends and strangers, thought that I killed Riley Giddens — and I guess they still do.

Chapter 30
Homecoming

The whole thing was so disturbing that I could not sleep and I mounted up and left. I had entertained visions of riding in with Nate and Green with the roundup as if I were a new hand and surprisin' everyone, but that would not happen now and I rode for the ranch in th' dark.

Of course, I had an alibi, but to testify to that would mean ruin for Cindy and subject her to a lifetime of ridicule and ostracism. I could not — would not — let that happen.

Goin' home. It was such a bittersweet trip up th' mountain an' down into th' Far Pasture. I rode up to the line shack just at sunrise. Smoke was risin' from the chimney and there were horses in the corral. I "hallo-o-ed" and was invited in by a couple of strangers who had been hired by Bob. They were there t' watch cattle an' mend things around the place.

I didn't tell them who I was until I was

ready to leave. They were a little taken aback and though they were warm I also noticed a little reserve crept into their demeanor. I left them there and rode over the ridge for home.

It hadn't changed much, a little neater, a little busier. A troop of about six vaqueros rode out the upper end of the yard as I rode in the lower end. Bob Nealy was standing on the bunkhouse stoop watching them go and only noticed me as I approached.

"Got anything a hungry cowhand can do around here t' earn his keep?" I asked.

He glimpsed my way, started and looked hard at me again. "Tucker? Tuck Beavers, is that really you?" He grinned, gave a shout and fairly lifted me out of the saddle. "Tucker's home!" he yelled at the top of his voice. "Tucker's home!" He nearly deafened me still in his big hug.

"Yaho-o-o-o!" a boy yelled as the screen door to the bunkhouse banged into the wall and a youngster in boots and hat rushed out and almost bowled us over. The screen door never closed itself before a toddler pushed it back and stood watching us in wonder. Eda B. stood there in an apron, hand to her mouth, eyes wide.

"Josh Nealy, I hear you've taken over my bunk," I said and the boy laughed.

"Shore, Tuck, an' you ain't gittin' it back."

Eda stood there, the child in her arms. "Zenas, I want you to meet your uncle Tucker." The child clung to his mother and I hugged them both. Eda B. kissed my cheek and I had a wet place on my face from her tears.

"Joshua, what's all this noise?" I turned and there were Ma and Sue Ellen standing on the porch of the house. My sombrero had fallen off with Josh's rush and when Ma saw my face, she screamed. Sue Ellen was down the steps and running to us. She jumped in my arms and I took a step backwards and we sat down my sister's arms still wrapped around my neck tightly. There was a bunch of delighted babble all around and I scarce took any of it in until Ma spoke, "Sue Ellen, let that boy up from there and let me look at him," she ordered, as if we were little kids again in some kind of trouble. Sue Ellen got up laughing and brushed her skirt back down over her knees. "It was his fault, Mother, he shouldn't have surprised us so."

I stood up and took my mother in my arms. She was just as strong as ever, but I felt she was smaller in some way. It got very quiet for a few moments and there were a lot of tears to be wiped away. Ma stepped back and looked me over up and down. "I do believe you have grown some, Tucker, but you are limping. Are you hurt?"

I swear I hadn't taken more than two steps the whole time I had been on the ground, yet this mother of mine had noticed something about me no one else would hardly discern if I were walking down the street.

"It's just a little hitch, Ma, an' it's gettin' better."

"It's not a hitch. What is wrong, Tucker?"

I pretended to be a little boy and scratched my toe in the sand. "Aw-w-w-w Ma," and everyone laughed. Even Ma smiled.

"Josh!" Bob said. "Go get Joe and Bud!"

Presilla Nealy pushed her way through the crowd. "Stop hogging this boy and let me get a big hug." And she got as much as she gave. "You look very well, Tuck, but a little gamey, I'd say," she laughed.

"But Mrs. Nealy, I took a bath in th' Rio Grande," I protested in jest and everyone laughed.

"We'll get you some clean clothes while you take a bath," Ma said. "They will be on your bunk . . ."

"My bunk!" Josh yelled as he rode by.

"That boy! As I was about to say, come to the house when you are ready and we will all have a big meal this evening."

"Bob, you be sure to send someone to town and get Cindy and Rance," Presilla called as she hurried off.

He took up th' reins of my horse. "I got your horse, Tuck."

A thousand miles I had traveled with Cindy on my mind and I would pick th' day she was in town t' show up.

A TIME TO LOSE

The bunkhouse looked th' same as it ever did. I suppose you could walk into a hundred bunkhouses, and they would all look alike, a cowboy's home. Too many women around t' take a bath in the creek in th' daytime, so I set up a tub in the middle of th' floor and used up all of Eda B.'s hot water. It was still a cold bath. Sue Ellen knocked and passed my clothes through the door. "Let me know when you are decent, I'm coming in."

When I had my pants and shirt on, she came and sat on one of the bunks and asked a hundred questions. I had questions too and we talked for several minutes. The conversation paused while I tugged on my stiff new boots I had bought in El Paso.

"Tucker, Cindy and Rance got married."

It struck like a bolt of lightning, only there was no warning as it had been on El Me-

444

dio. I felt the blood drain from my face and sat down on the bunk. My hands got that tingly feeling and I felt dizzy. I don't remember that bullet hitting me as hard as this. "What did you say?"

"They got married at Christmas. We knew she was waiting for you and it like to have killed her when we heard you were dead — several people told us so and she wore black for a long time. Rance stood by her faithfully and it was mostly him that pulled her through her sorrow. He began to press her after she had gained some of her strength back and at Christmas she consented to marry him. They are living in town and Rance is running the old Giddens store for his dad."

How can I describe my feelings? I just can't, it isn't possible. Sorrow, fear, anger swirled through my emotions and left me weak and listless. Sue Ellen came and sat by me and took my hand. "I'm so sorry, Tuck, I know how much you love her and believe me she loved — still loves — you just as much. The tragedy is that she is married to another man instead of you."

We sat there like that for a long time. I watched a cricket crawl across the floor and could not say a word. Finally, "How am I going to go on with this, sis?"

She lay her head on my shoulder. "I don't know, Tuck . . . remember when Pa got killed and you took me up in your arms on that horse? I thought my world had ended, but your strength held me on that saddle and gradually it comforted me and I came to realize that though I had lost a huge anchor in my life that here — with family — was strength, though lessened by our loss. Lean on us, Tuck, lean on us and we'll get through this."

Sue got up and went to the cook house and brought back a steaming cup of coffee. I took a sip and realized there was more than sugar in it. "A little bracer won't hurt," she said with a smile. And I agreed. When I had gathered myself some, we walked toward th' house. Joe, Bud and Josh rode into the yard in a swirl of dust and their warm greetings cheered me some. I was grateful for that.

What a reunion we had and there was much happy talk and laughter. Nate and Green drove in the roundup mid afternoon and joined us. All afternoon we visited while the women prepared a big meal. When our hands rode in for supper they were invited to the big house. They appeared freshly washed and in clean shirts and we all sat

446

down at the long table on the back porch. Bob sat at the head of the table at Ma's insistence and offered a blessing. It was short and there was a catch in his voice when he thanked the Lord for my return. We ate and laughed and talked long into the night. I had to tell all about my adventures and when I told about getting shot, Josh hollered, "Show us your scar, Tuck."

I told them about Conly and the Mexican Beaver Ranch partnership. The men were pleased at the possibilities that gave us.

I had bought handmade black lace rebozos for all the women in the family and I gave Presilla two of them. What Sue Ellen had said about leaning on family proved true for the next days, but the storms were not over and in the end, I was forceably removed from the family circle and their support. That's why I am here.

CHAPTER 31
TRIAL

A SEASON TO HATE

A great weariness came over me in the days following my return and I was content t' sit on some stoop and watch the world go by. Ma and the girls attributed it to my trip and my wounds, all the while knowing it was my heart that was ailin'. Men are not so sensitive to those things unless it happens t' them an' they were after me all th' time t' go look at this or that on th' range. Sometimes I would go, but mostly what I saw there was Cindy and me up to somethin' or other. Times it was just her, riding sidesaddle. Once or twice I imagined I felt her knees bumping my leg as I rode along. It scared me.

Little Zee took a likin' to me and was my constant shadow when I was around. He would sit at my feet and play for hours and howl bloody murder if I left him. Havin' him around was a comfort and I often took him ridin' with me. He chattered constantly and once in a while said a word or two in our language. He knew words like *getty-up, whoa,* and *let's eat.*

My first meeting with Rance and Cindy was really strained and strange. I've done my best to forget it. Sometimes I get flashes of visions of it or hear bits of our conversation in my head. There were harsh words and deep regrets spoken, but they didn't change anything or soothe feelings. After that I avoided contact with either one of them. My relationship with the rest of the Nealy family remained as warm and close as ever and I was grateful for that. Presilla made it a point to come sit with me and talk. She was a great comfort.

The county grand jury indicted me for the murder of Riley Giddens. Deputy George Ryles came out and arrested me. He was very professional about it, walked up the steps of the porch and handed me the paper. "Tucker Beavers, it is my duty to arrest you for the murder of Riley Giddens."

I read the paper, which said that I was to be tried for the murder of Riley at the fall session of Otero County circuit court. "What do we do now, George?"

"I have to take you to Tularosa an' th'

judge will set bail. You would probably be set free until court comes in session. If you'll come to the office before eight o'clock in the mornin', we can take the eight forty-five local and I'll bet we could catch th' five fifteen train back home."

Ma was awful upset and cried.

"Don't worry, Ma, I didn't do it. It'll all come out in th' wash," I said, but I wasn't all that certain.

Bob rode to town that evening and wired J. G. Burnett to be my lawyer. He returned a wire and said he would meet me at the courthouse. I was grateful that Bob went with me and he was helpful in introducing me to various officials at the bank and courthouse. J. G. Burnett was a heavy man who walked with a cane. He was softspoken and friendly, seemed to know everyone and made a point to speak to each of them. We were scheduled to go before the judge at three o'clock, so we sat in his law office and J. G. heard my story. His secretary took notes and wrote them up for Mr. Burnett. When he had them, he read them over, asked me a few questions and penciled in more notes on the papers. He took us to lunch and at two thirty we met Deputy Ryles at the courthouse. There were some formalities George had to go through to register me with the court clerk and just at three o'clock the bailiff came to escort me to the courtroom.

J. G. was at bar, which the judge's high desk is called, talking to the judge. The bailiff indicated a chair behind a table for me to sit in. My lawyer took his seat beside me, and the judge rapped his gavel and declared court in session. The county attorney stood and read the indictment to the court, gave it to the clerk and recommended that bail be set at two thousand dollars. Mr. Burnett stood and told the judge that I had voluntarily returned to the country from Mexico where I had ranch business, had lived peaceably in the county and did not pose a threat to flee. The judge questioned Deputy Ryles who said he did not think I was a threat to flee.

It got very quiet in the room and the judge thought a moment and wrote something down on his notes. "In the light of today's testimony and with my personal knowledge of this man's family, I do not think that the defendant will pose any danger to the public or to flee this jurisdiction. Therefore, I set bail at one thousand dollars and the trial date of October twenty-fifth, eighteen eighty-eight." He struck his gavel and said, "Court adjourned." We all rose while he left the room and Bob wrote a check for the bail. After that we went out to catch the 5:15 home.

There seemed to be a lot of preparation necessary for a trial and I made several trips to Tularosa to confer with my lawyer and make depositions and such. Otherwise, things went along smoothly and I worked hard on the ranch. It was good medicine for me.

The indictment seemed to be the event that galvanized opinions in the community and feelings ran high on both sides of the issue. John R. Giddens was sure I was the killer of his son and loud in his condemnation of me, making threats and dark promises of my fate. October twenty-fourth came soon enough and Bob, Presilla and Ma came to Tularosa with me. Feelings ran so high that the judge ordered me into protective custody during the trial and I spent my time out of the courtroom in jail.

The next morning we met with J. G. at his office and he said he was ready and optimistic about the outcome of the trial. Court began at nine o'clock, and we were all in our places when the judge took his seat. The jury was sworn in. Twelve people I didn't know were to determine my fate. The county attorney made his charge to the jury, and J. G. made a nice speech telling them how he was gonna prove I was innocent.

The coroner's inquest was read and entered into evidence. It stated that Riley Giddens had expired at 2:17 a.m., May 10, 1886, as the result of a severe beating he received by person unknown late on the evening of May 9, 1886. There were some other formalities that the court had to do that I didn't understand, but they took up the rest of the morning. After lunch, the trial continued. Bill Evans was called as the first witness and gave his testimony and was questioned by the prosecuting attorney.

Bill Evans: "I was just leaving Harvey's Saloon when I heard a shot down the street. When there was nothing else, I rode down there and saw somebody running around th' corner of Town Hall. There was a body lying on the ground in th' edge of th' street."

Prosecuting attorney: "Can you give a description of the man you saw running?"

B. E.: "He was about my height . . ."

P. A.: "How tall?"

B. E.: "Five foot eight or so, and wore a dark shirt and bibless overalls. His hair was short under his hat and he was white."

P. A.: "By white you mean . . ."

B. E.: "Oh — he wasn't Mexican."

P. A.: "Did you know who he was?"

B. E.: "Well, he looked an awful lot like Tucker Beavers."

It was J. G.'s turn to question Bill: "Bill can you describe what the men around Pinetop generally wear, day to day?"

B. E.: "Yes, sir, for work, we wear a plain shirt, denim overalls and boots."

J. G.: "Bib or bibless?"

B. E.: "Both, about fifty-fifty."

J. G.: "Did the man you saw running wear a gunbelt?"

B. E.: "No, sir."

J. G.: "No gunbelt in a country where almost every man carried?"

B. E.: "Yessir — I mean no sir, he didn't wear a belt."

J. G.: "Are you sure that the man you saw running was Tucker Beavers?"

B. E.: "Purty sure."

J. G.: "Bill, your testimony here could be the difference between a man living and hanging. *Can you be positive that the man who ran was Tucker Beavers?*"

B. E.: "No, sir, but he looked a lot like him."

J. G.: "Can you be positive it was Mr. Beavers?"

B. E.: "No, sir."

The prosecuting attorney came back and

454

asked Bill some more questions, but none of his testimony changed. The next witness was "Doc" Shull. He swore that I was the one he saw beating Riley and running away. When it was J. G.'s turn to question him, he asked, "Doc, how far away from the two men were you when you first saw them?"

Doc Shull: "I suppose it was fifty or sixty yards."

J. G.: "How much light was there?"

D. S.: "Th' Town Hall light was on."

J. G.: "How bright is it?"

D. S.: "It's just an average kerosene lantern."

J. G.: "Would you say it was bright where the men were fighting?"

D. S.: "Not so much, but I could see the man standing and what he wore."

J. G. looked at the back door to the courtroom and a man entered and stood at the door. "Doc, a man you and I know well just stepped into the room, can you tell me his name?"

Doc turned and looked at the man who stood silent and still. He squinted and peered at the man and finally said, "Why, I do believe that's Wayne Meaders."

J. G.: "Sir, will you please state your name?"

Man: "My name is John Williams."

The prosecuting attorney objected because the man had not been sworn in to testify, but the clerk advised th' judge that John Williams had been sworn in before court started. The judge nodded and instructed J. G. to proceed and he addressed the jury, "Gentlemen, the witness has just demonstrated that he could not identify a man well known to him who was standing not twenty-five feet from him, yet he said he could identify our assailant fifty yards away in the dim light of a lantern that was a good thirty feet from the scene of the fight," and he sat down.

"The prosecution rests, your honor," the prosecuting attorney said.

When J. G. called me as the next witness, the judge called the two lawyers to the bar and they had a whispered conversation. I could hear some of it where I sat, especially what th' judge said because he was facing me and I could read his lips some. One thing I did catch was when he said, "If he has an alibi, he will go free."

For a person who was used to working from can to can't, the business of court seemed awful leisurely, for the judge adjourned court until the next morning and it was just four o'clock. When I got up to leave, there were only a few people in the

456

audience, mostly my folks.

A TIME TO DIE

We went to J. G.'s office for a few minutes. "I'm very pleased with the way things went today, at best, they only have one witness who thinks he saw you running away from the killing. The only thing they can salvage from Doc's testimony is that the one who ran is the same one Bill Evans saw. I'm gonna put you on the stand tomorrow, Tucker, just to show the jury the kind of person you are. *But* if you have an alibi, it would wrap this thing up really quick."

Bob stirred in his chair and for a moment I thought he would speak.

"I have no alibi, Mr. Burnett, I was on my way to Mexico alone." It was the truth — almost.

After supper with the rest of the family and they had retired for the night, Bob walked with me and Deputy Ryles to the jail. Bob and I sat on the porch a while watching the nightlife and just chatting. Just before George took me inside, Bob leaned toward me and said, "I've thought back to th' night Riley was killed and it occurred to me that Cindy had gone into town t' stay with a friend. Tuck, I'm her father and I know how close you two were and I love

457

you both. If there is any chance that she could give you an alibi . . ."

"She can't give me any alibi, Bob, she must not testify." My legs felt like jelly and my stomach rolled.

Bob didn't say anything, just nodded, said good night and left. There had been no condemnation or anger in his talk and I marveled that he would suspect what we had done and not been angry.

George seemed awful nervous when he took me from the jail for the walk to the courthouse. When we stepped off the porch, two deputies followed us. It wasn't anything t' make a feller feel relaxed. As we approached the courthouse, a big loud crowd grew quiet and parted to let us through. There were comments from the crowd, some threatening and some encouraging. I suddenly realized that whatever the outcome of the trial was, I could no longer stay in this area.

As I stepped up on the first steps, someone shouted, "You murderer, I'm gonna kill you!"

George and I both turned around, George drawing his gun. The two deputies following were trying to push their way through the crowd, and John R. Giddens was standing there, a gun in his hand. He shot George and I rushed at him. He was almost within reach when he fired again and hit me square in the chest. Everything went black and the noise faded away.

When I could see again, Ma and Cindy were with me, my head cradled in Ma's lap. They both were crying. George had sat up and I was glad to see he wasn't hurt bad. The two deputies were hustling John R. away and the crowd was very still. I smiled up at Ma and squeezed Cindy's hand. "I love you both," I said and everything went black again. The next thing I knew, they had brought me here and here I've been eight years.

What about Rance's triple play? Well, it wasn't on the ball field and didn't have anything t' do with baseball. He claims his triple play was when he killed Riley, his mortal enemy that night, got away scot-free, and eliminated any competition for Cindy, though it took two years for that last "out" and he didn't do it unassisted.

A SEASON TO KEEP SILENCE

J. G. Burnett sat in his darkening office, a glass of bourbon in his hand. He rarely drank, but today was one of those days when a good stiff drink was called for — was necessary. He raised the glass with a shaky hand and sipped the strong drink. He looked at the glass and as if taking unpleasant medicine, took a bigger sip. Setting the glass down, he leaned back in his chair, looked at the ceiling and closed his eyes. Almost immediately the vision of the morning flashed before him. *When will they go away?* He heard the shouts, two shots blasted his ears and he turned to see two men lying on the steps, their lifeblood soaking through their clothes and the deputies wrestling a man to the ground. He felt again the shock of realizing that the two victims were George Ryles and Tucker Beavers. He saw again those two women pushing through the crowd and kneeling by Tucker, his mother, Mary Beavers, and the young woman, Lucinda Nealy Brown. His eyes moistened even now as his mind watched in horror as the young man died in their arms.

Opening his eyes and shuddering as if to dismiss those images, he sat up and looked at the glass. Slowly, he shook his head and shifted his gaze to the envelope lying next to it. In the gloom he could still make out the note written on the face of the envelope in a neat female hand. It read:

Dear Mr. Burnett: Please do not open this unless there is an urgent need for an alibi for Tucker for the night Riley was murdered.

He tapped it gently. By its very presence the letter confirmed his conviction that Tucker Beavers was not the killer of Riley Giddens, and that the killer was still free. Yet, the death of Beavers had the effect of ending any further investigation into the killing. In the minds of the law and the public, the killer was dead and the case closed. J. G. knew better. If he opened the letter, he would find a witness to confirm that Tucker Beavers was somewhere else when Riley Giddens was killed. The investigation would go on, the killer would probably eventually be found and justice served.

Still, the lawyer hesitated. *That poor girl,* he thought. *She had to choose between two men, the man she loved or the man she married and she would have chosen the man she loved if it became necessary. Now that choice isn't necessary and she stands a real possibility of spending the rest of her life married to the man that probably killed Riley Giddens.*

He could open the letter, J. G. could, and reveal the fact of Tucker's innocence, but was that his option? The note said if there was an urgent need for an alibi and there was no longer a need at all.

461

It would be good to note here that J. G. Burnett was a man of the highest fibre. He was one of those rare men in his profession who was scrupulously honest, highly responsible, a follower of the letter of the law. That is why he was so popular and his services in such high demand. (Even as he was being dragged away, the shooter, John R. Giddens, had called for him to represent him. "No!" J. G. had roared.) It's also why he was not a rich man.

No, he said to himself, *it is not my privilege to open this letter, it is the option of the one who wrote it to reveal her knowledge or not.* His mind made, he picked up the letter and walking to the cold stove, lit a match and burned the unopened envelope, dropping it into the stove as the last corner burned. *Now,* he thought, *I can finish that drink.*

A few days later a letter addressed to Mrs. Rance Brown arrived in the Mountain Beaver Ranch mail. Presilla gave it to Cindy the next time she visited. In part it read:

Please accept my sincerest sympathies for the loss of our dear friend, Tucker Beavers. I remain convinced that he was innocent of the crime he was charged with. It is possible that his innocence may never

462

be known.

Your Servant, J. G. Burnett.

AFTERWORD

Pinetop is gone, as are most of the ranches that used to populate these mountains and valleys. All you would find of the town are mounds of adobe slowly returning to the soil they once were, or there might be a foundation rock or two in the tall grass. You might dig up a worn-out wagon wheel hub and some pieces of iron fixtures here and there. Of course, the cemetery is still there inside its rusty cast-iron fence. The Beavers family members are buried there as are the Nealys, Meekers and Browns — Rance and his parents. Lucinda Nealy Brown lived many years after her husband died; she ran their store until it closed. She was quite an efficient manager and owned a large ranching operation which she sold at a goodly profit, keeping the land, when she was no longer able to manage it. She and Rance had no children and when she died, the land and improvements went to her many nieces

465

and nephews. Nobody comes and decorates the graves or clears away the tall weeds. Only the local historical society is interested in its preservation and knows just which three-thousand-acre pasture it is located in.

And there you have Tucker's story. Have you figured out where you have heard it before? I'll give you a hint: It is a ballad that has been sung now for many years. The poet took what we call "poetic license" with the events, but the basic facts are still there.

Why do we reference the seasons of life in the story? (They are not the song we are looking for, by the way.) Because of the monument that marks Tucker's grave. It is a broken column, signifying a life cut short. The inscription at the bottom reads:

Tucker I. Beavers, Jr.
Born Sept. 12, 1865
Killed Oct. 26, 1888

For everything there is a season,
And a time for every matter under heaven.
The Preacher, Ecc. 3:1

ABOUT THE AUTHOR

James Crownover has been a student of the American westward migration for many years. Upon retirement from a career in engineering, he has found time to write about that era. His first book, *Wild Ran the Rivers*, received two 2015 Western Writers of America Spur Awards for Best First Novel and Best Historical Novel. Students of history know that inside every major event in history are hundreds of smaller events performed with little or no notice by unknown men and women. James is convinced that these unnoticed people and the aggregate of their unnoticed labors are the essence of any great event in history. These are the people he wants to recognize and write about.

The employees of Thorndike Press hope you have enjoyed this Large Print book. All our Thorndike, Wheeler, and Kennebec Large Print titles are designed for easy reading, and all our books are made to last. Other Thorndike Press Large Print books are available at your library, through selected bookstores, or directly from us.

For information about titles, please call:
  (800) 223-1244

or visit our Web site at:
  http://gale.cengage.com/thorndike

To share your comments, please write:
Publisher
Thorndike Press
10 Water St., Suite 310
Waterville, ME 04901